Shit Happens

Shit Happens

GAVIN L JAMES

StoryTerrace

Design Grade Design and Adeline Media, London

First print January 2021

StoryTerrace

www.StoryTerrace.com

Dedicated to my boys, Bill and Oscar.

I would like to thank Rita and Carole for helping me to get my story on paper.

CONTENTS

PROLOGUE

Houston Heart Hospital, Texas, 1991

The rhythmic beeping of the hospital monitoring equipment was comforting, reassuring even. Although Steve was pale, his breathing was regular, and he appeared to be sleeping peacefully. A brief smile flitted across Rachel's face. She was the only one who called him Steve; everyone else called him Spanner, even his political rivals. It was a nickname that had endured since his school days, a combination of his name, Steve Tanner, and his love of mechanics. As she sat by his bed and watched the rise and fall of her husband's chest, she tried not to think too much about what she had done. The most important thing was Steve. Nothing else mattered. She had made the right decision. Not that she could change anything. It was far too late to turn back the clock and make different choices even if she wanted to, which she didn't.

Rachel closed her eyes briefly and thought about the turmoil of the past few weeks. So many times she had thought she was going to lose him, to lose everything they had fought for. Then, just as she'd been about to concede defeat, she had been thrown a lifeline, and she'd taken it. Rachel's expression hardened. Of course she had. She would have been mad to walk away from such a gift. She'd had no choice, not if she wanted to keep Steve alive, not if she wanted to achieve everything they had planned. None of those things could happen without Steve, and if he'd known the truth, he would never have made the same decision. He would have allowed his heart to rule his head. Steve had always been more emotional than her; she was the one who'd kept her eye on the ball, the one who'd kept their dream alive. Without her, Steve would never have made it this far, and with her help he'd have a lot further to go.

"Love you." His voice was weak, but in the unnatural silence of the hospital room it still made her jump.

"I didn't realise you were awake, darling." Her heart thudded uncomfortably against her ribs. Surely she hadn't spoken out loud?

"Not certain I am, really." He moved his head slowly and opened his eyes. "You look beautiful."

Rachel laughed and began to relax. It was alright, he hadn't heard anything. "I doubt it. I've been sitting here for hours, my hair needs combing and my face..." She stopped and reached for his hand. None of that mattered. "How do you feel?"

"Sleepy..." Steve squeezed her hand. "You must be tired too. You should go home and get some rest."

"I will, but not just yet."

He gave a drowsy smile. "I couldn't have got through any of this without you, Rachel." His clear blue eyes stared into hers, and she felt the familiar warmth in her stomach. He had always had the ability to make her go weak at the knees, ever since that first time. It had never changed. He was her world and she would do anything for him. Even as the words formed in her brain, her heart began its uneven dance again, making her feel lightheaded. She licked her lips and swallowed nervously. If he ever found out what she'd done, he would never forgive her. For a brief moment she wanted to pull her hand away from his and run from the room in case he could read her thoughts...

She took a deep breath, held his gaze and slowly began to relax. She could see now that the focus wasn't there. She often felt Steve could see right into her soul, but not now – his eyes were hazy, and she wasn't really sure he was even seeing her all that clearly. Her heart rate slowly dropped back to normal. She was allowing fear to influence her reactions, which was ridiculous. There was no reason for Steve to find out what she'd done. Only one other person knew the truth, and he was hardly in a position to say anything. Obviously, the strain of the past few weeks was getting through to her. A good night's sleep and she would be back to her normal self.

"Rachel? Are you alright?"

She realised his tone had shifted, concern replacing his relaxed sleepy expression, and she hastened to reassure him. "I'm sorry, I was miles away, thinking about what could have been…" It was only a partial untruth, and compared to the main lie it was nothing, but she still felt sick.

"I'm ok, darling, you have to stop worrying now. After all, I've survived worse."

Rachel shook her head. "It's not the same, you know it isn't."

Steve smiled faintly. "Maybe, but at least my body is 'used to recovering from trauma'."

Somehow Rachel managed a smile as he repeated the surgeon's words. Inside, her stomach contracted and her legs felt like water. If she never saw that revolting snake again, it would be too soon, but she could hardly say that to her husband about the man who had saved his life. Yet another secret, bound up with the first one, a web of lies that she could never allow to surface because it would destroy them all.

PART ONE

GENERAL BACKGROUND

Following the end of World War II, an era of suspicion and paranoia developed between the capitalist Western countries, dominated by the United States and the communist countries of Eastern Europe, dominated by the Soviet Union (USSR). This became known as the Cold War. There were many manifestations of this suspicion and paranoia from both sides, usually reactions to actions of the other side.

In 1949, the North Atlantic Treaty Organisation (NATO) was set up, the constituent members agreeing to mutual defence in response to an attack by any external party. In direct response, the Warsaw Pact was set up in 1955, and this was signed by the communist countries of Eastern Europe.

The Berlin Wall was erected in 1961 to prevent people moving from East to West Berlin. It was a physical representation of the division of East from West, and it confirmed the existence of an 'Iron Curtain' across Europe dividing the continent and the world into two ideologies: democracy and communism. The term 'Iron Curtain' was first used by Winston Churchill during a speech in Missouri in 1946.

One effect of this suspicion and paranoia in the United States during the late 1940s and early 1950s was the period of McCarthyism, during which many innocent people were accused of being communists and of spying on the US. Those accused often lost their employment, and others were imprisoned without any evidence against them. All federal employees had to be vetted before they could be employed.

In 1956, the people of Hungary began an uprising to remove communism from their country. The Soviet Union sent in tanks to regain control. In 1968, the Prague Spring in Czechoslovakia also led to Soviet tanks on the streets as the USSR determined to maintain their grip on the Eastern Bloc.

The arms race was also a direct result of the Cold War. The Cuban Missile Crisis in October 1962 occurred because the USSR supported the Castro regime financially, and in return they wanted to place missiles in Cuba. This was probably the closest the two superpowers came to direct military conflict during the Cold War.

Another manifestation of the Cold War was the 'The Space Race'. This was the race between the USA and the USSR to develop the ability to travel in space and to launch satellites, for various purposes, into the Earth's orbit. The Space Race started in 1957 when the USSR launched Sputnik 1 into space. This alarmed the US, because in their opinion it showed that the Soviets could launch intercontinental nuclear weapons. In response, NASA was founded in July 1958.

In September 1962, President J.F. Kennedy delivered his 'We Choose to Go to the Moon' speech to an audience in Houston, Texas. The challenged was to land a man on the moon before the end of the decade.

The culmination of the Space Race took place on July 20th 1969, when Neil Armstrong stepped onto the surface of the moon.

Over 500 million people around the world watched the landing on their black and white television sets. It is widely considered the greatest achievement of the US – and of mankind – in history, and it fulfilled Kennedy's dream. In the US, the Apollo 11 mission dominated the news for a number of days, giving the American people some respite from news of the Vietnam War, which was rarely good from an American perspective.

Communism in Asia was led from China under the control of Chairman Mao. The Domino Theory (the Domino Effect) was a Cold War policy that suggested communism would spread from a country to its neighbouring states, each falling like a set of dominoes. President Eisenhower applied this theory to Southeast Asia and especially Vietnam. This theory was also later used by Presidents Kennedy and Johnson to justify increasing military involvement in Vietnam. The wars in Korea and Vietnam were both intended to prevent the spread of communism in Asia.

Whilst the US news was dominated by the Vietnam War in the 1960s and early 70s, the rest of the world was focused on other issues. Unfortunately, these were often military and terrorist conflicts in other parts of the world.

Background to Vietnam War

In September 1960, the Communist Party of North Vietnam called for the liberation of South Vietnam from American imperialism. In November of the same year, John F. Kennedy narrowly defeated Richard M. Nixon to become the 35th President of the United States. In his inaugural address Kennedy made a pledge, "to pay any price, bear any burden, meet any hardship, support any friend, oppose any foe, in order to assure the survival and success of liberty."

The first two years of his administration were characterised by failures in preventing the communist expansion. Fidel Castro gained control of Cuba, and the Berlin Wall was erected, which effectively gave the Soviet Union control of Eastern Europe. President Kennedy felt the credibility of his administration in the US and with his allies was at stake, and he was therefore determined to prevent a communist victory in Vietnam. In an interview with the New York Times *in 1961, he stated, "We now have a problem making our power credible and Vietnam looks like the place."*

By 1963 there were over 15,000 American military advisers in South Vietnam. Unfortunately, Kennedy's administration was supporting a corrupt and incompetent President of South Vietnam, Ngo Dinh Diem, and an inept and corrupt South Vietnamese army. On November 2nd 1963, President Diem was overthrown and executed. Twenty days later, on November 22nd 1963, President Kennedy was assassinated and Lyndon B. Johnson became President of the United States.

After the execution of President Diem, there were numerous unsuccessful coup d'états in South Vietnam, leaving no effective government in the country. The Viet Cong were in control of much of the countryside, and Ho Chi Minh increased funding to the insurgents.

At first, President Johnson wanted Vietnamese forces to do the fighting with US support, but the South Vietnam army was ineffective, leading to an increased deployment of US forces. Under the Johnson regime, American involvement in the war increased massively. The United States Air Force began a bombing campaign in March 1965 which lasted three years, their plan being to, "bomb them [the communists] back to the stone age." In March 1965 US marines were introduced to Vietnam, marking the beginning of the ground war for the US. At that time, the American public and newspapers overwhelmingly supported this development in Vietnam.

The role of the marines was initially defensive and to support the South Vietnamese army. But following a number of defeats suffered by the South Vietnamese army, it became increasingly clear that they were incapable of defeating the North Vietnamese and the Viet Cong. General William Westmoreland advocated for using US troops in an offensive role instead of the South Vietnam army. He predicted victory by the end of 1967.

There was a huge build-up of US forces in Vietnam under his command. The initial deployment of 3,500 in March 1965 was increased to over 200,000 by the end of the year. In 1966 the number rose to 385,000, in 1967 486,000 and in 1968 536,000. As troop numbers increased in the combat zone, so did casualties. In

1965, 1,863 were killed in action, 6,143 in 1966, 11,153 in 1967 and 16,592 in 1968. For every soldier killed there were six injured.

By now public resolve in the US was beginning to wane, so in spring 1967, General Westmoreland addressed a joint session of congress in which he asked for government and public support for the war effort. Despite this, congressional and public support for the war continued to decline, especially as the Johnson administration was economical with the truth when giving press releases about the conflict. Military information officers only released information about successful operations in the war, so over time the public began to lose trust in these military announcements. The media coverage began to differ from what the Pentagon was saying, and a credibility gap developed.

In January 1968, the Tet Offensive began. Previously, the Lunar New Year (Tet) had been a time for a truce in the fighting. But in 1968 the North Vietnam army, the Viet Cong, launched a surprise assault on a hundred cities in South Vietnam, including Saigon. General Westmoreland's headquarters and the US Embassy in Saigon were also attacked. US forces responded quickly and eventually regained control of South Vietnam, but not without the loss of thousands of lives. The city of Hue was destroyed and over 6,000 civilians were killed. Although the Tet Offensive was a military 'failure' for the North Vietnam army and the Viet Cong, it was a political success.

General Westmoreland had been the face of the US military in Vietnam, the man who would deliver victory against the communists. He had featured on the cover of Time Magazine *three times and was named Man of the Year in 1965. In November 1967, he had stated that the war had reached a point, "where the end comes into view." So when the Tet Offensive happened less than two months later, the US public was shocked and confused by Westmoreland's previous statements. He lost all trust and credibility with the public. President Johnson and his administration also lost media and public support in the US and the rest of the world.*

Walter Cronkite said, "To say that we are closer to victory today is to believe, in the face of evidence, the optimists who have been wrong in the past. To say we are on the edge of defeat is to yield to unreasonable pessimism. To say that we are mired in stalemate seems the only realistic, yet unsatisfactory, conclusion."

Following Cronkite's report, President Johnson is reported to have said: "If I've lost Cronkite, I have lost middle America."

The Tet Offensive ended the career of President Johnson, who declined to run for re-election. Westmoreland was 'promoted' to Army Chief of Staff and replaced by his deputy Creighton Abrams.

Richard Milhouse Nixon was elected the 37th President of the United States on the promise of withdrawing the troops from Vietnam. He was inaugurated on 20th January 1969.

However, at the beginning of his Presidency there was an escalation of the war when Nixon ordered the bombing of Laos and Cambodia. Although Nixon did want US troops out of Vietnam, he didn't want South Vietnam to capitulate to communist forces. Nixon's plan was 'Vietnamization', a policy similar to Kennedy's whereby the South Vietnamese army would fight the war themselves, without US troops. The plan also included negotiations with the

Soviet Union and the People's Republic of China.

President Nixon struggled to push these policies through Congress because politicians and public alike were sceptical. Their views were reinforced by continuing bad news from Vietnam, including early reports on the My Lai massacre which began to appear in 1969.

While the war was waging in Vietnam, the United States was in turmoil. The 1960s was a decade of radical change and social upheaval. Opposition to the war grew in the US and many other Western countries. The public no longer believed what they were being told, and demonstrations against the war began as early as 1964. Burning draft cards was a common protest during the early part of the war, followed later by large demonstrations, many of them violent. Reports of massacres like My Lai and the secret bombing of Laos and Cambodia led to more suspicion and distrust of the military and politicians. The peace movement in the US was led by students, hippies, teachers, academics, journalists and many ordinary people. Peace marches followed in other countries including the UK, France, Germany and Australia.

The mood of America and the world was reflected in the music of artists such as Bob Dylan, Joan Baez, Janis Joplin, Neil Young, The Byrds, James Taylor, Joni Mitchell, John Lennon and others. The Summer of Love in 1967 and the hippie movement was a momentous social, cultural and political change, a reaction to the politicians driving the Vietnam War and their philosophy. This hippie culture came into public awareness and the peace movement became part of the mainstream in the Western world. The Woodstock festival of August 1969 was also used to protest against the war. The posters proclaimed, 'Three days of music and peace' and 500,000 people attended.

The 1960s was also the decade of the civil rights movement as African American people in the US fought for equality with their fellow countrymen. Protest marches, led by people such as Martin Luther King, were widespread. The most famous of these was the March on Washington in 1963, which was followed by Dr King's famous 'I Have a Dream' speech.

The 1960s was also a decade of assassinations in the USA. Medgar Evers, a WWII veteran and black civil rights activist, was murdered in June 1963, followed by President Kennedy in November. Malcolm X was assassinated in New York in February 1965, and in 1968 both Martin Luther King and Robert F. Kennedy were killed.

For those soldiers returning from Vietnam, life was not what they expected. Many soldiers had suffered badly from their experiences in Vietnam and had dreamed of coming home, but instead of being welcomed they were treated very badly. There was no welcome and no victory parades. Instead they were picked on and spat upon, and their chances of employment were considerably reduced by newspapers reporting that drug usage and alcoholism was common amongst Vietnam vets.

The North Vietnamese army had lost many thousands of troops during the Tet Offensive, and this reduction in numbers allowed the Nixon administration to gradually reduce the number of US troops in Vietnam. However, a US presence had to be maintained, so recruitment through the draft system was continued. Despite the background of social and political unrest, the Nixon administration reintroduced the lottery system for selection of conscripts. It was believed, at the time, to be the fairest way to select young men to be drafted to the army. In 1970, over 160,000 young men were drafted.

CHAPTER ONE

Omaha, Nebraska, 15 October 1969

Rachel Hanson hurried down the drive to catch the school bus. She was tall for her age, her body slim and athletic from years of playing tennis and other sports. As she strode purposefully towards the gates of the Hanson mansion, her long blonde hair fought to break free from the purple hair band and pins holding it in place. Rachel barely noticed. Today was much too important to be late. For once, her school bag was light. It was normally bulging with heavy books, but this morning some of them had been replaced with a change of clothes. The Moratorium to End the War protests were taking place all over the country today, including Omaha, and Rachel was determined to play her part and be there. Her biggest worry was trying to avoid anyone who knew her or her parents. This would be difficult because they were so well known, but not insurmountable if the march was packed, which she was sure it would be. The other problem was how to leave the school building without anyone noticing. Rachel had considered not going in at all, but then she wouldn't be there for registration, and if she didn't bring in a letter from her mother the following day, the school would contact her parents. She glanced at her watch and peered down the road. To her relief, the bus was now in sight. Now all she had to do was pretend this was just a normal day.

Emily Hanson, an attractive brunette who had kept her athletic good looks into middle age, stood at the bedroom window and frowned as she watched her daughter hurrying down the long drive. She was sure Rachel was up to something. Her daughter had barely eaten any breakfast and had spent the whole time glancing at the clock. When Emily had asked if she was alright, Rachel had flushed and looked guilty.

"She's really growing up, isn't she?" Mark was standing by her side, a proud smile on his face.

Emily turned towards her husband and helped him arrange his tie before answering. "Yes, she is." She hesitated and then said what she was thinking. "Do you think she has a boyfriend?"

Mark blinked down at his wife in surprise. "Well, she is sixteen now, so I suppose it's possible. You've told her all about the birds and bees, haven't you?" He smiled, trying to lighten the mood.

Emily nodded, but there was no answering smile. "Why wouldn't she tell us?"

Mark shrugged. "Perhaps it's only just started. You know what kids are like, Em, they don't tell us everything. It makes them feel grown up to have secrets."

"Or he's someone we wouldn't approve of?"

Mark frowned; the thought hadn't occurred to him. "I'm sure it's nothing, Em." He could see she wasn't reassured. "Why don't you ask Paul? He's pretty close to his sister."

Emily thought for a moment. "Yes, that's a good idea." She turned back to the window and peered down the drive. Rachel had reached the other side of the gates and was waiting for the bus. Emily wondered if her daughter was seeing one of the boys from school, perhaps one she travelled on the bus with. She hadn't spent a fortune on Rachel's education and tennis lessons, all so she could meet the right men, for her daughter to throw it away on some boy from the wrong side of the tracks. Emily stared down the drive for a few more seconds before making her decision. She turned back into the room, slipped on her shoes and quickly retrieved her coat and hat from the closet. "I'll see you later – have a nice day." She pecked Mark on the cheek, grabbed her car keys from the dressing table and hurried from the room.

Mark watched, bemused, then brushed it off. No doubt she would tell him what was going on later. Several minutes later, as he was about to leave the bedroom, Mark heard his wife's car speeding down the drive. He stepped back to the window, but there was no sign of Emily or Rachel.

Emily waited until Rachel boarded the bus before heading down the drive and following at a safe distance. If her daughter was up to something, Emily had a duty to find out what it was. The last thing she needed was for Rachel to do something that would ruin her future.

Outside Springfield, Nebraska

"She'll definitely be ready to race next spring then?"

Steve Tanner, known to friends and family alike as Spanner, nodded. He stepped back from the engine, stood up straight, wiped his hands carefully on the dirty towel resting on the roof of the Plymouth Roadrunner and grinned.

"Didn't I tell you she would, Pete? When have I ever let you down?" He didn't wait for an answer, instead ambling round to the driver's side, climbing through the open door and turning the key. The car started instantly, its engine roaring in the confined space of the barn, momentarily deafening them and drowning out the transistor radio.

Pete hesitated, torn between wanting to hear the rest of Janis Joplin's 'Summertime' and listening to the smooth rhythm of his car. Despite the stimulating effect Janis Joplin had on him, the car won.

"Do you want me to close the hood?"

Spanner pulled the door closed. "Yep, get in, we'll try her out."

Pete didn't need asking twice. The car had been little more than a wreck when he'd first bought her, but a month of Spanner's gentle nurturing and she sounded like a million dollars. He didn't know how Spanner managed it, not when he worked most daylight hours on the farm as well, but his friend was right: he had never let Pete down.

They had met at school. Spanner was tall, intelligent and good looking, his Scandinavian ancestry apparent in his blonde hair and clear blue eyes. Given his appearance Spanner could easily have been full of himself, but he wasn't. There was no hint of vanity or arrogance, just a friendly boy always willing to help others, which made him popular as well as admired. Pete had never been popular. An outsider by nature, he had a reserved and withdrawn nature the other boys saw as unfriendly and even uppish, and it took him a long time to make friends. But Spanner had seen past the shy veneer and taken Pete under his wing, the two boys linked by their love of cars. Pete loved speed – when he was racing, his insecurities vanished – but he had little interest in what went on under the hood. In contrast, Spanner wasn't interested in racing, but he loved tinkering with cars, making them go faster, improving their performance. It was the perfect match.

The Roadrunner was Pete's third car, bought specifically for racing in the Grand National Division. Pete's father had been heavily involved in hot rod racing until he'd been killed when Pete was two. Hot rod racing had also died not long after, but stock car racing had grown really popular, so despite his mother's objections Pete had persuaded Spanner to help him. The pair had joined NASCAR (National

Association Stock Car Auto Racing) for $25 in Pete's name. They'd even bought a copy of the 90-page rule book for $1.50 – not that there was much in it they didn't already know, having hung around the stock car racetracks for the last few years.

They had saved up and bought their first car, a 1967 Oldsmobile F-85. It had been in a crash and was quite badly damaged, otherwise they'd never have been able to afford it. Unfortunately, Pete had written it off nine months ago after taking a bend too fast; he'd emerged uninjured and, without consulting Spanner, had rushed out and bought himself a Pontiac Tempest, not because it had any more chance of winning than the Oldsmobile but because it was cheap. It was also dangerous and caught fire after a crash on Capitol Beach, the Lincoln County Speedway Track. Pete had been lucky to get out alive, but it hadn't put him off. Once he'd recovered from his broken arm, he'd gone straight out and bought another wreck. But at least this time he'd listened to Spanner's advice and this one stood a chance; well, it would do if Spanner worked his magic on it.

Spanner revved the engine, drove slowly out of the barn and down the track towards the gate. He liked working on the family farm, but he enjoyed tinkering with cars even more. Fortunately, it was quiet enough on the farm in the winter for him to spend time on his hobby. It also helped having three brothers who could fill in for him.

The track down to the gate was bumpy and uneven,

but Spanner barely noticed. He was focused on the engine noise. In the field to his right he was vaguely aware of Chris ploughing deep furrows with the old tractor. His brother glanced across and waved. Spanner returned the greeting and put his foot down. The engine responded immediately, and a slow smile of satisfaction spread across his face.

"Sounds good to me. What do you think?"

Pete nodded. "You're a genius, pal."

Spanner grinned. "Probably better start on the body then, or it'll rot before you get a chance to race."

Pete grimaced. "I thought we could go to the dance tonight?" His thoughts turned momentarily to Janis Joplin. If only he could find a girl like that…

Spanner turned the car around at the gate, opened the door and climbed out. "You drive, put your foot down and let's see how she goes."

Pete didn't need telling twice. He moved across, waited for Spanner to get in the passenger side, then revved up the engine. Mud flew everywhere, covering the gate and the car. "Ready?"

Spanner held onto the door handle and made a mental note to stick to fixing cars rather than racing them before nodding. Pete put his foot hard down on the accelerator. The car skidded in the mud before careering up the track at twice the speed they had come down.

Spanner closed his eyes and tried to listen to the engine, but all he could think of was whether he would actually get a chance to see how the car performed in a race. He never normally bothered to listen to the news, having little interest in what was going on elsewhere, but that had changed lately. Spanner wasn't stupid, he knew his future hung in the balance. Like the rest of his age group, he'd recently been through the army medical and had been passed A1. He was fit for duty. The Vietnam Lottery was scheduled for the first of December. If his number came up, he would be conscripted.

Village north of Da Nang, Vietnam

Sixteen-year-old Nguyen Xian Lien cowered in the corner of the makeshift bunker and covered her ears with her hands, hoping to block out the sound of the shells landing indiscriminately above. But she couldn't ignore the massive vibrations of the makeshift shelter, which shook every time a shell landed. Even worse were the sounds of the machine guns, the hollow clicks of the rocket launchers before they unleashed their cargo on the defenceless village, the sound of helicopters whirring overhead like angry birds. Only hours earlier she had been helping her mother in the kitchen, preparing food for their meagre meal, and now they were praying for their lives.

"Our friends will soon see them off, you'll see," Phuc, her older brother, sneered. Lien nodded but didn't answer. She was supposed to be brave. Her ancestors were warriors: they had fought off the Chinese, freed themselves from the French. Surely it wouldn't be long before the Americans too were sent back to their own country, their tails between their legs. Her thoughts drifted to the resistance fighters and her resolve strengthened. On many a midnight meeting in the clearings outside the village she had learned the revolutionary songs and been trained in what the independence fighters needed. She had played her part, stealing hand grenades and first aid kits from the visiting Republic soldiers. At the midnight meetings, her name had been added to the Blackboard of Honour, several handmade medals had been pinned to her shirt. She had needed to hide them afterwards, but it didn't matter. She knew what she was doing was right.

So far Lien had been lucky, and no one had spotted her stealing the enemy's equipment. Others had not been so fortunate. A couple of months ago, one of the older girls had been arrested while trying to steal ammunition. Lien had watched as she was dragged into a car, never to be seen again. The cadreman from the independence fighters had told them that they should not let themselves be captured – instead, they should hide in the tunnels and wait for rescue, and if that wasn't going to arrive in time they should kill themselves. Those captured by Republican soldiers were tortured and betrayed their friends. Only those who died before capture would be heroes. Lien had listened and nodded her head with fervour. She was fighting for freedom, like her ancestors; of course she should be prepared to die for her country.

By rights she should have been off fighting with the Viet Cong now – she was old enough – but somehow her father had managed to persuade them to let her stay in the village. Lien had been disappointed when he told her she was to remain instead of playing her part. However, she had been given new instructions. She was to act as a look-out and signal the freedom fighters if there were Republican soldiers or American patrols around. She was also to make false friends with the enemy soldiers, so it was easy to steal their possessions. Lien closed her eyes and wrapped her arms even more tightly around herself as the ground shook again. If only her father had let her go and fight, instead of cowering inside this bunker…

Outside Springfield, Nebraska

"Perhaps we should have gone to the anti-war march?" Spanner was watching Pete rub down the rust on the driver's door, but his mind was elsewhere.

Pete stopped what he was doing and glanced up in surprise. "Not like you to worry about politics."

Spanner shrugged. "I could get drafted in December. It's alright for you and Jamie. Apart from being a police officer, he's exempt for the moment because he's married with a kid, and you're medically unfit. I'm A1."

Pete thought for a moment. "Jamie's at the march, isn't he?"

"Yeah, he's on duty. Not sure that's the same as protesting." Spanner gave a wry smile.

Pete glanced at his watch. "We could go if you want. It doesn't start for over an hour."

"You're well informed?"

"It was on the radio before 'Summertime', " Pete flushed, "... before we tried the car out."

Spanner grinned at the soppy expression on his friend's face when he mentioned Janis Joplin, then stared at the car, undecided. He really wanted to check the acceleration again... but if he was drafted, all this would be for nothing anyway. He put down the cloth he had been using to wipe his hands and began taking off his overalls. "Come on then. You can drive." That way, providing they survived Pete's driving, they would definitely arrive there on time.

Omaha, Nebraska

Rachel was excited but nervous, and she glanced around to make sure there was no one around who knew her parents. They would be furious if they knew she had skipped school to be here, but how could she ignore something so momentous? Slipping out of school had proved easier than she had expected: she had waited for the end of the first lesson when they changed classrooms and just walked out. It had been nerve-wracking, walking through the corridors and down the stairs until she reached the toilets on the ground floor nearest the outside doors. She had dived inside, changed quickly, and, after checking no one was about, hurried through the doors, expecting at any moment to hear someone shouting after her. She hadn't realised she was holding her breath until she reached the gates. Then she had increased her pace and headed into the city centre, her long blonde hair now swinging freely in the gentle breeze. Rachel mentally congratulated herself. She had made it! She should forget about her parents, the school and all the trouble she was likely to be in and enjoy herself. Plenty of time to worry afterwards. The noise was growing as all around her people were chanting, "Give peace a chance, end the war," and after a brief moment of self-consciousness Rachel joined in. Within moments she had forgotten any embarrassment and was shouting as loud as anyone else.

"Here, take this." A tall skinny girl with long curly auburn hair, her jeans covered in brightly painted flowers, a rainbow-coloured smock reflecting the rhythmic movement of her body, handed her a placard. "I'm Jenny, by the way."

"Rachel..." She smiled and took the board, feeling more at ease with every passing minute. "Have you been to many of these?"

Jenny laughed, revealing white teeth and dimples on her freckled face. "I've lost count. Your first one?"

Rachel hesitated, wondering if she should lie and pretend she was an old hand at this, but instinct told her this veteran of protests would know immediately if she was lying. She nodded. "Yes… yes, it is." She had to shout to make herself heard above the chanting crowd.

"That's great!" Jenny touched her arm gently and smiled at Rachel's surprise. She leaned closer. "It means the movement is spreading, and when you tell your friends it will grow even more."

Rachel thought for a few seconds, then smiled back, before turning her attention to the march again and joining everyone else in chanting loudly. Jenny took her free arm and the two girls marched purposefully forward, their voices mingling with thousands of others.

A few feet away, Emily watched with increasing fury. Her first instinct when she'd seen her daughter leaving school in her ordinary clothes was to stop her, but she'd soon realised that if she did she would never find out where Rachel was going. Instead, she'd followed her. At first she'd been relieved that the only thing Rachel was guilty of was joining the march. Emily wasn't overjoyed, but it wasn't the end of the world – definitely better than an unsuitable boyfriend. She had begun to relax until she saw Rachel talking to the hippy. She was so busy watching Rachel that she wasn't watching where she was going. A sudden pain in her foot stopped her in her tracks and she cried out.

"I'm so sorry, ma'am." A short wiry black man was

apologising profusely. Emily stepped back in alarm, grimacing at the pain.

"I do hope I haven't hurt you?" He raised his voice so she could hear him above the chanting.

"It's fine..." Emily snapped and backed away. His face fell and she felt slightly guilty. He seemed genuinely sorry, and it was probably her fault. "Honestly, I'm not hurt."

"You're quite sure?" He still hadn't moved, and people were having to walk around them.

"Yes, yes..." She replied impatiently, suddenly realising she had lost sight of Rachel. He tipped his hat and moved away, but it was too late. Emily looked around her, frantically searching for Rachel, but she was nowhere to be seen.

Omaha, Nebraska

Pete drove at his usual speed, but they were lucky – there were no police about, they were probably all at the protest march. Spanner and Pete arrived just in time, parked up the car and joined the tail end of the march.

"Lots of hippies here," Pete remarked, unable to believe his luck. There was he thinking about Janis Joplin, and now he was surrounded by the women of his dreams.

Spanner grinned. "Glad to see you're taking this seriously."

Pete reddened. "I am, man; honestly I am. You know I don't want you to get drafted."

"No, you'd have no one to work on the car!" Spanner retorted.

Pete looked horrified. "You know that's not the only reason…" He broke off when he saw the big grin on Spanner's face. He punched his arm. "Right, you're joshing me."

"Of course I am. It's not your fault you've only got one kidney." Spanner raised his voice to be heard above the increasing noise from the protesters.

"I never considered myself lucky before, but now…" Pete fell silent. He'd lived with only one kidney since he'd lost it after an infection years ago. He hadn't let it affect his life that much, but now he realised that he was lucky. At least he wouldn't have to worry about the draft. He glanced across at Spanner, and for the first time he realised that one of his best friends might not be there next year.

Village north of Da Nang, Vietnam

It was several hours since the bombing, but Lien couldn't sleep. She wasn't sure whether there would be a gathering tonight, but she decided to take a chance and make her way to the clearing just in case. They had been lucky; the bombs had landed just outside the village, scorching the forest, leaving massive craters in the fields and killing two water buffalo, but at least this time no villagers had been injured or killed.

Lien climbed carefully through the window into the darkness outside and made her way silently to the clearing. Another advantage of being on the edge of the village: she didn't have to risk waking any other residents as she made her way to the meeting place.

The forest was silent other than the usual night-time sounds – bats, flying squirrels, red-shanked doucs high up in the canopy, pygmy slow loris crawling through the undergrowth in search of insects, fruit and nectar. Lien took her time. There was little chance of stepping on a python – thankfully, they were shy of people – but there was no point taking chances.

She could hear the chanting before she reached the clearing and she relaxed. If the Viet Cong were there, the Americans and their Republican lapdogs must be long gone.

"Here, take your flag." The cadreman didn't seem particularly pleased to see her, and for the first time ever Lien felt slightly annoyed, but then she remembered the lives the freedom fighters lived. Forever hiding from the enemy, never knowing who you could trust. Of course they were bound to be tense sometimes.

"I'm sorry to be late, I wasn't sure if you would be here..." She tailed off feeling stupid. What was the matter with her? Of course they would be there. The freedom fighters were always there to support the villagers, unlike the Republican soldiers who treated them like dirt, tortured and shot people at random, sometimes just because they were distantly related to a freedom fighter or someone suspected of being an enemy.

The cadreman narrowed his eyes. Lien suddenly remembered what she'd been told by the freedom fighters. *If you are seen to be too smart you will die, no matter who is questioning you. So play stupid, a silly farm girl who knows very little*. Lien lowered her eyes and spoke softly. "I am sorry, I wasn't thinking… the bombing…"

There was a brief silence before he smiled at her. "Of course, Lien." He lent forward, his eyes boring into hers. "But just remember who your friends are." He turned away and began issuing their new instructions. Lien took a breath and was surprised to find she was sweating. She ignored her rapid heartbeat and concentrated on what he was saying. They were to meet here at midnight in a few days' time, and then they would visit the other villages, singing their patriotic songs and waving the Viet Cong flag. The VC needed to recruit more fighters; it was her patriotic duty to help.

CHAPTER TWO

Omaha, Nebraska

Officer James Meyer stood motionless near the town hall steps, his eyes roving restlessly over the crowd amassing in front of him. The noise was deafening, but everyone seemed in good humour. He could see people smiling and laughing in between chants, and he relaxed his grip on his weapon slightly. The last time he'd seen so many people on the streets of the city was after a policeman had shot Vivian Strong at the Logan Fontelle Public Housing Project back in June. But that hadn't been peaceful. Over two hundred people had rioted, looting stores, smashing windows, pelting cars. James had been relieved it had been the National Guard's responsibility to subdue them.

He stared into the crowd. So many people, from all walks of life. His eye was caught by a well-dressed young girl with long blonde hair standing next to an attractive auburn-haired hippy in jeans and colourful smock, because they were such an incongruous couple. The two were chatting away, seemingly oblivious of the crowds. For a brief moment, James envied them and their freedom to protest. He too was against the war, something he was careful to keep to himself. His brother had already died in that faraway place, and a cousin had lost a leg. He'd only avoided military service himself by luck. If he hadn't made Linda pregnant… James smiled as he thought about the shotgun wedding his father-in-law had insisted on. If he'd realised at the time how lucky he was to be married with a child when all his friends were being drafted, he would never have fought so hard against it. He didn't love Linda, not really. Not with that overwhelming, never-look-at-another-woman feeling, but he liked her, and he did love their daughter, Tammy. James knew how lucky he was, and he would do everything to look after and protect them both.

He glanced back at the two girls, who were chatting away. The crowd was still good natured, although the chanting was growing louder. As he continued to monitor the demonstrators, Jamie suddenly spotted two familiar faces near the back. Despite his need to keep a watchful eye on the protesters, Jamie grinned. Of all the people at the march, he hadn't expected to see Spanner and Pete. The three had been friends since school, drawn together by a love of stock car racing, and even Jamie's marriage hadn't put a stop to that. Then he remembered that Spanner was on borrowed time. He'd been passed as fit by the army, so it was probably only a matter of time before he was drafted; it could be as early as December. No wonder he was there. James sighed. Unfortunately, even if the protesters finally got their way, it could be too late for Spanner.

James looked at his watch. Not long now and the speakers would arrive. Then he would be relieved and expected to mingle with the protesters, just to make sure no one had any plans to cause trouble. With a bit of luck, he could take the opportunity to have a chat with Spanner and Pete then.

Omaha, Nebraska

Rachel felt like she was walking on air, breathless with an excitement she'd never felt before. The march had finished, but she was still on a high. She didn't want it to end. Jenny watched her new friend's face with amusement. "How about we go and sit in the park? I'll introduce you to some friends of mine."

Rachel nodded, delighted the day wasn't over yet. "Thank you, that would be amazing."

"What made you decide to join us today?" Jenny was genuinely interested. Rachel was obviously reasonably well-off, though her expensive clothes were understated: neat knee-length dress and cardigan, her coat slung carelessly over her arm.

"I heard about it on KOI." Jenny looked slightly confused. "The local radio station?"

Jenny nodded. "Ah, ok. I'm not from around here

originally. I'm staying near the Old Market with some friends."

Rachel's eyes widened in surprise. Her parents frequented the French Café; they'd taken her there a few weeks earlier as a special treat when she and her tennis partner had won a doubles match in the club tournament. The view from the floor-to-ceiling windows still stuck in her memory. From there she'd gazed down on the brick-built buildings and cobblestone streets, a movie house, antique shop, artist studios and galleries. The place that had really caught her eye had been a large artisan space where various stalls sold handmade crafts. She would have loved to walk around, but her mother would have been horrified if she had suggested it, so she'd kept her thoughts to herself. Maybe this was her opportunity...

"I'd love to have a look around..." Rachel couldn't believe she'd spoken out loud. "Sorry, that sounded very presumptuous." Rachel held her breath and wished the ground would open up and swallow her. How could she be so stupid? And it was all going so well... To her relief, Jenny laughed.

"If you want to come and visit us, you're more than welcome. We can take a walk around together, if you like?"

Rachel relaxed. "Wow, that would be really neat – if you don't mind."

"Of course not. So, what did you think of the march?"

"It was awesome. Are there any more planned?"

Jenny smiled. "Yes, there's a big rally being organised for next month in Washington."

"Really? Like this one?" Rachel's heart skipped a beat.

"Yes, but much bigger." Jenny stopped and gazed intently into the younger girl's eyes. "We're determined to make Nixon keep his promises. He only got elected because he said he'd pull our troops out of Vietnam, and yet he's escalating the war by going into Cambodia." A flush of passion coloured her cheeks, and she paused as if out of breath.

Rachel didn't answer. She didn't want to admit that she never paid that much attention to the news.

Jenny seemed to realise her discomfort. "Sorry. I just get really annoyed when I think of all our poor boys being sent out there."

"Do you think the president will listen?"

Jenny shrugged. "He can't ignore us if we're right outside his door, can he? Oh look! There's Bob and Debbie." She waved her arm and increased her pace towards a couple of young people sitting on a park bench. Rachel followed close behind, trying to look more confident than she felt.

"This is my new friend Rachel." Jenny introduced everyone before surreptitiously taking a hand-rolled cigarette from Bob. "Boy, I need this." She inhaled deeply and let the smoke out slowly before offering it to Rachel.

Rachel hesitated, but she didn't want her new friends to think she was a child, so she took the cigarette and hesitantly put it to her lips.

"Just inhale, it's magic," Jenny smiled encouragingly.

Rachel nodded and did as she was told. The harsh taste of marijuana caught in her throat, but somehow she managed not to cough. Instead she breathed the smoke deep into her lungs before handing it back to Jenny. She was vaguely aware of everyone watching her, then everything became blurred and hazy. "Wow," she managed, before groping her way onto the ground.

"Great, isn't it?" Jenny was sitting beside her, reefer still in hand.

Rachel nodded and then wished she hadn't as her head swam again. But at the same time, she was aware of a growing feeling of warmth, of relaxation, of intense happiness. Jenny smiled and handed her back the reefer. Rachel tried again. This time she didn't feel the need to cough and she closed her eyes in pleasure.

"Fuzz!" The urgent whisper pulled her out of her reverie. The reefer was snatched from her fingers, and she opened her eyes to find a policeman heading towards them.

James headed towards the group sitting on the park bench. He recognised the two girls he'd seen earlier. The others looked like any other hippies, probably from the Old Market district. The young girl on the grass had a vacant expression on her face, and he sighed. The distinctive smell of marijuana hit him, but was gone as quickly as it had appeared, blown away by the cool autumn breeze.

"Afternoon, officer." The hippy with the auburn hair he had seen before smiled up at him.

"Miss." He touched his cap. "I hope you're not smoking anything you shouldn't?"

Jenny managed to look affronted. "Of course not, officer."

"Mmm. Well, you'd better look after your friend. She looks a little unwell."

Jenny glanced at Rachel and bit her lip. Rachel was indeed looking rather green. "She's just had her first cigarette," she improvised. "I don't think it's agreed with her. But don't worry – we'll look after her."

James hesitated. He didn't really have the time or inclination to bust them for smoking dope, but his fellow officers would not be so lenient. "I'd suggest you move on now, ok?"

Jenny breathed a sigh of relief and stood up. "Yes, officer, we were just about to do that. Thank you."

She watched as James moved off and reached down for Rachel's arm. "Come on, Rachel, you have to go home."

Rachel stood up carefully. She was feeling better now, but she was horrified at the fact she could have been arrested. Her parents would kill her if they found out what she had been doing. But it had been fun, and she now knew what she wanted to do with the rest of her life. She wanted to make a difference, to change the world. The first step would be to get to the march in Washington.

Omaha, Nebraska

Charles Brandon Peterson blew the girl a kiss goodbye before letting himself out of the door, a satisfied smile on his face. That was the best sex he'd had in a while. Shame he was going to have to say goodbye. But she was starting to get clingy, and that was the last thing he wanted. It wasn't as if there weren't plenty of other women around who were more than willing to take him to their beds. With his Swedish good looks, cropped blonde hair, blue eyes and easy smile, Charles was very popular with the opposite sex, and he was more than happy to take advantage of this. He had always been able to charm the ladies; it was his father he had trouble with. He scowled. His father was constantly on his case, forever telling him what to do, always reminding him that he had the family name to live up to. He much preferred his mother. He could wrap her around his little finger, but it was a shame she wouldn't stand up to his father.

By the time he reached his Alfa Romeo GTZ2, Charles's good mood had evaporated. He climbed in, slammed the door and drove off at speed. He hadn't got very far before the sirens started. Charles cursed, but he reluctantly pulled over to the side of the road and waited.

"Can I see your driving licence please?" The policeman was polite, but Charles wasn't in the mood. If he got another ticket his father would hit the roof; he might even take away his car.

"I'm not sure why you've stopped me. I haven't done anything wrong."

"You were speeding, sir. Your licence, please." The policeman had recognised Charles now, and his fist clenched. Another spoilt brat who thought he could get away with breaking the law because Daddy had money.

Charles was about to argue when he realised there was no point. He took out his wallet, pulled out his licence and slipped a $100 bill into it. "Here you are, officer," he smiled.

The policeman stared down at the money and hesitated. He glanced around. There was no one about, no one watching. He had a young family; a hundred dollars was a lot of money. He licked his lips and wiped away the sweat that had suddenly appeared on his upper lip. The money disappeared into his pocket and he handed back the licence.

"My mistake, sir. Just make sure you stick to the speed limit, please. Have a good day."

Charles watched him walk back to the patrol car and grinned. Money always talked.

CHAPTER THREE

Omaha, Nebraska

Come on people now, smile on your brother, everybody get together, try to love one another right now...

Rachel lay on her bed listening to The Youngbloods on her transistor radio and wished she had some marijuana and could roll her own reefers. If only she'd been allowed to go to Woodstock... Jenny had told her all about it. All those amazing artists, the icons of the age, all in one place, and she had missed it because she was too young. Rachel sighed. Being 16 was the pits, especially when she felt much older. She was top of her class in all subjects and she knew exactly what she wanted out of her life. But she was still young enough to want to have some fun.

Her new friend Jenny was like a breath of fresh air. Much to her surprise, Rachel had managed to keep her attendance at the protest march and her new friendship a secret from her parents. They definitely wouldn't approve of Jenny, so it would probably be best if they didn't meet her just yet – or ever. In any case, it was rather nice to have a secret, something her parents didn't know. It made her feel grown up. Her thoughts wandered back to the main discussion at the commune, the upcoming protest march in Washington. She was determined to go, but the question was how to travel all that way without her parents knowing. They would never agree if she asked them.

The knock on the door made her jump. "Yes?"

Her older brother opened the door and leaned in. "Hi sis, just to let you know I'm taking you to tennis tonight. Mom has a headache."

"Ok, thanks Paul. I'll be ready in about 30 minutes."

"Ok, I'll meet you downstairs in 30." The door closed and he disappeared.

Rachel felt the usual surge of irritation when Paul mentioned driving her anywhere. It wasn't that she was ungrateful, just annoyed that her parents wouldn't let her take lessons so she could drive herself. Her parents had paid for them both to have expensive educations, and they supported her sporting activities, especially her tennis. But it was still Paul who was the most important. As soon as he was old enough, he had learnt to drive, and when he'd passed his test their parents had bought him a car. They wouldn't even let her have lessons. Not that being able to drive would have helped her get to Washington, because she would still have to find a good excuse to disappear for a couple of days. If only her parents gave her the same amount of freedom they did Paul. He could come and go as he pleased, whereas she had to ask permission for everything.

The music had changed now: Bob Dylan's 'Lay Lady Lay' interrupted her thoughts and for a moment she closed her eyes and allowed the music to relax her. She really needed to get some dope of her own. It wasn't as if she couldn't afford it, she had her allowance. The thought of spending the money her parents gave her on dope was exhilarating, exciting and nerve-wracking all at the same time, and she savoured it.

The track finished, Rachel turned over and lay on her side, her thoughts returning to Paul. It wasn't that she didn't love her brother, she did, but it was infuriating that her parents concentrated all their ambitions on him, convinced he was going to be someone important. She was sure they were right, and that was good. She would like to see Paul do well, but that didn't mean she too couldn't shine. Rachel was determined to prove her parents wrong about her. What was the point of having an expensive education if she couldn't use it? She was worth so much more than just being some rich man's wife, having his children and basically becoming a younger version of her mother. A life like that would drive her mad. She wanted more and now was the time to get it. Times were changing, women were beginning to fight back at last. She was grateful to her parents for giving her a good start in life, but despite this they still expected more from Paul than her.

The radio switched to the Fifth Dimension and 'Aquarius/Let the Sunshine In' filled the room. Rachel closed her eyes and thought about the future. Her new friends had really opened her eyes to all the injustices in the world. Their conversations were so much more stimulating than those of her other friends. All they wanted to talk about was boys and who they were going to marry. She had been bored with that before, but now she felt completely disconnected from them. She wanted to make a difference to people's lives, and she couldn't do that if she allowed her parents to marry her off to the first rich idiot they found.

Well, that was a problem for another day. Today's problem was to find a way of getting to Washington. Jenny had said she could go with them in their VW camper van, but she couldn't just disappear for several days. Her parents would be worried sick if she just went without telling them, and if she left a note, they would notify the police and then her new friends would get into trouble and probably miss the march, or worse. Rachel shuddered at the thought. There had to be a way. Maybe she could ask one of her friends to say she was with them? Rachel thought carefully. That might work, unless her parents decided to check on her. But they would only do that if they were suspicious, and there was no reason for them to suspect anything if she was careful. Her heart beat a little faster. And provided they didn't check up too soon, she would already be in Washington and there would be nothing they could do. There would be hell to pay when she got home, but it would be worth it.

She glanced at the clock and stretched. She had better get ready. At least this was something Paul couldn't do. Rachel smiled. Tennis was something she was very good at; not as good as Billy Jean King of course, but certainly good enough to allow her to mix with the great and the good at the most prestigious of Omaha's private tennis clubs.

Rachel stood up and hurried towards the closet to look for her tennis wear. She would find a reason to go into the city tomorrow and tell Jenny she was going to come with them. Then she would work out which of her friends was the most trustworthy and set up her alibi.

Outside Springfield, Nebraska

Spanner finished his beer and glanced down at his cards. He had a lousy hand, but it didn't really matter as they weren't playing for money. "I'm out." He put the cards down and glanced at Pete and Jamie, who always took the games more seriously than he did.

Pete followed suit. "Me too."

Jamie smirked. "Thanks guys!"

"Make the most of it, you won't win next time," Pete grumbled, but his comment was good-humoured.

"I hear they're planning a massive anti-war march in Washington next month. Are you going?" Jamie was opening his beer, but he was watching Spanner carefully.

Spanner shook his head, his good mood evaporating.

"No, probably not. I can't really take time off for that as well as for working on the car. It's not fair on Dad."

"What's he gonna do if you get drafted?" Jamie drank deeply from his bottle.

Spanner shrugged. "Chris is already working full time; Andy will have to step up. He's nearly 16, so it won't hurt him. Anyway, he loves working on the farm, so I don't think that's much of a problem." He sighed. "But that's different to me just taking time off to go on some march." He changed the subject. "How's Tammy?"

Jamie grinned. "She's getting big now, three years old going on twenty." They all laughed. "She's just like a miniature Linda, real smart. But I would say that, wouldn't I?"

"You're lucky, Jamie." Steve was surprised to find that a part of him envied his friend, not just because he wouldn't have to worry about being drafted, at least not yet, but because he had a daughter. Spanner quite liked the idea of having a daughter, someone to protect and look after. Having a son would be even better... He pushed the thoughts away. There was no point thinking about the future. He might not have one.

"We could go together, the three of us?" Pete suddenly interjected.

Spanner was about to reiterate the reasons he couldn't leave the farm when he stopped. Maybe he should go. If everyone made excuses not to protest, the war would just continue, possibly for years, and then it wouldn't only be his life it affected – it would be his brothers' too. He owed it to them.

Omaha, Nebraska

Emily watched Rachel climb into Paul's car before heading back to bed. Her headaches were becoming more frequent. If they carried on like this she would have to see the doctor again; the tablets he'd given her were taking longer to work each time. She closed her eyes and winced. This headache was different, it hadn't come out of the blue like they often did. It was probably a result of worrying about Rachel. After she'd lost sight of her daughter at the protest meeting, she'd come home and tried to work out whether she should confront her daughter or not. She had eventually decided to hire a private detective to follow Rachel and find out if she was still seeing that hippy girl. To her horror, the man had reported that her daughter had gone straight to the Old Market District and disappeared into one of the old tenements. Emily was shocked, and for once she didn't know what to do about it. If she waded in and forbade her daughter from seeing *those people*, Emily shuddered, she was likely to make things worse. Rachel had inherited her mother's stubborn streak and her father's quiet determination. The two characteristics together would be lethal if they weren't properly channelled. Emily already knew that her daughter resented the attention they gave to Paul; the last thing they needed was to alienate her even further.

As the tablets gradually relaxed her and she drifted off, Emily found her thoughts wandering to how she'd been at Rachel's age.

Like her daughter, Emily had been very pretty, intelligent and athletic, an extrovert who excelled at all sports, which made her very popular and compensated for her family's lack of money. Emily's main sport had been tennis too, and this had enabled her to cultivate the friendship of the sons and daughters of the wealthy and powerful. She spent her summers playing at elite country clubs, which was where she met Mark. The young men liked winning trophies and loved partnering Emily. Not only was she pretty, she also played well. To supplement the money from her family, Emily worked in the kitchen of a local hotel. She had chosen this deliberately because she was unlikely to be seen by any of her rich friends if she was in the kitchen, and an added bonus was that she learned to prepare and cook food. Emily loved the expensive things in life, but she hadn't yet worked out how to afford them. She had no intention of spending the rest of her life slogging in the hotel or marrying one of her many suitors who were nice but poor and had no prospects. It wasn't until Mark Hanson arrived for dinner one evening with his family in a chauffeured limousine that the idea struck her.

Emily immediately recognised Mark from the tennis

club. He was one of the quiet boys, not particularly good at tennis, but he was handsome. Emily made a mental note to find out more about him. Her athletic ability allowed her to gain a scholarship to the Municipal University of Omaha and she proceeded to study American History, but she hadn't forgotten Mark and she continued her enquiries. Discovering he was the grandson of the founder of Hanson, Brown and Jensen, a financial firm that could trace its history back to 1890 and provided tax advice and dealt with the accounts of most of the big corporations in Omaha, made him even more interesting.

In July 1950, Emily had attended a barbeque at the tennis club to raise money for Korean refugees. Emily wasn't that interested in the cause; she was more concerned about taking the opportunity to get to know Mark Hanson, and she wasted no time in putting her plan into action. The first step was ensuring she and her partner Grant won the mixed doubles. Grant was delighted and needed little persuasion to introduce Emily to one of his friends. Emily found Mark very shy, so she took it slowly, keeping his drink topped up and being very attentive. Emily was careful to only drink orange juice, wanting to keep her wits about her. This could be her only chance – and it worked. Mark had gradually relaxed and even allowed her to take him onto the dance floor.

Emily smiled as she remembered their first kiss. Mark had suggested they get some fresh air away from the crowded dance floor and Emily agreed. In the darkened area of a tennis court they stopped. Mark was quiet, and he made no move to touch her. Emily decided to take things into her own hands and just hope she had read Mark correctly.

She turned towards him, put her arms around his neck and gently pulled him down to her lips, allowing the kiss to linger for quite a few seconds. It was Mark who broke the kiss, and for a moment she thought she had ruined everything. Mark had gazed down at her for what seemed like an eternity, before suddenly bending down towards her again, holding her tightly and kissing her roughly on the lips. Emily had felt his excitement and she relaxed, allowing him to continue for a few minutes even though she didn't like his roughness. Mark moved his hands to caress her body. Emily allowed him to run his hand over her breasts, once, before stopping him and suggesting they go back inside. She could feel his disappointment, but she knew she had done the right thing. If she'd given in then, she might have lost him. For the rest of that summer Mark and Emily had been inseparable, but she had always remained in control. If he got too excited, Emily would gently relieve him and convince him it was safer that way.

While Mark was away studying at Cornell University for two years he had written to Emily regularly, and she had always replied promptly, trying to make her letters as amusing and interesting as possible. Emily shuddered again as she relived that awful time, terrified as she was that she would lose him to some wealthy Ivy League socialite.

Emily opened her eyes and stared up at the ornate ceiling. Rachel may have thought her parents were fixated on Paul's career and didn't care about her, but she had no idea. Emily's ambitions for her daughter far outweighed those she had for Paul. Paul was moderately clever, and he was amenable. He would do what he was told to keep the peace. It was Rachel who had the brains of the family, and Emily had every intention of exploiting that to further the family's fortune. The question that was causing her headaches was how she was going to keep her daughter in line.

CHAPTER FOUR

Village north of Da Nang, Vietnam

The helicopters came early in the morning, the whirring blades lifting her sun hat and scattering the village children as they landed in the grasslands and unloaded their men. Lien watched from the river, seated on her favourite water buffalo as it plodded slowly along, seemingly unfazed by the noise. Lien counted the men as they jumped off the machines, their weapons cradled in their hands, their rucksacks weighing them down, and watched as they ran towards the few patches of vegetation that provided them with cover. Lien frowned as she reached 50. This was the biggest force she had seen so far. She watched as the men settled into their hiding places and wondered what they were waiting for. She didn't have to wait long to find out, as in the distance she spotted more Americans coming down from the hills. The helicopters hadn't yet taken off, and she realised they must be there to collect the soldiers coming down.

Her heart skipped a beat and she felt a frisson of excitement. Normally the exchange was quick and precise from regular practice and the machines were gone almost as quickly as they had arrived, but not this time. She stared again at the men tracking down from the hill and estimated it would be at least another ten minutes before they were down. If she was quick, she could give the signal…

Lien stood on the small hillock outside the village and scratched her nose before removing her sun hat and fanning herself twice. She replaced the hat, climbed down and waited. Within seconds there was a rustling noise behind her, and a freedom fighter appeared.

"What is it?" He looked furious at being summoned.

"The American helicopters are waiting to pick up their men, they will be at least another five minutes." Lien spoke so quickly she feared he might not understand. She opened her mouth to repeat it, but his expression had changed completely and before she could say anything else, he had gone.

Lien slumped back down on the hillock, her breath coming in short gasps as she realised the consequences of what she had just done. If the VC ambushed the Americans and anyone had seen her contacting the freedom fighters, or even talking to them, they would destroy the village and kill everyone in it.

She took a deep breath and tried to calm herself. How could they have seen her? She had slipped away from the buffalo and swum down the other side of the river out of sight of the Americans. They couldn't possibly have seen her. They were too busy watching in the other direction for an ambush.

She was still trying to convince herself when the sound of explosions shattered the silence followed by rapid machine gun fire, rocket launchers, grenades exploding. Smoke drifted lazily upwards in the distance, and then she heard something else. Above her head a gunship appeared, spitting fire and tearing up the bushes and trees on the other side of the village. It flew lower, and then the bullets were ricocheting off the ground in front of her. There was nowhere to go, nowhere to hide. If she moved, she would be hit. Lien covered her ears and crouched down as far as she could, but the bullets raced across the ground toward her. Instinctively she closed her eyes and waited for the pain.

She was still waiting when the gunship moved away, and the noise began to fade into the distance. Lien opened her eyes cautiously and took her hands from her ears. They were buzzing and everything sounded like it was coming from a long way away, except... She shook her head. She must be imagining it. But no, it was definitely there. Lien could hear screaming, a long cry of pain that reverberated around her head, and reached deep into her soul... and it was coming from just in front of her.

Omaha, Nebraska

"Thanks for the lift, Paul." Rachel climbed out of her brother's red Chevrolet Corvette.

"No problem, sis." He watched as she hurried towards the tennis club, paused briefly at the door to wave and then disappeared inside. His mother would be very disappointed he hadn't asked Rachel if she had a boyfriend. But it was hardly something he could just blurt out. He was reasonably sure she wasn't seeing anyone, although… Paul frowned. Actually, now he thought about it carefully, perhaps his mother did have a point. Rachel was acting a little strange. He shrugged. It would have to wait until the next time he was with her, and he would have to try and find the right way of asking or he wouldn't get a straight answer.

He was about to turn the car around and drive away when there was a loud roar behind him. Paul glanced in the mirror and watched as an Alfa Romeo raced up the drive and into the small car park before pulling up sharply. The driver climbed out, reached back inside and took out a tennis racket. As he straightened up, Paul grimaced. Charles Brandon Peterson, Rachel's doubles partner, was unmistakable: tall athletic build, short blond hair, arrogance in every step as he strode towards the club. What on earth Rachel saw in him, Paul had no idea. In fact, he couldn't understand why the ladies had any time for Charles. The man was completely insufferable. Paul was about to drive off when an idea popped into his head. He shook his head. No, surely not? A wry smile crossed his face. No, Rachel had too much sense to get involved with Charles. Although his mother would probably approve if she did.

Paul sighed; she certainly wouldn't approve of his friend. He eased the car out of the car park and headed into the city. Traffic was light and it wasn't long before he pulled up outside an expensive apartment block. Paul drove into the underground parking lot and parked in his usual place. The garage was silent, and he didn't pass anyone on his way to the elevator. Once inside he pressed the button to the tenth floor and waited patiently as he ascended. The tenth floor was also deserted, and Paul made his way quickly to his friend's door, checked there was no one about before pressing the doorbell. The door opened almost immediately.

"Paul, you're late. I was beginning to think you weren't coming."

Paul looked apologetic. "Sorry, I had to drop my sister at the tennis club first." He stepped quickly inside, closing the door behind them.

Rachel was busy practicing with one of the other boys when Charles reached the court. He tossed his towel onto the chair and strolled nonchalantly out onto the court.

"I'll take over now."

Rachel nodded at the other boy. "Thanks, Aaron. I'll see you next week." She turned towards Charles. "It wouldn't hurt you to be polite."

Charles looked surprised. "I thought I was." He smiled and threw a tennis ball over the net to her. "You can serve first."

Rachel nodded; there was no point arguing with Charles, he never listened to anyone except himself. Her first serve was down the line, but Charles still managed to return it and Rachel found herself running all over the court. For the first time in days, she forgot about the march and concentrated her attention on making sure Charles didn't beat her. It was a forlorn hope – she had never beaten him before, and the first game soon went the way of previous games, although she did manage to win two points.

Charles watched Rachel running around the court opposite him and tried to ignore his feelings. Rachel was a very attractive young lady and he was determined to have her one day, but he had to be careful. Rachel wasn't some waitress or shop worker, her family had money, so he had to tread carefully. Unfortunately, she seemed immune to his charm. He would have to try harder. The thought amused him. He had never had to try hard for anything. If it didn't fall into his lap, he would just take it.

Village North of Da Nang

Lien peered anxiously into the trees wishing the noise would stop. It seemed to be getting louder, but she still couldn't see anything. Her ears were beginning to hurt, but there was no movement in front of her. She shook her head and the noise changed vibration slightly. Lien grimaced. It was no good, she would have to leave her place of safety. She couldn't stand that noise for much longer.

"Lien, are you hurt?" She jumped and looked behind her. Phuc was standing there, concern on his face.

She shook her head slowly. The noise vibrated again.

"Then stop screaming!"

Lien gaped at him in shock, then he slapped her across the face and the noise halted abruptly. "Are you sure you aren't hurt?"

Lien nodded, relieved the terrible screaming had ceased but unsettled that the noise had been coming from her and she hadn't even realised.

"We have to get back to the bunker. If you are found out here..." He left the rest of the sentence unspoken. Lien nodded and suddenly found the strength to move. She stood up and followed Phuc back to the house, helped him move the cooker and climbed down the steps. The bunker was full, not only with her family, but with several freedom fighters. Lien recognised a couple from the midnight meetings, and she smiled at them.

"Where have you been?" Huy, her father, was furious.

"Tending the cattle, father, I had to leave them when the fighting started." Lien was surprised to find the lies rolled off her tongue effortlessly, although she was careful not to look at Phuc. She squeezed in next to her parents and looked down at the floor. Her head was still spinning, and every time she thought about what she'd done, her heart started pounding.

Above them the bombing continued. The house shook intermittently, the rattle of machine guns grew closer and Lien felt sick. At one point she looked up to find Phuc smiling at her, and she made an effort to return his smile. All she could think of was how many people were dead because of her actions. If she could turn the clock back, she would, but it was far too late for that.

Omaha, Nebraska

"That's wonderful, Rachel." Jenny reached out and hugged her. "I'm so pleased you can come with us."

Rachel dumped her coat on the floor and eased herself down onto one of the large cushions in the living room. She had told her parents she was going to Vanessa's after school, so she had a few hours of freedom. Vanessa was more than happy to cover for her, convinced Rachel had a boyfriend, an assumption Rachel was more than happy for her to believe if it meant she could spend time with her new friends.

"How'd you get your parents to agree?" Bob was stretched out on the pile of cushions strewn on the floor, watching Debbie swaying rhythmically to the Mamas and Papas album playing on the rather battered record player in the corner of the room. Posters of Che Guevara, Indian gods and Buddhas adorned the walls, competing with beaded curtains, cotton throws and wind chimes. By the large floor-to-ceiling window, numerous plants bathed in the late afternoon light. As 'Dream a Little Dream of Me' started, Bob exhaled a cloud of smoke up into the brightly painted ceiling, leaned forward and handed the reefer to Rachel.

"No sweat." Rachel took the cigarette gratefully and inhaled the smoke deep into her lungs. She didn't want to lie to her new friends, so she hoped that would suffice. She had been planning to ask Vanessa to cover for her, but then she'd realised there was no need to actually arrange anything. If her parents checked with any of her friends, they would soon find out she was lying anyway so why involve anybody else in her lies. She would just say she was going to one of them for a long weekend and hope they wouldn't check up at all, or at least not before she had left Nebraska.

"Will they be alright with us going earlier?" Jenny asked.

Rachel's heartbeat quickened slightly. "Earlier?" She inhaled deeply again before reluctantly passing the reefer to Jenny. She would have liked to smoke a bit more, but she was still new to the etiquette of joint smoking and didn't want to be called a bogart.

"They're planning to hold a March Against Death starting on Thursday evening, so we're going to leave here on Tuesday morning."

Rachel nodded. "No, that'll be cool." She lay back, closed her eyes and thought as quickly as the marijuana would let her. She would have to tell her parents she was staying overnight instead. A smile spread over her face, as she realised that this would actually be easier. No one would bother looking for her until the Wednesday morning, and by that time they would definitely be out of Nebraska and well on the way to Washington. There would be hell to pay when she got home, but she'd worry about that then. "What time do we leave?"

"As early as possible, to give us plenty of time," Bob answered. "About nine?"

"I'll be here." Rachel stared up at the psychedelic painting on the ceiling, her eyes tracing the patterns. She smiled over at Bob. "Can I buy some dope off you?"

Bob grinned. "Sure, honey, how much do you want?"

"Just a couple of grams please – oh, and some Rizlas..." Rachel breathed a sigh of relief. She'd been nervous of asking.

She was vaguely aware of Bob standing up, and then he was squatting down beside her. "Here, $5 worth, that ok?"

"Super, thank you." Rachel sat up, put it in her bag and took the cash from her purse.

"Don't get caught." Jenny was looking concerned. Although Rachel didn't look like she smoked, if she was stopped, she could still be given seven days in jail.

"I won't." Rachel thought carefully for a moment before slipping the small bag and packet of Rizlas down into her boot. She winked at Jenny, glanced at her watch and sighed. "I'd better go, or I'll miss the bus."

She got slowly to her feet, wishing she could savour the fuzzy feeling in her head a bit longer, gave Jenny a hug, waved to Bob and Debbie and headed for the door.

"Bye Rachel, take care."

Rachel turned back and beamed at them. "See you next Tuesday morning at nine." As she headed down the stairs to the street, her heart was pounding with excitement. Only a week to go and she would be on her way to Washington. She couldn't wait.

CHAPTER FIVE

Omaha, Nebraska

"Another goddamn speeding ticket?" Jonathan Brandon Peterson glared at his son as he threw the ticket on the large antique desk in front of him.

Charles shrugged. "Just some stupid cop trying to make his name." Having avoided a speeding ticket on the day of the anti-war demonstrations, he'd fallen foul of another policeman a week later. Unfortunately, this one hadn't been interested in taking his bribe.

Jonathan slammed his hand on the desk, making Charles jump. "And you tried to bribe him? For Christ's sake, Charles, what the hell is the matter with you?"

"It normally works."

For a moment, Jonathan was speechless. He stood up and walked around the desk until he was face to face with his son. Charles swallowed nervously and stepped back. "I have lost count of the times we've had this conversation. This is your last warning. One more ticket and the car goes." Charles breathed a sigh of relief. "And you can thank your mother for that. If it was up to me, you'd be walking now!" Jonathan added furiously, walking back to his chair.

Charles debated whether now was a good time to ask his father about an increase to his allowance, and then decided it probably wasn't.

"Are you still here?" Jonathan barked.

Charles spun on his heel and headed for the door. He would leave it a couple of weeks, then ask about a raise. At least he still had the car, which meant he could go and visit Dorothy. She was always sympathetic, and he could do with cheering up.

Village north of Da Nang, Vietnam

The American soldiers were everywhere, their helicopters landed and took off constantly, and Lien lived in constant fear that she would be discovered. She was sure her father was suspicious, mainly because Phuc was treating her with respect instead of his usual disdain for his younger sister. It was rather nice to have her brother admiring her, but she wasn't sure it compensated for the terror that at any moment the Americans would arrest her.

"Lien!" The loud whisper broke into her thoughts and she spun around. Phuc was standing by the door, a smile on his face. Lien was still struggling to get used to her brother's smile, it wasn't something she'd seen much of growing up.

"I am going to join the fight. Tell our parents that they should be proud of me, and if I die for the cause I will always be remembered."

"But what will we say to the Republicans?" Lien was horrified. The Republican soldiers knew who lived in each house, they had been coming to the village regularly over the past few years. It wouldn't take long for them to miss her brother and then take reprisals against the rest of the family.

"Tell them I was killed in the bombing and you have buried me."

"But how...?"

Phuc took a step towards her and lowered his voice. "Tell our father to dig a grave and for you all to mourn."

"But surely you should wait until there is some more bombing?" Lien shook her head.

Phuc frowned, and Lien realised he hadn't given any proper thought to this. Typical Phuc, impetuous as always. Somehow, she had to persuade him to delay his departure. "If you go now, it will be obvious you have gone to join the VC."

The stubborn expression she recognised so well crossed his face and he shook his head. "It is my duty to fight for us, Lien. You have played your part; now it is my turn to make the family proud."

"We won't be proud if we are all dead, will we?" Lien was furious that not only had he mentioned her without checking there was no one around, but that he was prepared to put them all at risk just to compete with her.

"It's alright for you – you're a girl, and still you have helped destroy our enemies…" Phuc had raised his voice, and in panic Lien grabbed his arm and dragged him inside.

"Are you trying to get us all killed?"

"No, I am trying to make you and my family proud." Phuc pulled his arm away from her. "You have no idea…" He stopped abruptly at a sound behind him and the horrified expression on Lien's face. Swallowing nervously, he whirled around.

Washington DC, USA

Rachel, Jenny, Bob and Debbie had arrived in time to join the estimated forty-thousand protesters walking down Pennsylvania Avenue to the White House, each carrying the name of a dead American soldier or a Vietnamese village that had been destroyed. The march was silent, only punctuated by the sound of six drums playing funeral songs. They finished in front of the Capitol Building, placing the placards in coffins, but there was no sign of the President.

"I don't understand why he doesn't come out and speak to us." Rachel sounded bewildered. She had never experienced anything like this. The journey east had been exciting enough, her heart palpitating wildly until they left Nebraska, despite the copious amounts of cannabis she'd smoked. She'd never travelled this far from home before, and while a part of her was terrified, she was also finding the whole experience exhilarating. To her relief, the VW had made good time, Bob driving more quickly than she'd expected. Rachel peered out of the window, ostensibly watching the changing scenery, but in reality checking there were no police cars following them. Marijuana flowed freely, and soon they had to open the windows of the camper van because it was hard to see where they were going. She watched as the plumes of smoke were carried away by the cold air, and then they were over the county line and she finally began to relax.

Jenny sighed. "They say another ten thousand American boys have died since he came to office. So much for ending the war."

"Not to mention innocent Vietnamese." Debbie was on Rachel's other side and she leaned in. "My Lai was a disgrace; I am so ashamed to be American."

Rachel didn't answer for a moment. She'd been brought up to be patriotic, and although she was against the war, she found it difficult to criticise her country. But these were her friends, and she was entitled to her opinion. "There are horrible people everywhere, Debbie, the massacre was carried out by individuals. You can't blame the country."

Debbie stared at her in astonishment and, forgetting where she was, raised her voice. "Surely you aren't defending them?"

"Shhhh!" The censure came from some people following behind them, their placards held high as they marched in silence.

"Sorry." Rachel flushed, half-turned towards them and apologised.

The three men nodded but didn't reply. Rachel turned back, feeling embarrassed.

"Don't worry, you're right about not blaming everyone for the mistakes of a few," Jenny whispered in her ear. Rachel gave her a grateful smile and turned her attention back to the march. It was still silent for the most part, and she felt guilty for breaking the solidarity.

"Well, that was quite emotional, wasn't it?" Steve was surprised by just how much the march had affected him. They had arrived early, intending to find somewhere to stay, but instead they'd found the March Against Death and joined in. Apart from some silly girls chatting in the middle, the protest had been silent, which had made it all the more powerful.

"Peaceful, too." Jamie sounded surprised.

"I thought more people might be here." There was disappointment in Pete's voice.

"Well, the main event is on Saturday, so we'll see how many turn up for that," Steve grinned. "Come on, let's get some sleep, and perhaps we can have a look around tomorrow before it all starts." The three men headed towards the Smithsonian Museum complex which, like many other buildings including schools in Washington, had opened up their doors to offer the protesters somewhere to sleep.

Village north of Da Nang, Vietnam

"What does she have no idea about?" The Republican soldier stood in the doorway, his face unsmiling, hands on his weapon.

"You made me jump. Don't you ever knock?" Lien was so terrified that the soldier had heard Phuc's words about her that she completely forgot about playing stupid and spoke without thinking.

The soldier moved closer, his rifle ominously raised. Phuc was still speechless. Somehow, Lien pulled herself together and rolled her eyes. "If it's any of your business... we were having the usual family argument. My brother was just moaning about having to live here with us all, not having his own house yet. He wants to move to the city, but I said that it would break our father's heart if he does."

"What's in the bag?" The soldier didn't sound convinced, but he had lowered his rifle.

"Just some clothes I wanted my sister to wash before I left for the city, but she refused." Phuc had regained some of his confidence.

"Because you can't just leave without telling our parents, and I'm not sticking up for you," Lien snapped at him.

The soldier was standing undecided. "For heaven's sake, Phuc, show him your clothes!" Lien raised her voice and reached for his bag. "Look, I'll show you." She began undoing the bag. Phuc grabbed the bag and yelled back.

"Leave my stuff alone, I'll show him." He threw the bag on the floor and began undoing it. "You're always interfering..."

The soldier shook his head, his grin betraying his amusement. He backed towards the door, glanced around once more and left.

Lien stared at the vacant doorway for several seconds before groping her way back to the wall. She leaned against it, breathing heavily, her eyes closed. Phuc smiled at her. "That was very good thinking, Lien."

She opened her eyes and shook her head. "We were lucky. Surely you can see what I mean now, about how careful we have to be?" He didn't answer and Lien snapped. "If you must go, at least wait until there is still bombing or some fighting."

"But I don't need to wait now. Thanks to you, if I leave, they will just think I have gone to the city."

Lien shook her head. "It's still too dangerous Phuc... If you don't care about me, then at least think about our parents."

"But the Republican dog will say that he heard us arguing about going to the city..."

"We don't know that. He could be killed or moved

somewhere else." Lien was running out of arguments. "Please just wait until the bombing starts again. I am sure it won't be long, then you can go..."

"Go where?" Lien's father suddenly appeared in the doorway making them both jump. Lien moved to the door, her heart pounding uncomfortably against her ribs, and closed it firmly. She'd had enough shocks for one day.

Phuc faced him. "Yes, father, I can't stay any longer. I have to fight the invaders. I was going to leave now, but Lien insists that it is better if I wait."

"Wait for what?" Huy sounded confused. He smiled at his son. "It is your patriotic duty to fight the invaders."

Lien exhaled noisily, conveniently forgetting her own actions had already put them all in danger. What on earth was the matter with the men in her family? She had always looked up to her father, but now he was being as reckless as Phuc. "But not to get us all killed father. If he goes now, we will have trouble explaining his disappearance. It's better to wait until there is some more fighting, then we can pretend he has been killed."

Huy thought for a few seconds, then nodded. "Yes, your sister makes sense." He focused his attention on her, stepped closer and lowered his voice. "Was it you, Lien?"

Although she didn't want to lie to her father, Lien tried to look confused. "I don't know what you..."

"Who told them about the Americans?"

Lien hesitated. Then she nodded, slowly.

Huy smiled, reached out and patted her shoulder. "You did well, my child."

Lien shook her head and swallowed nervously. "Not if the Americans find out."

"They won't." He turned to Phuc. "Your sister is right; you will go when the next battle takes place."

Phuc hesitated. Would it always be like this? His sister taking precedence over him? He had to do something to make his father realise that it was he, not Lien, who would make the family proud. He forced himself to smile. "Yes father."

Omaha, Nebraska

"What do you mean she isn't there?" Emily snapped. She listened carefully and pursed her lips. She really hated apologising. "I'm sorry, I must have misunderstood. I'll try her other friends." Emily replaced the receiver and folded her arms. She hadn't made a mistake; Rachel had lied to her. But Emily had no intention of letting anyone else know that. She fought down her anger and tried to think rationally. Where would Rachel go that she didn't want her parents to know about? She picked up the phone and dialled. A few moments later, she was through to the private detective.

"I need to know where she's gone."

"If she's missing, shouldn't you call the police?" The detective didn't sound very happy.

"She's not missing, she's made very deliberate plans to go somewhere that she doesn't want us to know about. She told me she was staying overnight, so she should have been back today. If she's not back tonight I may have to call the police, but I would prefer to find her before that. What about those hippies she was hanging around with?"

The detective sighed. There was no point arguing with Mrs Hanson when she was in this mood. "I'll go straight over to the Old Market District and see if she is there."

The phone went dead, and Emily put the receiver down. She was sure in herself that Rachel was ok, and that she would return home when she was ready, but it was better to be safe rather than sorry.

Washington DC, USA

"Ho, Ho, Ho Chi Minh, Viet Cong are going to win."

The chants grew in volume as the protesters made their way to the National Monument. There were few clouds in the blue sky, the keen wind tugged at the flags of the protesters as their voices rose in unison. *"1,2,3,4, we don't want your fucking war!"*

"I've never seen so many people!" Rachel had to shout to make herself heard. All around her people were chanting loudly, waving home-made flags, placards and banners carrying message of peace, pictures of Ho Chi Minh, the protesters spanning all ages, black and white, young and old.

Jenny laughed. "They can't ignore this – there must be half a million people here."

Rachel was about to answer when the crowd stopped chanting and began singing instead. Rachel peered through the crowd; she could just make out Pete Seeger in the far distance leading them in John Lennon's 'Give Peace a Chance'. *"Are you listening Nixon? Are you listening Agnew? Are you listening Pentagon?"* His voice could be heard clearly in between the choruses of protesters singing, *"All we are saying... is give peace a chance."*

Rachel sung her heart out for the ten minutes the anthem lasted. All thoughts of home and the trouble she was likely to be in were forgotten as she gave herself completely to the cause.

Further back in the enormous crowd, Spanner and Pete were busy waving their own banners, *Get us out of Vietnam, Peace not War, Bring our soldiers home,* hastily put together on the Friday after they'd arrived. "Pleased you came?" Jamie yelled.

Spanner nodded. "Definitely. Feels good, doesn't it, to be part of this?" He leaned towards Pete. "Enough people here for you?"

Pete laughed. "Too right." He peered up towards the stage and turned his head in an attempt to hear what was being played. He didn't have to wait too long, as the crowd around them began singing loudly. As soon as he recognised the words to Country Joe and the Fish's famous anti-war anthem, Pete joined in with enthusiasm. "*"And it's one, two, three, what are we fighting for? Don't ask me, I don't give a damn. Next stop is Vietnam. And it's five, six, seven, open up the pearly gates. Well there ain't no time to wonder why. Whoopee! we're all gonna die.*" As the chorus died away Pete glanced across at his friends, expecting to see them singing along with everyone else. On his left, Jamie was waving his banner and shouting loudly in time, but although Spanner was waving his banner, he wasn't singing. Pete was about to ask why when he realised he already knew the answer. For Pete and Jamie this was a protest against a distant war, one that probably wouldn't really affect them at all. They could show their support, be part of a moment in history, sing anthems and protest songs, march in time with their friend, but unlike him, there was little danger of them being drafted. For Spanner, this was real life. This was his future. In a couple of weeks' time he would be sat in front of his family's small black and white television watching the draft lottery, his future decided by the fall of lottery balls. He reached out and gently punched Spanner's arm. He wanted to offer his friend support, to tell him it would be alright, but he couldn't.

Spanner slowly refocused his gaze and brought his thoughts back from the dark place the words of the song had taken him to. He was too young for his life to be over, there were things he wanted to do – he didn't know what they were yet, but he did know he didn't want to die.

Omaha, Nebraska

"The hippies have gone to Washington, to some protest march. They left Thursday morning and Rachel was with them." The detective's report was matter-of-fact, concealing his own sense of relief. He would have preferred the police to be involved in case Rachel really was missing; he certainly didn't want to be responsible.

Emily closed her eyes for a moment. Thank goodness, at least she was alright, or had been when she left for Washington. "Thank you. Is this the march they've been talking about on the television and radio?"

"Yes, the Moratorium Against the War. Massive turnout by all accounts, about half a million."

"Yes, so I heard on the radio. Alright, thank you. Send me your bill and I'll settle it." She put the phone down, clenched her fists and cursed. Goddamn stupid child. What on earth was she doing going to Washington with a load of hippies? Anything could happen to her. Emily stared stonily out at the extensive grounds, but for once the view didn't have its normal cheering effect. Instead, she was considering what to do about Rachel. She had to ensure this was the last time her daughter pulled a stunt like this, or she would put all Emily's plans for the future at risk.

"I'm not getting anywhere with our little problem." Mark strolled in from his study and watched his wife with concern. He had spent the morning chasing anyone he could speak to in an attempt to pull some strings. The draft lottery was coming up in two weeks, and unless he could do something about it, Paul could be drafted.

Emily frowned; for a moment she couldn't think what he was talking about. Then she remembered. The draft lottery. How on earth could she have forgotten? This was all Rachel's fault. If she hadn't been concentrating on her daughter... Her face paled. "If we can't find someone to help..."

Mark nodded and put his arms around her. "I'm sorry, Em, I've spoken to everyone I know. No one can do anything."

Emily shook her head and pulled away. "That's ridiculous, there must be something—"

"Senator Harley said he might be able to help if Paul's name comes up, but until then..." Mark shrugged helplessly.

"So we have to wait for fate to decide his future?" Emily slammed her fist onto the table, making the phone jolt. As if she didn't have enough problems.

Mark looked at her, confused. It was rare for Emily to lose her temper. "Is there something else going on?" He asked, after a long pause.

Emily met his eyes, wondering how to explain Rachel's stupidity. Mark had always been softer on their daughter than her, but she was sure that even he would draw the line at this. She had spent years trying to convince Mark that Rachel's education was equally as important as Paul's, that their daughter was just as intelligent, and now Rachel had blown it all by behaving like some stupid spoilt brat.

"Rachel has lied to us. She's not at school, she didn't spend the night at her friend's house. She's gone to Washington to join in some anti-war march."

Mark's eyes widened. "Washington? On her own?"

"No, with a bunch of hippies."

Mark looked even more astonished. "Hippies? How the hell did she meet them?"

"Last month at the march in the city." Emily rushed on before he had the chance to ask any more questions. "When I thought she had a boyfriend... I knew she was up to something, so I followed her... then I hired a detective."

Mark's eyes narrowed. "And you didn't think to mention this before?"

Emily faltered. "I thought it was just a phase she would grow out of."

There was a silence, which Mark broke. "Is she alright?"

"How the hell do I know?" Emily snapped, taking him by surprise. "I have no means of contacting her. We'll just have to wait until she comes home."

"And what if she doesn't?"

Emily stared at him in horror. That Rachel wouldn't come back had never occurred to her. "I'm sure she will..."

"Well, let's hope so!" Mark stormed off. Emily watched him go and shook her head. All her carefully laid plans were starting to fall apart because of that stupid war. Mark was seemingly unable to prevent their only son being drafted, and their daughter had gone completely off the rails.

CHAPTER SIX

Village north of Da Nang, Vietnam

It had been quiet for a couple of days and Lien had kept her head down, not even going to the midnight meetings. Despite hating the invaders of her country, she still felt guilty about the death of so many American soldiers. She knew they were the enemy, but her inner voice kept reminding her that they were still someone's son, someone's husband, brother, father. She sat astride the water buffalo as it made its slow path down the river, and again thanked Lord Buddha that as yet there had been no reprisals. It seemed the Americans had not realised anyone in the village had been the cause of their ambush. She prayed every night that this would continue.

"Are you still feeling sorry for the enemy?" Phuc's scornful voice interrupted her thoughts. He was walking alongside the riverbank.

Lien shook her head and lied. "Why would I feel sorry for them? They are invaders, and soon we will drive them out. Don't be so stupid. I was thinking about the future when our country is no longer at war."

Phuc was taken aback by her vehemence. Perhaps he was wrong about his sister. He had been sure she was regretting her actions. "Yes, you are right – we will defeat them, the sooner the better." He sighed. "I just want to go."

Lien drew a breath. Not this again. "We've agreed you are to go as soon as there is some fighting." She tried to speak calmly, even though she wanted to get off the buffalo and beat her brother with the stick she carried to keep the animals in check.

Phuc pursed his lips and kicked the grass and reeds on the edge of the bank. "It's taking too long." He peered at her from under his conical hat. "Maybe I should help things along..."

Lien stared at him in shock. She swallowed nervously. "What do you mean?"

Phuc shrugged. "I don't know... I could shoot one of the Republican dogs, that would start things off."

"And get you killed." Lien was beginning to have serious doubts about her brother's sanity. "I thought you wanted to fight the invaders, throw them off our soil, send them back where they came from? Killing one random soldier won't achieve that."

"Then perhaps we could do something better?"

Lien looked at him sharply. "We?" Since when did her brother think she was worthy of being included in anything?

"Together we could make a difference." He was smiling

now, the petulance gone.

Lien had started to shake her head when she suddenly caught herself. If she agreed with Phuc, it might prevent him from doing something really stupid. She didn't need to actually do anything, just pretend to go along with him. If nothing else, it would stop him thinking she'd gone soft on their enemies. "You're right, we should be fighting for our homeland." She was about to add that they should check with the VC first, to make sure they didn't compromise any of their operations, but as she had no intention of actually doing anything, there was no point.

Phuc smiled. If he could carry out a bigger operation and kill more soldiers than the last ambush had done, he would be the hero of the family, and they would soon forget about Lien.

Omaha, Nebraska

Rachel walked apprehensively up the long drive to her home and wondered what punishment awaited her. The euphoria from the past few days had worn off, and even copious amounts of marijuana couldn't take the edge off her nerves. The journey back from Washington had been too quick for her liking, and now it was time to face the music.

She was almost there when Paul appeared from behind the house, making her jump. "Oh boy, are you in trouble!"

Rachel blanched. "Did they call the police?"

Paul laughed. "No, Mom had a private detective on you."

"So they know where I've been?" Rachel wasn't sure that was such a bad thing. At least she wouldn't have to explain.

"Protesting with a load of dirty drugged up hippies in Washington."

Rachel flushed. "They aren't dirty."

Paul burst out laughing. "But they are drugged up?"

Rachel flushed even more. Paul stepped closer. "If you've got any dope, you can always give it to me until the heat's off."

Rachel shook her head. "No, I didn't think bringing any back here would be wise." She looked at him closely. "Do you smoke then?"

Paul hesitated, then nodded. "Of course, but I'm careful. You know what they're like."

Rachel was about to answer when the front door opened. The butler stood there, his face stern. "Your parents wish to see you in the drawing room immediately, Miss Rachel." His English accent always sounded more pronounced when he was being formal. Rachel sighed.

"Thanks, Tremayne." Rachel debated whether to say she wanted to get changed first, then decided it was best to get it over with.

"Good luck, sis." Paul disappeared down the drive and she wondered briefly where he was going before following Tremayne towards the drawing room.

Outside Springfield, Nebraska

Spanner stood outside the barn he used as a workshop and gazed out over the fields. All was quiet. He refocused his gaze on the lane, but there was no sign of Pete. Spanner looked at his watch and frowned. It was unusual for Pete to be late. He lit a cigarette and inhaled deeply, his thoughts on the protest in Washington. While they had been amongst the crowd he had felt an incredible sense of power, of being part of a momentous movement that would bring about change and save lives. He'd been convinced that the President would listen to them. How could he fail to be moved by the outpouring of anger, grief and the overwhelming determination for peace, for a better world for his generation and for Vietnam? But nothing had happened, the war had continued, the lottery would still take place, nothing had changed. They had effectively been completely ignored, and he didn't understand how that could happen. Weren't their voices important? He was still ruminating when he heard a car heading up the track. Good, Pete was here at last. Spanner stepped forward to greet him and stopped short. It wasn't Pete, it was a police car. He froze and wondered briefly if he was about to be arrested for going to the demonstration, then his common sense reasserted itself.

The car pulled up and to his surprise Jamie stepped out.

"Jamie?" Spanner laughed in surprise and relief. "I didn't

know you were coming up today, but you know you're always welcome. Pete's not here yet..." He stopped as he finally registered that Jamie was in uniform and driving a patrol car. His thoughts immediately went to his family, but they were all on the farm as far as he knew. He peered at his friend and his heart skipped a beat. Jamie wasn't smiling. If anything, he looked shocked. Spanner cleared his throat and ground out his cigarette on the earth. "Is something wrong?"

Jamie nodded. "Yes... yes, I'm real sorry, Spanner..." He stopped, unable to find the words.

"You're scaring me, pal." Spanner tried to smile, but his heart was pounding.

"It's Pete, he... he crashed on the highway."

"Crashed?" Spanner relaxed slightly. "I've told him so many times not to drive so fucking fast. Did he walk away from this one or is the lunatic in the hospital?"

"He didn't make it, Spanner."

"What d'you mean he didn't make it?" Spanner stared at him.

"He's dead, died at the scene before the ambulance could get to him." Jamie had reverted to his official self in an attempt to block out the horror of what he'd seen.

"Were you there?" Spanner was still trying to make sense of what he had heard.

Jamie nodded. "Yes. He took the curve too fast, spun off and hit a tree head on. There was nothing I could do."

He closed his eyes and tried to hold back the tears. He had attended many accidents, but none had been of people he knew. He opened them again, unable to unsee his friend's almost unrecognisable face and twisted body mangled in the car. "I couldn't believe it..."

Spanner was still motionless. "I don't... it can't be..." He fell silent, reached for his cigarettes and offered one to Jamie. Jamie moved next to him, leaned back against the barn and the two men smoked in silence for several moments.

"He was on his way here?" Spanner spoke eventually.

Jamie nodded. "Yes, I should think so. I was on patrol..." He slammed his fist against the barn. "I've pulled him over a couple of times on that stretch of road and told him to slow down. If I'd given him a ticket both times he wouldn't have even been on the road because he'd have lost his licence. This is my fault."

"That's bullshit, Jamie, and you know it." Spanner shook his head and gave a wry smile. "Pete was always going to kill himself at speed, whether on the track or off it."

"Yeah, but..."

"But nothing. Pete was driving too fast, his fault, not yours. You need to let it go, Jamie."

Jamie didn't answer. Even though deep down he knew Spanner was probably right he couldn't help feeling guilty, and nothing would ever change that.

Omaha, Nebraska

"I can't understand what is going on in your head. I thought you were intelligent." Emily barely gave Rachel time to walk through the door before unleashing her fury. "Anything could have happened to you with those hippies. I've had to employ a private detective to find out where you were. And lying to us. How long has that been going on? I suppose you've been smoking marijuana and God knows what else with those subversive idiots. Listening to all their poisonous views… and as for going off in a camper van with them. They could have taken you anywhere, sold you into prostitution…" Rachel couldn't stop herself smiling. Emily shook her fist at her. "You think this is funny? Have you no idea what the publicity could have done to your future? You would have been in all the newspapers, on the radio, you would have been ruined, all the plans I had…" Emily took a breath and tried to calm down. It wouldn't do to let Rachel know of the plans she had for her, certainly not until she'd grown up. She changed tack. "You could have been arrested – you weren't, were you?" Emily stopped long enough for Rachel to shake her head. "As if we haven't got enough to worry about. Your brother could be drafted in a couple of weeks, and you pick this time to go galivanting off with a load of subversive morons."

"If we can stop the war, Paul won't be drafted." Rachel couldn't believe her luck at being handed such an opening.

Emily stared at her, for once unable to think of a reply.

"That's hardly the point, Rachel," Mark interjected. "We were worried sick about you, and as your mother said, anything could have happened to you."

"I'm sorry, Dad, I should have left you a note." Rachel faced her father.

"But you didn't, because if you'd left a note, we might have been able to stop you." Emily stepped between them.

Rachel focused her attention on Mark. "I'm sorry you were worried, Dad. I didn't mean to upset you." She looked at Emily. "And I know you must have been concerned, Mom, to employ a private detective and not call the police." She paused to let her words sink in, the implication clear that her mother cared more about their reputation than her safety. Then she continued, using the lifeline her mother had inadvertently given her. "But this was something I had to do. The war is wrong. Nixon was voted in on a promise to end the war and bring our soldiers back home, but all he's done is escalate the situation and send even more boys like Paul out there. And now they are holding this stupid draft lottery. Paul's my brother, I had to do something to try and stop him being drafted." Rachel could see her parents were weakening, so she pressed home her advantage. "I'm really sorry, I know I should have told you, but I was frightened you would say no and then I wouldn't be able to go – and I would have felt so useless, not being able to help Paul at all. You've brought me up to know the difference between right and wrong, and the war is wrong. I couldn't ignore it." She lowered her head and peered through her lashes.

Emily exchanged glances with Mark. She wasn't entirely convinced by Rachel's confession that this had all happened because she was trying to stop the war to save Paul. Unfortunately, she'd allowed her own concerns about her son to give her daughter a way out.

She was still trying to decide what to say when Mark spoke. "Well, we can understand that, Rachel. But in future you must tell us if you are planning anything..." He saw Emily's expression and rapidly changed direction. "Obviously you won't do anything that stupid again, will you? Your mother is right. If anything had happened to you... We love you very much, and we're only trying to protect you." He put out his arms and Rachel stepped forward and snuggled up against him. She kept her eyes down and didn't look at her mother. Her father might have believed her, but she was reasonably certain that Emily had not.

CHAPTER SEVEN

Omaha, Nebraska

Paul finished his drink and poured another. His nerves were on edge, and no amount of alcohol or marijuana could deaden the feeling of dread in the pit of his stomach. It was December 1st, the night of the draw, and the reality that he could be drafted had suddenly hit him. He knew his parents had been frantically trying to get him off the list, but so far they had been unsuccessful. He would just have to hope and pray that his number didn't come up.

"It will be alright, Paul." Heine Rosenberg watched his friend with concern.

"You've got a crystal ball, have you?" Paul started rolling another reefer.

"You'll never be able to drive home if you have any more."

Paul shrugged. "I'll get a cab, then. As long as I am there to watch the farce, no one will care what state I am in."

"I'm sure that's not true, Paul. You said yourself that your parents have been trying to get you excluded."

"They haven't succeeded though, have they? So much

for all their influential friends."

Heine frowned. He had no idea what to say to help. He wished he could be with him during the broadcast, but that could never happen. All he could do was to try and sober Paul up and make sure he got home in time and in a reasonable state.

Paul lit the reefer and drew the smoke deep into his lungs. "Well, if all else fails I could always tell the army the truth." He began to giggle.

Heine watched him in horror. "The truth?"

"That I am not suitable for the army because I'm a faggot." He collapsed into more giggles until the laughter turned to tears. Heine reached over and put his arms around Paul. If only it was that simple Paul could have done that ages ago and saved himself all the stress. Unfortunately, telling his family that he was gay would cause even more heartache than being drafted, and as for telling the army...

Village north of Da Nang, Vietnam

"You can't be serious, Phuc? It's a ridiculous idea, and completely unworkable." Lien had listened to several ever-more elaborate schemes to attack the invaders, and none of them made any sense to her. They all carried absurd amounts of risk and would have ended up with the whole family being shot, and that was even if they were lucky enough to succeed.

Phuc glared at her. "Well, you come up with something then!"

Lien nodded. "I'll think about it, I promise." At least if she came up with something it might work, and they might all survive to see a future without foreigners in their country. Unfortunately, she couldn't think of anything. Since the ambush, the Americans were much more cautious when they set up patrols. The helicopters barely spent any time on the ground and the soldiers were heavily armed, hyper vigilant, never relaxing their guard for a moment. To attempt another ambush in those circumstances would be asking for trouble. The patrols also followed no discernible pattern that she could see, they seemed to arrive at random, so it wasn't possible to plan in advance. "We need to be patient."

Phuc spat noisily on the floor. "I think you're scared."

Lien bit her tongue. She wanted to say, *Of course, I'm scared. Only a fool doesn't feel fear.* But if she did, her brother would take that as a sign of weakness, and then he would do something himself and get them all killed.

Omaha, Nebraska

Charles undid the zip on his trousers and smiled down at the girl tied to the bed in the hotel bedroom he had rented earlier that afternoon. He was willing to pay her, but she was still not being very cooperative. When she'd served his food in the restaurant earlier in the day he'd piled on the charm, and it hadn't taken long for her to agree to meet him in the hotel across the street later. Unfortunately, when she'd arrived, she had made it clear she didn't want to go any further than a quick kiss and a fumble through her clothes. That wasn't what Charles was expecting, so he'd plied her with alcohol and, when she was barely conscious, he'd tied her to the bed with her stockings. But fucking a lifeless body wasn't much fun, so he'd waited for her sober up a bit and then offered her money to let him do what he wanted. It was obvious the girl was terrified, but for some reason that made it even more exciting, so he'd got out some more money and threatened to tell the police that she had solicited him if she complained. He had spared no time in telling her just how rich he was, and that no one would believe her word over his.

"Come on, Dorry, or whatever your name is. Try and look like you're enjoying it, for fuck's sake." He threw his trousers and underwear on the floor before grabbing her chin and forcing her to look up at him.

The girl stared up at him with fear in her eyes and began

to struggle. Charles smiled again. "That's better, much more interesting. No, don't close your eyes, I want you to watch me... There's a good girl..."

An hour later, Charles let himself out and hurried down the steps to the lobby. That was definitely more fun than he'd first expected. And the girl had been well paid for her time. He glanced at his watch and increased his pace. It was that lottery thing tonight. As he had nothing to worry about, he would quite enjoy watching it. Thank God his parents knew the right people.

Omaha, Nebraska

Rachel smoked the last of her marijuana while listening to the radio and Bob Dylan's 'Blowing in the Wind'. Tonight would decide her brother's future, and that of so many other men. If only she could be out there protesting, instead of being stuck in her bedroom, unable to go out unless it was to school or the tennis club. Thank God for Paul keeping her supplied with dope and acting as a go-between with her and Jenny. Hopefully, her mother wouldn't keep her locked up for much longer. Perhaps she should appeal to her father? He had always been more reasonable. Rachel thought about it and shook her head. She would wait and see what happened tonight. As much as she wanted her freedom again, she knew that Paul was their biggest concern at the moment, and she genuinely didn't want to get in the way of their efforts to prevent him being drafted.

She glanced at the clock, switched off the radio and headed downstairs. Her parents were sitting in the living room. The television was already on, *The High Chaparral* playing on NBC although neither of her parents were watching. There was no sign of Paul.

"Have you seen your brother?" Emily was looking worried. Her head was starting to throb again. The doctor had now decided that it was caused by her hormones, and once she finally stopped menstruating the headaches would go away. Unfortunately, she still had a few years to go, so somehow she would just have to put up with them.

Rachel shook her head. "No, not since this morning."

"He should be here. This affects him…" She fell silent.

Rachel glanced at her father, but he too was looking worried. Rachel shivered. It wasn't like Paul not to be on time for anything. He had always been the amenable one, unlike her.

"If he's not here soon, we'll have to call the police."

Rachel blinked at her mother in shock. "He's not even late, Mom…"

"Do you know where he went?"

Rachel shook her head. "No, Mom." As she answered, Rachel realised she actually had no idea who her brother's friends were, and she felt guilty. She had been too wrapped up feeling sorry for herself to have given him much thought. Another thought occurred to her. What if he had run away to avoid the draft? She had heard people were going to Canada... Then she realised that was ridiculous. They hadn't even drawn the lottery yet. Plenty of time to run away if his number came up, no point doing it before.

Outside Springfield, Nebraska

The Tanner family sat in front of the black and white television and gazed apprehensively at the small screen. Normally the TV was a source of entertainment, something to draw the family together in the evening, but not tonight. Spanner's thoughts were on Pete. Although he'd attended his best friend's funeral the previous day, he still couldn't believe his friend was dead, and he was struggling to concentrate on the farce unfolding in front of him, even though he knew his future depended on it.

"I still think this is a stupid idea." Jean Tanner was a plump woman in her mid-forties with greying hair, horn-rimmed glasses and florid cheeks, a legacy of years spent outside in the fresh air of the family farm.

"It's supposed to make things fairer, Mom," Spanner replied, trying to make himself concentrate. "By making it a lottery, no one can say it's only the poor that are being sent over there." He had no idea why he was bothering to explain things; it wasn't as if he wanted anything to do with this. Given a choice, he would spend his life on the farm, tinkering with cars, maybe meet a nice girl and settle down… He glanced around at his family, and for a moment he felt cold. It wasn't just he who could be drafted. His two younger brothers would soon be of age, and even if he was lucky, they couldn't all be. His thoughts turned back to Pete. His friend's death seemed so much more real and important to him than this.

"We're all rooting for you." Chris punched his arm affectionately. Anthony gave him a nervous smile. At 17 and 15 respectively, they could both be facing the same fate if the war continued to drag on.

Spanner tried to smile back, but found he couldn't. He felt sick. Instead he nodded, and finally put Pete to the back of his mind and focused his attention on the tiny screen. It was strange that his future was about to unfold before him, and it all depended on a lottery, on whether fate chose to be kind to him. The room was hazy from cigarette smoke, its pungent plumes added to by Spanner as the moment of truth grew closer. He could feel the heat from the large log fire blazing in the hearth. Its reassuring warmth would normally lull him into a relaxed state, but not tonight.

As the moment drew closer, Spanner finally forgot about Pete and concentrated on what was happening. He realised Roger Mudd, the CBS correspondent, was speaking, took another anxious drag of his cigarette and listened. "This is the first draft lottery in 27 years, the first since World War II. Any young man between the age of 19 and 26 is eligible to be drafted into the armed forces of the USA, and the lottery is based on birth dates." Spanner tuned out and watched the blue capsules containing the dates of the year being drawn from a large glass container. The capsule was opened, and the date read out. The date was then placed on a large board on the wall. The dates were given a number in the order they were drawn, from 1 to 366, one number for each day of the year. The lower numbers were drafted first. High numbers might never be drafted, if the war ended soon enough.

Spanner held his breath as each capsule was opened, and then let it out slowly as someone else's birth date was drawn. The first twenty had been drawn, he wasn't safe yet. He could feel the rising tension in the room, his father's frantic puffing on his old pipe, his mother's almost inaudible gasps of relief as each date that was placed on the board meant another momentary reprieve, taking him another step towards safety. Even Johnnie and Ruth were quiet, although at five and eight respectively he knew they probably didn't really understand the momentous events unfolding before them. Terry, who was 13, and Annie, who'd just turned 11, did understand up to a point, and he saw them exchange nervous glances. It didn't help.

Spanner lit another cigarette without looking away from the screen. As the smoke rose towards the ceiling the next blue capsule was opened. He held his breath. The date was read out. August 10th, number 21. Spanner stared at the screen in disbelief. His birthday was 10th August, and in 1970 he would be 21. The irony didn't escape him. He exhaled slowly. Despite his tension, he hadn't really believed they would call out his number this early – fate had always been good to him. But now it seemed to have deserted him completely. Yesterday he'd watched his friend being buried, today his life had been taken out of his hands. Spanner glanced around at the stunned faces of his family. His mother was already crying, his father was staring at him, searching for words. His siblings were sitting in stunned silence. Spanner breathed in another lungful of tobacco, glanced around the room, and somehow managed a smile. "Well, it looks like I've been drafted. Me and about a million others."

CHAPTER EIGHT

Omaha, Nebraska, 1970

It was a bitterly cold Monday morning when Spanner and his family arrived at the magnificent Art Deco Union Pacific railway station in Omaha, but neither he nor his family noticed the beauty of the building as they hurried through it towards the military station, where the buses that would take the new recruits to their training were waiting.

Christmas had been awful. Jean had tried to make it one to remember, insisting that all mention of the war be avoided, but all Spanner could think of was when his Order to Report for Induction would arrive. His life was no longer his own, and he found it difficult to pretend to enjoy the celebrations. He had seen Jamie briefly the day after the draw, and his friend's sober reaction had said it all. The 'greetings' letter had finally arrived on 28th December ordering him to attend the Military Entrance Induction Station in Omaha at midday on January 5th 1970; it was the same place he'd attended his medical. From there, he would go straight to Basic Combat Training, more commonly known as 'boot camp'.

Spanner glanced around the station; it was packed. There were young men everywhere, as well as lots of young ladies in school uniform. As his gaze moved restlessly over the crowds, he realised that one of the girls seemed to be looking at him. For some reason this lifted his spirits, and he smiled at her. It was nice to have something else to think about, even briefly. Although she was some distance away, Spanner could still make out the faint blush covering her pretty face. He was about to raise his hand and wave when his father spoke.

"Do you have enough money?" Robert Tanner was stone-faced, struggling hard to hide his emotions. Spanner hurtled back to reality; the girl was already forgotten.

"Yes, I'm fine, Dad. Don't worry." Spanner shook his father's hand, then turned to his mother. Jean was unable to hold back her own tears, he could see the moisture glistening on her cheeks. "I'll be fine, Mom, please don't get upset." He had hoped his mother wouldn't be able to see just how nervous he was, but obviously not.

"This is for you." Jean suddenly leant towards him, took his hand and pressed something into it. Spanner looked down in surprise. It was the ring his mother always wore. She never took it off. The ring was old, from their 19th-century German ancestors, and had been handed down through the generations.

"I can't take this, Mom..."

"I want you to. It will keep you safe, son." She kissed

his cheek and hugged him tight before stepping back and staring hard at him, as if trying to imprint his image on her mind.

There were suddenly so many things Spanner wanted to say to them all, but there was no time. He slid the ring onto his little finger and raised his hand to his siblings. "Look after Mom and Dad for me, be good and don't forget to write!"

His siblings, normally so noisy, were strangely silent, even the younger ones. That, more than anything, was in danger of bringing tears to his eyes. He blinked them angrily away, turned and made his way to the buses laid on by the military for their transfer to the induction station.

Omaha, Nebraska

Rachel yawned and tried to ignore the dull ache in her head as she and the other pupils in her class wandered through the station. She wished the all-girls private Academy of Omaha had not chosen today to take the pupils on a trip to visit the city's historical buildings. Thanks to Paul, she had managed to sneak out the previous evening and see Jenny. The two girls had chatted and smoked into the evening and Rachel had been so stoned when she came home that Paul had had to smuggle her into the house. Unfortunately, this morning her head was like lead, and she wanted nothing more than to go back to bed and sleep for hours. They had already visited the Krug Brewery, which had been built by German immigrants and had made Omaha a major centre for brewing in America, followed by the Ackerhurst Dairy Barn. Rachel had tuned out as their teacher explained how it was built in the Dutch style in 1935, reflecting the Dutch influence on Midwest architecture. They were now walking through the station, and Rachel was wondering when she could get some coffee in the hope of clearing her head.

"This building was designed to express the strength, power and masculinity of the railroad..." the teacher droned on. Rachel hid another yawn.

"I know which masculinity I prefer." Vanessa's voice was close to her ear, although it was unlikely the teacher would hear above the noise in the station. Rachel glanced at her friend, who checked the teacher wasn't watching before indicating large groups of young men milling around. Rachel grinned, her throbbing head momentarily forgotten.

"Wow, what are they all doing here?"

Vanessa shrugged. "I have no idea..."

"Did you have a contribution, Vanessa?" the teacher snapped. Vanessa blushed but didn't answer. "Well? Please do enlighten us."

"She was just saying that this place is amazing, the views are incredible, and we should definitely spend longer here," Rachel answered quickly. Vanessa nearly choked, but managed to turn it into a cough.

The teacher fixed the girls with a stern gaze, but as she

couldn't see anything wrong with Rachel's statement, she let it pass and continued her lecture. Rachel and Vanessa exchanged glances and resumed their appraisal of the young men. "He's nice." Rachel's eye had been drawn to a tall athletic man with blonde hair. He seemed to glide as he moved quickly but effortlessly through the station. *So masculine*, she thought to herself. He suddenly turned his head and their eyes met briefly, piercing blue eyes that took her by surprise, and he gave a distracted smile. Rachel blushed furiously and smiled back. Then he was gone, lost in the throng of young men all heading in the same direction. Rachel wondered where they were all going, and then it struck her. She paled. "Oh my God, they're all draftees."

Vanessa smirked. "Well, they're certainly fit for service."

Rachel stared at her friend. "Those poor bastards are being sent to war. Don't you care?"

Vanessa looked astonished. "Well, there's nothing I can do about it, is there? And you have to admit, they really are better to look at than the architecture."

Rachel shook her head in disgust and moved away before she said something she might regret later. If only Jenny was there, she would have understood Rachel's feelings. Thinking about Jenny and the previous evening gradually relaxed her. Thank goodness for Paul. If he hadn't agreed to take her... she frowned. It hadn't occurred to her last night, but Paul had also been trying to escape the house. She knew he was dreading getting a letter telling him to report, even though his number had been quite high. Now she thought about it, he was always disappearing out, had been for several months now. Perhaps he had a girlfriend? Rachel smirked. Obviously not a suitable one, or he would have brought her home to meet the family. She would have to ask him. It was nice to think she wasn't the only rebel in the family.

Omaha, Nebraska

On arrival at the induction centre, Spanner was directed to a large assembly hall. He glanced around nervously; there seemed to be hundreds of young men all looking as worried as he was. He wasn't sure whether that was comforting or not. He was still thinking about it when his attention was drawn to a podium at the end of the hall.

A soldier was stepping up onto the rostrum, clearly about to speak. Spanner watched as he glanced around the hall for a moment before shouting, "Quiet, please!" Everyone fell silent.

"Welcome everyone, you've all been drafted into the armed forces of the United States. In a few minutes we will check your documents, and then you will be told which basic training camp you will be assigned to." There was a pause, during which there was complete silence. "Along the walls you will see letters. Please go and stand in front of the letter that corresponds to your family name." He stepped back down and Spanner headed towards the letter T, joining the other two men already standing there, and waited patiently for his turn.

"Name!"

"Steven Herz Tanner." He handed over his documents, which were checked carefully by the soldier.

"You've been assigned to Ford Leonard Wood for your Basic Combat Training." He looked up. "Your transport has been arranged, and it's coach number five outside. It will leave at 1500. Don't miss it!" he barked, making Spanner jump. "Any questions?"

Spanner shook his head, then felt obliged to say something. "No, sir." He took his documents and moved away. Although the hall was full of men producing documents and others milling around like him, waiting to see what would happen next, there was relatively little noise. Spanner frowned, then realised it was probably because no one knew anyone else and they weren't bothering to introduce themselves because they could all be going somewhere different. Eventually, the soldier who had given them their initial instructions reappeared and climbed back onto the podium.

"Ok," he shouted, and what little noise there was subsided. "Most of you will be travelling to Fort Leonard Wood in Missouri. It's a long journey, and you will need something to read and something to drink. There is a shopping mall half a mile away where you can purchase what you require for the journey. Your transport leaves at 1500. Please do not miss it. There is no other way to get to Fort Leonard Wood today."

Steve hesitated for a few moments, then followed some of the others to the shopping mall where he bought some Coca-Cola. Then he hurried back to coach stop number five and climbed onto the waiting bus.

"Do you know how far it is?" he asked the man sitting next to him.

"About 400 miles, I think they said." There was silence, then he spoke again. "I'm Tim, by the way."

"Steve Tanner, but everyone calls me Spanner." Steve had contemplated losing his nickname, but right now it felt familiar, something to hold onto when everything else was changing.

"Spanner?" Tim raised an eyebrow.

"It's been my nickname since I was a kid, because my neighbour said I should have been born with a spanner in my hand."

"Ok, Spanner, pleased to meet you... although I could think of better things we could be doing than being hijacked by the US Army and dragged off to one of their numerous indoctrination camps."

It was Spanner's turn to look surprised. Tim grinned. "Don't tell me you want to be here?"

"No, I don't..." Spanner sighed heavily and thought back to Washington and the protest march, how powerful they had all felt, convinced they were going to make a difference, certain that they would stop the war – and yet nothing had changed. A few weeks later and here he was, he and hundreds – no, thousands – of others, all at the start of their journey to Vietnam.

Village north of Da Nang

"Can I help you with that?" Lien hadn't heard anyone approach and she jumped. She squinted into the sunlight and saw a tall American soldier smiling down at her. Behind him, she spotted three other men spread out along the river bank, their attention focused on the surrounding countryside. Lien's first instinct was to tell him to get out of their country, to go home to wherever he came from, but she bit her tongue. There was no point antagonising him, and she certainly didn't want to make him suspicious. She had too much to hide.

Instead, she made an effort to smile. "Thank you." She handed him her pole on which were balanced two heavy paniers of rice and bananas, which he lifted effortlessly.

"My name's Doug, what's yours?"

"Lien."

"Well, I'm real pleased to meet you, Lien."

Lien was silent, unsure how to answer. "I am sure you would prefer to be back in America?"

He frowned. Lien realised her mistake too late and mentally cursed before attempting another smile. "I'm sorry, I didn't mean to be rude. I just meant that it must be hard to be away from your family and all those you love."

Doug relaxed slightly and nodded. "Yes, it is." There was a long silence. Lien tried to think of something else to say. This was the closest she had actually been to an American and she was sure she should be filled with rage, but for some reason she didn't feel anything except a mild curiosity. She hunted around for something to say. It had just occurred to her that if she was friendly towards him, he might let something slip she could use to help her brother and the freedom fighters.

"Do you live in a big city in America?"

"Yes, I'm from Detroit in Michigan. I work... I used to work in a car factory."

Lien glanced back at the rice fields, at the lush vegetation bordering the edge of the track, the broad-leaved banana plants waving gently in the breeze, at the thick jungle, wooded hills and mountains in the distance, and for the first time she saw it as a stranger would. She had no idea what it was like to live in a big city, but it must be completely different to this. She waved her arm in a sweeping gesture. "Then this must be even more strange to you?"

"Yes, it is," Doug said again, smiling down at her. "It's a beautiful country, Lien. It must be real hard being stuck in the middle of all this fighting for so long. I can't imagine what it's like."

Lien stared at him in astonishment. He wasn't supposed

to be sympathetic. "Yes…" She was about to say more when she fell silent again. What if this was a trap? He might be trying to get her to say something about supporting the freedom fighters. "But life is what it is."

"I don't think I could be so calm if it was my country."

Lien started to feel annoyed. "What do you want me to say, that I hate the fighting, that I wish you would all go home and leave us in peace?" She regretted her words as soon as they left her mouth. So much for trying to be friendly... she was a complete failure as a spy. She risked a glance up at him, expecting him to be angry but to her astonishment he was laughing.

"That sounds a bit more honest to me, that's how I would feel."

Lien was even more confused. They walked in silence for several moments.

"I'm sorry if I've upset you. I didn't mean to."

"No, you haven't. I just…" She stopped abruptly, unsure how to say what she was thinking.

"You just expected me to not give a damn about how you felt."

Lien peered up at him, there was a broad grin on his face that she found herself mirroring. "Yes, yes I did."

"We're not all like that, Lien. Most of us just want to survive long enough to go home." The sincerity in his voice was unmistakable, and left her feeling strange, like the world had suddenly turned on its head. She took a deep breath.

She could almost hear Phuc's scornful voice in her head. *Surely you aren't going to fall for the invading pig's lies?*

Of course not, Lien answered him in her head. She had just been taken by surprise. It wouldn't happen again. She suddenly realised she was almost home.

"This is my village."

Doug stopped and handed her back the pole with her crops. "I don't want to cause you any problems by coming into your village. It's been nice to meet you, Lien. Perhaps I'll see you again if I'm out this way patrolling." He spun around and began walking away.

Lien watched in astonishment and a certain amount of confusion. He had been nothing like she was expecting. He had treated her with respect, and was much politer than many of the Republican soldiers. She shook her head. She was being ridiculous; he was an invader and she was supposed to be fighting with the VC to get rid of them. What on earth was the matter with her? She should have taken the opportunity fate had given her. If she had made more of an effort, she might have been able to use him to get information. But instead, she had wasted the time she had spent with him feeling sorry for him because he was a stranger. Thank goodness Phuc was nowhere to be seen.

Doug and the rest of the patrol watched her disappear into the village from a safe distance. He hoped his Lieutenant was wrong about the girl; she was very pretty, and she had seemed quite nice. He waited until she had gone from view, and then gave the signal to his men. They headed quickly back to where their unit was camped out to report that he had made contact with their main suspect in the recent ambush.

CHAPTER NINE

En route to Fort Leonard Wood, Missouri.

Other than his few days in Washington with Pete and Jamie, this was Spanner's first time away from home. He took a sip of his Coke and waited for the bus to leave the station. For a brief moment, he thought back to the girl who had smiled at him in the station. She was very pretty, and although in school uniform she was probably not much younger than him. In another life, he might have tried to speak to her. At least she had provided a brief moment of happiness and normality in this strange new world. *"If you're going to San Francisco. Be sure to wear some flowers in your hair..."* The music, coming from someone's pocket radio, interrupted his thoughts and made him smile, bringing back his memories of the protest march and his friends.

"Turn it up, pal!" Tim called out. "Might as well enjoy our last few hours of freedom."

The music grew louder, and someone started whistling. Another man began humming, and Steve wondered if anyone would start singing. He took a breath... perhaps he should start… He had just opened his mouth when the driver climbed aboard. "Turn that crap off! This is a military bus, not a fucking hippy waggon!"

There were various low mutterings and murmurings, interspersed with swear words, but the music came to an abrupt halt. Spanner glanced at Tim. "Looks like we've had our last days of freedom!" Tim looked furious, but there was nothing any of them could do.

The bus started up and slowly eased its way out of the station. As they left the coach stop Spanner's ring glinted in the winter sunlight coming through the bus window, and he focused his attention on it, his thoughts on his family. He slipped it off and examined it carefully; he'd never had the chance before. It was gold and plain on the outside, but on the inside of the band there was some writing, which was difficult to read because it was so worn. He peered closer and realised it was a date and a name: *1879, Karla Herz.* He recognised the surname because it was his middle name. Steve Herz Tanner. He replaced the ring on his finger. He'd better not lose it. His grandmother and her family had come to Nebraska in the early part of the 20th century; he didn't know much about his father's side of the family except that they too had come from Germany. Perhaps if he survived this, he would try to find out some more about his ancestors. They were his roots, after all.

The bus thundered on. Spanner gazed out of the window as it picked up speed, watching the fields and countryside roll past. Occasionally he saw men working in the fields and he thought about his own life on the farm. He hadn't realised how lucky he had been until now. The farm had been where he'd learned to repair machines. His mother said he hardly ever rode his bicycle, he was always removing the wheels, fixing the brakes and generally repairing it. As he grew older, he did the same with the tractors and other farm machines. He had learnt how to mend most machines on their land, and it was there that a neighbour remarked how he must have been born with a spanner in his hand. Spanner smiled to himself. From that day on, he'd been known as Spanner Tanner to everyone except his mother. He was called Spanner at school by the pupils and the teachers alike and by his stock car racing friends. Even his father and his siblings called him Spanner. And now… now he would ensure that any new friends he made would also know him as Spanner. Perhaps then he wouldn't feel so isolated from everything and everyone he had ever known. Feeling depressed, he turned to Tim. "So what are you going to do when you come home again?"

Tim thought for a moment. "I'd quite like to study medicine, so I'm hoping to get involved with the medics while I'm out there. Might as well get a head start and do something that will be useful for me when I get out." He grinned. "Obviously you'll want to do something with machines?"

Steve nodded, his depression lifting slightly as the idea

occurred to him that it might be possible to do something other than killing people he had never met.

Secret Camp, north of Da Nang

"What did you think of her?" Lt Jenson Cox poured out some coffee and handed it to Doug.

Doug shrugged. "Just your average gook peasant. Pretty, though."

Jenson didn't smile. "Just because she's a looker doesn't mean she's not guilty."

"No, sir." Doug flushed. He thought for a moment. "It's hard to say, to be honest. She's quite wary, it was hard to engage her at first, but that could be normal." He sighed. Heaven only knew what was normal in this godforsaken country. If he was perfectly honest, he'd actually felt a bit sorry for her – it must be awful living in a war zone for years on end – but it might be best not to say that to the Lieutenant. "I think I need to get to know her better before I can make any kind of judgement."

"Then do that. We lost close on 50 men to that ambush, Cunningham. Our orders are to make sure they don't get away with it."

"Yes, sir." Doug paused before asking the question he was dying to know the answer to. "What happens if we find out she is guilty?"

Jenson's eyes bored into his. "Then we pay her village

a visit, find out who else is involved, where the nearest VC camps are, and arrest her."

Doug nodded, feeling relieved. He had no time for anyone helping the VC, but this was his first special forces mission after being seconded from the infantry, and having heard about the My Lai massacre he had been looking for reassurance that wasn't normal operating practice.

Jenson glanced sideways at his young sergeant and wondered if Cunningham would cause him a problem. They were fighting a war against a ruthless enemy: there was no room for compassion.

Omaha, Nebraska

"You can't keep drinking like this, Paul." Heine was becoming increasingly concerned about his lover. If Paul carried on like this, he would end up doing something reckless. Homosexuality was illegal in Nebraska and if his friend wasn't careful, he could be arrested and subject to the psychopathic offender law, where anyone convicted of sexual offenses was investigated to see if they were a psychopath. If it was decided he wouldn't benefit from treatment, he could be sent to prison indefinitely. It wasn't only Paul that would be at risk, either. If his lover was arrested, Heine would be in danger too.

"It's alright for you, you're too old to be drafted," Paul snapped.

"And you think that makes it any easier? I love you, Paul, to think of you going away to war..." Heine fell silent. It wasn't just the dangers of Paul going to war, it was all the young men he would be with. Homosexuality was illegal in the armed forces too, but he was sure it wouldn't stop them. It wouldn't have made any difference to him.

"I'm sorry, I didn't mean..." Paul trailed off. He stood up. "Perhaps I should go?"

"You've only just arrived, and you haven't eaten yet."

Paul looked into his lover's eyes and felt guilty. It wasn't Heine's fault, and he didn't want to hurt him. "You're right – I'm sorry, Heine, I'm behaving like a pig. Let's eat, and you can tell me all about your day."

Heine breathed a sigh of relief. He had averted another crisis, but for how much longer? Perhaps he should end the relationship now before they both ended up in prison?

Paul sat down at the table and tried to put his fears to one side and concentrate on the wonderful meal Heine had cooked for him. If it was just his relationship with Heine that was the problem, they could move to another state where the sodomy laws were more relaxed. But he couldn't avoid the draft, wherever he moved, and his parents' attempts to protect him had so far failed miserably. He didn't blame them, he knew they were doing their best, but if they didn't succeed soon, he would have to take matters into his own hands.

Fort Leonard Wood, Missouri

The journey had seemed endless. They had made two stops so the men could use the rest rooms and stretch their legs. Some were still suffering from excess alcohol, the after-effects of goodbye parties, and others, like Spanner, just hadn't slept for fear of the unknown.

At the first stop, Spanner bought the latest edition of *Time* magazine. There was an article on the Vietnamization of the South Vietnam army, and the problems it was causing. The article said that 877,000 South Vietnam soldiers had been equipped with M16 rifles. They had also been provided with 50,000 vehicles and 50,000 radios. Spanner thought about the work involved and wondered how to be sure of getting himself transferred away from the infantry to something more mechanical, like the maintenance of army vehicles and other equipment.

It was very late when they finally arrived at their new home. They were met by other soldiers and ordered to a barracks close by and allocated a bed. "15 minutes to lights out. Reveille is at 6 a.m. Welcome to your new life!"

Steve was sure he wouldn't be able to sleep in a room with so many others, but within minutes of his head hitting the pillow he drifted off, his last conscious thought of the pretty girl in the station.

The following morning, the new conscripts were officially welcomed to Fort Leonard Wood, introduced to their drill sergeants, and had their first experience of army food.

"This is the beginning of your transition from civilian to soldier and consists of eight weeks of basic combat training. The first three days are for induction, beginning with the Oath of Allegiance." The officer looked over the men assembled before him and raised his voice. "Step forward in turn, insert your name and repeat after me." Spanner waited patiently; and then it was his turn.

"I, Steven Tanner, do solemnly swear that I will support and defend the Constitution of the United States against all enemies, foreign and domestic; that I will bear true faith and allegiance to the same; and that I will obey the orders of the President of the United States and the orders of the officers appointed over me, according to the regulations and the Uniform Code of Military Justice. So help me God." Even as he said them, the words sounded almost unreal to Spanner, but it was a timely reminder that his life was no longer his own.

An hour later, Spanner watched in the mirror as his hair was cropped close to his scalp. Around him, the other men were shorn in the same style. He barely recognised himself now; once he put on his uniform, he would be indistinguishable from anyone else. "Done." The barber whipped off the towel and shook it onto the floor, where Spanner's blonde hair joined the growing pile of clippings. Without bothering to look back, the barber pointed to a door at the end of the hall. "Go through there and they'll sort out your uniform."

Spanner did as he was told, and after lining up for what seemed like hours and collecting various items, he eventually found himself in another room, his arms full of clothes. In front of him were rows of desks and men being interviewed. Spanner turned to the man behind him. "What now?"

His companion shrugged, but a soldier standing at ease by the door quickly explained.

"Most of the troops in Vietnam are in a support role. Only one in seven are combat troops. This is to find out where you can be most useful."

Spanner nodded. That made sense. Maybe this was his chance to make sure he could do something he would enjoy. He was still thinking about how to go about it when he was called to the next vacant table.

"Steven Herz Tanner?" The soldier barely looked up.

"Spanner..."

The man looked up from the form in front of him. "Sorry?" He sounded, and looked, tired and bored.

"Spanner, that's what everyone calls me." The words formed of their own volition. The soldier was still looking confused, so Spanner took his chance. "I'm good with mechanical things, it's what I do, so the nickname."

"It says here you work on a farm?" The soldier looked sceptical. He had already marked Tanner down for a combat role, given he was a farm worker and looked physically fit.

"It's my parents' farm, but I maintain all the vehicles and farm equipment. I also do up cars for stock car racing." Spanner spoke with more confidence than he felt. He had a feeling it was really important to get this soldier on board, or he would end up wasting a year of his life in an infantry regiment.

To his relief, it looked like his boldness had paid off. The soldier was looking more interested. "So how long have you been looking after the vehicles?"

"Since I was about ten. I started on bikes and worked my way up." He decided at the last moment not to smile. He had a feeling the man opposite probably didn't have much of a sense of humour. He was probably used to people trying to get out of the infantry by making things up, and Steve was wondering how he could prove he was telling the truth when the soldier nodded. "Ok, we'll send you to one of the mechanical engineering units. They can try you out. If you're lying, they'll soon sort you out." His eyes held Spanner's, who finally relaxed and smiled.

"Thank you, sir. They won't be disappointed, I promise."

The man gave a half smile back. "Let's hope not, soldier." He wrote illegibly in the notes of Spanner's form and handed them to him. "Next!"

Spanner walked away, a broad grin on his face. For the first time since he'd been passed A1, he felt almost optimistic about the future.

CHAPTER TEN

Village north of Da Nang

Lien looked up in surprise. "Doug?" She had seen him a couple of times after their first meeting, but then he had disappeared. At first she'd looked out for him every day, but as the days had passed she'd come to the conclusion that she'd done something wrong. Lien was furious with herself. She'd had the perfect opportunity to use the American, and somehow she'd messed it up. She was only grateful that Phuc didn't know, or she would never have heard the end of it. Lien resolved to be more careful in future – that was, if she was lucky enough to get another chance.

He smiled. "You remembered my name."

Lien flushed. "Yes." Having made the decision that if she saw him again she would do what she was supposed to, Lien was surprised to feel nervous. As a descendant of generations of women fighting against invaders in their country, she was determined to play her part: to be friendly and see what information she could find out. It was no different to making friends with Republican soldiers, so she had no idea why she should suddenly feel intimidated by what she was planning to do. She glanced back at the men with him; they looked to be the same soldiers as before, but none of them made eye contact.

"Can I help you again?" He indicated the heavy panniers she was carrying on the pole across her shoulders.

"Thank you. Are you becoming more used to my country now?"

Doug laughed as he placed the pole across his shoulders. "Not really, but I still find it beautiful." He began walking towards her village and Lien fell in beside him. Behind them, the rest of the patrol closed in. Lien glanced back again, and this time gave a tentative smile, but no one responded. Feeling uncomfortable, she decided to ignore them and concentrate her attention on Doug. He was obviously in charge, so he was the one to target for information.

"Do you not miss your home?"

Doug nodded. "Every day, but I guess we all have to make the most of where we are, don't we?" He glanced down at her and winked. "Someone I knew once said something like that."

Lien looked up, saw he was laughing and found herself joining in. "Do you remember everything people say to you?"

"Only if they are said by beautiful women."

Lien flushed even more.

"I'm sorry, I didn't mean to be rude or sound

disrespectful." Doug stopped and let out a slow breath. "I'm inclined to say exactly what I think."

"You didn't... I am just not used to..." Lien fell silent.

"Don't you have a boyfriend... a young man?" Doug whistled. "Sorry I am doing it again. Asking way too many questions."

"It's alright, I just have to get used to you." Lien gasped at her own boldness, and wondered if she'd overdone it. She reddened and looked down at her feet. "Now I am sorry; I am being very forward."

Doug took her arm gently. "No, Lien, it's nice. I'd like to get to know you too, if that's alright?"

Lien hesitated. She knew she wanted to say yes, but she was starting to question her own motives. It would be perfectly acceptable to get to know him if she was going to use him to further the cause of the freedom fighters, but was that the only reason for her interest in him?

Doug held his breath and wondered if he'd pushed too hard. He'd been sure she would say yes, so he wasn't certain why she had suddenly pulled back. "I'm sorry – I don't want to cause you any trouble..."

Lien made up her mind. "You won't." She smiled. "I would like to get to know you too." She let out her breath. The words had been spoken. She only hoped she would not regret them.

Doug relaxed. Thank goodness for that. He had been wary of pushing things, so after speaking to her regularly for a couple of weeks he had pulled back and left it for two weeks before contacting her again. It had been a risky strategy, and for a moment he thought he'd blown it.

Omaha, Nebraska

Rachel bounced the tennis ball, focusing on a point on the boundary line on the opposite side of the net and standing up on tiptoes. She raised her racket, threw the ball into the air and slammed it over the net, watching in satisfaction as the serve landed just inside the court lines before bouncing out and eluding her opponent. The spectators erupted in loud applause, amid some cheering from Rachel's friends. "Yes!" she yelled. Charles was never very demonstrative and always seemed to take winning in his stride, so she intended to shake his hand as normal. To her complete surprise, he lifted her high into the air and swung her around in triumph.

"Goodness, I've never seen you so pleased!" Rachel sounded so astonished that Charles decided to explain. He placed her gently back on the ground, leant closer and spoke softly in her ear.

"Between you and me, I can't stand Harold White. He's a real arrogant pig."

Rachel was pleased Charles wasn't looking at her face, as she found it difficult to stop herself laughing out loud. Charles calling someone else arrogant had to be the epitome of irony. On the rare occasion she'd played against Harold, she'd always found him quite pleasant, and certainly nothing like as pretentious as Charles. She wondered what Harold had done to upset Charles, not that she was particularly interested. She was just pleased they'd won the indoor tournament. She was looking forward to the party later, her only regret being that she couldn't invite Jenny. The thought amused her; she knew Jenny would hate mixing with the tennis club set, especially Charles.

They walked to the net together and while Charles shook hands with Anita, Rachel shook Harold's hand. "Well played, Rachel. Charles is lucky to have you on his side. He'd never have won without you."

Rachel grinned. "Thanks Harold, but I'm sure that's not true." She shook hands with Anita and prepared to walk away when she realised that something was going on between Charles and Harold. Their hands were still locked, and they were glaring at each other. As she watched, Charles pulled his opponent closer and Harold used his free hand to push him away.

Conscious of the watching crowd, Rachel grabbed his arm and spoke close to his ear. "Come on, Charles, let's not spoil the match."

The two men remained locked together, their eyes boring into each other.

"For Christ's sake, Charles, everyone's watching!" Rachel's voice had risen an octave. Charles finally seemed to remember where he was, let go and stalked off the court.

The applause had died down as the spectators realised there was an altercation on the court. Rachel could hear people commenting, and she felt her temper rising. "What the hell is it with you two?" She turned back to Harold, but he was already walking away in the opposite direction to Charles.

Anita shrugged. "Don't worry about it. I think it's something to do with a girl."

"Oh, ok. Why doesn't that surprise me?" Rachel smirked. "Judging by Charles's reaction, Harold was more successful?"

Anita grinned. "He's a lot less pompous than Charles. Given the choice, who would you rather go out with?"

Rachel laughed. "No contest." After a moment, the laughter faded from her face. "Charles is a pig. He treats women like they're his private property. I saw him harassing one of the waitresses here a few weeks ago because she wouldn't go out with him. I think he must have gotten her fired, because I haven't seen her since."

"That's awful!" Anita looked horrified.

"His parents have so much money he thinks he can get away with anything, and he normally does." Rachel became conscious that the spectators were still watching them. "Come on, we'd better go in and get changed for the dinner and party."

Anita nodded and the two girls walked slowly off the court together. Rachel's euphoria at winning the trophy had faded, and she wondered briefly if she could slip away without anyone noticing. In her heart she knew there was no chance of that, because they would be awarded the trophy at the dinner – she could hardly miss that. But once the formal dinner was over and the party started, she might be able to leave. If only Paul was coming to the dinner, she could get him to take her home. But Paul had been adamant he wasn't going to attend.

Rachel frowned. Ever since the lottery draw, her brother had been different. He used to be happy-go-lucky, but now he was jittery and on edge. He'd always been sarcastic, but there had been humour in his comments. Now there was an edge to them, a bitterness that hadn't been there before. She couldn't understand why. His number had been high in the draw, so his chances of going to Vietnam were quite small, unlike those poor men she'd seen at the station. For a brief moment an image of the tall blonde man with the piercing blue eyes popped into her head, and she wondered where he was now. Then her thoughts returned to Paul and she resolved to talk to him. But that was tomorrow's problem. Tonight's was to find a good excuse she could use for leaving early.

Secret Camp, north of Da Nang, Vietnam

"You are absolutely certain it was her?" Doug knew he probably shouldn't question his commanding officer's decisions, but he couldn't help himself.

Jenson stared at him in disbelief. He'd been having doubts about Cunningham's suitability for this mission since speaking to the other men on the patrol. They believed that the sergeant was much too friendly with the suspect. Jenson knew that had been the plan, but he had expected Cunningham to keep an emotional distance. He had hoped he was wrong but…Jenson took a breath and tried not to show his irritation. They were too close to completion to change the plan now, a plan which depended on Cunningham's relationship with the girl. It was that friendship that would get them into the village before anyone became suspicious, and that could save the lives of his men and their support troops. He needed Cunningham on side. "Yes, I'm afraid all the evidence points that way. She was seen on the riverbank by several men after they were helicoptered in, and then she disappeared. 15 minutes later, the men coming down from the hills were ambushed."

Doug shrugged. "She could have been scared and just run away?"

"Except she was seen standing outside the village a few moments later. She didn't run away to hide. She's also been seen several times at night heading into the jungle. Where do you think she's going? For a fucking walk?" Jenson snapped, his resolution to control his temper forgotten. "You need to accept the truth, Cunningham. She's not the little innocent you seem to think she is. She'd hand you over to the VC without a second thought."

Doug realised he'd gone too far and flushed slightly, embarrassed. In any case, it sounded like the Lieutenant was right, and as much as he would have liked to believe Lien was an innocent, he was going to have to accept she wasn't. "When do we go in?"

"Just sorting it now with base. We'll need more support; we don't know what we'll find there."

Doug nodded. "Do you want me to carry on seeing her?"

Jenson thought for a moment. He wanted to say no, but that might make her suspicious. "Yeah, don't see why not. Just be careful you don't give anything away."

"Ok." Doug headed back to his own tent, his thoughts on Lien. He still hoped the lieutenant was wrong, but it was looking increasingly unlikely.

Fort Leonard Wood, Missouri

Spanner crashed into his bunk and closed his eyes, relieved to be back in the barracks after yet another exhausting day. It had been a gruelling month, one he'd rather forget, although probably not as bad as he'd actually imagined before arriving at the training centre. He had hoped that when he told them about his skills, they would immediately reassign him to something more suitable. But the army didn't work like that. Before he did anything, he needed to complete basic training, so he had joined everyone else on the routine training which would last eight weeks.

The first month had been a shock to the system. Spanner had always thought he was fit, but he had soon learned that his idea of physical fitness wasn't the same as the army's. Getting fit involved numerous marches, runs, and assault courses. But that wasn't all. Alongside being taught how to look after their uniforms, shine their boots, fix their beds and look after their field equipment, they also learnt how to shoot their M16 rifles, throw hand grenades, read maps and utilise their C-rations. Every Saturday, there were the dreaded weekly inspections where everything, including the barracks, was checked. This was part of a competition in which the winning barracks were given an evening pass to go into the local town. Spanner's barracks had yet to win, but it was having the desired effect: the men had gone from being individuals to a cohesive unit. Spanner had also learnt how to salute, stand to attention, march and parade, and he'd learnt the rules of war.

The one thing he had adjusted to easily was getting out of bed every morning at 5 a.m. Living on a farm had prepared him for early mornings, unlike some of his new friends, and rising early was strangely familiar. Like everyone else, Spanner's first attempt at the physical combat proficiency test had been a total failure. He'd looked at the challenge and considered it reasonably easy until he'd realised there was a time limit to each activity. Covering 36 rungs on the overhead ladder in 60 seconds, followed by crawling on his stomach for 40 yards in 36 seconds and then a mile run had taught him a valuable lesson: not to assume anything would come easily.

But that was a month ago. He opened his eyes, looked up at the bunk above him and smiled. He had survived the first four weeks; only another four to go and then, hopefully, he would be doing something he loved instead.

"Chow's up!" The words brought another smile to his face. The hardest adjustment had been to get used to four weeks on C-rations. He'd been used to fresh food on the farm and his mom's cooking. C-rations were nothing like his mother's cooking. These were the canned meals for use in the field, which usually consisted of a can of some basic fare, a can of fruit, a packet of some type of dessert, a packet of powdered cocoa, a small pack of cigarettes, and two pieces of chewing gum. At first he'd found it difficult to digest the food, but he was so hungry at the end of each day that after a while he no longer noticed what he was eating. It was just fuel to get him through the day.

Spanner swung off the bunk easily and headed after the other men. One thing he had learned was not to hang around when food was about. He caught sight of himself in the mirror as he hurried out of the barracks, and wondered if his family would recognise him when he finally got some leave. The constant physical training had toned his body, his face was slimmer, and he was feeling rather proud of himself. He had finally passed. Now he just had to get through another four weeks here and he would be sent to train on his own speciality, which he hoped and prayed would be engineering of some sort. The thought of being sent to Vietnam as a combat soldier haunted his dreams.

CHAPTER ELEVEN

Village north of Da Nang, Vietnam

"I saw you talking to that pig."

Phuc had waited until their parents had left before grabbing hold of Lien and shouting at her.

"You want to set up an ambush, don't you? How else am I supposed to find out what patrols they are planning if I don't talk to them?" Lien was so annoyed she forgot to be cautious and raised her own voice.

Phuc peered at her, a suspicious expression on his face. "You are telling me you are spying?"

"What else do you think I am doing?" Lien hoped he couldn't see into her heart. In her more honest moments, she was beginning to find it difficult to distinguish between her duty and her pleasure.

"You looked like you were having a fun time with the American pig to me." Phuc didn't sound convinced.

"He's not going to let anything slip if he doesn't trust me, is he?" Lien snapped back.

"And have you found out anything?"

"Not yet, but I have only seen him a couple of times."

"I can't wait any longer. It has been two months since you persuaded me to wait and you haven't come up with any ideas."

"It's not that easy." Lien wrenched her arm away from him.

"Then try harder. You have until the end of the week and then I am going anyway."

Lien took a deep breath. Surely not this again. It was like talking to an idiot. "But if you just disappear…"

"Then you should all come with me."

Lien stared at him in disbelief. "How can we?"

"I will suggest it to our father. He is the head of this family, not you." Phuc stormed out, leaving Lien gazing after him in despair. She didn't want to leave her home or her life, not if she didn't have to. She tried to calm herself down and think about it carefully. Would her father really agree to leaving everything they had and joining the other fighters, hiding in tunnels, living from hand to mouth, never knowing where the next meal would come from, never knowing when they would be attacked? The more she thought about it, the more Lien realised Phuc was dreaming if he thought their father would ever agree to it. If it was just her father, Phuc and Lien then maybe, but he wouldn't want that life for their mother or the younger children.

Lien took a breath. She would have to find out something from Doug. The problem was that she didn't know when he would appear. The first few times had been quite close together, then there had been a long gap. She had no means of finding him as she had no idea where his camp was. Lien frowned and thought about their conversations. He always asked her questions, never told her anything about himself, other than the fact he came from a big city, and she was wary of asking him direct questions about what he was doing in the area.

She suddenly felt uneasy. He was always with the same men, the same number of men – the patrol never got any bigger. Surely if they came from one of the big camps the number of men on the patrol would change, and wouldn't there be different men? She was sure these were always the same. Her pulse quickened slightly. The more she thought about it, the more unnatural it seemed. She had grown up with Republican patrols, they always varied: although the man in charge might stay the same, the patrol was rarely made up of exactly the same men. That was what made it hard to get close to them, to find out their secrets.

Her mind was now working overtime. Perhaps these men did not come from the main camp. Maybe Doug was one of those special soldiers that she had heard the freedom fighters speak of. They lived in the jungle for weeks on end, gathering information about her friends so they could be attacked. Lien clenched her fists. Phuc was right after all – she had allowed her personal feelings to get in the way of her duty. She should have reported the presence of Doug and his men to their friends straight away. What if she had left it too late? What if he already had enough information about them to bring in an attack on the village?

Omaha, Nebraska

Charles sat at the bar drinking whisky; he was still fuming over his earlier encounter with Harold White. Despite winning the trophy, he still felt the man was laughing at him. He downed the last of his drink and ordered another, his thoughts on the previous summer and the cause of their dispute. Her name had been Margaret and she was very pretty: long blonde hair, green eyes that sparkled when she laughed and her body… Charles felt the familiar rage boiling inside him. She had been sitting in this very bar, having a drink with him, laughing at his jokes, enjoying his company, and he had been looking forward to bedding her that evening. He'd excused himself to go to the toilet, and when he'd returned Harold was sitting in his seat and Margaret was no longer interested in him. Charles had been so shocked he hadn't really reacted, not even when Margaret left the bar with Harold. He'd sat back down and ordered another drink, and it was then he'd become aware of the whispers, the looks, the sniggering going on behind his back. He had looked around; no one had made eye contact, but he was sure they were all laughing at him. That was when the rage had really taken hold.

Fortunately, their paths rarely met. Harold wasn't a member of this club, he belonged to another, just as prestigious, but on the other side of the city. He'd only been there that evening because he'd been playing a match. Charles had spent weeks trying to plan his revenge, but Harold came from an old Omaha family too – he wasn't a nobody that Charles could bully. As time went on Charles had gradually put the memory of his humiliation to the back of his mind, but seeing that bastard on the court today had brought it all back. Even trouncing Harold at tennis hadn't given Charles the satisfaction he craved, because even in his moment of triumph the asshole had implied Charles had only won because of Rachel. Charles finished his drink, ordered another and peered around the room. What he needed was something to take his mind off Harold. His eyes alighted on Rachel, who was standing by the window staring out at the courts. For a moment she reminded him of Margaret. Same long blonde hair and green eyes, and she was certainly pretty enough…

Rachel had been unable to find a good excuse to leave the party, so she had finally decided that as she was stuck there, she might as well enjoy herself. She gazed out at the tennis courts and thought how pretty they looked all lit up. There was going to be fireworks later, and they would all congregate outside to watch. Meanwhile she had nearly finished her drink, bought for her by one of her older friends.

"I hope you are not drinking alcohol, Rachel?" Emily appeared by her side and peered at the glass in her daughter's hand.

"It's only a small glass of wine, Mom."

"You are underage, Rachel; you shouldn't be drinking."

"It's just one glass, and I think I deserve it," Rachel pouted. Then, realising that sulking and arguing probably wasn't the best way to get her mother on her side, she tried a smile instead.

Emily hesitated. Rachel had played really well today. She was very proud of her daughter, and she didn't want to make a scene. "Well, alright. Just the one, then." She patted Rachel on the shoulder and walked off, leaving her daughter staring after her in astonishment. Now all she had to do was to make her one glass appear to last all evening.

"Want a top up?"

"Goodness, did you just read my mind, Charles?" Rachel laughed and lowered her voice. "We'd better make sure my mother doesn't see us, though."

Charles took her arm and led her towards some tall ferns and other green plants decorating the spacious room. "Wait here for a moment, no one will see you behind the plants. I'll get you some wine while you finish that one, then we can swap the glass over."

Rachel looked at him in surprise. It wasn't like Charles to be so helpful. He had been her tennis partner for several months, but their conversations usually consisted of him telling her what to do and sarcastic jibes when she messed up a shot.

Charles bought a bottle of wine and headed quickly back towards Rachel. He was still thinking about Harold's parting shot, that he'd only won the match because of her. Charles checked no one was looking and carefully refilled her glass.

"Thank you." Rachel was even more surprised that Charles had bought a whole bottle. "Aren't you having any?"

"I've got some whisky." They clinked glasses, and he watched as she drank deeply, then glanced around nervously, presumably for her mother. He grinned. "Perhaps we could go somewhere a bit quieter?"

Rachel raised her eyebrows and he hastened to explain. "I was thinking it would be nice for you to enjoy your drink without having to worry about your mother!"

Rachel nodded. "Yes, I suppose so." She was still trying to work out why Charles was being so nice to her, but the wine was making her feel warm inside and it would be lovely to be able to relax and enjoy a drink without having to keep checking her mother wasn't about to pounce on her.

"We could go out on the terrace."

Rachel thought for a moment. "It's a bit cold."

"You could get your jacket." He was already taking her arm. Rachel was about to object when she realised that his touch was rather nice; it was adding to the fuzzy feeling inside her. She glanced up at him and wondered why she'd never noticed how attractive Charles was before. Probably because he was always so obnoxious towards her, treating her like a child who needed to be told what to do all the time. But now... now he was looking at her in a different way, and Rachel decided she rather liked it.

"Alright." She handed him her drink. "I'd better meet you outside, as my parents might see me if I come back in here with my jacket on."

Charles watched as she walked quickly across the room and smiled. The evening was definitely looking up. He was feeling better already. His smile broadened, and then the expression on his face froze and his earlier rage resurfaced with force.

Village north of Da Nang

"Why did you not tell us this before?" The cadreman looked annoyed, and Lien took a deep breath.

"I was hoping to find out information from him. It was only when I gave it some thought I realised that these were not normal patrols and then I thought I should tell you." Lien was relieved that Phuc was not there. She didn't know what she was going to tell him yet; it would depend on the freedom fighters.

The two cadremen walked away from her and held a whispered conversation. They were too far away for Lien to hear what they were saying. Then one of them came back. "You will carry on making friends with him. Try and find out where they are and what they are doing."

"Do you want me to follow them?" Lien hoped they would say no, as she had no idea how to follow someone without being seen, but she thought she had better ask.

"No, your brother Phuc can do that. Then if he is caught, he can say that he is worried about your honour."

Lien licked her lips nervously. Phuc would be furious that she had gone to the cadremen without telling him. He would see it as a betrayal, as her trying to stop him becoming a hero. Then she realised she didn't need to tell him. She could pretend this was her idea. Lien nodded. "Yes, of course. I will tell him immediately."

She hurried back to the village. At least they didn't seem suspicious, and now she had an excuse to talk to the American so that even Phuc couldn't accuse of her of doing it for the wrong reasons.

Omaha, Nebraska

"Are you going home already, Rachel?" Harold caught her arm as she hurried across the room.

Startled, Rachel pulled back, then she laughed in relief. For a moment she'd thought it was her father. "No, I'm just going to the restroom."

"In that case, can I book a dance for later please?"

Rachel smiled. "Yes, of course you can." She glanced around, making sure her parents weren't watching her. At first she couldn't see them, then she spotted them in the corner talking to one of the senators. They were probably still trying to get Paul off the draft list. She breathed a sigh of relief. At least if they were occupied with that they wouldn't be watching her. "I won't be long." She disappeared through the doors.

Charles watched in fury. How dare Harold speak to Rachel? He wondered what the bastard had said to her. Whatever it was, it had made Rachel laugh. He clenched his fists and walked slowly towards the door. He had almost reached the door when Harold's voice rang out.

"Drinking on your own again, Charles?" The words were loud enough for Charles and several others in the vicinity to hear.

Charles stopped dead, torn between wanting to get to Rachel and find out what Harold had said to her and the desire to punch his rival in the mouth. Revenge won, and he stepped back towards him.

"I don't think my drinking habits, or whom I am drinking with, have anything to do with you."

"You just looked at bit lonely," Harold grinned.

Charles glared at him for several seconds, then realised people were starting to watch them. He was tempted to throw caution to the wind and just hit Harold, but if he did that Rachel would slip through his fingers and he would probably never get a better chance than tonight to bed her. He took a breath and walked slowly away.

Rachel stared up at the stars and wondered how much longer Charles was going to be. She felt like she had been waiting for ages on the terrace. She was about to go in when she heard footsteps and he appeared. Rachel smiled. "I thought you'd changed your mind!"

Charles smiled back. "No, I just stopped to talk to someone. I didn't want to leave too soon after you, or it might look suspicious."

"I think we're quite safe. My parents are talking to one of the senators. They're trying to get Paul out of the draft." She held out her glass.

Charles tried to ignore the anger still coursing through him and poured out some more wine. "To our success."

Rachel smiled and they clinked glasses. "To many more." They sat drinking in silence for several minutes, then Rachel shivered.

"Are you cold?" Charles moved closer and put his arm around her.

Rachel relaxed against him. The wine was starting to go to her head, and she closed her eyes.

"Shall we go for a walk?"

Rachel frowned and opened her eyes. "I was just getting comfortable." She peered up at him and he leant closer, his lips brushing hers. It felt nice, and Rachel responded. Charles pulled back, leaving her confused. "It's a little too public here..." He indicated the windows of the clubhouse behind them. Rachel nodded. The warm feeling was growing inside, and she wanted him to kiss her again. But he was right, she didn't want her parents watching her. Rachel stood up, swayed slightly, finished the rest of her wine and allowed him to take her arm.

CHAPTER TWELVE

Village north of Da Nang

Phuc watched the tall American pig wave goodbye to his sister and head back the way they had come. He gave them a few moments to get clear of the village before following at a safe distance. To his surprise, they were easy to tail. He'd expected them to be more wary, but they barely checked behind them at all. He began to grow bolder and allowed himself to get close enough to hear them talking; not that he understood most of what they were saying, because they were talking too fast and he didn't recognise all of the words they were using. Phuc clenched his fists as he crept hurriedly through the undergrowth. It was a shame he didn't have a gun, then he could shoot them all – except that wasn't what Lien had told him to do. He began to feel annoyed. Why was he taking orders from his little sister, anyway? His frown lifted to be replaced by a broad smile. Never mind Lien's orders. He would follow the soldiers to their base, go back and get the rifle he'd hidden outside the village, and come back and kill them all. Then he would be a hero.

"How far back is he now?"

"A few yards. He's getting careless, he's much closer than he was to start with." The two men at the back of the patrol had spotted Phuc almost immediately. "I'll tell the Sarge." The older man raised his voice slightly, "Sarge, we've got a tail."

Doug didn't turn around, but he nodded and cursed under his breath. "Right, Collins, keep formation. There's a bend half a click further on. When we get there, double back and come up behind him."

"Will do." Collins glanced across at Jenkins and the two men exchanged a smile.

Omaha, Nebraska

Charles opened the back door into the club house and let Rachel in. He led her down a short corridor and then opened another door. Rachel stepped inside and looked around in confusion. The room was dark, the only faint light coming from outside the windows. "Where are we?"

"It's the storeroom. Here, have another drink." Before she could answer he filled her glass with more wine.

Rachel giggled. "I'd better not have any more, I'm feeling a bit drunk."

"Don't be silly, you're just enjoying yourself. You're entitled to celebrate, aren't you?"

"Yes, that's very true, but I have to go home with my

parents, and although I can get away with saying I've had one glass of wine, I can't roll up drunk out of my mind!"

"It'll wear off before you go home."

"You think?" Rachel giggled again. "I'm not sure it will..."

"Well, I could take your mind off it?" Charles leant closer and before she could answer, he pulled her in and kissed her. His arms were warm, and as they encircled her Rachel relaxed and kissed him back with increasing passion. Charles was surprised by her response; he'd half expected her to push him away. His slid his hand down to her bottom and pulled her closer to him. Rachel struggled briefly, but he was still kissing her, and eventually she stopped fighting and gave in to the strange feelings coursing through her body.

Emboldened, Charles moved one hand to her breasts and began squeezing gently. Rachel stopped kissing him, pulled back and pushed his hand away. "No... you mustn't."

"Don't be silly, I'm not going any further...."

"I don't think we should...."

"It's alright... don't worry... I promise I won't go any further...."

As Rachel pushed his hand away again, she recalled hearing one of her friends complaining that keeping her boyfriend under control was like struggling with an octopus. She hadn't understood at the time; she did now. Charles's hands seemed to be everywhere.

"I think we should go back to the bar." She no longer felt drunk, and she was remembering her earlier comment to

Anita about the way Charles treated women. She was also starting to regret allowing herself to be alone with Charles.

"For goodness' sake, Rachel, it's not like I'm the first, is it?" Charles snapped. "You're not a baby."

Rachel opened her mouth to argue that no one had ever touched her like that when she fell silent. She didn't want him to think she was a child. Perhaps she was being silly, and anyway he was only touching her outside her clothes. She stopped struggling and Charles eagerly replaced his hand on her breast, squeezing until he found her hardened nipple. "See, you are enjoying it..." He spoke urgently, his hand had now found its way inside her bra, and he was pulling at her nipple, making her gasp.

"No... please... you're hurting me..." She tried removing his hand, but he was too strong. He shoved her back against the wall with his free hand, the fingers on his other hand pinching her nipple hard and making her whimper in pain.

She opened her mouth to cry out, but he leant forward and forced his tongue into her mouth. Rachel could barely breathe, and she flapped her arms, unable to push him off. Charles suddenly let go of her breast and began pulling up her dress.

Rachel managed to push him back briefly "No! Charles...."

"Shut up!" Charles slapped her across the face. Stunned, Rachel froze, and Charles grabbed hold of her underwear and pulled hard, ripping them off and dropping them on the floor. As the shock wore off, Rachel suddenly realised what was happening and instinctively raised her knee, catching him in the groin. His erection vanished as he groaned in pain and momentarily let go of her.

Rachel moved away from the wall and tried to orientate herself. The room was dark, but her eyes had adjusted now to the low light level and she could see the door a few feet to her left. She stepped quickly towards it, but she was too slow. Charles grabbed her from behind, spinning her round and shoving her down on her knees so her face was level with his crotch. She was vaguely aware he was undoing his zip and then he forced himself in her mouth, making her gag. He began moving back and forth, his hands tearing at her hair. For a few seconds Rachel was in complete shock, unable to believe what was happening to her. Then she tried moving her head away, but he tightened his grip on her head, forcing himself deeper and deeper inside her mouth. Tears rolled down her cheeks, but still he carried on. Then suddenly he stopped, pulled out, and shoved her onto the floor on her stomach. Rachel was so shocked she barely registered what he was doing until she felt him straddle her legs and push up her dress.

Rachel opened her mouth to scream, but Charles grabbed her hair, pulled her head back and whispered loudly in her ear. "If you scream, I will tell everyone about your faggot of a brother." Rachel gasped, her brain racing and for a moment she forgot what was happening and stopped struggling.

Charles laughed. "Ha, you didn't know, did you? Well he

is, he's a filthy fucking queer. Bet your parents would love to know that, wouldn't they?"

"You're lying..." Rachel was so shocked she wasn't struggling anymore, and Charles took the opportunity to shove her legs apart.

"Then scream and we'll find out, shall we?" He let go of her head, slid his hands under her crotch, and quickly raised her hips off the ground.

Rachel began struggling again; Charles slapped her hard across the buttocks and, as she gasped and briefly stopped fighting, he forced himself inside her. He felt a second of resistance and a feeling of euphoria flooded him as he realised he was her first. He hadn't expected that...

The pain took her breath away and she began sobbing. "Please... please stop..."

Charles laughed again. "You're loving it really, Rachel; don't pretend you aren't. You girls always make such a fuss about sex, but you love it as much as we do." He thrust harder. "And now, thanks to me, you're a real woman. You should be fucking grateful..."

Village north of Da Nang

Phuc had no idea what hit him. One moment he was running along the edge of the track, using the undergrowth to conceal himself from the enemy, the next he was lying on the ground, his head spinning, a grinning pig staring down at him. He tried to get up, but one of them kicked him in the ribs and he doubled up in agony.

"What the fuck are you doing, boy?" Collins' southern drawl was always more pronounced when he was taunting or bullying someone.

"I don't know what you mean." Phuc struggled to get up again, but the boot on his stomach made him cry out in pain.

"You were following us. Why?" Doug pushed Collins out of the way and glared down at him.

"I wasn't…" Phuc began, before the boot caught him in the ribs again.

"Enough, Collins. He's just a boy!" Doug took Collins to one side. "Wait there, and don't kick him again, ok?"

Doug didn't wait for an answer. He stepped back to the boy curled up on the ground. "Look, kid, if you don't tell me why you were following us, I will have to hand you over to my friends. I'm sure you don't want that?"

Phuc stared up at him. He wanted to be brave and say nothing, but he was in so much pain. He thought back to what Lien had said when she'd told him to follow them.

"My sister..."

Doug frowned. "Your sister?"

"I wanted to know what your intentions are towards my sister." Phuc spat the words out.

Doug relaxed slightly. "You're Lien's brother?"

Phuc nodded. "Yes."

Doug sighed. "Get up and go back to your village."

"Sir, with respect, what are you fucking doing?" Collins had stepped forward and raised his rifle.

"You heard him; he's just looking after his sister."

"And you believe that... sir?" The faint hesitation before the 'sir' irritated Doug.

"Yes, I fucking do. Now back off, Collins, and remember the bigger picture." He turned back to Phuc. "My intentions are not dishonourable, I promise. You don't need to worry."

Phuc stood up slowly, his heart beating hard against his ribs. Was it a trap? Would they shoot him as soon as he walked away?

"Go back to your village." Doug's eyes bore into his, and eventually Phuc looked down. He turned slowly and began walking back in the direction of the village. At every step he expected to hear the sound of gun fire, but nothing happened and eventually he risked turning around. He was alone. The soldiers had gone.

Fort Leonard Wood, Missouri

To his surprise, Spanner was actually enjoying himself now the eight-week basic training had finished and he'd been assigned to the United States Army Engineer School. Once he'd shown them his mechanical and engineering skills, he hadn't looked back. Fortunately, the USAES was also located at Fort Leonard Wood, so he hadn't had to travel anywhere else. The army were delighted with his obvious talent and wasted no time in letting him loose on their vehicles.

"Come on, Spanner, hurry up and make a decision." Jim Bonner was staring at his cards and waiting for Spanner to do something. Jim was the most impatient man Spanner had ever met. He was from the Bronx, and as far as Spanner could tell he only had three interests other than engines: baseball, women and beer.

"Relax man, there's no rush." Kurt Jackson stretched, yawned and smiled lazily at Jim, who glared back. Kurt was the opposite of Jim, a laidback surfer from California who made no secret of his hatred of war. Somehow, despite their totally different personalities, the three of them had become good friends, united by their love of anything to do with engines.

Spanner grinned at the furious expression on Jim's face, glanced back at his hand and threw them down on the table. "I'm out." It was a good job he wasn't playing for money, as he rarely won a hand.

"You're no fun at all, Spanner." Jim turned his attention back to Kurt. "Well, what about you, you lazy bum?"

Kurt winked at Spanner, gave a theatrical sigh, and dropped his cards on the table with Spanner's. "Nope, that's me out too."

Jim shook his head and stood up. "Sorry guys, I am going to have to find some better competition!"

"Good luck!" Spanner waved a hand as Jim stomped off down to the other end of the barracks. He quirked an eyebrow at Kurt. "I don't know why he bothers with us."

"No, we're not much good, are we?" The two men laughed. Kurt sighed. "God, I hate this fucking place."

Spanner shrugged. "It could be worse. They could have put us in the infantry."

"That's what I like about you, Spanner, you always see the positive." Kurt stood up, stretched and stared out of the window. He was missing home, missing the surf and getting to the point where he'd kill for some dope, as ironic as that seemed. "Have you any idea when we're likely to ship out?" At least then they would get a 48-hour pass.

Spanner shook his head. "No, not heard anything. But it can't be too much longer. We're pretty much up to speed on everything they've got here, including the helicopters." A smile crossed his face. Working on the helicopters had become his favourite job, and he was hoping he would be sent to an air base so he could carry on doing that job.

Omaha, Nebraska

The room was silent. Charles's parting words were that if she said anything to anyone, he would make sure her brother went to prison for his unnatural acts. Rachel stared at the floor. She couldn't think about Paul, not now. Tears streamed silently down her face. Her body was aching, her face hurt where Charles had slapped her, but her mind was in more pain. Outside she heard a clock chiming and she shivered. She would have to go home soon. She couldn't stay here all night, but how could she leave this room? How could she go back up to the bar and pretend nothing had happened?

Rachel stood up slowly and glanced down at her dress. It didn't look torn, just creased. She took a step and then remembered *he*… she couldn't even think his name… had ripped her knickers off. She peered on the floor, spotted her underwear lying near the wall, took a tentative step towards them, picked them up and stuffed them in her bag. Rachel took a breath and glanced around the room. If only there was a mirror. She must look awful, and if she was going to act as if nothing had happened, she had to look normal. Rachel let out a low moan of pain. How could she pretend everything was the same as it had been just a few hours ago?

Rachel was conscious that time was passing, and she tottered towards the door. Opening it took all her strength, but outside in the corridor everything was quiet as she walked slowly back the way *he* had brought her earlier and made her way outside. Rachel had already made the subconscious decision that going back to the bar was out of the question. Her only other option was to go to her parents' car and pretend she'd had too much to drink. She choked back a sob. Why should she have to lie? There was money in her purse, enough to get a taxi and go to the police station and report him.

Her heart began to beat faster. And what if he carried out his threat to expose Paul? Perhaps it wasn't true? Rachel shook her head slowly. Even if it wasn't, the publicity would be awful for Paul and for her parents. Thinking about the rape was too painful, so she tried to concentrate her thoughts on Paul, thinking back to how he had never brought a girl home, was almost always in the company of men... Rachel sighed as she came to the conclusion that, unfortunately, it probably was true. It would explain Paul's secrecy, why he never said where he was going when he offered her lifts and never had any girlfriends despite his good looks. If only he was there so she could talk to him – not that she could tell him what Charles had done. Tears rolled down her cheek again, and then Rachel realised she had reached her parents' car. It was time to make a decision.

Village north of Da Nang

It was early morning, and Phuc and Lien were sitting quietly in the living space of their hut, discussing the events of the previous day. "You are *sure* they believed you?" Lien couldn't believe her brother had been so careless as to get caught. But she was even more worried that they hadn't arrested him, and that he was seemingly unhurt apart from some bruised ribs. When he'd returned the previous day, Lien had wasted no time in hurrying to the meeting place in the jungle and leaving a message for the freedom fighters, but as yet they hadn't contacted her. She had spent a sleepless night going over everything Phuc had said, and she still wasn't satisfied.

"Why else would they let me go?" Phuc tried to ignore the pain in his ribs.

"I don't know." Lien was about to say more when the sound of helicopters interrupted her thoughts. She glanced up, not unduly worried as they flew over frequently. She was about to say more when the door flew open and several American soldiers rushed in. Phuc half rose from his seat on the floor, but was shoved violently back down. Two of the men hurried through to the other rooms, and the next moment her parents and two younger sisters were dragged into the room and forced to sit crossed legged on the floor, their hand on their heads.

"What do you want?" Huy's voice trembled, but the need to protect his family gave him courage.

"We've come for the VC sympathiser who arranged for our men to be ambushed a few weeks back. Ring a bell?" Lieutenant Jenson Cox's voice was icy cold as he peered around the room, his eyes finally coming to rest on Lien. He stepped towards her and leant forward, his eyes boring into hers. Lien shrank back, horrified that they knew what she'd done – and then a horrible thought struck her, and she felt sick. She glanced at Phuc.

"Did you tell them, brother?" Lien spoke quickly in the local northern Vietnamese dialect, hoping the Americans wouldn't understand.

Phuc answered in the same dialect, hurt and disbelief in every word. "How could you possibly think I would betray you, Lien?"

"Shut the fuck up or speak English." Collins moved towards him and used the butt of his rifle on Phuc's already bruised ribs. Phuc cried out and Lien acted instinctively, jumping up and shoving the soldier away from him. Collins lost his temper and hit out with his rifle, catching her on the side of the face. For a moment Lien lost her balance, but somehow managed to stay on her feet. She could feel something trickling from her mouth, and when she put her hand up to wipe her face she realised she was bleeding.

"How dare you hit my daughter?" Huy forgot his fear, stood up and pushed Lien behind him, shielding her with his body. Jenkins raised his rifle and knocked Huy flying. Lien rushed to her father's side, but before she could reach him she was dragged away and dumped unceremoniously in the corner of the room. She tried to get up, but was held down by strong arms. Lien struggled in vain before looking up to see Doug staring down at her. "Stay down, Lien, or you'll get hurt."

"I thought you were my friend."

Doug flushed. "And I thought you were an innocent girl just trying to make the best of the situation she found herself in. Looks like we both lied, doesn't it?"

"You have no idea what it's like to live with foreign invaders ruling your life." Lien spat back at him. They had obviously already decided she was guilty, so she might as well tell them the truth. "Yes, I called in the ambush, and while I did not mean for so many to be killed, I don't regret it. You come over here to our country in your thousands, take over our cities and fight your wars on our soil. You destroy our villages, set fire to our crops, maim our animals with your bombs and kill us for no reason. Your soldiers rape our women, dishonour our men, and then you wonder why we want to fight back. If someone invaded your country, wouldn't you do everything you could to throw them out?" Lien ran out of words and fell silent.

There was quiet for a few seconds. She was pleased to see Doug looked uncomfortable. Then there was a strange sound which she eventually realised was someone clapping. She looked past Doug to the officer in charge who was watching her, a sardonic expression on his face. "Bravo, well done… " he laughed, but there was no humour in his eyes.

Lien tried to hold his gaze, but the fury in his eyes took her breath away. Her bravado disappeared as quickly as it had come, and her fear returned. He walked over to her and crouched down. "Thank you for confessing, it will make our job so much easier." He smiled at her, then suddenly grabbed her hair and pulled her to her feet.

CHAPTER THIRTEEN

Omaha, Nebraska

"What on earth are you doing out here?" Emily stared at her daughter in surprise and not a little irritation. "We have been looking for you for ages."

"I thought you were already here, so I came out… and then there didn't seem much point going back inside in case I missed you." Rachel was careful to stand in the shadow of the light in the car park. It was a struggle to sound normal, but she tried.

Mark opened the car doors, Emily climbed into the front while Rachel eased herself carefully and gratefully into the back seat. As Mark started the car and pulled out of the car park, Emily turned around, peered at Rachel and frowned. "Are you alright? You look a little peaky." Even as she spoke, Emily realised *peaky* didn't begin to describe Rachel's pallor or the strain in her eyes.

"Yes, I'm fine…"

"Are you drunk?"

Rachel felt the first stirrings of irritation. What kind of

mother immediately thought her daughter was drunk if she didn't look well? She was tempted to say no, but if she did her mother would keep questioning her and, until she'd spoken to Paul, she didn't dare risk telling anyone what Charles had done to her. On the other hand, she wasn't drunk and she didn't see why she should pretend she was. "No, I just feel a little sick. I think it was something I ate."

"Hm," her mother snorted, "More likely something you drank!"

Rachel didn't answer. When she'd first seen her parents walking across the car park to her she'd had to fight so hard to stop herself running towards them and pouring out her pain and distress, but now... now she was glad she hadn't. Her mother would probably say it was her own fault for having a drink. She closed her eyes, but all she could see was his face laughing at her. She opened them quickly, blinked the tears away and looked out of the window instead. As Emily fought down her fury, she felt Mark's hand on hers and she glanced across at him. He shook his head gently and she sighed. Just like Mark to make excuses for Rachel. It would be a different story if it was Paul.

Village north of Da Nang

Lien screamed in pain and Jenson slapped her hard. "Shut up, bitch. You killed my friends. Did you really think you were going to get away with it?" He shook her violently and she screamed again.

"Sir..." Doug spoke urgently.

"Outside, Cummings, if you can't handle it." Jenson snapped without looking at him.

"Sir, I really think...."

"I don't give a flying fuck what you think, Cummings. I'm in charge here, unless you want to change that?" This time he let go of Lien and turned to face Doug. Doug swallowed nervously; he was aware of Collins moving closer, but he held his ground. "I'm sure we don't want this to get out of hand, sir. She's confessed, so why don't we just arrest her?"

Collins laughed. "You really are fucking naïve, *sir*..."

Cummings spun around to face him, and then a shot rang out.

Fort Leonard Wood, Missouri

"Orders have arrived!" Jim stuck his head into the hut, the Bronx accent even more pronounced than normal.

Spanner watched as the other men leapt off their bunks and took a deep breath. This was the moment he had waited for, so why wasn't he running across the floor with the other men? Because deep down, he didn't really want to know. Once he left his bunk and joined the others, his fate would be decided: he would be going to Vietnam.

"Come on, Spanner, might as well find out." Kurt was standing by the side of his bunk waiting. "I'm not in a great hurry to find out either, but we might as well see what fate has in store for us."

"Yeah, I guess so." Spanner eased himself up slowly, and the two men headed towards Jim, who was waiting impatiently by the door.

"Da Nang." Spanner shrugged and read the rest of his orders before smiling. "Yes! I've been assigned to a helicopter squadron, gun crew and maintenance." Gun crew wasn't great; it meant riding shotgun on missions, something he wouldn't be looking forward to, but at least he would get to do some maintenance when he wasn't flying. He started to relax; it could have been worse.

"Me too." Kurt breathed a sigh of relief. At least he would be with someone he knew. "Jim?"

"Yep. Me too!"

Spanner relaxed even more. He had been hoping they would all be together, but he hadn't dared believe it. He glanced back down at his orders, quickly scanning the rest of the information. They would fly from Oakland to somewhere called Cam Ranh Bay airbase and from there onto Da Nang.

"And we get a pay rise," Spanner grinned. He had already

been saving his basic pay of $90 a month, and he quickly calculated that with his basic pay of $200, plus overseas pay of $65 and combat pay of $30, he would be earning just under $300 a month tax-free, the majority of which he could save as everything he needed was supplied by the military: food, medical and dental care, clothing, even cigarettes. If he was careful, he could come home from Vietnam with some money behind him.

Omaha, Nebraska

Rachel couldn't sleep. Every time she closed her eyes, all she could hear was Charles laughing and taunting her. Even worse, she could see his face, the cruelty in his eyes… She eventually reached a decision. Whatever the consequences, she was going to report Charles to the police, because she was sure she was not his first victim and she wanted to stop him before he did the same to someone else. Talking to Paul would have to wait until she returned.

She got off the bed, picked up the paper bag with her dress and underwear in, and quietly opened her bedroom door. The house was silent. She breathed a sigh of relief – the last thing she needed was to speak to her mother, not until she'd been to the police station, anyway – and hurried down the stairs to the telephone, where she rang the local taxi firm and told them she would be waiting by the gate. The house was still quiet when Rachel let herself out of house and hurried down the drive.

The precinct was busy with drunks and prostitutes, and Rachel had to force herself through the doors. "I want to speak to a detective." Her voice shook and she fought back tears.

"Can I take your name?" Jamie smiled at the young girl in front of the desk. She seemed vaguely familiar, although he didn't know where he'd seen her before.

"Rachel Hanson."

"And why do you want to see a detective?"

Rachel hesitated and then took a breath. She was going to have to tell the detective. She lowered her voice and leant forward. "I was attacked... raped." The word was out, and tears trickled down her cheeks.

Jamie tried not to react. He glanced into her eyes and saw the fear and pain and his heart went out to her. But he had to remain impartial. "Do you know the name of the man who attacked you?"

"Charles Brandon Peterson."

Jamie was unable to stop himself reacting this time. His heart sank. Charles' father virtually owned Omaha. She would never make a charge stick against him. "Are you sure you want to do this?"

Rachel stared at him. "What do you mean?"

Jamie knew he was on thin ice, but he felt obliged to tell her the truth. "Charles's family are very important... it might be hard to..."

"Get anyone to take me seriously?" Rachel's tears dried up and she felt the beginnings of anger. "So he gets away with it because of who he is? I thought you were supposed to uphold justice?"

Jamie lowered his voice and leant towards her. "I would like nothing better than to see him locked up, but it won't happen. No one will take him on. The only person who will get hurt is you."

"And you think I'm not hurting now?" Rachel spat at him.

"Is there a problem, officer?" A short, balding detective stepped towards her.

"No sir... I was..."

"I've been attacked, and I want to report it." Rachel turned towards him and spoke loudly.

"Then please come this way." Detective Barnes gave Jamie a puzzled look and indicated Rachel follow him into an interview room, where she sat down at the table opposite him. There was silence. Rachel fixed her eyes on the table and tried to get her thoughts into some sort of order. It had seemed so simple when she had first walked into the precinct...

"So why don't you tell me what happened in more detail." Detective Barnes took out his notebook and pencil and waited.

Rachel continued to stare at the table and finally found the words. "I was raped at the tennis club this evening."

The detective put away his notebook and stood up. "If

you'd like to come this way, miss, we need to gather the evidence from your clothes and your person, and then we can do the interview."

Village north of Da Nang

Lien screamed. Doug ducked down behind the large stove. The shot had come from close range, one of the bastards must be armed… Doug was furious that he'd tried to protect them… then he realised the shot had come from the Lieutenant, and Lien's father lay bleeding on the ground. "What the hell…?" He began to stand up.

"Better decide whose side you're on, Sergeant!" Jenson aimed at Lien's mother and sisters and began firing. Lien screamed and Collins turned his weapon towards her. Doug fired instinctively, knocking Collins off his feet. Jenson spun around and let loose a volley of bullets which ricocheted off the stove and rebounded, catching Jenkins, who went down, blood pouring from a hole in the centre of his forehead. Doug felt something in his arm, and he began firing back, vaguely aware that Lien was still screaming, and her brother was crawling toward the door.

"Take Lien with you –" Doug managed to yell at him before another bullet caught his shoulder. Jenson was firing indiscriminately, and Doug took his chance. He began firing at the general area the bullets were coming from, and then everything went quiet. Doug slid to the floor and tried to breathe. His chest hurt, and when he glanced down at his uniform, he could see blood pooling on the ground. He stared up at the ceiling and wondered if Lien and her brother had escaped, then everything faded to black.

Omaha, Nebraska

It had seemed like forever since she'd first arrived at the precinct, so Rachel was surprised to find only a couple of hours had passed. She had handed over all her clothes, which they told her would be examined for any blood that they could use to get a blood group from, then she'd had her fingerprints taken for elimination purposes. The officer fingerprinting her told her that they would look for prints on her handbag. The most embarrassing part had been when the doctor had examined her, and they had taken photos. Rachel had wished several times that she hadn't bothered, but she was sure the worst was over now. All she had to do was to tell the detective exactly what happened and then Charles would be arrested. She knew she would have to go through it all again in court, but it would be worth it to take the supercilious look off that bastard's face.

She sat down at the table and waited while the detective found the place in his notebook where he had been writing before. He looked up. "Right miss, could you tell me exactly what happened?"

Rachel took a deep breath, fought back the tears that

threatened to overwhelm her again and looked down at the table, head bowed. "We had been attending a dinner and dance to celebrate winning a tournament. We went outside for a drink, but it was cold, so he suggested we went inside, and he took me into the storeroom..."

When Rachel eventually finished, she looked up. The detective was still scribbling in his notebook. Rachel realised she was clenching her fists and she slowly unclasped her fingers.

He eventually stopped writing and looked across at her. "Thank you. Can you tell me the name of the man?"

Rachel hesitated then looked him in the eye and spoke firmly. "Charles Brandon Peterson."

North of Da Nang, Vietnam

Lien and Phuc walked all night. Lien was in total shock, trying to process that everyone in her family, apart from Phuc, was dead. She and her brother had only survived because of Doug, who had seemingly died to save them, which didn't make any sense at all. This was all her fault, hers and her stupid brother's, and yet they were the only ones left. Everyone was gone...

"Why did that bastard save us?" Phuc's growl echoed her thoughts as they fought their way through the jungle. "What did you do for him that he chose you over his friends?"

"I didn't do anything." Lien's voice trembled. "I hardly

knew him. You have to believe me. I don't understand it either. He tried to save us, but I was responsible for the death of his friends. Why didn't he just do what they wanted and shoot us?"

Phuc didn't answer. He was becoming increasingly convinced that his sister had dishonoured herself with the invader, and that she was now lying to him. Nothing else made sense. "If our friends could see you now, they would be horrified that you have betrayed us!" He spat at her.

Lien stopped and cried out. "Why don't you believe me? Nothing happened. Whenever I saw him the other men were always there. In any case, how can you think so little of me?"

"You must think I am stupid!" It wasn't a question, and Lien made no attempt to answer. "You were going to find out their patrols so we could ambush them. Obviously, there was only one way you could get that information." Phuc had stopped too and was glaring at her.

Lien shook her head. "No... no, that isn't what happened..." Tears ran down her cheeks and she flopped down on the ground, put her hands over her face and began sobbing.

Phuc stared at her in fury. He wanted to leave her in the jungle, to run away, go and join the VC like he'd wanted to, but he felt responsible for her. "Get up!" She didn't move, so he bent down and pulled her to her feet. "We need to find our friends before the Americans send out search parties and we are caught."

Lien stopped crying and looked at him in horror. "You think they are looking for us?"

Phuc laughed, a harsh raucous sound that was nothing like his normal laugh. "They'll have every helicopter for miles searching for us. They won't want to admit that one of their own killed them, so we'll get the blame."

Omaha, Nebraska

Rachel shook her head, unable to believe what she was hearing. Her breath came in short bursts as she fought down her panic. "I don't understand...?"

"It's quite simple, Miss Hanson. It would be your word against his, there are no witnesses. You didn't tell anyone at the time, you waited until this morning to come and report it." He sighed and gave what he obviously intended to be a fatherly smile. "I appreciate you might regret your indiscretion, but to accuse a man of rape, just because you wish you hadn't got drunk and given in to your desires... well, I am sure you can see what I mean." He smiled again.

Rachel was so angry that for a moment she forgot her pain and embarrassment at having to discuss something so mortifying with a man she didn't know. "Are you saying you think I am making this up?"

"I am not accusing you of anything, miss, just suggesting

that you think about whether you really want to go ahead with this."

"Because he's got lots of money?"

The detective's smile faded. "That's a very serious accusation, Miss Hanson."

"And rape isn't?" Rachel snapped.

"There's no need to lose your temper, Miss Hanson. I suggest you go home and think about this carefully. If it goes to court, you will have to give evidence. Because the man you are accusing is the son of a well-known citizen, your name will appear in all the newspapers. Do you really want that? What about your parents? What do they think? To be honest, I am surprised they have agreed to you coming here..." He watched her face carefully, then smiled again. "Ah, you haven't told them, have you?" He stood up. "Go home, Miss Hanson, and put this down to experience. In the future, don't drink too much or put yourself in situations you can't handle." He pointed to the door.

Totally shocked, Rachel stood up and walked slowly towards the door. The detective waited until she'd gone back into the main reception area before tearing out the pages of his notebook, screwing them up and chucking them in the waste bin.

"Are you alright?" It had been a long night, but Jamie had kept an eye out for Rachel, having a feeling she would need a friendly face. One glance at her face confirmed his suspicions and he guessed the interview had gone as he had expected.

Rachel looked across at him and shook her head. "No. He thought I was making it up." She was still stunned, unable to make sense of the detective's attitude. "At least, I don't know if that's what he thought, or if he was just saying that because he didn't want to do anything about it." Her eyes met Jamie's. "You warned me..."

"I'm so sorry, Miss Hanson. Really I am. If it makes any difference, I believe you. I..." He trailed off and was hunting for something else to say, something that would help, when the detective came out. He beckoned Jamie over. "Destroy the evidence. Mark the ledger to say it was destroyed because the complaint was unsubstantiated." He glanced at Rachel, who was still standing at the counter. "And get rid of her – just another time waster, too much to drink and regretting her actions." He spun on his heel and disappeared through the door.

Jamie stared after him for a few seconds, wishing there was something he could say to make the detective change his mind, and then an idea came to him. "Wait outside for me. I won't be a minute." Rachel was exhausted, and knowing it had all been a waste of time was too much. Tears rolled down her face as he disappeared. Rachel bowed her head and walked slowly outside. All she wanted was to go home, but the young officer had been so nice, and it wasn't his fault the detective was a gutless bastard. She walked through the large doors, down the steps and leant back against the wall, and wished she could die.

Jamie appeared a few moments later, glanced around and handed her a large box. He knew he was breaking all the rules, but hopefully they wouldn't notice it was missing, especially as he had marked up the ledger to say the evidence had been destroyed.

Rachel looked confused. "What's this?" She started to undo the lid.

Jamie stopped her. "Your clothes and the other evidence they collected, including the doctor's statement and the photographs from the Polaroid camera. Things might change in the future – maybe other women will come forward saying the same thing, perhaps…" He'd been about to say that maybe they'd get some detectives with balls, not lackies, but that wouldn't be wise. "Don't touch anything. Leave everything in the box and hide it away somewhere, out of sight so it doesn't upset you, but don't get rid of it."

Rachel looked up at him in surprise. "If you think it's worth it?"

Jamie nodded. "Yes, I do. We never know what the future holds…" He looked embarrassed. "Try and forget what he did, Miss Hanson…"

"Rachel." She somehow managed a smile.

Jamie nodded. "Rachel. I'm Officer James Meyer. Jamie." He reached inside the top pocket of his uniform and handed her a card with the precinct phone number on it, and his name.

"Just ask for me," he said. "What I was going to say,

Rachel, is don't let him ruin your whole life. He isn't worth it."

Rachel rubbed her eyes with the heel of her hand. "I know, but it's not that easy. I'm going to have to see him all the time and know that he's laughing at me, laughing at what he's done, laughing because he thinks he's untouchable."

"He won't always be." Jamie smiled. "Things have a habit of sorting themselves out. Look after yourself, Rachel, and if you ever need someone to talk to, give me a call."

Rachel felt tears forming again, and she brushed them away. "Thank you, that's really kind of you."

Jamie shook his head. "I'm only sorry we've let you down. If it was up to me..." He stopped again. There was something about Rachel that was making him reckless.

"Goodbye, Jamie."

He watched as she walked slowly out of the precinct and wished there had been something useful he could have done, other than offer meaningless platitudes and someone to talk to.

Washington, USA to Cam Rahn Bay, Vietnam

Spanner, Jim and Kurt finally boarded a chartered Flying Tiger DC-8 Stretch at McChord AFB, Washington at the beginning of April. The interior partitions had been removed, and it was all coach seating. They made their way to the back and sat down; the aircraft was so long it was like looking down a giant drain.

Spanner thought back to their flight instructions. They were due to fly first to Yokota Airbase in Japan to refuel, and from there to Cam Rahn Bay. Once there, they would board more aircraft for the flight to the Marble Mountain Air Facility at Da Nang and the 213th Helicopter Squadron, the unit he and his friends had been assigned to.

Spanner closed his eyes and thought back over the past few months and how his life had changed so completely. He would give anything to be back on the farm, to be spending his free hours tinkering with cars, planning for the next races with his friends. Well, with Jamie, anyway. Spanner still struggled to accept that he would never see Pete again. His thoughts wandered back to Jamie, and he wondered what his other friend was doing now. At least he hadn't got into any trouble with the police for attending the protest march in Washington, not that it had done any good. As far as Spanner could see, the politicians had completely ignored the people they claimed to represent.

That couldn't be right, surely?

Normally good-humoured, Spanner felt the familiar pangs of irritation when he thought about the march. He had given the whole thing lots of thought, because he couldn't understand why this particular instance of politicians ignoring the voters annoyed him so much. It wasn't as if he was a stranger to injustice, he'd seen plenty in his young life, but this was different and, at first, he couldn't work out why. Spanner finally realised that it was because he had been part of something that he had been sure would make a difference. His belief that the war would end had been absolute, and when nothing had changed he had taken it personally. If he survived Vietnam, perhaps he should do something different with his life, other than working on a farm? He smiled. Who was he kidding? You needed money to get into politics, so unless he made a fortune somehow, he wouldn't be able to make a difference to anyone.

One of the four stewardesses stopped by his seat. "Can I get you anything?"

"You can come over here, I've got something for you…" The girl ignored the ribald comment from the row behind, her attention focused on Spanner.

"No, I'm good, thanks. Sorry about that…" He indicated the row behind him. She smiled. "We get used to it. Just shout if you need anything…" She blushed slightly. "Food or drink, I mean."

Spanner grinned. "Will do; thanks, honey."

He watched her go from row to row, being careful who she leant over and who she chatted to. Then he lost interest, and his thoughts wandered to the lottery and how fate had deserted him. Spanner suddenly remembered the bright-eyed schoolgirl who had smiled at him in the railway station, and he wondered what she was doing now. No doubt getting on with her life, the brief eye contact between them long forgotten. Spanner's thoughts left the past and moved to the future, to what was facing him. He had always thought he would be scared knowing he could be killed, but now he thought about it, he was actually more scared of killing someone else.

PART TWO

CHAPTER FOURTEEN

Omaha, Nebraska, May 1970

Rachel stared at the television in disbelief. Surely she must have misheard. She glanced at her parents, who were looking equally shocked. Emily spoke first. "Did he really just say we invaded Cambodia two days ago?"

"Sounds like it." Mark shook his head. "I know we've been carpet bombing the country for ages, but we didn't actually have any boots on the ground."

"So the war is escalating, not finishing?" Rachel was sure she knew the answer, but she wanted confirmation.

"Yes, it would seem so." Her father exchanged a glance with Emily before addressing her firmly. "I know you feel very strongly about this, Rachel, but please don't go off on any more demonstrations."

"You think we should just let Nixon get away with extending the war, making it even more likely that Paul will be drafted?" Rachel stood up and glared at her father.

"There's nothing you can do, Rachel. The last demonstrations didn't make any difference, did they?" Emily interjected before Mark could answer.

Rachel transferred her glare to her mother before storming out of the room and slamming the door behind her.

"I really don't know what has got into her lately." Emily was furious, but she was so fed up of continually arguing with her daughter that she made no attempt to follow her. "Is it me, or has she been unmanageable since the tennis dance?"

Mark nodded. "She does seem to be behaving out of character. Do you think something happened at the dance?"

Emily thought for a moment; it hadn't occurred to her. "Like what? I know she was drinking wine..." She frowned. "Goodness, you don't think she has a drink problem?"

Mark laughed. "No, of course not. If she had we'd be able to smell alcohol!"

"Yes, of course." Emily smiled briefly. "But there is something..."

"It's probably just her age, she'll get over it." Mark returned his attention to the television. Emily fixed her eyes on the screen, but she was no longer watching. There was definitely something going on with Rachel, and she would find out eventually.

Rachel headed up to her bedroom, slammed the door, threw herself on the bed and burst into angry tears. She hated her parents, she hated the President, and most of all she hated Charles fucking Peterson. She wiped her eyes and blew her nose on her handkerchief – and she hated fucking crying all the time, too. Ever since that night, she'd found herself tearful over the most stupid things, sometimes crying for no reason at all.

She reached for her cigarette tin, pulled out a rizla and the small stash of dope she had left and began rolling herself a small reefer. She couldn't smoke in her room, the smell was too strong, so she would go out into the grounds and down to the lake. The small jetty had become her refuge lately, a peaceful place where she could sit and smoke and try and forget the world. The last few weeks had been awful, and although there were several times she wanted to tell Jenny, something held her back. The thought of explaining everything in detail again was too much, so when she was with her friends she took the opportunity to smoke copious amounts of marijuana and try and forget for a few hours.

Bizarrely, the only person she felt able to unburden herself to was a comparative stranger: Jamie, the police officer. The first time she had rung him she had almost hung up before he answered, but he had persuaded her to meet him in the park near the precinct. She had considered not turning up, but she had been so desperate... and she was eternally grateful she had. They had now met three times, and the freedom to be herself, to talk to someone who knew what had happened, had kept her sane. Being able to vent her rage at Charles, something she couldn't do anywhere else, was briefly liberating. He sat with her while she cried. If it hadn't been for Jamie, she wasn't sure she would have been able to cope at all.

She stood up, left the room and went downstairs, her thoughts returning to Nixon and the war. Whatever her parents thought, she wasn't going to just sit back and do nothing. She let herself out the front door and headed down the driveway. She would go and see Jenny instead and see what they could do to let Nixon know he couldn't keep ignoring them.

213th Helicopter Squadron, Marble Mountain Air Facility, Da Nang

The helicopter flew over the fighting on the ground several feet below for the second time, and Spanner, seated near the open door, peered down, took a deep breath, leant forward and began firing the machine gun. They had already landed briefly and disgorged their cargo, a new patrol with their equipment, but had then had to take off again after coming under attack. The men on the ground, waiting to be picked up, had finally fought off the assault with the help of Spanner and Kurt firing relentlessly down on the enemy. The helicopter was pitching and rolling wildly, and Spanner found it difficult to keep his aim true, several times having to remove his finger from the trigger for fear of hitting his own side.

Even at that altitude he could hear the screams of the

wounded and dying, which he did his best to block out. The helicopter finally approached the ground, and Spanner stopped firing for a moment as men climbed aboard, but his eyes roved restlessly over the rugged terrain, watching for any signs of the VC.

The helicopter finally lurched back up into the air, and then they were on their way back to Marble Mountain. Spanner relaxed slightly and sat back in the seat. He still had to keep an eye out for VC shooting at them from the ground, but the most dangerous time had passed.

Omaha, Nebraska

"The President has definitely overstepped the mark this time. According to the papers, he didn't even bother to tell the Secretary of State or the Defence Secretary what he was authorising." Jenny was pacing up and down in full flow, and Rachel watched her friend enviously. Jenny was always so sure of herself.

"Congress are saying he has illegally widened the scope of our involvement in the war. He should have held a vote." Bob stopped smoking long enough to contribute to the conversation and handed the joint to Rachel. She inhaled deeply.

"What are we going to do?"

"I don't know yet, Rachel," Jenny smiled at her, "but doing nothing is not an option. I will find out what demonstrations are happening, and then we can go and join them." She frowned. "What about school?"

Rachel shrugged. "This is more important." Her mother wouldn't see it like that, but she would worry about that afterwards. In any case, she was doing this for Paul… Rachel sighed. She still hadn't found the courage to ask her brother if he really was homosexual. It wasn't something she could just drop into the conversation, and the opportunity hadn't arisen. She realised Jenny was talking to her.

"Sorry?"

"You don't mind getting into trouble again?"

Rachel inhaled deeply, forgot about Paul and smiled. "No, not at all."

My Khe Beach, Da Nang, Vietnam

The bar was heaving, and Lien was rushed off her feet serving drinks to what seemed like a never-ending succession of Americans. My Khe Beach, or China Beach as the enemy called it, was the place where the troops came to get some rest and relaxation from combat, an R&R resort.

Lien still found it strange that she should be working in the enemy's midst, and she struggled to think back to how her life had changed over the past few weeks. After the murder of their family, Lien and Phuc had fled through the jungle and various VC secret tunnels for several days until they had reached the outskirts of the city. Despite Phuc's fury and his determination to have revenge, Lien was quietly confused. She would never tell Phuc that – out loud, she agreed with everything he said – but in the privacy of her mind she constantly questioned the events that had taken her family. She couldn't understand why Doug had given his life to save her and her brother. It made no sense at all. She was also riddled with guilt. If she hadn't signalled their friends about the Americans and they hadn't ambushed the enemy, her family would still be alive. But she couldn't talk to Phuc about her guilt either. As far as he was concerned, they were fighting a war; there was no room for pity for the enemy, only merciless revenge for the invasion, rape and pillage of their country. Lien wished she could see things in black and white too, but for her there were too many shades of grey.

She smiled at the two Americans as she handed them their drinks and took their money. They told her to keep their change and she thanked them, but she didn't make eye contact. She'd seen the other girls fawning over the enemy, and although she was ambivalent about them, she had no intention of getting involved with any of them. She owed her family that much. Unfortunately, before they had emerged from the tunnels they had met with one of the freedom fighters who had given them food, money, clean clothes and instructions for their new lives, and she knew it would probably only be a matter of time before the freedom fighters increased pressure on her to make friends with the enemy, to glean information she could pass back to them. Lien knew it was her patriotic duty to spy on her enemies, but she had no appetite for espionage. She just wanted to be left alone with her thoughts until she'd decided how she really felt about the Americans.

Omaha, Nebraska

The apartment block was in the rougher part of the city: peeling paint, graffiti, communal bins overflowing, garbage piling up by the entrance. The police arrived in droves, responding to an anonymous telephone call from a member of the public about sexual offences being committed in an apartment on the seventh floor.

Paul took another deep drag of marijuana, swallowed some more beer and gave himself up to the caresses of the skinny young man he'd met in one of the city's seedier bars earlier that evening. He was just beginning to enjoy himself when the door to the small apartment burst open and the police rushed in, guns drawn, and began yelling at the occupants to lay on the floor, arms outstretched.

Paul had no trouble obeying. He was already laying on the floor in a befuddled haze. The apartment smelled strongly of marijuana and beer, but that wasn't the reason for the police visit, although it would help with the charges against the two men who had been caught naked in each other's arms.

Paul made no attempt to fight back, instead pulling on his clothes and then allowing the police to handcuff him. His companion began crying as they forced him down the stone stairs to the waiting van, and Paul felt a glimmer of guilt. This was all his fault. Jerry had offered to satisfy him in the toilets, but Paul had persuaded him to bring him back to his apartment instead. If they'd stayed in the club, this wouldn't have happened.

"Come on, you fucking faggot." The policeman punched him hard in the stomach before forcing him in the van and slamming the door behind him. Paul crawled into the corner and slowly began to sober up. As the realisation hit him that there was no way back, he vomited.

213th Helicopter Squadron, Marble Mountain Air Facility, Da Nang

The helicopter landed safely back at the base, and Spanner allowed the tension to drain out of him.

"Christ, I could do with losing myself in the surf right now." Kurt slid out of his seat, ducked under the still-whirling blades and followed Spanner and Jim across the tarmac. The heat was oppressive and would apparently get even hotter over the next few months. Fortunately, the rainy season didn't start until later in the year.

Jim laughed. "Cold beer would be better."

Spanner didn't answer; he was wondering if there would be any mail today. It seemed like ages since he'd heard from home, although it was only a couple of weeks. Their arrival here already seemed like it had happened months ago, the jeering from jubilant GIs going home taking them by surprise. *"So long, sucker"; "Have a nice war, loser"; "Give us your wife's number, I'll keep her warm for you."* Not what he had been expecting at all. Having heard some of his father's stories about his own arrival in Hawaii during World War II, Spanner had expected the same camaraderie, not the weird feeling that he was the personal replacement some other poor sod had been waiting for so he could go home.

The locals had been even less welcoming. His first impressions were that men and women seemed to dress mainly in black with straw conical hats and worked alongside each other performing various manual tasks, chattering constantly. His second was that even the children hated them, making obscene gestures and shouting, *"Go home, Joe," "Charlie's gonna get you,"* and various unintelligible things he guessed weren't complimentary. Spanner had been confused by their attitude. He'd at least expected the citizens to be pleased to see them – after all, the Americans were there to help them save their country. He remarked on this to Kurt, who had been sitting next to him on the short bus ride, but his friend had just shrugged, lit another cigarette and hunkered down even further into his seat. Spanner didn't blame him. Unfortunately, he'd been unable to switch off, his eyes taking in every detail of the strange land in which he found himself.

On arrival at the base, they had waited in line for what seemed like hours as clothing was allocated and mountains of paperwork were filled in, and all the time hecklers around them continued to crow about going home, adding to his sense of despair, jealousy and growing feelings of homesickness. Finally, they were pointed in the direction of their sleeping quarters. As they marched towards them, he became aware of an appalling, pungent smell that permeated everything. It reminded him vaguely of the farm when they were muck spreading, but it was much worse. Despite having his friends with him, Spanner was now in the depths of depression. He found his bunk and crashed into an exhausted, dreamless sleep, only to be woken by a recorded version of reveille playing over the loudspeaker system the following morning. It was then that the smell had really hit him, making him retch. Although he had slowly adjusted to the constant odour of burning shit and rubber, he hadn't got used to the bitter, fuel-smoked taste of the food or the quinine-flavoured water filled with additives to prevent malaria and other diseases. It wasn't until he'd received some Kool Aid powder in his first care package from home that he'd found the water palatable.

"You're quiet, Spanner. You ok?" Kurt patted his arm,

jolting him back to the present.

"Yeah, sorry – was thinking about our friendly welcome when we first got here, and that god-awful smell." He sighed. "Seems like we've been here forever now, so long I barely even notice it."

"Each day is another day closer to going home," Jim joined in. "We get some leave soon and we can go to China Beach. I've heard the women are pretty hot there, very obliging." He winked.

Spanner chuckled, his bad mood forgotten for a moment. "Don't you ever think of anything except getting laid?"

Jim looked horrified. "What else is there? Apart from some good beer and baseball on the tele…"

"You haven't lived if you don't surf..." Kurt began, to the immediate groans of his companions. He stopped, chuckled and added, "And you really need to try some dope."

Spanner didn't respond. Knowing his own views on drugs, he was sure Kurt only said it to wind him up. Jim grinned, but didn't answer either as the three men reached the hangar and picked up their orders for the rest of the day. Spanner glanced down at the list of repairs needed and breathed a sigh of relief. If only he could spend all his time in the hangar, this war would pass so much quicker. Unfortunately, there were the constant patrols, the never-ceasing stress of going out into the unknown.

When he'd first been allocated his task as gunner in the helicopters, he'd heard tales of men having reoccurring ulcers, and it hadn't taken him long to understand why. It wasn't fear of dying that kept him awake at night. It was the gut-wrenching terror that he would make a mistake while he was maintaining or repairing the helicopters, that the machine would break down while they were in the air, or be damaged by ground fire and forced to land. The fear that they would be stranded in the middle of a VC controlled area, that they would survive to be captured and tortured, imprisoned somewhere in China, never to go home again. Just thinking about it brought him out in a cold sweat. Even landing in a so-called safe area could result in death or horrendous injuries from the numerous traps the VC left. According to his training, the VC marked these with broken leaves or a certain alignment of twigs. But unless you knew what to look for, every step could lead to death. Punji sticks, sharpened bamboo sticks smeared with urine or faeces to infect the victim, placed in the bottom of a hole and covered with a thin frame so the soldier would step on it, go through and land on the sticks. Snake pits were common, as were booby-trapped flags; when the Americans captured their flags they would blow up. One of the worst he'd heard about was the mace, which was a two-foot wooden ball weighing about 40 pounds and covered with metal spikes, which swung down from the tree to impale the person who'd triggered the trip wire.

Spanner swallowed nervously, licked his lips and stopped by the helicopter he'd been tasked to work on this afternoon.

A brief smile crossed his face, his fear momentarily forgotten as gazed up at the Sikorsky HH-3E, or the Jolly Green Giant as the men called the fast rescue helicopters. They had a crew of four men: pilot, co-pilot, flight mechanical engineer and a gunner, were armed with two 7.62 M60 machine guns and could carry 25 passengers and two attendants. But from Spanner's point of view, the most interesting part of the machine was its two General Electric T58-GE-5 engines, which gave it a top speed of one-hundred-and-seventy-seven miles per hour. He'd often wondered if it was possible to make it go even faster, but that wasn't why he was there. His job was to make sure the Jolly Green Giants were fuelled up, ready to take off at a moment's notice and mechanically sound. There was no room for error; not only were the crew relying on his expertise, so were the men they were risking their lives to go out to rescue, and Spanner took his job very seriously. Being stranded anywhere in Vietnam was extremely dangerous – the whole country was effectively enemy territory. He put on his overalls, readied his tools, pushed his earlier fears to the back of his mind so he could focus all his concentration on the task in hand, and started work.

CHAPTER FIFTEEN

Kent State University, Ohio

Rachel hadn't expected Jenny to find something so quickly, but to her astonishment she hadn't even left their apartment when news came up on the transistor that demonstrations had already started at Kent State University in Ohio. Jenny's eyes had lit up as the news went on to inform them that the park-like space called the Commons at the centre of the campus was filling with hundreds of protesters, people speaking out against the war and President Nixon. Jenny, Bob and Debbie had quickly discussed the idea of driving down there while Rachel waited anxiously for their decision. At least if they went now she wouldn't have to go home first, and by the time her parents realised she was missing they would be over the state line. To her relief they had left almost immediately, and for the first time in weeks Rachel forgot about Charles and began to think about the future, a future where she could really make a difference to the world.

By the time they arrived, there were police everywhere and reports of students throwing bottles at police cars, stopping traffic and lighting bonfires in the streets overnight.

"What's going on?" Bob pulled up at one of the roadblocks and yelled out of the window of the VW camper van.

"We're having problems with the police. They don't want us demonstrating." The student was young with dark hair, wearing a psychedelic t-shirt and jeans. "Have you come to join us?"

"You bet!" Bob yelled back.

"You can park up over there if you like." The student indicated an empty building lot further down the road. "The mayor has declared a state of emergency and closed all the bars, which has just increased the number of people who have turned up to protest!" He laughed.

"He's also asked the Governor for help." A pale girl with short curly hair piped up from behind the barricade. Rachel could just make out a long suede coat with a fur trim over jeans and a multi-coloured blouse. As she spoke, Rachel could hear shouting, and she leaned out of the window and peered into the distance, trying to see what was going on.

"Bastards are using tear gas on the streets nearer the university, trying to get the crowds back on the campus." The dark-haired man had come out from behind the barrier and was smiling at her. He handed her a reefer. "Welcome to Kent State University... I'm Jeff."

"Rachel." She smiled back.

Jenny glanced across the van at Rachel, her eyes alight with excitement. "Looks like we've come to the right place, Rachel!"

Omaha, Nebraska

"What the hell are you talking about?" Mark shouted down the telephone, furious that he'd been woken in the middle of the night for what he assumed was some misunderstanding. He listened for a few seconds, growing pale. "That's ridiculous..." The voice on the other end continued for several minutes, and then Mark slammed the phone down.

"What is it, Mark?" Emily was standing on the stairs in her nightdress, watching with increasing concern. Mark rarely lost his temper.

He stared at Emily, wondering how on earth he could tell her. "Paul has been arrested."

Emily blanched. "Paul? Are you sure?"

"Of course I'm goddamn sure!" Mark snapped.

"What on earth for?"

Mark hesitated and then lowered his voice. "For unnatural sexual acts."

Before she'd even had time to fully process his words, Emily crumpled and slumped onto the bottom step, her face aghast. "No..."

"I need to telephone Simon." Mark tried to pull himself together. His son needed a lawyer and as soon as possible, before he said anything incriminating. He picked up the phone and began dialling.

Emily watched him in shock. There had been times she had wondered about Paul, but she'd never really given it serious thought. But now… he'd never had a girlfriend that she could remember. She wondered if Rachel knew. Emily frowned. *Where was Rachel? She must have heard the telephone ringing*. Mark was talking to Simon, so she headed back upstairs to her daughter's room.

She flung open the door and gasped. Rachel was not there, and the bed had not been slept in. Emily fought down her rising fury. Paul had been arrested for something so unspeakable she couldn't even think about it, and Rachel had chosen this night to go missing again… She leaned back against the door jamb and clenched her fists. What on earth had she done to deserve such ungrateful children?

Kent State University, Ohio

"Perhaps we should go home?" Rachel suggested.

Jenny responded immediately. "We've come all this way, Rachel. It was calm yesterday, there's no reason for it to kick off again."

Rachel didn't answer straight away. She had watched uneasily on Saturday night as students had burned down the ROTC building on the campus and as the protesters had clashed with firefighters who were trying to put the fire out. All around her the students and other demonstrators were cheering, but Rachel had remained silent. This wasn't what she had been expecting, and she wasn't entirely sure she was comfortable with the way the protest was going. The peaceful demonstrations in Omaha and Washington had been wonderful, Rachel had felt part of something amazing and there had been such a feeling of togetherness and love... but the atmosphere in Ohio was completely different. The National Guard had arrived while the rioting was in progress and several people had been arrested. On the other hand, Jenny was right, Sunday had been quiet, the sun had shone down and the tension between the protesters and the National Guard had seemingly faded away.

She shrugged. "Ok, I just prefer it when we protest peacefully. You saw the television coverage yesterday. All they talked about was the trouble and the people who were arrested, not what we are demonstrating against."

"She's got a point." Bob smiled at Rachel. "But we're here now, so we might as well stay for today. And you're going to get loads of shit, Rachel, for disappearing again anyway, so you might as well stay away as long as possible!"

Rachel grinned and punched the air. "Too right!" She laughed. "Ok, but if they get violent again, I think we should go home."

"Agreed." Jenny nodded.

Rachel craned her neck to see through the crowds of people in front of her. There were thousands of people thronging on the campus in front of the burned-out building, and facing them were armed National Guardsmen. There was someone speaking, but she was having trouble hearing because there was a policeman in a military jeep riding across the Commons shouting at protesters to disperse using a bullhorn. To Rachel it seemed that one moment all was peaceful, then someone started throwing rocks at him.

Rachel found herself being dragged forward by the crowd and she tried to pull back, but it was impossible. She lost contact with Jenny and the others as the protesters surged forward. She heard orders to fire, and tear gas drifted across the crowd, catching in her throat and making her cough. Her eyes were streaming now, and she was struggling to breathe. She tried to stop coughing, bending over double to try and get out of the noxious cloud still wafting over them.

"Here, take my arm… if you fall down you'll get trampled on." Like her, the student sounded breathless, but he managed to grab her arm and pull her upright. The protesters were now being forced up a hill. Rachel finally stopped coughing and nodded her thanks to her rescuer, before beginning to search frantically for her friends. But she couldn't see anything other than a sea of heads, and she was powerless to prevent herself from being dragged up the hill, then down the other side to what looked like a football practice field.

She could hear shouting and realised that the demonstrators, furious at being trapped against the fence, were throwing rocks at the National Guard again. Rachel managed to get herself to the edge of the crowd and resumed searching for Jenny. She watched as the soldiers retreated back up the hill to get away from the rocks still being thrown at them, and then, suddenly, they turned and began firing their M1 rifles.

All around people were screaming. Rachel gaped at the carnage unfolding in front of her. Although she'd thought the guardsmen were firing into the air, Rachel had instinctively ducked down. It wasn't until a few seconds later that she realised that some had deliberately fired at the crowd.

Outside My Khe Beach, Da Nang, Vietnam

"We have to keep on the right side of the Commander." Phuc sounded very nervous, which was making Lien even more anxious as they hurried towards the small settlement on the outskirts of the city where they had been summoned to meet Commander Hoang Kim Chinh. "Although he is not much older than us, he has been fighting for years and he has a fearsome reputation among the other freedom fighters." Phuc took a breath and lowered his voice, even though there was no one around. "I have heard many terrible things about him." Phuc sounded in awe rather than terrified. "He has removed tongues of traitors, ordered disembowelments, machete attacks on those who oppose him – he has even hacked off the genitals of village chiefs and sewn them inside their mouths for collaborating with the Americans."

Lien shuddered and fought down a wave of nausea. "He doesn't sound very nice," she said eventually. The freedom fighters near the village had always been friendly and had often helped them with their chores. She was finding it difficult to accept that their own people could do such horrible things. Any atrocities near them had always been carried out by the Republican soldiers. Surely their own people should not be behaving like that? Then she remembered other stories she'd heard but always discounted as enemy propaganda: a village chief and his wife had been distraught because their seven-year-old son had been missing for four days. The boy had suddenly reappeared out of the jungle and run across the rice paddies towards the village crying. When his mother picked him up, she discovered both of his hands had been cut off, and there was a sign around his neck threatening that if any of the villagers went to vote in the upcoming elections, something worse would happen to the rest of the chief's children. Lien had also heard that in a hamlet not far from the city the chief had his tongue cut out while his pregnant wife and four children were forced to watch. Then his genitals were cut off and sewn inside his mouth, while they killed his wife and rammed a bamboo lance through the head of each of the three sons, leaving only the five-year-old daughter alive.

Lien shuddered and began to wonder exactly who the

enemy was. Could she have gotten things so wrong? Her thoughts returned to Doug and how, although he was the enemy, he had given his life to save them from his companions. It was all very strange. She was still thinking about it when she realised they had reached the meeting place. She glanced around but couldn't see anyone, so she sat on a log and continued to think about the strange American who had tried to protect them from his own people.

"Miss Nguyen." Hoang Kim Chinh joined his hands together and bowed slightly.

Lien jumped to her feet, forgot about Doug and quickly returned the greeting. The Commander was taller than both her and Phuc, of slight build with a pleasant face. After Phuc's warning she'd expected someone who looked like a demon, but he was rather handsome.

They sat down and Chinh wasted no time in giving them their orders. To Phuc's disgust, his were no more than to protect his sister for the moment, as she was the one who would be able to find out what they needed to know. He felt the familiar jealousy returning. How could he be a hero if his sister continued to take the glory?

Lien was just as horrified but for different reasons. Somehow, she managed to keep her face expressionless as the Commander continued to outline the information they were looking for. "... in particular details of patrols, so we can ambush their helicopters." Chinh glanced at Phuc before smiling at Lien. Phuc didn't look very happy, and Chinh mistook his petulant expression as concern about his sister's honour. Chinh made a mental note to speak to him alone. The boy would have to learn that they were all warriors in this fight against the invaders, and his sister's honour was being sacrificed willingly in the fight for her country. He returned his attention to Lien. The girl was very pretty, and in different circumstances... He sighed, and with difficulty pushed his impure thoughts away. It would probably not be wise to become involved with Lien in any way. She had her duty to do and so did he, and he was sure she would do well. He'd already heard from their comrades further south that she had led several of the enemy into an ambush. Now they had killed her family in revenge, he was sure she would work twice as hard for their cause.

Lien could feel Phuc's eyes on her. Unlike Chinh, she was sure Phuc's fury stemmed from jealousy that the Commander was giving her work to do and not him. She ignored him, concentrated her attention on Chinh and nodded. "I will do my best, Commander."

"Good." He smiled again and stood up. "Come Phuc, we have things to discuss and your sister needs to get back to My Khe. Good luck, Lien. Anything you find out, pass to your brother and he will bring it to us." It made sense for Phuc to be the go-between, as being her brother it was natural for them to be seen together.

Lien watched them leave before heading back to My Khe. She had no idea how to talk to the Americans, even if she wanted to. And as for getting them to give her information... there was only one way to do that. Surely the Commander did not expect her to become a whore for them? Perhaps she had misunderstood? Unfortunately, she had no choice but to do what he wanted. Maybe there were other ways of getting information that did not involve dishonouring herself? She would have to watch the other girls and see how they behaved. Her thoughts returned to the Commander and she felt confused again. He seemed very nice, not like the devil she'd been expecting after Phuc's warnings. Perhaps her brother was wrong about him, or had just said those things because he was jealous of the man's rank.

Omaha, Nebraska

"Still no word on Rachel's whereabouts?" Mark downed his whisky and poured another before sitting back down in his leather armchair.

Emily shook her head. "Nothing. No doubt she'll be back when whatever demonstration she's at finishes." She had contacted the private detective she'd used earlier, and he'd reported back later that morning that Rachel had been seen leaving with her hippy friends. Emily had almost breathed a sigh of relief. At least she wasn't out sleeping with some boy. The last thing she needed was Rachel getting involved with some boy and getting pregnant. Going on anti-war protests wasn't ideal, but it was probably safer.

"Well, let's hope she's not gone to Kent State University." Mark slumped down in his chair.

Emily looked at him. "What do you mean?"

"They set fire to a building on the campus on Saturday night. Lots of arrests, apparently." Mark stared morosely at the newspaper.

Emily didn't answer. That was all she needed – Rachel being arrested too. She couldn't even think about Paul, she was so disgusted. He was still in a police cell awaiting a bail hearing in the morning. The way she felt about him at the moment, he could rot in jail. Mark had mentioned something about getting him treatment, but she had been too angry to listen. Good job she had always pinned her hopes and ambitions on Rachel. At least it would be, if her daughter hadn't suddenly taken leave of her senses too. Emily would have to somehow stop Rachel having anything to do with those blasted hippies in future. She should have done something after the last time, but she wouldn't make the same mistake this time. She would get them thrown out of their apartment and moved on out of the city, Mark had enough friends to make sure that happened. Then at least she could re-establish control over Rachel.

Kent State University, Ohio

The firing seemed to go for hours, although Rachel knew it could only have been a few seconds. When it finally stopped, she cautiously raised her head. It was then the sound of screaming swelled, and she could hear people shouting for doctors.

"I thought they were firing into the air?" She spoke to a girl next to her who shrugged, bewildered.

"So did I, but it looks like they were shooting at us." The girl was in shock, as were the other people around them. Rachel looked back up the hill; she could see people shouting, but the soldiers were no longer pointing their rifles in their direction. Rachel straightened up and headed back down to where people were yelling. There seemed to be separate groups gathering all over the field and she moved towards the nearest one. As she approached she saw someone holding their arm, blood pouring from an open wound. In front of him was a man lying face down, a hole in his back. Rachel gasped in disbelief; he was quite obviously dead. Rachel had never seen a dead body before, and she couldn't stop herself from staring.

"Rachel, thank God. Are you alright?" Jenny's normally pale face was ashen. Behind her Rachel could see Bob and Debbie, their faces reflecting her own. She was aware of shouting towards the edge of the field and police running, and then Jenny had grabbed her arm and was pulling her away. "We have to get out of here, Rachel."

"But..."

"She's right, kid, we need to leave." Bob had taken her other arm and Rachel allowed them to propel her towards other protesters who were fighting their way through the gates. As they made their way there, they could see other injured students and what appeared to be more dead bodies. Rachel had no idea how they got back to the VW, she was in too much shock to take any notice and only regained her senses when the van started up and Bob began driving. No one spoke. Rachel peered through the windows, watching the chaos outside: police cars, motorbikes, ambulances all rushing in the other direction. Rachel really wanted a smoke, but she knew that would be stupid. There was a good chance they would be stopped, so having the van reek of marijuana would not be clever.

Jenny turned on her transistor and they listened to the news. The shooting had lasted less than fifteen seconds, but four students were dead and nine others injured. Reports were emerging that one of the dead had been shot in the back, as had two of the injured. Rachel shivered. Peaceful protesting against the war had suddenly become deadly serious.

CHAPTER SIXTEEN

213th Helicopter Squadron, Marble Mountain Air Facility, Da Nang

The eastern world it is explodin', Violence flarin', bullets loadin', You're old enough to kill but not for votin'. Spanner smiled as Barry McGuire's 'Eve of Destruction' blared out from a radio further up the barracks. In his opinion it was still one of the best protest songs, even though it was several years old now. He finished reading the latest letters from his parents and siblings and lay back on his bunk, thinking about the protest movement back home. Despite some incredible protest songs and numerous demonstrations, nothing had changed. Even if it did, it was too late to save him. He was here now, and would be until next year, if he survived that long.

Spanner sighed. Vietnam was nothing like he'd thought it would be, but if he was honest, he hadn't really known what to expect. Perhaps he would form a different opinion when he finally had some R&R. There was lots of talk about My Khe beach, or China Beach as all the GIs called it. He only hoped it lived up the rumours he'd heard. For once he was in agreement with Jim. All he wanted to do was to relax, to be somewhere he wasn't under stress or pressure all the time, and to finally lose his virginity. That was something he hadn't shared with his friends. They had both seemed so worldly-wise that he had just gone along with them and pretended he was just as experienced. He closed his eyes and wondered what it would be like to feel a woman's arms around him, to feel her naked body next to his. He smiled. Not long now and hopefully he would finally find out.

Omaha, Nebraska

"Where the hell have you been?" Emily grabbed hold of Rachel's arm and pulled her into the large drawing room. Rachel tried to ignore the nauseous feeling in her stomach, which she assumed was probably fear.

"I went to protest against the war. Nixon isn't stopping the war; he's escalating it and before long Paul will be drafted too…" She stopped abruptly, conscious of a sudden change in atmosphere. "Has something happened to Paul? Oh my God, have they drafted him?"

There was a long silence before her father eventually spoke. "He's been arrested."

Rachel looked stunned. "Arrested? What for? Oh, I suppose he went to a demonstration as well?"

"Not exactly."

Rachel looked from one to the other and felt the first

stirrings of unease. She could hear Charles's voice in her head making accusations about Paul. She forced the image away and concentrated on her father. "What's going on?"

Her parents exchanged glances. "He's been arrested for having an unnatural relationship." It was Emily who finally answered.

Rachel was rooted to the spot, she felt dizzy and sick. "When..."

"Last week... he's been in custody since then." Emily took a deep breath. "We'll talk about that in a moment. You haven't answered the question. Where have you been?"

"Kent State University."

Mark gasped. "Are you alright? There were people shot dead there!" His voice rose.

Rachel nodded. "Yes, yes I'm fine... I saw the bodies... It was supposed to be peaceful." She fell silent.

"You could have been killed." For once Emily was speechless. While she had been worrying about Paul and feeling furious with Rachel, her daughter could have been seriously injured or killed.

Rachel was about to answer when the nausea rose up again and this time, unable to fight it down, she rushed from the room to the downstairs bathroom, lifted the toilet lid and began retching.

"What on earth's the matter, Rachel?" Emily was standing by the door.

Rachel shook her head, and then wished she hadn't. "I

don't know... I feel sick and dizzy."

Emily sighed. "Go up to bed and get some rest. We'll talk when you are feeling better."

Emily waited until Rachel had gone upstairs before returning to the drawing room.

"Is she alright?" Mark looked concerned.

"Yes, it's probably just shock."

Mark nodded and his thoughts returned to his son. He had no idea how they were going to get Paul out of the mess he was in. The state had very strict laws on sodomy, and Paul would now have to be referred for evaluation and treatment.

"What are we going to do about Paul?"

"I don't know." Mark frowned. "I think we have to try and prevent him going to court if we can; maybe we can agree to him having treatment first."

"What sort of treatment is it?"

"I don't know. But whatever it is, it has to be better than him spending the rest of his life in prison, doesn't it?"

My Khe Beach, Da Nang, Vietnam

Lien smiled nervously at the short, stocky dark-haired American, who had introduced himself as Howard, and shyly accepted his offer of a drink. Her heart was fluttering in her chest, and she could barely stop her hands from shaking as she took the cocktail and sat down at the table with him. After her meeting with Commander Hoang, her first worry had been about how she could just stop serving drinks to dance with a customer, but when she'd arrived back at work the manager had taken her aside and told her he had been given instructions that she was to talk to the Americans. Lien had been shocked at the power of the Commander and realised she was trapped. She would have to do what they wanted, but that didn't mean she would have to sacrifice her honour. She would just have drinks and dance with them. Lien tried to concentrate her attention on the American, but he was difficult to understand, and she had to keep asking him to repeat himself.

"Gee, honey, you're really hard work." Howard leaned forward and spoke slowly. "I said, how about we go somewhere so I can fuck you?" He put his hand in his pocket and pulled out a handful of dollars. "What's the going rate here?"

Lien gazed at him in horror while she tried to work out what was worse – letting this pig maul her, or upsetting the

Commander. Her disgust won and she stood up. "I am not for sale, pig." She spat the words at him and despite her trembling legs began walking away, her head held high.

"I just paid for you, you fucking bitch –" Howard caught hold of her and pulled her back towards him. She could smell the alcohol on his breath as he grabbed her hair and kissed her, forcing his tongue in her mouth. Lien struggled against him, but he was too strong. She was distantly aware of laughter, and she realised his friends were encouraging him.

"No –" she managed to free herself for a moment, but he slapped her and pulled her back towards him again.

"I think the lady said she wasn't interested." The voice rang loud in the sudden silence in the bar.

Howard let go of her abruptly, and Lien almost lost her balance.

"What the fuck's it got to do with you? She's just a whore."

"There's plenty of girls in here who'll be happy to go with you, why bother with her?" Spanner had drawn himself up to his full height and towered over Howard, but he was still trying to be conciliatory.

"Yeah, pal, she's probably not much good anyway." Kurt was standing to his right.

Spanner glared at his friend, who shrugged and murmured, "Sorry… just trying to help…"

"Loads of whores to choose from pal, why make trouble for yourself?" Jim joined in. Spanner groaned inwardly.

He'd been trying to avoid trouble, but obviously Jim hadn't realised that.

"You threatening me?" Howard had forgotten Lien now and was squaring up to Jim. A couple of other men came up behind him, and Spanner sighed. So much for his first peaceful night of R&R.

Lien stepped back further, wondering what on earth she'd done. It looked like the Americans were going to fight. Would she be blamed for that? What would the Commander say? Her heart beat faster against her chest, and she began to regret her hasty reaction. Perhaps there had been a better way to handle it?

"Look, why don't we all sit down and have a drink? No need for any trouble, not over a girl. There's plenty of them..." Spanner waved his hand vaguely in the direction of the bar, "and we don't want to end up in the clink, do we?" He was about to say more when Howard threw a punch. He was drunk, so Spanner dodged it easily, retaliating with a quick upper cut to his chin. Howard crashed to the floor and his friends stepped forward, fists flailing. Kurt and Jim moved quickly to restrain them and force them back towards their seats.

"Like our friend said, chill out and let's all enjoy our evening..." Jim glared at the two men, who exchanged glances and then slowly sat down.

Spanner breathed a sigh of relief and turned to Lien, who was still looking petrified. "I'm sorry, we're not all like him.

Can I buy you a drink by way of an apology?" He smiled. "You don't even have to talk to me, I promise."

Lien looked properly at him for the first time. For some reason, he reminded her of Doug; it wasn't just the cropped blonde hair, it was his easy smile and the twinkle in his blue eyes. She smiled back without thinking. "Thank you... I am grateful." Then she remembered what she was supposed to be doing, and she forced her smile to widen. If she had to drink and dance with any of them, he was as good as any. At least this way there was a chance the manager wouldn't tell the Commander about her failure with Howard.

Spanner couldn't help but feel pleased. He'd only offered out of politeness, but the girl was very pretty, and if he was going to have some female company, he could do a lot worse. "We'll leave you to it then, pal." Kurt winked at Jim, patted Spanner on the shoulder and they headed towards the bar.

"Thanks guys!" Spanner turned his attention back to the girl. "I'm Steve, but all my friends call me Spanner."

"Hello, Spanner. My name is Nguyen Xuan Lien – Lien."

Spanner tried to get his tongue around the whole name a couple of times, making her laugh. "Perhaps I'll call you Lien, if that's alright?"

Lien nodded. "Yes, of course." She began to gradually relax. Perhaps her duty wouldn't be quite so onerous after all.

Omaha Correction Centre, Nebraska

Paul sat on his bunk and stared at the bars opposite. Now he was completely sober, he was bitterly regretting his reckless decision to pick up a stranger in a bar. There were other things he could have done to avoid the draft, including crossing the border into Canada. Getting himself arrested for sodomy was the least intelligent, yet that was what he had done. He wondered what Heine was doing, whether he even knew that Paul had been arrested. It was unlikely, as no one knew about their relationship.

He turned round, lay back and fixed his eyes on the ceiling. What was going to happen to him now? He had heard rumours about aversion therapy, some which just involved counselling, others which were more invasive and some like electric shock treatment. But to even get 'treatment' he would have to get through the evaluation. If he didn't, he could be facing most of his life in prison, all because he preferred men to women. If only he lived somewhere like England. Heine had said that it was alright to like men there. You weren't locked up or punished. Paul shuddered and wished he could turn back the clock and make different decisions.

Omaha, Nebraska

Rachel lay on her bed and thought about Paul. He must be terrified, stuck in prison. She wondered what had happened for him to get arrested. Despite laying down she suddenly felt light-headed as a horrible thought crossed her mind. Charles had threatened to make Paul's proclivities public knowledge if she went to the police. Surely Charles hadn't reported him? Perhaps the detective had told Charles that she'd reported him? The fear that she was responsible consumed her for several minutes, before she realised that if that had been the case, her parents would probably have said as much. They hadn't given her any details, so it must have been something else. She wondered when they would let Paul come home. It could be weeks before he went to court; surely her parents wouldn't leave him in prison that long? Rachel shook her head. No. She was certain they would pay the bail money, however much it was.

Thinking about Charles had made Rachel feel sick again. She took a breath and tried to concentrate on something else, but it didn't work. Obviously that bastard had been right about Paul after all. Rachel clenched her fists. She didn't mind that her brother was different, he couldn't help it after all. But somehow, the thought of that animal knowing all about her brother made it seem sordid. Rachel took a breath and shook her head determinedly. No. Charles could only ruin her life if she let him, and she had already decided not to let anything that bastard had done to her affect her, and that would now include her relationship with Paul. At least Charles no longer had anything over her... other than saying she'd consented to sex with him of course, and with his money and connections everyone would believe him.

Her stomach heaved again, and she closed her eyes, willing it to go away. Why on earth did she keep feeling sick? She hadn't had much to smoke the previous day and she'd eaten normally. It didn't make sense. Perhaps it was something to do with her period... she'd felt nauseous a couple of times before, although she hadn't felt any cramps yet, but that must be it.

Rachel was just beginning to relax; obviously her period must be due, and all the stress of the weekend had made her ill. Then her heart skipped a beat and she frowned, her panic increasing as she tried to remember the last time she'd had 'the curse' as they jokingly called it. She forced herself off the bed, walked shakily to her dressing table and opened the top draw, all the time praying that she was wrong. Her diary was on top of her underwear and she pulled it out. A quick flip through the pages confirmed her worst fears and she sank onto the stool and stared at her ashen face in the mirror. She hadn't had a period since before the tennis tournament, before Charles had raped her. Yes, it could be the stress of what happened to her, but the absence of menstruation for two months and feeling sick could probably only mean one thing. She was pregnant.

CHAPTER SEVENTEEN

Omaha, Nebraska

"Simon thinks we can avoid court if Paul agrees to aversion therapy." Mark was pacing up and down the study. Emily breathed a sigh of relief. "Then it won't be in the newspapers?"

Rachel shook her head and fought back the ever-present nausea.

"You have something to say, Rachel?" Emily glared at her daughter. "This affects you too. If your brother's problems are splashed all over the papers, you will forever be associated with the scandal."

"Do you think I care about that?" Rachel spat. "Paul is my brother, I love him. I just want what's best for him."

"And you think we don't?" Mark rounded on her. "How will it help Paul to have everyone know about him? If he has the treatment, then he can carry on his life as normal and no one will be any the wiser."

"But he isn't ill! He doesn't have something that's curable! He was born like that. He prefers men, what's wrong with that?" Rachel stood up and glared at her father. "What damage will the treatment do to him? Have you read about what they do to people…" She faltered, not knowing how to phrase it. She'd been about to say *'people like him'* but that made her sound as bad as her parents.

"You don't know what you're talking about, Rachel." Emily moved in front of her and grabbed her daughter's arm. "We're doing this as much for you as for Paul. You don't need to be tainted by scandal, any more than Paul does."

Rachel pulled her arm free. If only her mother knew… "Have you asked Paul what he wants?"

Emily gave a harsh laugh. "I think your brother has lost the right to a choice, don't you?"

Rachel shook her head. "No… no, I don't. It's his life." Rachel stopped abruptly, realising she was no longer really talking about Paul. She had been thinking about herself. When she told her parents she was pregnant, they would do the same thing they were doing now. They would take charge and make all the decisions. She wouldn't have a say in her own future or that of the child's. Rachel's hand automatically went to her stomach as she recognised that this was the first time she'd thought about the baby growing inside her as a separate entity from its violent conception. Up until that moment, the baby had just been a disaster, an inconvenience that would ruin her life. But now…

"Rachel? Are you alright?" Emily was staring at her.

"Why did the police arrest Paul?" She had to know whether she was responsible, whether her failed attempt to get justice had brought this disaster down on her brother.

"Oh, for goodness' sake, Rachel, we've been through this!" Mark snapped.

"No, I know why, I mean was he with his…," she hunted around for the right word but could only come up with, "… boyfriend?"

"*Boyfriend*?" Emily sounded horrified. "I sincerely hope not. He was arrested in one of the seediest parts of Omaha with some drug addict." Her eyes narrowed. "What do you know about a *boyfriend*?"

Rachel shook her head. "Nothing, I just assumed he must have one… he's always out, I mean..." Her heart was racing, but at least it didn't look like this whole mess was anything to do with Charles taking revenge.

Emily scowled. She hadn't thought of Paul having a 'friend' but Rachel was probably right. Then she wondered why her daughter was so interested. "Why did you want to know who was with him when he was arrested?"

Rachel hunted for a credible reason. "I just thought if he did have a special friend, he might not know what had happened to Paul, so he might be worried." Rachel was making it up as she went along.

"Perhaps we should go and ask Paul so we can find him, put his mind at rest?" Emily's voice was dripping with sarcasm. Rachel flushed and looked down, then she raised her head and met her mother's gaze squarely. "Yes, perhaps we should."

Emily lost her temper. "Enough Rachel. Stop making stupid suggestions. If you don't have anything sensible to contribute, go to your room." Emily lost her temper.

"Actually, I thought I was making a sensible suggestion." Rachel realised she was quite enjoying annoying her mother. "You're making all these decisions about Paul's life and you aren't even going to consult him. Don't you think that's wrong?"

"Why should we ask your brother when all he's done is bring disgrace down on us all? He's obviously not capable of making adult decisions, or he wouldn't have got himself into this mess."

"So that's it? He's made one mistake and now you're going to make him pay?" Rachel lost her temper. "Don't you think that's unfair?"

"You're being ridiculous, Rachel. Next you'll be telling us that your decision to go on these stupid demonstrations is sensible!"

"At least I am doing something!" Rachel fired back.

"You'd be better off spending your spare time improving your tennis game and mixing with people like Charles Peterson. At least he's got a future, unlike your idiot of a brother."

"Charles?" Rachel suddenly found herself struggling to breathe. "Charles is a pig. I would rather be dead than spend any more time with that animal."

"Oh, for goodness' sake, Rachel, grow up!" Emily took a

step towards her, eyes blazing. "I suppose you'd rather be with your hippy friends?"

"Damn right I would." Rachel held her mother's gaze. "At least I'm safe with them."

"Safe? Safe?" Emily snorted. "They took you to a university where the National Guard opened fire!"

"But they didn't rape me!" Rachel's hand flew to her mouth and she stared in horror at her parents. Oh God. What had she said? Her mouth filled with bile and, no longer able to control herself, Rachel turned and fled from the room.

Outside My Khe Beach, Da Nang, Vietnam

"I hear you had some problems." Phuc didn't sound particularly sorry.

"It was nothing." There were times Lien didn't understand her brother at all. But she was more concerned about the reason why they had been summoned to meet the Commander.

"Lien, Phuc." Chinh suddenly appeared from behind one of the huts, making them jump.

"Commander." Lien greeted him in the traditional way, hoping he couldn't see the fear in her eyes.

"Please call me Chinh," he smiled. She really was very pretty, especially when she was frightened.

"Have we done something wrong?"

Chinh laughed. "No, you have done very well. The man you kept company with is at the air base from which the helicopters operate, so he will know patrol details. Much better than the first man, who was just an infantry soldier."

Lien stared at him in astonishment. She had found out that much about Spanner, but how did Chinh know? His smile widened. "I have spies everywhere, Lien."

"Of course." She breathed a sigh of relief. She wasn't in trouble, then.

"What else did he tell you?"

Lien had prepared herself for this question as soon as they had received the summons, so she answered with confidence. "He told me that he is a gunner on helicopters, and that he is also a mechanic repairing all army vehicles." She flushed. "He wants to see me again."

Chinh nodded. "That's good. You will become his favourite girl, the one he comes to My Khe to see every time he has leave. Do you understand?"

Lien's flush deepened. "Yes, Chinh."

"Good." He turned to Phuc. "You can go back now; I have things to discuss with Lien."

Phuc hesitated, then remembered his previous conversation with Chinh, in which the Commander had made it quite clear Phuc was not to interfere. He stood up and bowed before leaving.

Chinh reached out his hand to help Lien up, bringing her

close to him. “You are nervous of doing your duty, Lien?”

“No, of course not…” She stopped and lifted her eyes to his, then nodded. “Yes, Chinh.”

“Would you like me to show you how easy it is?” Chinh had changed his mind about not having anything to do with Lien. She was so pretty, and surely it would be better for her if her first time was with someone who would be gentle, someone who was on her side.

“I don’t understand…”

“It will be better for you if you know what to do. The first time can be difficult, but I can show you.” His eyes were mesmerising her. Lien could feel the warmth of his gaze deep inside her, and she made no move to escape as he moved closer and kissed her gently. Lien closed her eyes and forgot everything except the feel of his lips on hers.

Outside Da Nang, Vietnam

“We thought you were never coming back.” The latest patrol Spanner and Kurt had gone to pick up included several injured men, and it was taking some time to load them.

“We had to wait until it was safe to land.” Spanner’s eyes scanned the landscape, wishing they would hurry up. He wasn’t entirely convinced the VC who had lain in wait for their first attempt at landing had gone, although they had circled for some time before finally coming back in to rescue the patrol. Fortunately, they had had no men to drop off here; the drop zone further inland had been quiet and the landing uneventful. The helicopter had risen into the air and prepared to fly back to base when the message had come in to fly south and rescue a patrol under heavy fire.

He was about to say more when a burst of machine gun fire riddled the air above him, the bullets ricocheting off the metal body of the helicopter, narrowly missing him and the Lieutenant. As Spanner spun his gun round and fired in the general direction he thought the bullets had come from, the pilot took off, the machine swaying dangerously as he tried to avoid more gun fire. Spanner and Kurt began spraying the area with machine gun fire, but the bullets kept coming.

"To the left... over there..." Jim yelled, leaning out of the door.

"Get back in, you fucking maniac!" Spanner grabbed his friend and shoved him to the floor just as the helicopter banked suddenly, enough to have dislodged Jim if he'd still been hanging onto the frame, and then more bullets hit them. Spanner heard a cry from behind him, but he didn't have time to look. Thanks to Jim, he had finally spotted where the VC were hiding. He swung his gun around and aimed in the general direction of the smoke that was fast dissipating into the atmosphere, and opened fire.

There was a sudden silence, and he risked glancing back

into the body of the helicopter. One of the patrol was trying to bandage Jim's arm.

"You alright, pal?"

Jim nodded and Spanner breathed a sigh of relief before glancing around at the inside of the craft and offering up a quick prayer that the enemy fire hadn't done any serious damage. They were higher now and out of range of anything other than the 122-millimetre rockets the VC used with a variety of homemade launching systems, which made it easy to move around and difficult for the Americans and their republican allies to detect. Spanner shivered nervously and tried to banish the image of a 75-inch rocket hurtling toward them.

"Looks like you got them," Kurt nodded at him from the other side.

Spanner nodded but didn't answer, instead resuming his reconnaissance of the landscape below them. This was often the most dangerous time, because the VC would know which routes they used back to base, and that was where they would station their rocket launchers.

Omaha, Nebraska

Emily's first thought was that she must have misheard, but one look at Mark's shocked expression had confirmed the truth and for a few moments she had been rendered speechless.

"Did she really say that Charles had raped her?" Emily prayed Mark would shake his head and deny it, but he didn't. His expression had now changed, the shock replaced by fury.

"Yes, that's exactly what she said." He clenched his fists. "I'll kill the bastard." He walked to his desk, opened the top drawer and pulled out his model 19 Smith and Wesson.

Emily somehow pulled herself together. "Don't be a fool, Mark. You can't go and shoot Charles... you'll be arrested, and they'll send you to the chair." Mark ignored her; he was checking the gun was loaded. Emily tried again. "Mark, wait. We need to make sure of our facts. You can't just go and accuse someone from such a prominent family of rape, not on Rachel's word. We might have misheard, or she could be lying."

Mark gazed at her in disbelief. "You really think our daughter is lying? We both know she hasn't been herself since the tennis tournament."

"But it doesn't mean he raped her." Emily searched around for another explanation, anything to stop Mark. "Perhaps she just went too far and regretted it?"

Mark shook his head. "Then why say she was raped? Why bother to mention it at all?" He continued walking towards the door.

Emily frowned. Mark was right... and then the truth hit her. "Oh God. She's pregnant."

Mark stopped dead and turned around slowly. "Pregnant?"

"She's been sick for the last few days – that's where she is now, in the toilet."

"Pregnant?" Mark repeated. He walked slowly back to the desk and sat down. Emily waited for him to put the gun away, but he didn't. Instead he looked at her. "What's happening Em? What have we done to our children for them to behave like this?"

Emily shook her head. "I've been asking myself the same thing, and that was before this." She took a breath. "We could be wrong, so the first thing is to get Rachel back in here and find out the truth."

Mark nodded. "Yes. You're right." He replaced the gun in the top drawer and Emily let out a slow breath. Now all she had to do was to stop Rachel saying anything to inflame Mark. Emily made her way to the toilet, her brain racing. If that bastard really had raped her daughter, could she really stand by and do nothing? Emily snorted in derision. What could she and Mark do against the Petersons? They were the most powerful family in Omaha, probably the whole state. If they tried to report it to the police, they wouldn't believe them, not against the Petersons. No one would take their side; they would be ruined. This had the makings of a scandal even worse than Paul's. Everything she'd worked for, all her plans for the future would be in tatters. For a moment she felt like taking Mark's gun and shooting the bastard herself, but that wouldn't help. She had to keep calm and find a way to stop Mark losing his temper, even if it meant accusing her daughter of lying.

My Khe Beach, Da Nang, Vietnam

Lien walked slowly back to My Khe Beach, her thoughts on Chinh. She hadn't really understood what he'd meant, so when he'd taken her to the edge of the jungle and lain her down in the undergrowth, she'd been shocked. She did find him attractive, but she wasn't sure she really wanted to do this. But then she'd remembered his reputation, and that this was what she was expected to do with the American. She had convinced herself that Chinh was right and that the first time would be easier with him, so she had closed her eyes and not struggled.

"You were a long time." Phuc suddenly appeared beside her.

"I wish you wouldn't do that, you made me jump!" Lien snapped.

"You must have had a lot to talk about..."

Lien blushed. Phuc's eyes roved over her rather dishevelled clothes and shamefaced expression, and he shook his head in disgust. "Oh Lien, did the Commander want to have some fun with you?"

Lien flushed even more and Phuc's face grew puce

in fury. He slapped her across the face, knocking her off balance. "You have dishonoured our family; you are nothing more than mãi dâm."

Lien stared at him in shock and then anger. "You call me a hooker for doing something with our Commander, but it is ok to do the same thing with the enemy?"

"You do it with the enemy because it is your duty. The Commander just wanted to fuck you. I saw it in his eyes when he first saw you! And you are so easy, sister!"

Lien shook her head. "No, you are wrong."

"He wanted to fuck you first, before the American pig could dishonour you!" Phuc was shaking with rage.

Lien shook her head again and opened her mouth to argue, but she knew there was no point. He would not understand.

"Nothing to say, stupid Lien? Ha, because you know I am right." Phuc began pacing up and down. "I should kill him for dishonouring you."

Lien's eyes widened in horror. Phuc was irritating and sometimes she didn't like him, but he was all she had left. "No, brother, he would kill you."

"You should have thought of that before becoming a mãi dâm!"

"He said it would be easier if I did it with him first!" She blurted out and burst into tears.

Phuc shook his head again and tried to regain his temper. Lien was right about one thing; he couldn't take on the

Commander, and he couldn't undo what had been done. And soon she would do the same thing with the enemy. He sat down next to her and put his arm awkwardly around her shoulders. "Oh, Lien, you think you are so clever, but you are not. You are just a child, really. He needed a good reason to convince you to let him fuck you, and one that allowed him to justify it to himself."

Lien sobbed louder, but she didn't push him away. She wanted to believe Phuc was wrong, but deep down she was beginning to have doubts.

Omaha, Nebraska

Rachel sat on the floor in the toilet and hugged herself. She couldn't believe she had just blurted that out to her parents, and she was trying to work out what to do next. Outside the door she could hear her mother pacing up and down.

"You can't stay in there forever, Rachel. Please come out and we can talk about this." Emily was trying not to lose her temper.

Rachel didn't answer, but she knew her mother was right. The fact she was pregnant would have come out eventually, so perhaps it was best to get it out of the way now. She stood up shakily and unlocked the door. Emily didn't trust herself to speak, so she just indicated Mark's study and Rachel walked slowly towards the door. Her father was sitting at his desk and he looked up when she came in.

"Sit down, Rachel. I think you need to explain what's been going on."

Rachel nodded, sat down and waited while her mother came in and shut the door behind her.

"Well?" Emily stood in front of her, hands on hips, and waited.

Rachel took a deep breath and began talking in a monotone. "Charles raped me on the night of the tennis tournament. I went to the police that night to report him, but they wouldn't do anything about it. The detective implied I was lying, at least he did after I told him who had done it. And..." her voice faltered. "I think I'm pregnant."

There was a silence; the explosion she was expecting didn't materialise and she belatedly realised her parents must have already guessed that she was pregnant. Emily finally spoke. "Are you lying?"

Rachel stared at her in shock. It had never occurred to her that her mother wouldn't believe her. "How can you ask that? Do you really think I would lie about something so horrible?"

Out of the corner of her eye Emily could see Mark reaching for the drawer again. She had to say something to stop him. "I think it's much more likely that you have been having sex with one of your hippy friends, probably when you were smoking drugs and goodness knows what else. And that's how you got pregnant. You're making this up to try and blame someone else for your mistakes."

Rachel couldn't believe what she was hearing. She stood up. "No, that's not true. Charles kept filling my glass with wine, he bought a bottle at the bar, you can check. Then he took me to the storeroom and when I wouldn't sleep with him, he raped me and laughed – he said if I reported him, he would tell the police about Paul being queer."

Emily gasped and took a step towards her. "Is that why he was arrested?"

"I don't know!" Rachel began sobbing. "I don't think so. I'm sure Charles would have let me know if he had told the police, he wouldn't have been able to stop himself gloating!"

Mark was on his feet again, gun in hand, and Rachel screamed. Emily threw herself in front of him, yelling, "No, Mark, please. You can't shoot him; they'll send you to the chair."

Rachel's sobs grew louder. Emily turned towards her, grabbed her daughter' arm and shouted in her face. "Then stop making things up and tell the truth. Otherwise your father will die, and it will all be your fault!"

213th Helicopter Squadron, Marble Mountain, Da Nang, Vietnam

"You could have fallen out, you mad bastard." Now they were safely back at the base, Spanner couldn't believe how close Jim had come to falling out of the helicopter. A few seconds later and he would have been lost. He finished repairing the last of the holes in the underside of the machine and wiped the sweat from his brows.

Jim grinned. "I owe you a drink, pal – well, probably more than one. Although you were a bit late getting their base, or I wouldn't have been shot!" He laughed.

Spanner rolled his eyes, but an answering grin tugged at his lips. "You were lucky, but yeah, you owe me a drink. Thank God we're off tomorrow."

"Ahh, looking forward to seeing your girl again?" Kurt interjected, aiming a ribald wink at Jim.

Spanner jostled him gently. "You're only jealous!"

His friends laughed and Spanner smiled to himself. Yes, he was looking forward to seeing Leni again. In his mind's eye, he could still see her sitting opposite him, wearing the native costume known as an Ao dai, pronounced 'owzeye'. The high mandarin collar, tight bodice and skirt split to the hip showed off her shapely breasts and tiny waist, but it wasn't just her body that Spanner wanted to get close to. There was something about her that reminded him of a wounded deer, and he knew that he wanted to get to know her better before taking things any further.

Leni was very shy, and it had taken him a while to get her to say anything about herself. But eventually she'd told him that her parents and younger sisters were dead, and her only living relative was a brother. She had shown very little emotion when she told him about her family, and afterwards he'd had a feeling she'd regretted telling him that much. She hadn't explained how her family had died and Spanner hadn't asked. If they had been ill she would probably have said, so he assumed they had been killed. But by which side? Presumably she wouldn't be working at the beach if she supported the VC, but he couldn't take that for granted. The older, more experienced sweats had warned them to be on their guard with the Vietnamese girls, as some were working for the VC, looking for information or to set them up to be killed, and given Leni's history she might be looking for revenge. But Spanner didn't want to walk away. He liked her, so he'd decided it might be best not to know who had killed them.

Spanner knew he couldn't talk about what he was doing now, so he'd told her about his life before Vietnam. Talking about his family had helped at the time, made him feel less homesick, and he was looking forward to having the opportunity to chat to her again. After the way his compatriot had treated her like a boom boom girl, Spanner had been careful not to do anything other than talk, but he was hoping that this time she would dance with him and things might go further. But not until he felt she wanted them to. Spanner knew now that he could pay for sex anywhere in My Khe Beach, there were plenty of girls selling themselves for very little money, but that wasn't what he wanted. Spanner knew he was probably old-fashioned, but unlike his friends he wasn't just looking for meaningless sex; he wanted an emotional connection as well.

Omaha, Nebraska

Rachel gaped at her mother in horror, then looked at her father.

"I can't lie…"

Emily slapped her across the face and Rachel screamed.

"Leave her, Emily. It's perfectly clear she's telling the truth." Mark began walking towards the door.

"No, please don't!" Rachel's words fell on deaf ears. She stared at her mother in desperation, and as her father opened the door she gave in. As much as she wanted her father to kill Charles, nothing was worth him being arrested and killed by the state. She would have to find a way of getting her revenge on Charles another way.

"Alright… alright. I made it up…" Even as the words left her mouth Rachel regretted them. Saying she'd lied was like being raped twice. She slumped down on the nearest chair and put her head in her hands. Her face was still stinging from her mother's slap and tears ran down her cheeks.

Mark had stopped by the door, his heart pounding furiously against his ribs. He took a deep breath and turned around. Somehow, he managed to sound almost calm. "Rachel, I really need you to tell me the truth, sweetheart. Don't worry about the consequences. I have always taught you to speak the truth, haven't I?"

Rachel raised her head slowly. She wanted so much to tell the truth but if she did… "No. I lied." She couldn't look at him. "Mom is right. I smoked some dope and had sex with one of my friends."

There was silence and she risked looking up. Emily was looking triumphant, and in that moment Rachel hated her mother. She glared at her for several seconds before turning her gaze to her father. He was still standing by the door, gun in hand. Then he slowly walked back to his desk. Rachel breathed a brief sigh of relief before standing up and running from the room.

CHAPTER EIGHTEEN

My Khe Beach, Da Nang, Vietnam

"Spanner, it is nice to see you again." Lien realised it was true. Ever since she'd slept with Chinh she'd felt more alone than ever. Phuc's words had lodged deep in her soul, and she was sure he was right about the Commander's motives. Spanner's cheerful face and the twinkle in his bright blue eyes was like a breath of fresh air, and she felt her spirits lift. "I get you a drink and bring it over…" She blushed as she realised she had taken it for granted that he wanted her to sit with him.

Spanner beamed. "That would be great, Leni. I thought you might have forgotten me!"

Lien blushed even more. "No, no, I remember you very well." His eyes held hers and she felt a sudden warmth in the pit of her stomach. With difficulty, she looked away. "I get you drink. You take a seat at table."

Spanner floated over to the nearest table. He'd spent days wondering if Leni would be there when he finally had some leave and then, when his pass had come through, he'd worried that she might not be interested in him, or even worse, be with someone else when he arrived.

When she came across with the drinks and sat down, Spanner's smile broadened and then faltered. He didn't want anyone else commandeering her while he was there, but he didn't want to upset her, especially after what had happened the last time.

Lien caught his change of mood and wondered if she'd done something wrong. "Everything ok? You no like drink?"

"Yes – yes, it's perfect, thank you." Spanner paused, choosing his words carefully. "I don't want to upset you. I am hoping you can spend all the evening with me, just talking and maybe dancing... but I don't know if I have to pay anyone for your time?" He prayed she wouldn't misunderstand.

To his relief, Lien smiled. "Yes, you pay the barman."

Spanner relaxed and stood up. "I'll do that then." He strode across to the bar, and after a hurried conversation with the barman and an exchange of some dollars, he was on his way back. He downed his drink and reached out a hand. "As your time is now mine, shall we go for a walk along the beach, away from here?"

Lien stood up and allowed him to lead her out of the bar, her heart pounding with a mixture of nervousness and excitement.

Now they were outside, Spanner had no idea what to say to her, so they walked in silence until they reached the beach.

"It's years since I went to the beach." Spanner gazed out across the ocean, and for a moment thought how far away from home he was.

"I never see the sea before I come here. I no believe how big it is."

Spanner smiled and completely forgot his decision not to ask about her family. "What was your life like in the village?"

Lien's face lit up briefly. "When there was not fighting, it was fine. We not have much money, but we had food and our home, our animals." Her face fell.

"I'm sorry. I didn't mean to make you sad." Spanner slipped an arm around her shoulders but made no move to pull her toward him. Lien found the gesture comforting, and for a moment forgot he was the enemy. She began telling him how they had lived in the village and Spanner was struck by the similarities. Their farms might be thousands of miles apart and their crops and livestock completely different, but there was little real difference in their lives. Both had grown up in the country with the values of the land. He listened as she talked, occasionally commenting, until she suddenly sighed. "Then, one night American soldiers came and killed everyone."

Spanner gasped and Lien stopped abruptly. She wasn't supposed to have told him that. What on earth was the matter with her? She had forgotten who she was with. Now he would ask why, and she certainly couldn't tell him that. Unable to think what she could say next, Lien disentangled herself from his arm and hurried across the sand towards the sea.

Omaha, Nebraska

"We need to make a decision about the baby before you are too far advanced. How pregnant are you?" Emily had left it a few days before tackling what she saw as the next problem.

Rachel lay on her bed, took a breath and held her mother's gaze. "The tennis dance was three months ago, so I am sure you can work it out."

"For goodness' sake, Rachel, stop repeating the same lie. I thought we'd got past that."

"No, I said what you wanted me to say to stop Pop killing that bastard, but we both know the truth, don't we?" Rachel wondered where the strength to stand up to her mother was coming from. Perhaps it was being pregnant?

Emily gaped at her daughter in shock. Then she decided to focus on the problem instead. "I'll arrange for you to see my specialist, then we can get you into a clinic."

"What for?" Rachel knew exactly what her mother was implying, but she wanted to make her spell it out.

"An abortion, of course. You don't think you're going to keep it, do you?"

Rachel looked at her for several seconds before answering. "I'm not killing my baby. I'm keeping it."

My Khe Beach, Da Nang, Vietnam

"Where are you going, Leni?" Spanner called after Lien in exasperation, then followed, his boots sinking into the soft sand, slowing him down. Fortunately, there were few people about and it was easy to keep her in sight. Within moments he'd caught her up, standing close to the water's edge, just out of reach of the gentle rolling waves. "What on earth's the matter? Why did you run off?"

Lien stared out across the sea and tried frantically to think of an answer, but all she could think of was lying. Spanner took her arm and pulled her gently round to face him. "I'm sorry – have I upset you?"

Lien shook her head. "No, I'm sorry." She knew she couldn't afford to lose Spanner; if she did, she might have to be nice to someone she didn't like. The thought made her shudder and focused her mind. "They were killed in a bomb. The VC were in the field near our house and when the bomb dropped it missed them and hit us instead. My brother and I, we tended the buffalos so were not there." She stopped and hoped he would believe her.

"That's awful, Leni, I am so sorry." Spanner placed a gentle hand on her shoulder. "You must hate us."

Leni drew a breath and turned to face him. "No, not all of you. How can I? You did not drop bomb on us. Just as you don't hate all of us because of action of a few of my countrymen." Leni looked up into his eyes and was relieved to see he didn't appear to doubt her at all.

Spanner smiled down at her. "I'm sure I could never hate you, Leni." His eyes held hers and then he was leaning forward, his lips gently brushing hers. Leni felt a rush of warmth, a feeling of sudden exhilaration, and she put her arms around his neck and returned his kiss. Spanner allowed himself to enjoy the warmth of her body against his, then, reluctantly, he pulled back. "I don't want you to do anything you aren't comfortable with, Leni. I know I've paid for your time this evening, but it wasn't for anything more than your company."

Leni stood on tiptoes and put her arms back around his neck. "I am happy, Spanner." She blushed, and then forgot her shyness as he kissed her with increasing passion.

Omaha, Nebraska

Emily stared down at Rachel in shock, which soon turned to fury. "What?"

"I said I am not having an abortion." Rachel held her mother's gaze.

"You don't seriously intend to keep the *bastard*?" Emily was struggling to resist the urge to pull her daughter off the bed and slap some sense into her.

Rachel flinched at the word *bastard;* but she nodded anyway. "Yes. I am going to keep my *baby*. *Your grandchild*!"

She paused to let the words sink in. "And before you start asking me which of my hippy friends fathered it, none of them did. Charles raped me, but I still want to keep the baby, in spite of that. And nothing you can say will convince me to do anything different."

"We'll see what your father has to say about that." Emily didn't trust herself to stay there any longer. She spun on her heel and stormed out of the bedroom.

Rachel wondered whether they could physically force her to have an abortion against her will. She climbed off the bed and put the transistor on. Immediately, the room was filled with The Animals' 'We've Gotta Get Out of This Place'. Rachel gave a wry smile. She didn't think her parents could do that to her, but if they tried, she would just run away. As she lay listening to the music, she realised it was time to tell Jenny what had happened to her; then she would know if she had somewhere else to go.

My Khe Beach, Da Nang, Vietnam

Phuc clenched his fists and kicked the sand in fury. He couldn't believe his sister was actually kissing the enemy in public, and even worse, she looked like she was enjoying it. He had begun striding towards her, determined to stop her dishonouring their parents' memory any further, when he remembered Chinh's last words to him and he slowed his pace. In his mind, Phuc could clearly see the expression on Chinh's face and he shivered despite the warmth of the evening. When he'd first heard the rumours about Chinh he hadn't really believed them, although that hadn't stopped him repeating them to Lien. But now he was convinced they were probably true, which meant he couldn't do anything about the man seducing Lien with his lies, and he daren't interfere in Chinh's plan to use Lien to find out information.

Phuc turned away, stared out into the ocean and wondered what he could do to protect Lien that wouldn't get him killed. Chinh had ordered him to keep an eye on her, but he couldn't bear to watch them kissing. He found a couple of stones and threw them out to sea, but it didn't ease his temper or make him feel any better, nor did kicking at the waves. Phuc grimaced. Even shouting at Buddha wouldn't do any good. The only thing that would help would be to kill the American, and that was the one thing he couldn't do. Phuc frowned… at least, he couldn't until Lien had all the information she needed. Then she would probably be ordered to target someone else. Phuc thought carefully. There was a chance this American would be killed in any ambush that came from Lien's intelligence, but if he wasn't…. that would be the time to take his revenge. Phuc smiled. He wouldn't just kill that American, he would make sure he killed lots of them. If he was a hero, it would be harder for Chinh to tell him what to do, and then maybe he could stop Lien selling herself to even more Americans, and he would finally overshadow her achievements. It would be Phuc whose name people whispered in awe, not that of his sister. Feeling better, Phuc turned back, but Lien and the American weren't there. He scanned the beach frantically and then the path alongside the beach, but there was no sign of them at all. Phuc swallowed nervously. If anything happened to Lien, it would be his fault. Not only would he have Chinh on his back, but he would never forgive himself for not watching them as he was supposed to.

He hurried back to the path, but he couldn't see anything, there were too many people about, enjoying the evening air. Phuc felt sick. Where on earth had they gone?

Omaha, Nebraska

"Why on earth didn't you tell me, Rachel?" Jenny looked horrified. "I can't believe the police thought you were lying, and as for your parents... That's awful, almost as bad as being raped." She gasped. "I'm so sorry, I shouldn't have said that, I'm sure it's not true..."

"That's exactly how I felt." Rachel patted her friend's arm and then wiped away her tears. "If it hadn't been for Jamie, I don't know what I would have done."

"He sounds really nice." Jenny didn't know what to say. "I'm so sorry, Rachel. Is there anything I can do?"

Rachel gave a small smile. "My mother is trying to force me into an abortion, but I'm not having one."

Jenny looked even more shocked. Rachel sighed. "Yes. I know it would probably be the sensible thing to do, but it's not the baby's fault. I can't kill it."

"Then what are you going to do?"

"I'm keeping it, no matter what they say." She took a breath. "You asked if there was anything you could do?"

"Yes, anything, Rachel. Do you want me to try and persuade your parents?"

Rachel shook her head and gave a harsh laugh. "They think it's all your fault I'm pregnant. No, I was going to ask if I could live here if they won't listen." She held her breath.

"Of course you can." Jenny patted her arm reassuringly, then her expression changed slightly. "I'll have to tell Bob and Debbie what's going on though, if that's ok?"

Rachel nodded. "Thank you, you don't know how happy..."

The door to the living room burst open and Bob stormed in, followed closely by Debbie. Bob looked furious, something Rachel had never seen before.

"What's the matter...?" Jenny began before he threw a letter down in front of her. Jenny picked it up and read quickly. "I don't understand. Why are we being evicted? We don't owe any rent; we haven't had any problems with the police. It doesn't make sense."

Rachel felt cold. "Can I see?"

Jenny handed it to her.

Rachel read the letter quickly and tried to dislodge the

awful thought that had popped straight into her mind... that her mother had done this to force Rachel into line, to ensure her daughter had nowhere to go and no one to turn to for help.

My Khe Beach, Da Nang, Vietnam

The sand felt warm on Lien's skin as she lay back and gazed up at Spanner. They had found a deserted part of the beach that was now in darkness, apart from the light of the crescent moon, high in the cloudless sky above them. Spanner smiled down and tried to control his excitement. "Are you sure? I don't want to do anything unless you're certain."

Lien took a breath and nodded, before bracing herself for the pain and discomfort. If she didn't go through with it now, she never would, and then Chinh would be angry and she would have failed her country. Lien reached up, put her arms around his neck and pulled him towards her. Spanner didn't need any more encouragement. His lips met hers and he forgot the war, his homesickness, the next patrol – nothing else mattered except Lien. The taste of her lips, the fragrant aroma of her perfume mingling with the warm smell of her skin filled every sense.

Spanner lay back on the sand and smiled up at the night sky. Even in his wildest imaginings, he'd not expected the first time to be like that. As they'd walked along the beach he'd worried that something would go wrong. What if he didn't know what to do, or worse, couldn't perform?

Lien curled up in Spanner's arms, even more disorientated than she had been before. If only she'd saved the first time for him. He had been so gentle, as if he'd been frightened he would break her. *Unlike Chinh, who had been quite rough.* The thought took her by surprise. She'd tried not to think too much about him once she'd realised Phuc was right about the Commander using her, but sex with Spanner had been loving, a completely different experience, and she didn't regret anything. In fact, she wanted Spanner to make love to her again, because she'd enjoyed it. Lien wondered if that made her a traitor. She closed her eyes briefly, pushed her unsettling thoughts away and concentrated on enjoying the warmth of his body next to hers.

"Thank you." Spanner eased himself up on his elbow and gazed down at her.

Lien smiled up at him. There was enough light from the moon for her to see the loving expression on his face, and she felt a rush of happiness. She reached up a hand and gently stroked his face.

"Will you be my girlfriend?" The thought of having to share her with anyone else was something Spanner couldn't bear to contemplate.

"Yes, I would like that." Lien felt she would burst with excitement; he was so kind and thoughtful, of course she would love to be his girlfriend.

"It won't cause you a problem at work?" Spanner sounded concerned.

Lien frowned and returned back down to earth. In normal circumstances she might have had trouble with the manager, but as she was supposed to be using Spanner to get information, it wasn't likely to be an issue. "I don't think so. My manager is quite good, unlike some of them." Lien hoped he would believe her, because she didn't want to lie to him anymore. It had been bad enough lying about her parents and sisters. Suddenly remembering her family and how they had died made her feel sick, and her confusion returned. How could she feel something for this American when she was supposed to be avenging her family and working to throw the enemy out of the country?

"Are you sure? I really don't want to cause you any problems." Spanner had seen the change in her expression, and was concerned it was because he'd asked her to be his girlfriend.

"You won't." Lien pushed the disturbing thoughts to the back of her mind and concentrated her attention on him. "When will you next have leave?"

Spanner relaxed. "Not sure yet, but if you give me your address, I can write to you and let you know."

"That would be excellent." Lien's face lit up again. "And I can write back to you. Then even when I don't see you, I can write you and read letters from you."

Spanner grinned. "Yes, it will almost be like being

together." He leaned forward and kissed her again, and Lien forgot all about her earlier confusion.

CHAPTER NINETEEN

Omaha, Nebraska

The atmosphere in the study was poisonous and Rachel wished she could just walk out, but she had to make it quite clear to her parents that she was keeping the child.

"Rachel, honey, your mother is right." Mark let out a deep sigh. "It would be much more sensible not to go through with this pregnancy."

"It's my body, my child." Rachel glared at him. "You can't make me kill my baby. I won't let you."

"Rachel, no one is going to make…"

"For heaven's sake, you're being ridiculous." Emily snapped, interrupting him. "Trying to make a point when all you're doing is throwing your life away." She took a breath, put her hands on her hips and faced her daughter. "If you are *so* determined to keep the bastard, you can leave here and support yourself."

"Emily?" Mark interjected, a shocked expression on his face.

"If she won't see sense, then she can look after herself."

Emily spun around to face him. "Perhaps that will teach her that she doesn't know everything."

"So now you're threatening me?"

"No, just pointing out the facts of life," Emily shouted. "If you're living here and we're paying for everything, you do as we say!"

"And I don't have any say in my own life at all. How is that fair?" Rachel yelled back.

"Life isn't fair, Rachel, the sooner you realise that the better." Emily grabbed hold of her daughter's shoulders and shook her. "It's damn hard, and tying yourself to a bastard child is not going to make it any easier."

"Get off of me!" She wrestled her mother's hands away from her shoulders and moved backwards. Emily made to follow her, but Mark stood up and placed a firm hand on her arm. "I think we should all calm down."

"You can pack your things and move out as soon as you've found an apartment. We'll pay your allowance for the next six months, and then you are on your own." Emily brushed his hand away and continued as if he hadn't spoken.

"Emily, please... I think we should discuss this." Mark was looking almost as distressed as Rachel felt.

"We've been discussing it endlessly. Rachel is determined to ruin her life and I am determined not to watch her do that, so this is the only solution." Emily swung back to face him. After realising that Rachel was not going to listen to them, she had finally come to the conclusion that the only way to force Rachel back into line was to threaten to throw her out. With hindsight, she realised she should probably have discussed it with Mark first so they could have presented a united front, but it was too late now. She turned towards Rachel again. "Are you still here? I would suggest you go into the city and try and find somewhere affordable to live."

Rachel didn't move. Her mother couldn't really want her to leave home. She waited for Emily to say it was all a mistake, but nothing happened. For a brief moment Rachel wondered if she was wrong. Perhaps she should just do what they wanted...

"Oh, and don't think you are going to live happily ever after with those degenerate hippy friends either, as they won't be here."

Rachel stared at her, the bombshell that her earlier suspicions had been correct momentarily rendering her speechless. Then she found her voice. "You got them evicted?" Her shock was gradually replaced with growing anger.

Emily shrugged. "They're a disgrace and have no business being here."

Rachel gazed at her in disgust. "I can't believe you would do that." Rachel looked at her father, waiting for him to support her, but he didn't say anything. She gave a wry smile and shook her head. "Perhaps I'll go with them, then. At least they have morals and ideals, both of which seem to be sadly lacking here." She walked out of the room.

There was a brief silence before Mark rounded on Emily. "What the hell have you done? What if she goes with them?" Mark was furious.

"She won't." Emily spoke with a confidence she didn't feel.

"You'd better hope you're right!" Mark spat before striding purposefully toward the door. "I can't believe you did all this without consulting me." He shook his head and walked through, slamming it shut after him.

North of Da Nang, Vietnam

The patrol had only been out a few moments when they came under attack from the ground. The first missile missed the helicopter by inches, as the pilot swerved at the last minute. Spanner was thrown violently back in his seat but managed to keep hold of the machine gun. Heart pounding, his mouth dry, Spanner peered nervously down at the rich vegetation, trying to see where the danger was coming from, but the large green banana leaves, bamboo, vines and flowering shrubs provided a perfect hiding place and he couldn't see anyone.

The next rocket came from a different direction. "Shit..." Spanner moved his weapon around, and this time spotted some movement in the jungle below. As he lined up to fire the movement ceased. Spanner concentrated on where he thought the mobile launcher might have gone and opened fire. He could see the bullets ricocheting off the ground, but he couldn't tell if he'd hit anyone. He was still looking when he heard the familiar sound of the Huey on his left, its guns blazing, and he leant back in his seat, breathing hard. The gunship would sort them out now; he could relax until they reached the exchange zone. He glanced at the men from the patrol who were about to be dropped and felt sorry for them. He could see the fear in their faces and, not for the first time, he was grateful he wasn't in the infantry.

The helicopter swung to the left and continued deeper into the interior. Spanner found his thoughts wandering to Leni and the night they'd spent on the beach. He had relived making love to her many times, and each time his feelings grew stronger. He'd written to her since then, giving Leni an address to reply to, but he hadn't heard anything yet. Hopefully there would be something when he got back to base... *if* he got back to base. Spanner couldn't help adding the codicil as he always did, a sort of insurance policy against presuming they would return unharmed, which seemed like tempting fate.

"Landing in five." The voice in his headphones sounded calm. Spanner felt the usual nervousness in his stomach and licked his lips. His fingers tightened on the machine gun and he began scanning the terrain below, searching for anything out of the ordinary, anything that could indicate they were about to fly into a trap. The small clearing looked to be safe as the helicopter circled once and then lowered gracefully down until it reached the ground. While the patrol on board hurriedly disembarked, the returning men rushed out of the bushes and climbed aboard. The whole process took less than five minutes, and then the helicopter was climbing back up into the sky. Spanner kept scanning the area as they headed back to the coast, but all was quiet, and his thoughts returned to Leni. With a bit of luck he would have some time off soon, and then he could make love to her again.

Omaha, Nebraska

Emily watched Mark leave the room and then groped her way to the nearest chair. She hadn't expected Rachel to defy her, she'd been sure that threatening to throw her daughter out would do the trick. She slammed her fist on the arm of the chair and cursed loudly. There had been a point when she'd thought Rachel was going to give in, and then she'd mentioned the hippies. If only she'd kept her mouth shut – but she'd been so determined to make Rachel realise that she was totally dependent on her parents that she hadn't thought it through. Emily thought for a moment. Obviously arranging to have the hippies evicted hadn't been one of her better ideas, but it was one she could undo. She stood up, walked to the desk and picked up the phone.

Upstairs, Rachel sat on her bed and thought about the conversation with her parents. The longer she sat there, the angrier she became. How dare her mother threaten her and her friends? She had gone too far this time. Rachel glanced around her bedroom and wondered what to take with her. She would pack a suitcase and make her way to Jenny now. Wherever her friends went, she would go too. If she never saw her mother again it would be too soon. And as for her father… he had made no attempt to support her. Obviously neither of them wanted her here, so she would go and stay with people who did want her. She stood up, pulled one of her suitcases down from the top of the closet and began packing some clothes.

"I'm sorry. I shouldn't have tried to have your friends evicted." Emily had come in without knocking.

Rachel spun around, shot her mother a quick glance of disbelief and scorn, shook her head and carried on packing.

Emily saw the suitcase and felt sick. She tried once more. "Rachel, I know you don't believe me, but I am only trying to do what's best for you. I've spoken to my contact and they're withdrawing the eviction notice."

"Only because you thought they would leave the city and I would go with them." Rachel sneered.

Emily wanted to argue, but she realised if she didn't say the right thing now she could lose her daughter forever. "Yes, you're right. You're my daughter, of course I don't want you to go!" She searched frantically for something else she could say that would make Rachel change her mind.

"Too late. I'm leaving as soon as I've packed. I'll come

back for the rest of my things once I'm settled." Rachel glared at her mother. "If that's ok, of course?"

My Khe Beach, Da Nang, Vietnam

Lien was finding it hard to concentrate on the customers, her thoughts constantly drifting back to Spanner and the evening she'd spent on the beach with him. The sex had been nothing like she'd expected. After her experience with Chinh she'd braced herself for the pain, but there hadn't been any. Instead she'd felt aroused, every sense in her body alive. Several times during the following days she had found herself smiling for no reason, and after every shift in the bar she couldn't wait to return to her small room, think about him without constant interruptions and reread his short letter. Lien could remember every word, but reading it made her feel so much closer to him.

She wondered if he had received her letter yet. It had been hard to write in English, but she had done her best. Maybe he would have some more leave soon? Her smile broadened, until she realised that the customer in front of her thought she was smiling at him. She handed him his drink, took the tip he gave her with a nod and muttered her thanks, hoping he would not take that as an invitation.

"Say, honey, you wanna join me?" He indicated one of the tables. Lien glanced at her manager, hoping he would come to her rescue, but he didn't. Reluctantly, she crossed the floor and sat down at the table with the middle-aged American. She glanced at his uniform and an idea came to her. He was older than the bar's normal clients; perhaps he had some information that would be useful. That way she could salve her conscience and provide her countrymen with intelligence without compromising her relationship with Spanner.

Correction Facility, Omaha, Nebraska

Paul watched as the guard unlocked the handcuffs and breathed a sigh of relief. It looked like his parents had finally succeeded in getting him out of prison. Simon, the family lawyer, was waiting for him on the other side of the gate.

"Your corrective therapy starts next week. Until then, you are on parole. If you breach the conditions in any form, they'll bring you back here and there will be nothing we can do to get you out. You do understand that, don't you?" They reached his car and he unlocked the doors.

Paul nodded and climbed in. He had no intention of ending up back in prison, but he would have to find a way of visiting Heine, or at least get a message to him. His lover must be frantic with worry. Perhaps he could ask Rachel to go for him? Paul had a feeling that she was the only member of his family who wouldn't be disgusted with him.

Emily was waiting when he arrived home, disapproval written clearly on her face.

"I'm sorry, Mom." Paul waited for the explosion of rage, but it didn't come. He glanced around. "Where's Pop?"

"He's gone out."

Paul sighed; it was even worse than he had expected. Obviously, his father couldn't even face him. "Rachel?"

"She's moved out."

Paul blinked at Emily in disbelief. He must have misheard. He gave a nervous laugh. "Sorry, I thought you said she'd moved out?"

"She has. She's pregnant and won't get rid of the bastard, so I threw her out."

Paul didn't move. He was beginning to wonder if he was in the right house. He'd only been in prison a short time and everything was different. "Rachel's pregnant? How? I mean whose is it?"

"Some hippy bastard. She's gone to live with them. Good riddance." Emily took a step towards him. "And if you know what's good for you, you'll keep away from her. You're in enough trouble, and you need us to support you or you'll be back in prison."

"Are you telling me I can't visit my own sister?"

"Not if you want to continue living here." Emily glared at him, daring him to argue.

Paul looked away. If they threw him out, he would go back to prison. As much as he wanted to see his sister, he had no option but to do what his mother wanted, at least until he was no longer on parole.

My Khe Beach, Da Nang, Vietnam

Phuc had been watching Lien from outside the bar, anger clouding his expression. It was obvious that something had happened to put a smile on her face. He couldn't ever remember seeing her look that happy. She had been like that ever since the night he'd lost her and the American pig on the beach. He'd searched everywhere and had eventually given up, returning to the small room he shared with his sister just before dawn, only to find her fast asleep. Phuc had wanted to shake Lien awake, but what could he say? She was only doing what Chinh had ordered her to. He peered through the growing crowd of Americans and clenched his fists. He could see her dancing with one of the customers – presumably she would sleep with that one too, if she was ordered. His father would be turning in his grave, even if Lien did claim she was doing it for their country.

Phuc was fed up with Lien dishonouring the family, but he was powerless to stop her. Even more worrying was her friendship with the American called Spanner. He had even written a letter to Lien, a letter she had hidden from Phuc, making him worry that his sister was not just doing her duty. He had waited until she had fallen asleep before reading it, not that it had contained anything very important, just an address for her to reply to.

He was also fed up with being treated as second-best to

his younger sister. Anyone could lay on their back and fuck the enemy; it didn't take any brains. Phuc was determined to make Chinh take him more seriously, but while he was babysitting Lien he couldn't prove his worth. If only there was something he could do...

Omaha, Nebraska

Rachel arrived at Jenny's with her suitcase, just after the landlord had contacted them to say their eviction notice had been withdrawn.

"Rachel! Look, the landlord says we can stay after all..." She suddenly noticed the bag. "Oh Rachel, I'm so sorry, here's me waffling on and you must be in bits. I take it they won't listen to you?"

Rachel shook her head. "No. They threw me out..." She indicated the letter. "It was her, my mother, she tried to get you evicted."

Jenny gasped, her brow furrowing as she processed the information. "So why has the landlord changed his mind?"

"I told them if you left Omaha, I would go with you, so she stopped the eviction." Rachel bit her lip. "I'm so sorry you've had all this trouble because of me."

Jenny grinned. "No sweat, Rachel, at least we don't have to move now!" She reached out and took Rachel's suitcase. "You can share my room until you can go back home."

Rachel stopped. "I'm not going back. I'll find somewhere

of my own. They're going to pay my allowance for six months, so that should be enough to pay the rent until I can find a job and support myself and the baby."

Jenny smiled. "Then you can share my room until you find somewhere. There's no rush, so you can save up your allowance and then the money will last longer."

Rachel smiled in relief. "Thank you so much. That's a really good idea about saving the money – if you don't mind, of course?"

Jenny smiled. "Of course not." She gave Rachel a big hug.

For the first time since the row with her parents, Rachel began to feel better. "It's so nice to have people who believe me and want me around."

"You'll always be welcome here, Rachel. Come on, I'll show you the room." She was about to lead the way when the doorbell rang. Jenny stepped back and opened the door.

"Dad?" Rachel stared at him in surprise.

"Hi sweetheart, I'm so sorry…" He put out his arms and after a brief hesitation Rachel stepped towards him and snuggled down into his arms. He held her for several moments before patting her head and looking at Jenny. "Thank you for looking after my daughter. She's lucky to have such good friends."

"That's not what your wife thinks." Bob had come into the hall, a hostile expression on his face.

Mark faced him. "I'm real sorry you got an eviction notice. It won't happen again. I give you my word."

Jenny glanced back at Bob and shook her head slightly. Bob nodded. "Ok, that's cool." He took a breath. "Thanks for sorting it out."

Mark sighed. "I'd like to take the credit, but I didn't do anything. My wife did; she regretted what she'd done so she got it reversed."

"Only because she didn't want me disappearing with my friends," Rachel snapped.

"Yes, you're right, that was the reason, but I am real glad she did, honey. I don't want to be estranged from you. Is it ok for me to visit you here?"

Rachel hesitated. "What about Mom?"

"She doesn't know I'm here – and I'd prefer to keep it that way."

Rachel smiled and nodded. "Suits me." She stopped and looked at Jenny. "Is that ok?"

"Of course it is, Rachel. This is your home now, you can see anyone you want."

The barb wasn't lost on Mark, who gave a wry smile. "Thank you." He turned his attention back to Rachel. "I'll help you financially as well, just let me know what you need."

Rachel breathed a sigh of relief; paying her own way had been her biggest worry. "Thanks Pop."

"Just make sure your mother doesn't find out."

Rachel hugged him again. For the first time in ages, she felt there was a small light at the end of a very dark tunnel.

CHAPTER TWENTY

Outside Da Nang, Vietnam, September 1970

Phuc shivered nervously as he faced Chinh in a small hut on the outskirts of the city. "But the information she gets for you from the other men is good?"

"That isn't the point," Chinh growled. "She was told to get close to the American, which she has done, but none of the intelligence she has given us comes from him. It's been months now and we've had nothing."

"Are you sure?" Phuc regretted questioning the Commander the moment the words had left his mouth. He fumbled for something to say that would rectify the situation. "I'm sorry, I did not mean to imply… I will tell Lien she must do better, sir."

"See that you do." Chinh glared at him. "He is in the perfect position to know when the patrols are going out, yet we have not had anything about them at all. Anyone would think your sister has forgotten her duty." The accusation hung in the air between them.

Phuc could feel sweat forming on his top lip and he cursed Lien for putting him in this position. "I'm sure that's not the case, sir. He is very much in love with Lien, I have seen his letters. Perhaps he is just very cautious and doesn't say anything." Phuc was sure that wasn't the case at all. Chinh was correct in his appraisal of the situation. His stupid sister was in love with the American, and despite repeated efforts on his part she wouldn't listen to him at all. Lien was putting both their lives in danger, and he would have to make her see sense somehow.

Chinh stood up. "This needs to change, or I will need to reassess your usefulness to the cause."

Phuc swallowed nervously and stood up too. "I will make her see where her duty lies, sir."

Chinh stared at him for several seconds, then nodded. "See that you do. I will meet you back here in a week to find out what progress you have made." He walked out, leaving Phuc staring at the floor in growing fury. All Lien had to do was to provide some useful intelligence, and she couldn't even do that because she had given her heart to an American who would no doubt drop her without a second thought if she did anything to upset him. Phuc frowned, and then smiled. He had been looking at the problem from the wrong angle.

Omaha, Nebraska

Rachel glanced at her reflection in the mirror and gave a wry smile. Even though she'd watched her stomach growing over the months, she barely recognised herself. Thank goodness there were only a few weeks left before she gave birth. The apartment was small compared to her family home, but she'd grown used to living in a small space after sharing a room with Jenny over the summer. She had finally felt ready to move into her own place a month ago, and with Jenny's help she had found a two-bedroom apartment not far from her friends and moved in two weeks earlier.

Rachel was still getting used to being completely on her own, but strangely enough she was rather enjoying her own company. She spent a lot of time thinking about what kind of job she would be able to do after the baby was born. Jenny had offered to help with babysitting, but Rachel knew she had to find something more formal, which meant finding a job that paid enough to afford a nanny. She'd had a good education but she had no experience yet, so it might be hard to find something.

The doorbell rang and she walked slowly to answer it.

"Hi sweetheart, how're you doing?"

"Hi Pop, getting bigger." She leaned towards him and he hugged her. Mark had been visiting her weekly ever since she'd moved out, without her mother's knowledge. She also knew he would help pay for a nanny if she asked, but she wanted to do things herself if she could.

"I bought you a few bits of food."

Rachel smiled. "Thanks, Pop. How's Paul?"

Mark sighed. "He's ok, I guess." Paul had managed to pass the psychological test, so at least he wouldn't be going back to jail, but he had changed. He was no longer the happy, amenable boy he'd been before. At least he'd avoided the draft so far. The army had decided he wasn't psychologically fit, which seemed bizarre to Mark. Like the hero in the Arlo Guthrie song, 'Alice's Restaurant, Massacree', who was turned down for the draft as he'd been arrested for dumping garbage, Paul was not moral enough to join and kill people. "I've suggested he come and see you now he's no longer on parole."

Rachel's face lit up. It was so long since she had seen Paul. "That would be great, Pop, please encourage him."

"I'm sure he will, he just has to make sure your mother doesn't find out."

Rachel gave a harsh laugh. "She still hates me then."

Mark shook his head. "She doesn't, Rachel..."

"You don't have to keep defending her, Pop." Rachel saw the pain in his eyes and stopped herself from saying any more. It must be hard for her father being stuck in the middle all the time. And as for poor Paul, he must be climbing up the walls by now. "Has Paul found any work yet?"

"Not really. He's volunteering for the Democrats at the

moment as they get ready for the House of Representatives elections on November 3rd, but it might lead to something more permanent."

Rachel laughed. "I bet that pleased Mom!"

Mark smirked. "No, not really." Emily's comments when she found out Paul was not only supporting the Democrats but actually volunteering to help them win were probably best forgotten, especially as she had said how much of a disappointment both her children were.

"Do you think they'll take the three seats in Nebraska?" Rachel had felt a sudden stirring of interest.

Mark shrugged. "Unlikely, but it's possible I suppose. Nixon isn't very popular, and Robert Denny has retired so there's a new man running, Charles Thine." He thought for a moment. "But he's untried, so anything could happen. There's also an independent running, a woman, Claire Armstrong Callan, so that could split the Republican vote."

Rachel nodded, her thoughts on politics. She'd almost forgotten her ambition to make a difference in the world. If Paul was volunteering for the Democrats, perhaps he could get her a job too. It might mean relying on her father financially for a bit longer, but it would be worth it in the end.

213th Helicopter Squadron, Marble Mountain, Da Nang, Vietnam

Seeing Leni every time he had leave had made the summer pass much quicker than Spanner could ever have imagined. He could hardly believe it was the beginning of September. Halfway through his tour already – he could only hope the winter went just as quickly, and then it would be time to go home. The thought no longer made him feel as happy as it used to, and Spanner let out a heavy sigh. If someone had told him when he arrived in Vietnam that he would be in two minds about going home, he would have laughed and thought they were mad. But if he went back to the US, what would happen to Leni? The army made it virtually impossible for the men to marry local girls, and he could hardly stay in the country when his tour of duty was up. Leni wouldn't be allowed to come to America either, so the only alternative was to move to a country that would accept both of them, not that he knew of one.

Spanner thought back to the day he'd given Leni his ring, the precious family heirloom his mother had given him the day he'd left for Vietnam. He'd wanted Leni to know how much he cared for her, and that whatever happened he would always look after her. With hindsight, perhaps he shouldn't have made a promise he might not be able to keep, but he didn't regret giving her the ring. It was the nearest he could get to marrying her. He explained to her that 'Herz' meant heart in German, so he was giving his heart to her, and that Herz was also his grandma's name.

Unable to find a solution, Spanner put his worries about the future to the back of his mind, a problem for later, and reached for his mail. He frowned. There was one from his mother, another from Leni, and one whose handwriting he didn't recognise. It had a local postmark, how strange. He shrugged and decided to read the unknown one first.

Your girlfriend, she fucking many men

Spanner stared at the few words in astonishment and then growing anger. How dare anyone malign Leni like that? Obviously, it was someone who was jealous... although how they had got his address was a mystery. It must be someone close to her, or him? Spanner glanced suspiciously around, suddenly wondering if the letter had come from someone he knew. Then he thought about the wording and realised it had to have come from a Vietnamese national. Furious, he tore it up, threw it in the bin and reached for Leni's letter.

Darling Spanner
I miss you so much when you are not with me. I can't wait for you to have leave again so I am not lonely. My bed seems big when you not here, so much space and so quiet. Do you think you will be at Beach soon? It seems long time this time, please write soon
Your loving Leni

Spanner smiled, momentarily forgetting about the anonymous note. It had been three weeks this time; extra patrols and more maintenance had meant he hadn't been able to get to see her. But he would be there in three days. He reached for some paper and quickly scribbled a note to let her know.

My darling Leni, thank you for your lovely letter. I love hearing from you, makes me feel close to you even though I can't hold you in my arms. I can't wait until we see each other again either so you will be pleased to know I will be there on Saturday. I am so lucky to have found you, I was feeling very lonely until I met you, but now I always have something to look forward to. I spend hours reliving our time together while I am waiting for the next leave, and I can't wait to make new memories with you.

Just think my darling, not long before I take you in my arms and make love to you again. Look after yourself and I will be counting down the hours.

All my love
Spanner

Spanner reached for an envelope, quickly wrote the address and climbed off his bunk. He would read his mother's letter after he put this in the mail to Leni.

My Khe Beach, Da Nang, Vietnam

Phuc read the latest letter from the enemy to Lien, put it back in the hole in the floorboards where Lien hid all the American's letters, and cursed. Either Spanner hadn't received Phuc's anonymous note or he hadn't believed it. He would have to try something else. But what? Phuc thought back over the letters he'd read, looking for a clue, something else he could use to put a wedge between them. If Spanner started questioning Lien, she might come to her senses and start doing her duty again. Chinh was not known for his endless patience and Phuc had to give him an answer in a couple of days. Lien was only sleeping with Spanner, which was how he knew she had forgotten her duty and had become a traitor. If he couldn't come up with an idea Chinh would lose his temper and then he feared Lien would be punished or even killed. Although he was jealous of his sister, and desperately wanted to prove he was more of a hero to the country than she was, Lien was still his sister and it was up to him to save her. If he couldn't persuade Lien to see sense, he would have to find a way of making her see Spanner as the enemy again.

Phuc watched Lien working in the bar, his thoughts on one of the earlier letters. Lien had mentioned trust, he couldn't remember the context, and the American had said something about making his own mind up about people he met. Perhaps that was the answer. Spanner had not believed the note because it was anonymous. Maybe he would only believe someone he had met. Phuc thought hard. Lien had never introduced Phuc to the American, so if he found a way of befriending Spanner, he could gain his trust and then begin feeding him lies about Lien. It would be difficult because Spanner spent all his time with Lien, but Phuc was sure there was a way. He just had to find it.

Omaha, Nebraska

"Paul!" Rachel threw her arms around him. "I've missed you so much."

"You too, sis." Paul realised it was true. "I can't believe I am about to be an uncle." He smiled at her. "So, who's the father, or is it a secret?"

He was completely unprepared for her reaction. Rachel paled and her smile faded.

"Rachel?"

"Didn't they tell you?"

Paul shook his head. "No, Mom just said some hippy had got you pregnant and..." He stopped short. "That's not true, is it?"

Rachel shook her head. "No." She took a breath. "I was raped at the tennis club. Mom wouldn't believe me, she wanted me to have an abortion and I refused, so she threw me out."

Paul was looking shocked. "Oh God, sis, if I'd known I would have been along to see you sooner." As he spoke, he recalled his mother's threats about letting him go back to prison, and wondered if that was true. Not that it mattered now. "Who was it?"

"Charles Peterson."

Paul looked even more shocked, then his expression hardened into bitterness. "No wonder they didn't want to believe you. Did you report it to the police?"

"Yes, but as soon as I told them who it was, they didn't want to know either." Rachel wondered if she should tell him about Charles' threats to make his sexuality public, but she didn't want him blaming her for his problems, so she said nothing.

Paul shook his head. "That's awful. I can't believe our parents didn't support you."

"Well, Pop comes to see me regularly, but Mom... well, you know what she's like."

Paul nodded, then a thought crossed his mind. "Why do you want to keep the baby? I don't understand."

Rachel didn't answer straight away. She sighed. "I didn't at first, the baby was just part of the rape, but Mom kept telling me what to do, going on and on and what was worse, not believing me. Then one day the baby suddenly became real, a person in its own right, nothing to do with that bastard. I can't explain it, maybe it's the maternal instinct or something. I felt that he or she didn't do anything wrong, so what right did I have to kill it?"

Paul nodded. "I think I understand that, but aren't you worried that…" He stopped, unsure how to say what was in his mind.

"That I might hate it, that it might remind me of Charles?" Rachel shrugged. "I don't think I will. But if I do, then I will have it adopted."

There was a long silence, then Paul changed the subject. "What are you going to do after the baby's here?"

"You mean am I going to find a job?"

"Yes."

Rachel laughed. "It's funny you should ask; I was hoping you might be able to help."

Paul frowned. "Me?"

"I'd like to work with the Democrats."

"You want a job with the Democrats?" Paul repeated and then laughed when Rachel nodded. His mother would be absolutely furious if both her children were working with the enemy. "I've just been offered a permanent job with them, so I will see what I can do."

Rachel's face lit up. "That would be brilliant, Paul. I don't mind what it is, I just need a start."

"Leave it with me." Paul thought for a moment. He'd been planning on finding out how Rachel felt about what had happened to him – he was reasonably sure she would be supportive, but he wanted to make sure before he asked for her help. But the conversation seemed to have led him here, so he would take a chance. "Perhaps you could do something for me in return?"

CHAPTER TWENTY-ONE

My Khe Beach, Da Nang, Vietnam

Lien stared at the manager in disbelief. She had been waiting for weeks to see Spanner, and now Chinh had called her to a meeting. She debated whether to send the Commander a message saying she was meeting Spanner so couldn't go, but she had a feeling that might not be wise. Lien had sensed Chinh was not happy with her lack of intelligence from Spanner, despite providing plenty of information from the other customers. Unfortunately, she had to do as she was told, but hopefully she would not be long. She would leave Spanner a note saying she had been called away, although what could possibly be so important that it meant cancelling the date they had both been looking forward to? Lien thought hard and came up with the only thing she could think of. "I am supposed to be meeting the American tonight. Do you have some paper I can write him a message on?"

The manager hesitated and Lien began to panic. "I am seeing him on the Commander's orders, he will be annoyed if I upset the American."

The manager sighed, nodded and reached for some paper. Lien wrote quickly.

"My darling Spanner, I am so sorry to keep you waiting but I receive word that my brother is ill, and I have to go to him. I will be back as soon as I can, please wait for me. Your loving Leni."

She handed the note to the manager and headed toward the door, feeling nervous. She couldn't understand what was so important that Chinh had suddenly called her to see him. She hoped she wasn't in trouble.

Phuc watched Lien leave and smiled. The first part of his plan was working. He glanced at his watch. The American should be here very soon, then he could put part two into action.

Omaha, Nebraska

Paul pulled up by the kerb a block away from Heine's expensive apartment and waited while Rachel climbed out of the car. He couldn't wait to see Heine again, it had been so long, their only contact a brief letter he'd sent explaining what had happened and that he would be in touch once it was safe. Heine had replied immediately, but that had been their only correspondence; neither man wanted to risk being caught.

"He's on the 10th floor," Paul repeated, glancing around nervously.

Rachel smiled. "I haven't forgotten. Now you need to go away so no one sees you here. I'll meet you in the restaurant as soon as I've finished." She waited until he'd driven off, then walked slowly toward the address Paul had given her.

Rachel reached the 10th floor, found the apartment, pressed the bell and waited.

"Yes?" The man who opened the door was several years older than Paul and not what she'd been expecting at all. Rachel checked the corridor was empty and smiled. "Are you Heine?"

The man frowned. "I am – who are you and what do you want?"

Rachel ignored his hostility, relaxed slightly and smiled. "I'm Rachel Hanson, Paul's sister."

Heine looked shocked but didn't say anything, so Rachel lowered her voice. "He sent me to say he's in the restaurant around the corner if you'd like to join us for lunch."

Heine's face lit up. "He's really there?"

Rachel smiled again. "Yes, he thought it might be better if I came too. He wants to give you my address so you can meet there or use it to write letters."

"I'll get my jacket." Heine suddenly looked much younger and Rachel could see why her brother loved him. It was obvious he felt the same about Paul.

My Khe Beach, Da Nang, Vietnam

Spanner hurried towards the bar, his heart racing with excitement. The last three weeks had dragged without any prospect of seeing Lien, but that was all over now, and he was looking forward to 24 hours of happiness. He glanced to his right and then left and began crossing the road, his thoughts on Lien and how much he was looking forward to making love to her. The next moment he felt someone shoving him to the ground, and a Vespa hooted loudly as it shot past him, missing him by inches. Spanner was aware of someone shouting and he shook his head to clear the ringing in his ears before glancing to his left, where a young Vietnamese man was laying on the ground, holding his arm and grimacing.

"Hey buddy, are you ok?" Spanner rolled over and knelt by the youngster. "You saved my life."

Phuc ignored the shooting pain in his left shoulder and leg where he'd landed on the road and managed to smile. "No problem. I... ouch..." He winced.

"Here, let me help you up." Spanner held Phuc's arm gently while he stood up. "Are you badly hurt?"

Phuc moved his arm gingerly. It hurt, but he didn't think it was broken. He tried walking on his leg; again, it was sore, but he didn't appear to have broken anything. "No, just some bruises. I am glad you are ok, sir."

Spanner glanced across the road to the bar where Lien would be waiting and was torn. He wanted to see Lien, but he couldn't just ignore the young lad who'd just saved his life or at least saved him from certain injury. "Let me buy you a drink." Spanner smiled. "My girlfriend works over there, come and sit with us and have a drink and something to eat, it's the least I can do."

Phuc looked like he was about to argue. "I insist on buying you a drink, you can't go without letting me say thank you."

Phuc hesitated again, and then decided he had done the reluctance bit enough and smiled. "Thank you, sir, that would be nice."

"Spanner, that's my name, not sir." Phuc nodded and allowed Spanner to help him across the road and into the bar. Spanner seated him at one of the tables and headed toward the bar looking for Lien.

"She left this for you, sir." The manager handed him the note and glanced across at Phuc. He recognised Lien's brother from an earlier meeting with Chinh and he wondered what was going on, not that it was any of his business.

Spanner read the note and failed to conceal his disappointment. Damn it to hell, he cursed under his breath. Then he remembered the boy and sighed. At least he had some company while he was waiting for Lien to come back. He hoped her brother was ok and she wasn't too long, though.

"Here, I bought you some beer, is that ok?" Spanner

placed the two glasses on the table. "My girlfriend has been called away, something about her brother being ill. Oh well, shit happens." He smiled at his rescuer. "So what's your name, buddy?"

"They call me Phuc."

Spanner nodded. "So why don't you tell me all about yourself, Phuc?" He wasn't that interested, but at least it would pass the time.

Omaha, Nebraska

Rachel soon forgot any awkwardness and found herself drawn to Heine's dry humour and his obvious love for her brother. "You can meet at my place if you want, if it will make it easier."

Heine thought for a moment. "I would need a reason to be visiting you."

Rachel nodded. He was right. There must be something they had in common. "What do you do for a living?"

"I'm a freelance newspaper reporter, I also write political articles for various magazines."

Rachel grinned. "That's perfect, then. Paul is working for the Democrats now and once I've had the baby I want to work for them too. Having a newspaper reporter as a friend would be perfectly normal."

Heine smiled. "Your sister's not just a pretty face, is she, Paul?"

Paul laughed. "No, she's the one with the brains, I've got the good looks and the charm!"

Rachel joined in the laughter. Her mother would hate to see her sitting with Paul and his friend. Emily had done everything she could to cut Rachel off from her family, but it hadn't worked. One day Rachel would take great delight in telling Emily how her father had visited and supported her while she was pregnant, and that she'd seen her brother regularly, but not yet. Revenge would be all the sweeter if she waited.

Outside Da Nang, Vietnam

Chinh watched Lien leave the hut and let out a slow breath. It had been hard to keep his hands off her, but it would not be appropriate to sleep with her again, however much he might want to. He couldn't justify it to himself or he would have pushed things with her. He had half hoped Lien would take the initiative, then he could argue that she had wanted sex, thus letting him off the hook, but she had seemingly not understood his suggestive remarks. Chinh stood up and began pacing up and down. There was something about Lien that unsettled him. He didn't normally have any difficulty controlling his sexual urges with the female fighters, but Lien...

He glanced at the clock and wondered how Phuc was getting on. He hoped the boy had succeeded, because Lien was on her way back now. If he'd given into his urges he could have kept her in the hut longer, but unfortunately she didn't seem interested. Chinh clenched his fists and wondered if his first impressions had been right after all. Lien was in love with the American and had forgotten her duty. The next time he saw her, he would have to remind her whose side she was on.

Lien made her way quickly back to the beach, her brain racing, and her heart pounding with fear. Thank goodness she had put Spanner's ring on a chain round her neck under her clothes before arriving at the hut. Chinh would have been sure to have noticed it on her finger, and then who knew what he would have said? As it was, the Commander had gone on and on for what seemed like ages about the poor quality of her information and why hadn't she got more out of the American. Lien had done her best to defend herself, but she was worried that he wouldn't keep letting her see Spanner unless she gave him something – but she couldn't do that. What if Spanner were killed because she'd told them when he was taking out or collecting a patrol? Perhaps she could make something up? Lien shivered. That might work once or twice, but if she kept giving Chinh the wrong information he would lose patience, and then she and Phuc would be at his mercy.

But that wasn't her only problem. Chinh had spent a lot of time staring at her and making suggestions that she had ignored, pretending she didn't understand. Lien knew exactly what he wanted, but the thought of sleeping with him again made her feel sick. If only she didn't have to see him again, but she couldn't avoid it, not unless she moved further away. But even then the VC's reach extended far into Vietnam, so wherever she went he could probably find her. Lien felt tears forming and she shook her head angrily. There had to be a way to stop him wanting to have sex with her, if only she could find it.

Omaha, Nebraska

Jamie took the last of the boxes of files the detective had given him to take down to the incinerator in the basement, his thoughts on Rachel. He reached the door to the storeroom and let himself in, switched on the light and waited a few seconds to make sure no one had followed him, because he wanted to check the files before he destroyed them. He had overheard one of the detectives moaning about Charles Peterson, and he was hoping to find something that could help Rachel.

Jamie checked through the paperwork quickly and eventually found what he was looking for: a file from a young girl claiming Charles Peterson had raped her. Jamie's heart beat a little quicker as he read through the details, and then he reached the detective's conclusion and cursed. The detective was sure she was lying, so he'd told her to go home and forget all about making false allegations about an innocent man or he would arrest her. Jamie took out the statements from the girl and the doctor and put them in the box with the evidence they had collected. He placed the box in with the empty ones and put everything else in the incinerator. When he'd finished, he took the stack of empty boxes back upstairs to the ground floor where he checked no one was watching before diving out of the side door and placing the full box in the trunk of his car. He was sweating with fear by the time he re-entered the precinct, but after a few moments it was obvious no one had seen him.

Jamie returned to the front desk, his heart rate slowed back to normal, and he began dealing with the next person. He would hide the box at home. It was obvious Charles would carry on his assaults, why wouldn't he if he kept getting away with his crimes? But Jamie had no intention of letting him keep avoiding justice. Once he had collected the evidence from enough women, he would make sure someone took him seriously and investigated. The hardest thing would be waiting until he felt he had sufficient evidence to have Charles Peterson arrested and charged.

CHAPTER TWENTY-TWO

My Khe Beach, Da Nang, Vietnam

Much to his surprise, Spanner was enjoying talking to Phuc. "So, do your family live in Da Nang?"

Phuc nodded. "My sister does, the rest of my family are dead."

Spanner was shocked. He only knew two people in Vietnam, and both had lost their families. "I'm real sorry to hear that..." He was debating whether to ask how they'd died when Phuc volunteered the information.

"Americans suffered bad ambush near our village, there was shooting..." He trailed off. "I understand their anger, but it was hard." He sighed, then smiled. "Then we came Da Nang to start new life. My sister, she works here."

Spanner was so shocked about Phuc' family he missed the last part of the conversation. He knew atrocities went on, after Mỹ Lai, everyone did, but to meet someone who'd had his family killed... "I'm not sure I would have risked myself to save the life of someone you must see as an enemy." As he spoke the words Spanner felt the beginnings of unease.

Phuc looked horrified. "Goodness, Spanner, please don't think that, sir. You are here to help us fight the enemy. I can't blame every American for the actions of a few. Our own forces have also made mistakes in our villages. It's war, shit happens..." He smiled. "Isn't that what you say?"

Spanner managed a small smile. "Yeah, shit happens." He shook his head. "I'm so sorry, Phuc."

"Please, Spanner, you mustn't be sad, you are my friend yes? I buy you drink this time." Phuc waited for Spanner to ask about his sister, but he didn't, and he realised eventually that the American was so shocked about the revelations about his family that he'd missed the part about Lien. Phuc would have to repeat it. "I usually work in different part of city, but I have time off today, so I am hoping to see my sister. It is nice to have company while I wait."

Spanner looked surprised. "Your sister works here?

Phuc smiled. Time to drop the bombshell. "Yes, her name is Lien. You know her?"

Omaha, Nebraska

"Vietnamisation, ha!" Jenny was sitting crossed-legged on the floor in Rachel's living room, a large reefer in one hand, Jimmy Cliffe's 'Vietnam' playing softly in the background. "They must think we're stupid!"

Rachel stopped listening to the lyrics that always made her cry and nodded. "I know. They surely can't think we won't see through the lies they keep telling us. Reducing our troop numbers and saying the South Vietnamese are now the only ones fighting and that we're just there for training. What a load of crap!"

"Exactly." Jenny leaned forward and handed Rachel the joint. "The Australians are protesting against their government's involvement; I wish we were doing the same. It's gone so quiet over here."

"There must be something we can go to." The baby kicked hard as Rachel spoke, and she smiled. Obviously, the baby agreed.

"I saw in the newspaper that there is a group of about a hundred war veterans marching through New Jersey. Apparently, they are re-enacting the atrocities carried out by US troops out there. The marchers are heading toward the anti-war rally on Labor Day at Valley Forge. We're leaving tomorrow, if you want to come with us."

Rachel didn't hesitate. "You bet. I'll get packing."

Jenny grinned. She hadn't thought for a minute that Rachel would say no, even though it wasn't that long before the baby was due.

"Good – we'll pick you up in the morning."

My Khe Beach, Da Nang, Vietnam

Spanner didn't move for several seconds. Phuc was Lien's brother? That explained the coincidence about their families both being dead, but not why Lien had lied to him about how her family had died. Then he remembered the note Lien had left him. It said she had gone to see her sick brother.

Spanner glanced around nervously. Everything seemed normal, but the warnings he'd received from the old sweats about local girls using them and setting them up were suddenly crystal clear in his mind again. He realised Phuc was watching him closely, so he made an effort to speak normally. "Lien's your sister? Wow, that's a real coincidence. She must have told you about me?"

Phuc looked confused, then a smile appeared on his face and he started laughing. "You are Lien's boyfriend! I can't believe it! She didn't tell me name, just that she was seeing really nice American. Now I definitely need to buy you a drink to thank you for looking after my sister."

"Thanks, a beer would be great." Spanner reached into his pocket and pulled out his cigarettes. He needed a smoke badly, while he tried to work out what was going on, if anything was. Maybe it was just all a coincidence? But that didn't explain where Lien was now. After saying she was desperate to see him, why would she suddenly disappear?

He glanced around nervously again, but everything seemed the same as usual. The bar was filling with Americans, it was unlikely anyone could suddenly kidnap him.

"Spanner, I am so sorry…" Lien rushed towards him and threw her arms around him before he could react.

"Lien, I'm so pleased you're back. Chinh and I thought it was about time I met your boyfriend." Phuc spoke quickly in Vietnamese.

Lien backed away from Spanner and stared at her brother in horror. "What are you doing here?" She answered in the same language, before the significance of his words hit her. In a flash, she understood why Chinh had called for her, but why did they suddenly want Phuc to meet Spanner and… oh God… Lien felt dizzy, there was a strange feeling in her head and she struggled to stay upright. Her note had said she'd gone to visit her sick brother. She could see the growing anger on Spanner's face and she spoke quickly in English. "What you doing here Phuc? I had message saying you were sick? I have been everywhere looking for you." She took a step towards him. "You have ruined my evening with Spanner, I waste my time worrying about you when I could be here."

Phuc looked confused. "I don't understand?"

"Nor do I." Spanner spoke with a calm he didn't feel.

"I get message saying Phuc is sick. I go three buses to find him but when I get to his work he not there. I look everywhere, I think something bad happen to him." She began to cry. "And all the time you here." She wiped her tears away and took a step towards her brother. "You do this deliberately to stop me seeing Spanner."

"No Lien, I came to see you because I wanted to see your boyfriend. You always talking about him, I wanted to meet him, make sure he look after you properly." Phuc smiled at her, his tone earnest, but his eyes were cold.

"I don't believe you." Lien was starting to get hysterical. What if Phuc had said something to make Spanner doubt her love? She couldn't stand it if he no longer wanted to see her.

"Leni, honey, he saved my life. I nearly got hit by a scooter, he pushed me out of the way. I wanted to buy him a drink." Spanner reached out and took her hand. "Why don't you come and sit next to me and we can stop wasting what's left of the evening."

Lien looked down at him and breathed an inward sigh of relief. She sat down on the chair near him and tried to get her heart to stop pounding. Her brain was still racing, though. What were Chinh and her brother up to? And why did she still feel sick?

Valley Forge, Pennsylvania

"It's was fine all the way through Morris and Sommerset Counties, we had loads of support but here..." the exhausted-looking man spat on the floor. "All we got was abuse. I don't understand these people, they don't seem to care what's going on."

Rachel shook her head in disgust. "It's a Republican stronghold, that's why. We need to get those bastards out of the House of Representatives."

"I agree, but not sure how."

Rachel fell silent. She was so used to mixing with people who were anti-war it was a bit of a shock finding that not everyone agreed with them. She felt sorry for the veterans, who looked disillusioned and were becoming increasingly bitter at the opposition and hostility they had encountered.

"We weren't even sure if anyone would turn up here." Another of the men chipped in. "We did a demo at White Horse Station with two of us posing as guerrillas. We showed how they were treated by a patrol, but hardly anyone turned up to watch."

"And those that did said they were disgusted at us for disgracing our uniforms." They had been joined by another soldier, a tall man with blond hair who sat down next to Rachel. She looked into his eyes and could see the exhaustion and something else which she couldn't identify. "We handed out fliers that said: *A US infantry company has just come through here. If you had been Vietnamese, we might have burned your house, shot you and your dog, raped your wife and daughter, burned the town and tortured its citizens.*" He scowled. "I was shot down twice out there, it's hell on earth. I'm lucky to be alive, but no one gives a shit."

"We do." Rachel smiled at him. "We support you all the way."

He smiled at her, the exhaustion temporarily clearing from his face. "Thanks. It's really appreciated, even more so when we get so much crap from everywhere else."

Rachel blushed. "It's our duty to support you."

"So what about your husband, does he believe in our cause too?" The man glanced around.

"I'm not married." Rachel met his eyes squarely and waited for the usual reaction she got when people found out she wasn't married.

The man looked slightly embarrassed, then grinned. "There's hope for me, then?"

Rachel looked confused and he hastened to explain. "I just meant that if you're not married, I don't have to worry about a jealous husband interrupting us."

Rachel smiled back at the unexpected reaction. "No, there's no one. I'm Rachel, Rachel Hanson."

"Martin Bremner. Pleased to meet you. I'm from West Virginia, what about you?"

"Omaha, Nebraska."

"Wow, that's a long way to come for this." He indicated

the small turn-out of protesters.

"We just wanted to show support. I'm with my friends Jenny, Bob and Debbie. We drove down yesterday."

"So, when's the baby due?"

"Next month."

"What happened to the father?" Martin looked horrified. "I'm sorry, that was really rude. I have a bad habit of saying what's on my mind. Just tell me to mind my own business."

Rachel smiled. "It's ok. Most people think exactly the same, but don't ask." She hesitated and wondered whether she should tell the truth or lie. There was something about Martin that she liked, and she didn't want to lie to him. She took a breath. "I was assaulted."

Martin gasped in shock and there was a moment's silence. Rachel was just beginning to regret her honesty when he spoke again. "I'm sorry, that's awful." He took a breath. "I'm going to be nosey again, and you don't have to answer. But why did you decide to keep the baby?"

Rachel sighed. "Good question, and I don't mind answering, although I'm not really sure except that it's not the baby's fault, and I couldn't bring myself to kill it."

Martin was quiet for a moment. "I think you're very brave."

Rachel looked astonished. "You've been in a war, you said you were shot down twice – that's courage. I'm just doing what millions of women do, I'm having a baby."

He decided not to push the point. "Your parents must be

great. There's so much stigma about women having babies when they aren't married."

Rachel gave a harsh laugh. "My parents didn't want to know – well, my mom doesn't, anyway. They threw me out when I told them, wouldn't believe I'd been raped because of who the man was. My dad came round later, he helps me out with money thank goodness, but I haven't seen my mom for months and she doesn't know that Pop visits. I'm going to get a job once the baby is born so I can support myself." Rachel wondered why she was pouring out her life story to a perfect stranger; she wasn't even stoned, which always loosened her tongue. She and Jenny had decided to leave the dope in the van, knowing that many veterans didn't approve of drugs. Rachel sighed. She could really do with a smoke now.

"That's dreadful." Martin shook his head. How could her own parents not believe her? And to throw her out...

Rachel shrugged. "Shit happens, right?"

The saying reminded him of Vietnam, and he smiled. "Yes, it does." He looked into her eyes. "I know we live miles apart, but I'd like to keep in touch, if that's ok?"

Rachel nodded and was furious to feel herself blushing. "I'd like that. I'll give you my address."

Martin smiled back, suddenly feeling much less tired. He had been beginning to wonder why he had bothered to come on this march, but now he felt much better. He watched as Rachel took her diary out of her large tapestry bag and scribbled quickly before handing it to him. Martin read it before folding it neatly and placing it in his top pocket. "Thanks, Rachel."

213th Helicopter Squadron, Marble Mountain Air Facility, Da Nang, Vietnam

Spanner lay on his bunk and thought about the last 24 hours. It had certainly been eventful, and not in a nice way. He wanted to believe Lien was telling the truth about where she'd been, but she had lied to him about how her family had died. He rolled onto his back, knuckling his forehead. He could understand she might not want to talk about it, but given the circumstances of their death, why would she want an American boyfriend? Had he been set up? He thought back to the time he had spent with her and was even more confused. She had never tried to find out any information, she never asked questions about his job or the airbase, although she'd had plenty of opportunity to do so. Her only questions were about his family and his life in America. If she was a spy, she wasn't a very good one. He thought back to how she was when he made love to her, the expression in her eyes and on her face, and he was convinced she wasn't acting. Maybe he was blowing things out of proportion and everything was just as it appeared.

His thoughts returned to the message from Lien saying

her brother was sick. Obviously, someone had it in for her, probably the same person who'd sent him the anonymous note. But he would ask her about her family next time he saw her, just to make doubly certain she wasn't hiding anything.

CHAPTER TWENTY-THREE

My Khe Beach, Da Nang, Vietnam

Lien stopped being sick into the bowl in her room, placed it on the floor by the bed, and wondered what on earth she'd eaten to make her so ill. She had been sick every morning for three days now, ever since the last time she'd seen Spanner. Perhaps he had it too? They had eaten the same food over the few hours he was off. She would write and ask him. Her heart sank as she relived that dreadful evening, and she still didn't understand what Chinh and Phuc were up to. She'd nearly had a heart attack when she'd seen Phuc at the bar, and Spanner's story of Phuc saving his life didn't sound very likely either. It was obviously something he had cooked up with Chinh to get her out of the way so he could befriend Spanner. But why? That was her job, or it would have been if she hadn't fallen in love with him. She couldn't blame Phuc for her message to Spanner, though, it was just unfortunate that she had used Phuc as her excuse. Just thinking of how close she had come to losing Spanner was enough to make her feel sick and dizzy again.

Lien sighed and threw back the covers. It was time to get ready for work. Thank goodness the sickness was only in the morning, or she wouldn't have been able to work. Lien climbed out of bed and then stopped dead as a horrible thought struck her. Although she had been sick every morning, she normally felt better as the day wore on. Her heart began racing again as she thought hard and tried to remember the last time she'd bled. Lien felt cold fingers of dread clawing at her insides. It was ages ago... *Oh Lord Buddha, please don't make it so*. Tears ran down her face as she imagined Spanner's reaction to the awful news that she was pregnant. Even if he wanted to stand by her, he wouldn't be able to. She knew the American army wouldn't let him marry her. Her own people would shun her for having an Amerasian child and Phuc... Her stomach contracted even more. Phuc would be absolutely furious with her for bringing dishonour on their family. He would disown her, and she would be on her own. She wouldn't be able to work, because no one would want to spend time with a pregnant woman. She was ruined. Her life was over.

Lien curled up in a ball and began sobbing. In her mind she repeated her prayers but there was no answer.

Omaha, Nebraska

Rachel gazed into the mirror and thought about Martin Bremner. The last thing she had expected was to meet someone on the march. Not that he was a boyfriend or anything, at least not yet. Maybe after the baby was born. Her heart leapt and then sank as she thought about kissing him. She had no idea how she would feel about anything intimate with a man after what Charles had done. Just thinking about it made her hands sweat and her heart beat faster in terror. What if she could never have a relationship with anyone?

The baby kicked and moved. Rachel automatically placed her hand on her stomach and took a deep breath. She would face that problem when the time came. She would concentrate on having the baby and finding a job before she worried about anything like that. Martin might not even contact her when he got home and thought about the complications of getting involved with someone like her. Rachel caught herself. She sounded like her mother, dismissing someone because of the hand fate had dealt them. She was determined that the rape would not define her life, so she would stop worrying about something that hadn't happened yet and concentrate on making sure she had everything she needed for the baby.

Outside Da Nang, Vietnam

"The best way is a bicycle bomb." Chinh stared into Phuc's eyes. "You can park it outside the bar and detonate it from across the road. No one takes any notice of bicycles. If we use enough explosive, we can kill plenty."

"What about Lien?" Phuc was quite excited about blowing up the Americans, but he didn't want Lien to get hurt. He was also confused as to why Chinh had suddenly decided to kill Spanner. He didn't mind, he hated the American for what he had done to Lien. She had chosen him over her duty. Maybe that was why Chinh had decided to act. Perhaps the American's death was meant as an example to anyone who thought love was more important than country. And one less enemy soldier meant one less pig to throw out of the country. What was more, Phuc would be a hero for once, and then Lien would have to take notice of him.

Phuc returned his attention to the Peugeot bicycle Chinh had brought into the hut. Like most of the bikes they used to move supplies, the frame had already been strengthened by adding metal struts which reinforced the front forks and increased the suspension. It was now capable of carrying up to 440 pounds, not that they intended to use that much explosive, or they would blow up most of My Khe Beach. When used to transport supplies through the jungle, a wooden stick of bamboo would be lashed to the handlebars and used to steer the bike, but the explosive didn't take up much room, so Phuc would ride the bike as normal. The seat, which had been removed for carrying supplies, had been replaced now, and no one could tell by looking at the machine that it was any different from a normal bike.

"We'll pack the explosive in bags and attach it to the bike here." Chinh indicated baskets at the back and front. "You can ride to the bar, park up and wait until you see him arrive."

Phuc nodded. Spanner was due to meet Lien later that afternoon. Plenty of time for him to position the bike and wait out of sight.

Omaha, Nebraska

Rachel read through the letter from Martin again and smiled. She couldn't believe how quickly he had written to her, and the thought made her feel warm inside

My dear Rachel
I do hope you don't mind me calling you dear, but the more I thought about you the more I realised how much your presence at Valley Forge lifted my spirits. I was feeling so disheartened after the hostility we met on the march that I was thinking of giving up protesting. We don't seem to be getting anywhere. Some of my friends are even talking about joining some of the more violent groups, but then you came along.

I hope you are keeping well and still looking forward to the birth of your baby. I forgot to ask what you were hoping for although I suppose it doesn't really matter as long as you are ok, and the baby is healthy. You must be getting excited now, although a couple of my friends say their wives just wanted the baby to be born by the time they reached the last month because they were fed up being pregnant.

If you agree, I will come and visit once the baby is born? Obviously, I will give you time to settle into being a mom and getting over the birth, but I can't wait to see you again.

Yours

Martin

Rachel placed her hand on her stomach and looked at herself in the mirror. Martin was right about one thing: she was excited, but not just about the baby. She was also looking forward to seeing him again. She thought back over the past year and how difficult it had been. But now things seemed to be looking up, and she had not missed her mother at all. Rachel's smile faltered. She would never forgive her mother for not supporting her, although the rejection had made her stronger and more independent in the long run. But the pain of her mother's behaviour would never completely leave her, and Rachel swore she would never make the same mistake with her own child.

My Khe Beach, Da Nang, Vietnam

Lien hurried toward the bar, her thoughts on how she was going to tell Spanner she was pregnant. What if he didn't want to see her again? Lien fought back tears. Not that it really mattered what he thought – she was ruined anyway and there was nothing Spanner could do to help, even if he wanted to. Perhaps she shouldn't tell him yet. She had a feeling he was still worrying about something. If only she knew what Phuc had said to him, but as she hadn't seen her brother, she hadn't had a chance to ask.

The beach was crowded, there were people everywhere and she was running late. The last thing she needed was to keep Spanner waiting again, not after last time. She increased her pace, dodging the numerous pedestrians enjoying the sunshine.

Spanner walked slowly toward the bar, his thoughts on how to find out whether Leni was lying to him. What a difference a few days had made. From hanging on her every word, and dying to see her, he was now apprehensive; he wasn't sure he could cope with finding out she had been using him the whole time. He could only hope he was wrong.

"Everything alright, Spanner? You normally can't wait to get together with Leni." Kurt had been watching him closely and he was concerned that his friend wasn't his usual happy self.

Spanner forced a smile. "No, everything's fine. Just wondering what I'll do when it's time to go back home."

"No point worrying about that now, man, anything could happen before then." Kurt patted him on the back. "You'll sort it, you know you will. Have you told your family about her?"

"No, didn't seem much point, not unless I can take her home with me, which isn't very likely." Spanner sighed and glanced around. The sun was shining, the area was packed with people; he could see surfers riding the waves, fellow soldiers enjoying the brief break from war, and slowly his spirits rose. He was sure Leni wasn't guilty of anything – he had just let his imagination run away with him. "You coming for a drink first?"

"Nah, think I'll save that until later, can't wait to get into the surf. It's the one time I forget I'm in this shithole and I can pretend I'm back home riding the waves in California!"

Spanner smiled. "Enjoy. See you later, then?"

"Count on it, buddy." Kurt was about to head off towards the beach when he spotted Leni. "Hey, that's Leni, isn't it?"

Spanner peered through the crowd and grinned. "Yeah, see you later man."

"Yeah, have fun." Kurt had his eyes on the surf.

Spanner headed towards Leni, a smile on his face. He reached the door to the bar and waited for her.

Omaha, Nebraska

Rachel was busy getting her suitcase ready for the hospital when Paul arrived, followed a few moments later by Heine.

"Are you ok?" Paul looked at the suitcase in concern.

Rachel laughed. "Yes, I'm fine. I thought I'd better get my hospital bag ready, just in case."

"Phew, thought I was going to have to deliver a baby for a moment," Heine laughed.

"Heaven forbid!" Rachel joined in. "I realised I've been putting it off."

Paul looked confused. "I don't understand?"

Rachel sighed. "It's one thing being pregnant, but to suddenly have a baby relying on me for everything without someone else to share that with..." Paul was about to argue, but she didn't give him a chance to speak. "I know I have you both, and Jenny, but it's not the same. You won't be here all the time; it will just be me. To be honest, I'm a bit scared."

"I think that's only natural, Rachel, even married people have that fear. But you *will* cope. You are one of the strongest people I've met." Heine smiled. "Look how you stood up to your mother and how you've survived when many a girl would have been defeated." He reached out a hand and patted her shoulder. "And we are all here to help. You only need to ask."

Rachel placed her hand on his. "Thanks, Heine, and

you too Paul. I know I will work it all out, but it's just a bit daunting thinking about all that responsibility."

"Well, if things go well with Martin, you might not have to do it all alone!"

"I wish I hadn't told you about him now!" Rachel threw a mock punch at Paul and started laughing, only to suddenly double up in pain. "Oh my God..."

"Rachel? Are you ok?"

Rachel moaned, took several quick breaths and then the pain subsided. She looked up at Paul, her face ashen, and he could see the apprehension on her face. "I think the baby's coming..."

Paul paled. "Isn't it too early?"

Rachel was about to argue when the pain came again. She breathed through the contraction, her mind racing. The doctor and the labour and delivery nurse had said the first pains were ages apart, but these were very close. Perhaps there was something wrong? Then she remembered that the nurse had told her labour pains sometimes gave backache. She'd had backache on and off since she'd woken up, but she'd thought nothing of it. "Can you take me to the hospital?"

Heine nodded. "Of course, the car's outside."

"Can you ring the midwife and tell her I'm on my way to the hospital, Paul, while I get my things? The number is by the telephone."

Paul disappeared into the living room while Heine

reached for the suitcase. "Looks like it was a good job you packed after all. Is it ready?"

Rachel nodded.

"Good, then we'll take you to the hospital as soon as Paul is finished." He held out his arm and Rachel took it gratefully. It looked like she wouldn't have any more time to worry about becoming a mother.

My Khe Beach, Da Nang, Vietnam

Phuc was watching carefully from the other side of the road. He saw Spanner reach the bar, and then Lien came into view and he cursed loudly. If he set the bomb off now, he would kill Lien too. He thought quickly and shouted to her. "Lien!"

Lien stopped walking and looked around to see who had called her. It had sounded like Phuc. She hadn't seen him since the day he had apparently saved Spanner from the scooter. She hesitated. She wanted to see Spanner, but she also wanted to find out what Phuc was up to. Curiosity won. She waved at Spanner. "Go in, I be in in a moment."

Spanner nodded, opened the door and stepped inside. Lien looked around for Phuc, and finally spotted him on the other side of the road. She began crossing the road and had almost reached him when the ground shook, she was vaguely aware of a tremendous noise, a whooshing sound and a strong wind that knocked her to the ground. Then everything went black.

Kurt had already stepped onto the beach, his thoughts on the surf, when there was a massive explosion. He threw himself flat on the sand and then raised his head cautiously and began looking for the enemy. But other than hundreds of shocked civilians, there was no other threat. He stood up carefully and glanced around. It must have been a bomb. The centre of the explosion was clear: the front of one of the seafront bars had been blown clean away. He headed towards it, wanting to move people away in case there was another bomb and to see if he could help. There was wreckage strewn everywhere – broken tables and chairs, splintered glass, blood and severed body parts littered the pavement together with nails and bits of iron. All around people were screaming and shouting, but for Kurt the world had suddenly stopped turning. He took another step forward, stared at the wrecked building in growing horror and fought for breath. "Oh shit... Spanner... please God, no... SPANNER!"

PART THREE

GENERAL BACKGROUND

The year 1970 was in many ways a continuation of the 1960s in the United States. The war in Southeast Asia had dominated the news, and protests against the war had continued in the USA and around the world.

The music of the time also continued to reflect the world, with one of the most iconic anti-war songs, 'War' *released by Edwin Star. The final album of Simon and Garfunkel was released in 1970. 'Bridge Over Troubled Water' went on to become one of the best-selling albums and singles of all time.*

The space programme continued, with the most gripping event taking place on April 13th when Apollo 13 announced, "Houston, we've had a problem." An explosion had occurred on board, and for six days the world watched the progress of the space craft and its final safe return to earth.

Other events in 1970 included the Boeing 747 Jumbo making its maiden commercial flight, and Concorde making its first supersonic flight. The Aswan Dam was completed.

The world population reached 3.63 billion.

1971 could well be considered the start of the digital age. The Microprocessor was released by Intel. The pocket calculator was released by Texas Instruments. The first CAT scanner was produced by EMI. The voting age in the USA was reduced to 18 years old. Walt Disney World opened in Florida. Apollo 14 and 15 made successful journeys to the moon and back and the Soviet Union launched the world's first space station, Salyut 1.

On June 13th, The New York Times *published the Pentagon Papers. These publications showed that the American government had been lying to the people in relation to the Vietnam War. The papers showed American involvement in military attacks that were unknown to US citizens. These made the Vietnam War even more unpopular in the US. 60% of the population were now said to be against the war.*

1972 was the year the Olympics were held in Munich. Although American swimmer Mark Spitz won seven gold medals at the games, the 20th Olympiad will be remembered not so much for sport, but for a terrorist attack in which 11 Israeli athletes were killed by Arab gunmen.

In Washington D.C. on June 17th, five men were arrested for burglary of the Democratic National Committee headquarters, also known as the Watergate building.

HBO was launched in the US. Atari launched the video game PONG. Digital watches went on sale. The VW Beetle became the biggest-selling car of all time, with over 15 million sold. Apollo 17 landed on the moon, the last manned mission to the moon.

In Vietnam, the last American ground troops went home, and Richard Nixon was re-elected President of the USA by a landslide.

By 1973, inflation in the world's economies was having a serious impact on industry and employment. OPEC had raised the price of oil in Western countries because of their support of Israel in the

Yom Kippur War. This led to recession. The cost of a barrel of oil in 1972 was $3.60. By 1975, the cost of a barrel of oil had rocketed to $13 per barrel, the biggest percentage increase in history. Due to this price increase, the Japanese car industry thrived because of the smaller and more efficient engines in their cars.

In New York City, the World Trade Centre had become the tallest building in the world. The Sydney Opera house opened. Skylab was launched into space. Barcodes were introduced.

The Watergate Hearings began in Washington D.C. The 'Agreement Ending the War and Restoring Peace in Vietnam' was signed. The Paris Peace Accords led to the end of American military involvement in Vietnam and there was a ceasefire. All US forces were removed, and military bases were demolished. Prisoners of war were released.

By 1974, inflation around the world was spiralling out of control, leading to a world-wide recession. Richard Nixon resigned as President on August 9th before he could be impeached. President Gerald Ford was Nixon's replacement, and he gave Nixon an unconditional pardon for his misdemeanours.

Muhammad Ali fought George Foreman in Zaire. The fight was known as the Rumble in the Jungle, and Ali defeated Foreman in the eighth round.

In 1975, inflation in the UK was 24% and the price of petrol had increased by 70%. The government tried to control inflation by raising interest rates. The Bank of England rates were 11% and in the US they were 7.25%. Oil had now reached $13 per barrel. US Apollo and Soviet Soyuz docked in space and cosmonauts and *astronauts shook hands.*

In the UK, Margaret Thatcher became leader of the Conservative Party.

Sony introduced video tapes. JVC introduced a different system. Motorola obtained a patent for the first cell phone. Microsoft became a registered trademark. Bill Gates and Paul Allen developed a BASIC program. BIC launched the first disposable razor.

The Vietnam War ended at the end of April 1975. The North Vietnamese army overran South Vietnam. South Vietnam surrendered and the country was united as one country. Saigon was renamed Ho Chi Minh City.

Fighting ceased in Vietnam for the first time in nearly 40 years.

CHAPTER TWENTY-FOUR

Saigon, Vietnam, April 1975

Lien glanced around nervously to make sure there was no one watching before setting light to the box which contained all her letters and photos from Spanner. As she watched the fire burning her happy memories to ashes, she allowed the tears to fall. The only thing she had kept was Spanner's ring; it was on a chain around her neck, but even that would probably not be safe now. She would have to hide it somewhere until it was safe to wear it again. Lien thought back to the day Spanner had given her the ring, the day he'd promised to look after her. Unfortunately, fate had decided that her destiny would be to follow a different path, one that didn't involve the man she loved. Lien wished she could wipe away the memories of that terrible day her life had ended, but they were firmly etched in her mind, every detail crystal clear and never to be forgotten.

Lien had come round to find herself laying on the road. All around she could hear people screaming and shouting, and there was a dreadful smell of burning and something else she couldn't identify. She had climbed to her feet slowly and stared in horror at the remains of the building opposite. It had taken her a moment to recognise it was the bar where she worked and then she couldn't breathe. She had glanced frantically around, but there was no sign of Spanner. As she fought for air, struggling against the tightening of her chest, she replayed the moments before she'd passed out. Spanner had been waiting for her and then someone had called her name, she had stopped and told him to go in without her. "No... no..." She felt like she was drowning, she couldn't speak. "Spanner... Spanner?" Dazed and confused, her words were little more than a whisper. At first, she couldn't move, then her lungs finally filled with air and she took a step towards the devastation.

"What the hell are you doing?" Phuc had grabbed her arm and was dragging her in the opposite direction.

Lien glared at him and tried to break away. "I have to get to Spanner."

"He's dead, just like the rest of the fucking enemy." Phuc had lowered his voice, but she could still hear the triumphant tone.

Lien felt dizzy suddenly, his voice coming from a long way away, she could barely breathe as the truth hit her. "You? You put a bomb there? You caused this?" She was struggling for air again, her surroundings spinning out of focus.

"You should have listened to me, Lien. I told you to do your duty!"

Lien fought to remain conscious. She could hardly believe

what she was hearing. Phuc couldn't have done this, not just to stop her seeing Spanner. All those people dead and injured because of her? She moved suddenly, wrenching her arm free. "I have to go to Spanner..."

Phuc grabbed her again. "I've told you, he's dead. Like all the other pigs."

"No, nooooo..." She turned towards the wreckage just in time to see someone carrying out a body. Her heart leapt. The man looked like Spanner's friend Kurt and... and he had Spanner! She could hear him calling for a doctor, so Spanner must be alive. *Thank you, Buddha. Please let him live.* Lien began to struggle, she had to go to him, but Phuc had taken her arm again and she couldn't break free this time. "Let me go, he's over there, I can see him." Tears were streaming down her face, and she was starting to shout, but she didn't notice. She just wanted to get to Spanner. Lien had almost freed herself when there was a sudden pain in her head, and everything went black again.

She had woken up sometime later to find herself in a hut, her arms and feet tied with rope and Chinh staring down at her. There was no sign of her brother.

"Good. You are awake."

The events of earlier flooded her mind: the explosion, Phuc gloating, Spanner's friend carrying him outside and shouting for a doctor.

"Where's Phuc?"

"Doing something for me." Chinh's voice was calm.

"If you promise not to run off, I will untie you."

Lien hesitated, then nodded. She would listen to what he had to say, then go back to the beach and find out what had happened to Spanner.

"The American is dead; the bar is gone." Chinh's eyes bored into hers. "You made such a fuss that Phuc had to knock you out, so you can't go back there yet in case anyone remembers. I'm sure you don't want your brother arrested for his heroic deed, do you?"

Lien couldn't speak, a mixture of fury and despair overwhelming her as she tried to comprehend how her brother could kill all those innocent people, just to stop her being happy.

The small fire had gone out now, the ashes blowing skyward in the wind, and Lien came back to the present. She wiped her tears away and wished she could extinguish the pain and memories as easily. When she had eventually returned to the beach, she'd discovered that Spanner had survived, but was badly injured and had been taken to Japan for treatment. She didn't want to write to him in case it drew attention to her or Phuc, so she waited patiently for him to come and find her, or at least write to her. Lien was sure it wouldn't be long, but as the weeks passed and she heard nothing she began to lose faith. Chinh had found her another job further along the beach but all Lien was interested in was hearing from Spanner. As the months passed and she heard nothing, Lien had clung to the belief that it wasn't his fault and she'd continued to wait. Even after the Americans had withdrawn their troops three years earlier, Lien kept believing he would reappear.

But now she knew he would never return. The war was virtually over, and the VC had won. A few years ago, she would have been celebrating, but instead she was terrified.

Omaha, Nebraska

Spanner finished checking the latest delivery of Toyota cars before walking towards his office. There were rarely any problems with the cars, but he liked to personally guarantee anything he sold, which meant checking them all carefully. His first two franchises selling low gasoline consumption Japanese cars in America were doing well against the gas-guzzling American vehicles, and he had plans to set up several more. He headed into the washroom to clean up and check his appearance. He had a busy day coming up, with newspapers and local radio station coming to interview him about his new scheme: a 50% discount on all vehicles for veterans of the Vietnam war. Spanner still thanked God every day for his miraculous recovery from the bomb at My Khe Beach, and he wanted to make sure as many other veterans as possible benefitted from his good fortune.

He gave a wry smile. Not many people thought he was fortunate when they saw the scars on his face and watched him walking with a stick, but Spanner knew he was lucky to be alive. Not because he could remember that awful day, but because Kurt had told him – he had no memory of Vietnam at all. He hadn't remembered Kurt either, or Jim, but his friends had kept in touch by letter after he was moved to Japan for extensive operations. The medics had told him it was Kurt who had dragged him outside and kept him alive while they waited for help to arrive. It was Kurt and Jim who had written to him regularly while he spent months in hospital recovering. Kurt had remained in touch and was now working for him, but Jim had fallen off the radar. Spanner frowned as he wondered yet again where his friend was now. Jim had begun drinking heavily a few months earlier, and despite Spanner's attempts to help him he had slipped further and further into alcoholism. Then one day he'd vanished, and despite concerted attempts by Spanner and Kurt to find him, they had been unsuccessful. Spanner was still searching, but he didn't hold out much hope.

Spanner peered at his face in the mirror. Despite the scars, he had changed little facially over the years; his hair was still blonde, his blue eyes as piercing as ever. He was never short of female company, although none of them lasted very long. Spanner didn't have time to nurture a long term relationship, he was too focused on making his business successful so he could use the profits to make a difference to other veterans. He had yet to meet a woman who shared his passion for veterans, but he didn't mind. Having read several books on Buddhism while he was recuperating in

Japan, Spanner accepted that nothing remained the same, so eventually the right woman would come along.

He removed his overalls, washed quickly and dressed in his shirt, suit and tie. While his face had stayed mostly the same, his body was a different story – although still toned, it was covered in scars from the bombing and the subsequent operations to save his life. Several bones in his left leg had been broken and although they had healed, he still couldn't manage without a stick. Spanner didn't feel sorry for himself, though; so many other veterans had lost limbs, he considered himself lucky that he still had his leg and could walk, even if it was with a limp. He walked back into his office and lit a cigar, another legacy of his time in Vietnam, even if he didn't know how the habit had started. When he'd been recovering his friends had sent him boxes of them, along with letters to cheer him up.

Spanner wished he could remember something about his time in Vietnam, but it was a complete blank. He remembered things from before the draft, but nothing after that. The doctors had said his memory might still come back, but it was over four years now and if he was honest, he didn't really care anymore. Maybe it was better not to remember.

Kurt drove the last of the cars onto the forecourt, parked up and climbed out. He could see Spanner in his office talking on the telephone, and he wondered if that was the first of the journalists ringing to interview his friend about his special deal for veterans. Hopefully, Spanner would be successful, and it would not backfire on him. The way veterans had been treated during and after the war in Vietnam was appalling. The public behaved as if those men had chosen to go to that awful place, as if they'd had a choice. Even thinking about it made him furious.

Unlike Spanner, Kurt could still remember every detail of his term in that hell hole: the beautiful lush shades of green which in normal times would be calming, but here were just somewhere the enemy could be hiding, waiting to ambush and kill or maim unsuspecting Americans; the smells of mud and water buffalo and human excrement; the blood and leeches. Every night when he closed his eyes, he could smell cordite, he could hear the sounds of an enemy mortar being launched at them, the roaring of shells from the 16-inch guns. In his head he was still in the helicopter, staring down at jungle burned with napalm, watching the green AK-47 tracer bullets ripping up the ground and the bodies of the patrols they went to rescue. Music was the worst – even now, a song could send him right back to the jungle to the worst atrocity he'd witnessed, when the helicopter he'd been on had crashed. Kurt took a deep breath and tried to clear the images of the children from the orphanage being burnt alive by the VC for helping them after they'd crashed, the smell of burning flesh... His breath came in ever-shortening gasps and he felt dizzy, unable to clear his mind of the sight, the smell... Kurt leant back against the car and tried to concentrate on something else.

"Kurt? You ok, buddy?" Spanner had spotted his friend doubled over by the car and rushed out. Kurt didn't answer and Spanner realised he was back in the jungle. "It's ok, buddy, you're in the US, you're safe. It's not happening now. Come back to me, pal." He kept speaking calmly and patiently, and eventually Kurt managed to bring himself back to the present.

"What happened?"

"You were back in 'Nam. Do you want to talk about it?" Spanner felt his usual frustration that he couldn't understand how Kurt felt because he couldn't remember anything. He doubted Kurt would tell him anything this time either, but he would keep asking. He guessed this was something to do with the helicopter crash that had happened after Spanner had been injured. Kurt had told him that he and Jim had crashed in the jungle and had to wait to be rescued. Spanner wished he knew what had happened there, but neither Kurt nor Jim would talk about it.

"Sorry. I'm ok now."

"If you're sure?"

"Honestly, Spanner, you've got things to do. It's an important day. I'm perfectly ok now, I promise."

Kurt waited until Spanner had returned to the office before allowing his thoughts to turn to Jim. He could understand why his friend had become an alcoholic; there were times he too was tempted to drink to block out the things he'd seen. So far he had resisted the temptation, relying mainly on marijuana to keep the nightmares at bay and help him sleep.

As the newspaper reporters began to arrive, Kurt thought about Spanner and how lucky it was for him that his friend had survived the bomb. If not, he would probably have gone the same way as Jim. Kurt exhaled slowly as he allowed his thoughts to go back to that dreadful day and his certainty that Spanner would be dead when he'd frantically fought his way into the wreckage of the bar. He'd been astonished to find his friend still breathing, but in danger of falling masonry as the ceiling started to cave in. Kurt had carried him all the way to the entrance and placed him carefully on the sidewalk opposite, put pressure on his wounds to stop the worst of the bleeding, and waited for the medic to arrive. Fortunately, Spanner had been close to the bar when the explosion happened. If he'd been near the door he would have been killed outright.

While the medics were treating Spanner, Kurt had looked around for Lien, but there were so many people he couldn't see her. She hadn't been by the bar, but there were several bodies in the building and Kurt feared she was dead. He had dreaded telling Spanner, knowing how his friend loved her, so when it became clear Spanner had lost his memory Kurt and Jim had decided not to tell him about Lien. They knew he hadn't mentioned her to his family so why upset him?

Omaha, Nebraska

Rachel glanced around the small Democratic Party office and smiled. Even now, three years later, she couldn't quite believe that she was being paid to work somewhere she loved. It had taken some time and help from Paul and Heine, but the Democratic Party had finally welcomed her even though she was an unmarried mother. At first Rachel had feared the stigma would prevent her having any type of career, but things had gradually changed in the past few years and it was no longer so unacceptable to have had sex outside marriage. She was still on the bottom rung of the ladder, but Rachel had every intention of rising to the top. She just had to find a way of doing it.

Her passion to change the world for the better had found a home, although it was happening much too slowly for her liking. America was a mess – thanks to Nixon people had lost all confidence in the government. Ford hadn't helped by pardoning him, and in her opinion was not doing a good job of running the country; the economy was stagnant, and unemployment and poverty were rife. Rachel couldn't wait for the elections next year, and she was dying to know who the Democrats would put up as their candidate for President.

She looked down at her desk, finished answering the last of the letters and put them in the mail. Answering veterans' letters always reminded her of Martin and the beginning of her journey to where she was now. There had been so many issues Rachel had wanted to fight for: women's rights, gay rights, an end to poverty, equal opportunities. But she'd soon realised that she needed to concentrate her attention on one thing if she was going to be successful. Thanks to Martin, she'd found her cause and had thrown herself into it with enthusiasm. If only he was still here to see what he'd inspired. Rachel felt the familiar mixture of anger and sadness that was always there when she thought of Martin. It had been his passion for the cause, to get American troops out of Vietnam, that had brought them together. And it was the cause that had ultimately been responsible for his death. She sighed and thought back to the heady days of their protests, and in particular, Operation Dewey Canyon III.

The veterans had named their protest after secret US operations in Laos, and in April 1971 they had gathered in Washington, local chapters coming together from all around the country, and Rachel had felt privileged to join their supporters. Even now, she could remember their disgust after Nixon questioned whether they really were veterans and how hundreds had tossed their prized war medals at the Capitol Building. Martin had been among those who had occupied a senator's office and had been arrested with over a hundred others. The protests had not stopped there – the day after Christmas, Martin and 14 other anti-war veterans had occupied the Statue of Liberty and flown a US flag upside down from her crown. Two days later, nearly a hundred other veterans clashed with police in Washington and were arrested while trying to occupy the Lincoln Memorial.

Rachel felt tears forming in her eyes and blinked them angrily away. As American troops were gradually withdrawn from Vietnam, their cause had shifted to fight the appalling way returning servicemen were treated by the public. Vilified, spat on in the streets, discriminated against for employment and housing... the catalogue of injustice had grown exponentially as the media and government seemingly turned against the men who'd been sent to fight a war that had torn the country apart. The fact that the majority had not had a choice had been quickly forgotten. Only the atrocities carried out by a tiny minority were remembered and referred to frequently, while those carried out by the enemy were forgotten. Rachel sometimes felt as if she were fighting a losing battle, but she owed it to Martin to keep fighting.

CHAPTER TWENTY-FIVE

Saigon, Vietnam

Lien had given Spanner's twins her surname, so at least they had birth certificates. Born almost exactly four years earlier, six months after the explosion, Lien knew she had to make a decision about their future. Her daughter, Nguyen Quy Vy, looked very much like her and could pass for Vietnamese, but her son, Nguyen Thanh An, couldn't. He was the spitting image of his father, blond-haired, long-limbed and blue-eyed; she couldn't see any Vietnamese in him at all. His appearance had already caused them so many problems – the Vietnamese detested Amerasians – but they had somehow survived. Now the threat to their lives was due to get a thousand times worse. There was a chance An could get them all killed, because the communists truly despised Amerasians. To them, Amerasians were a reminder of the hated Americans who had killed their friends and family and destroyed their country, a state that was now bankrupt. Because of the chemicals the Americans had sprayed on the land, people were unable to grow food, so many were starving. Large swathes of the countryside had been destroyed by Agent Orange. Lien had no idea what the future held, but her instincts told her that An would be a greater threat than she could cope with, and therefore she had to give him up.

The question was what to do with him. Fortunately, he was white and good-looking, unlike some of the black Amerasians who were treated even worse, but if she were going to find an orphanage for him she had to do it quickly before they were overrun. The thought of giving up her son was so heart-breaking Lien wasn't sure she could really go ahead with it. Maybe if she'd done it straight after he'd been born it would have been easier, but then she had been so sure Spanner would come back for her. She'd had four years with An, watching him grow, seeing Spanner in his face, his gestures, his expressions... To suddenly hand him over to someone else would kill her, but she had no option. Lien took a deep breath and called the twins to her. She would leave Vy with her friend and take An to the Buddhist temple on the hill. At least that way he would have a future. And if things weren't that bad under the communists, she could always come back for him.

Omaha, Nebraska

"And you don't think singling out Vietnam veterans for special treatment will damage your business?" The reporter was young, his tone aggressive, and Spanner forced a smile.

"Why should it? Vietnam veterans are constantly being discriminated against for being sent, against their will, to fight an unpopular war. The politicians that lost the war have successfully managed to misdirect the blame for the war, the loss of our country's prestige and their incompetence, onto our troops. Unfortunately, *some* media outlets have been unable to see this, which is rather sad." Spanner held the reporter's gaze until the young man looked away. Spanner smiled again. "Any other questions, gentlemen?"

"You think veterans aren't to blame for losing the war then?"

Spanner sighed, took a breath and focused carefully on the young reporter. "You look to be early 20s, am I right?"

The reporter shrugged. "I'm not sure what that has to do with anything."

"I was sent to Vietnam when I was 19. If the war had still been going on you would have been sent there too. You wouldn't have had a choice. You would have been forced to put on a uniform, to go thousands of miles to fight an enemy that thought nothing of maiming women and children to control the population. You would have been given orders that you obeyed or you'd be put in prison. If you disobeyed in the field, you could get yourself and your friends killed. You would not have been in a position to make decisions that could win the war. You were just cannon fodder. Still think *all* veterans are responsible for the war and deserve to be punished?"

There was silence. Spanner looked at the reporters and was pleased to see some of them were agreeing with him, although others didn't look convinced. He braced himself for another attack.

"I think your discount is very commendable, Mr Tanner."

Spanner breathed a sigh of relief. He smiled at the older man. "Spanner, please – it's what everyone calls me."

"Do you think the government should do more for veterans, then?" another man asked, and Spanner nodded. He began outlining his ideas for how veterans should be treated and forgot the middle-aged, balding reporter who'd come to his aid.

Heine waited until the press conference was finished and the other reporters had left before approaching Spanner.

"Mr Tanner – Spanner," he smiled, "could I have a word, please?"

Spanner recognised the reporter who'd supported him and nodded. "Sure, come into the office. I could do with a smoke and some coffee."

Saigon, Vietnam

Lien stumbled down the hill and somehow made her way back to Minh to pick up Vy. Her heart was breaking, and she kept reliving the last few moments with her son. His face when she'd left, the expression on his face so like his father's, the blue eyes so trusting as he raised his tiny hand and waved goodbye. Tears ran down her cheeks unchecked as she recalled the monk's last words. At first, he'd hesitated to take An, but after she'd given him all the money she had for the temple, he'd agreed. "He can stay here with the other boys, and he will become a monk when he is older." The words haunted her, it wasn't the life she'd envisaged for her son, but at least An would live and he would be treated well by the monks. There would be none of the regular abuse Amerasians suffered, which would probably get worse now. She only hoped Vy's Vietnamese appearance would be enough to keep her safe.

She wiped her eyes and took a breath. The rumours about the communists could be wrong, things might not be that bad and she might be able to go and rescue him. But first she had to find some more work, because she had no money left for food. Lien felt an overwhelming despair that threatened to bury her, then she took a deep breath and raised her head defiantly. She had survived after Spanner disappeared; she would get through this too.

Her thoughts returned to those dark days, her fury with

Phuc when she realised he'd been responsible and her fear and loathing of Chinh. She hadn't seen Phuc since that day and, after she'd told Chinh she was pregnant a few weeks later, she hadn't seen him either. With no job, she had lost the room she had been living in and ended up sleeping in the market. It was here her prayers to Buddha had finally been answered. She had met Du'o'ng Thu Minh, an older woman who had a shop selling various cooking and healing herbs and roots. Minh had taken her in and looked after her, treating her like the daughter she had always wanted. If it hadn't been for Minh, Lien had no idea what would have happened to her. After the American troops finally withdrew, Minh had made the decision to move further south to Saigon and she had taken Lien and the children with her. Lien knew Minh wouldn't throw her out if she didn't have any money, but Minh had already supported her through her pregnancy and Lien preferred knowing she was paying her own way. In any case, no one knew what would happen once the communists finally took control, so it would be better to have a job and some money before that happened just in case they had to move again.

Omaha, Nebraska

"Jamie, it's lovely to see you again." Rachel stepped back so he could come in. "Richie! Uncle Jamie is here."

Richie came running to the door, a big smile on his face. "Uncle Jamie!"

"Hi Richie, I swear you get bigger every time I see you." He swung the boy up into his arms and gave him a big hug before setting him back on the floor and turning his attention back to Rachel. "I can't stay long, but I have some more things for you."

Rachel's face changed and she nodded. "Go and play with your toys, Richie, we'll be along in a minute." She waited for her son to disappear through the living room door before speaking. "He's still doing it, then?" She clenched her fists and shook her head. "I can't believe he keeps thinking he can get away with treating women like this."

"That's the problem, he does keep getting away with it."

"I thought he'd gone away to study medicine?"

"He had, but he's back now, working at the local hospital. Apparently he's training to be a surgeon."

"It's just so wrong, Jamie." Rachel took a breath and tried to quash her anger. It would only bring back the overwhelming sense of helplessness thinking about the rape always made her feel. "Do you think we'll ever have enough to convict him?"

"I don't know, but we can't give up. We'll keep collecting

evidence and hope that somewhere along the line he'll make a mistake." Jamie turned back to the door. "I'll get the stuff out of the car and we can put it with the other boxes."

Rachel waited for him to come back, her thoughts on Charles Peterson and the growing number of crimes against women that they knew about. There were several gaps when he was elsewhere, and Rachel wished she had access to police departments in the other places he had been living.

"Do you think he only does it here?" She watched as Jamie added the box to the others.

Jamie shrugged. "It's possible. He may not risk it elsewhere in case Daddy's money doesn't talk loudly enough there." He smiled at her and changed the subject. "How are you now?"

Rachel gave a wry smile. "You mean am I still mourning for a criminal?"

Jamie shook his head. "You know that's not what I mean. I care about you, Rachel, and I understand why you fell for him, but what he did..."

Rachel interrupted him. "He felt like he was left with no option, Jamie, and to be honest I can see why he would feel like that, but I know you can't agree with me."

"I took an oath to uphold the law, Rachel, I can't condone what Martin did, even if I wanted to." Jamie was beginning to wish he hadn't mentioned anything now. He wished Rachel would look at him the way she did when she mentioned her ex-boyfriend. Obviously, she was still in love with him. Jamie sighed inwardly. He had spent years fighting to keep his feelings for Rachel hidden so they didn't ruin their friendship. It had been hard when she'd fallen in love with Martin Bremner, but at least then he could tell himself she was happy. Now she was on her own again he was back to square one, fighting his feelings all over again.

Omaha, Nebraska

Spanner finished reading the last of the articles from the press conference, put out his cigar and smiled. For the most part the publicity had been positive, apart from the young reporter he'd put in his place, but he'd been expecting that. He sighed. His natural inclination was to support the Democratic Party, especially after Watergate, but they needed to get rid of some of their young commies who hated the US Forces.

He thought of the woman Heine had suggested he meet. Apparently, she worked with the local democrats and was passionate about seeing Vietnam veterans better treated. Heine hadn't told him why. Perhaps her brother had been drafted, or a boyfriend, or her husband. Spanner shrugged. Whatever the reason, he was willing to work with anyone who could help their cause, and someone who was connected to a political party could be very useful indeed. He only hoped they hit it off – it would be so good to stop banging his head against the wall and really make a difference to people's attitudes and the way the country treated his fellow veterans.

Spanner sipped his bourbon and thought about how his life had changed since Vietnam. His earliest remaining memory was of waking up in a US army hospital just outside Tokyo. He'd spent months having operations and physiotherapy, but his leg wouldn't heal properly. Eventually they had sent him for a medical and decided that he was no longer fit for service. By then, as his year was up anyway, he had been discharged from the army. Spanner had planned to go home straight away but there was a long delay in processing his papers, so he had taken a room in a hotel in Tokyo and set about exploring the city. Although he couldn't wait to return to the farm and see his family again, a part of him had been quite pleased at the delay. He had not been looking forward to going home and enduring all the pitying looks when people saw his injuries. If he'd known he would be spat at and cursed by people in the street when he did return, just for being a Vietnam veteran, he would have been even more delighted at the opportunity to stay in Japan.

Spanner pushed the unpleasant thoughts to the back of his mind and relived his time in Japan instead. At first, he had worried that he would have to use his savings to keep him going, as his army pay had stopped. But the delay had been the best thing that could have happened to him. While walking around the city he'd found a Toyota showroom and begun looking at the small cars. The elderly owner, Miyoshi Yosai, had come out and begun talking to him. It seemed Yosai was looking for a new mechanic, and as Spanner was looking for some money to keep him going until he flew home, he'd been delighted when Yosai had offered him a job.

The relationship between the two men had grown quickly into a strong friendship. Spanner became a regular guest in Yosai's home, and he and his wife treated Spanner like the son they had never had. By the time his papers came through, Spanner was enjoying his work so much that he had decided to remain in Japan. As time passed and the international situation deteriorated, the price of oil went through the roof. It was then that Spanner had a brainwave. The large American autos he'd grown up with and worked on were gas-guzzlers, whereas the compact Toyotas used little fuel and were very reliable. Perhaps there was a market now for these small cars in his own country. Filled with excitement at repaying Yosai's kindness and friendship towards him, Spanner suggested the idea. His friend thought about it for several seconds then suggested that Spanner set up a franchise in the US at his expense. Spanner had been taken aback at Yosai's generosity, but he knew it was what he wanted, so he'd barely thought about it before accepting the chance fate had given him.

Spanner lit another cigar and sighed. The autos were selling well considering the country was in a recession, but the treatment of veterans had not changed at all. He still faced regular abuse, and he knew it was worse for thousands of others. He was becoming frustrated by his lack of achievement, but maybe this was about to change. He smiled. For some reason he had a good feeling about this Rachel Hanson, and he couldn't wait to meet her.

Saigon, Vietnam

"What on earth have you done?" Minh was horrified.

"An looks too American, he will bring trouble on us all." Lien was sobbing as she spoke. "It was the only thing I could think of to do, or we could all suffer."

"Better we all suffer together, you silly girl. Go and get him."

Lien stared at her in shock. "But..."

"Just go and get him, Lien." Minh snapped. "Whatever happens, we will face it together. Now hurry. If you go you can be back before nightfall, and with luck he wouldn't even remember that you abandoned him."

Lien nodded, her heart soaring. Minh was right – what on earth had she been thinking, giving her beautiful son away? "You're right, I'll go straight away." She hurried away while Minh watched.

"Where's An?" Vy tugged her skirt.

"Your mother has just gone to get him. He was staying with a friend," Minh answered, before picking Vy up and hugging her tight. She understood why Lien was scared, she was too, but to give An away...

Omaha, Nebraska

Rachel put Richie to bed, read him his bedtime story, kissed him goodnight, switched off his light and headed back to the living room where Heine and Paul were waiting. As she closed his bedroom door, she heard Paul talking.

"He looks so much like his father, Heine. I find it hard sometimes."

"But Richie isn't him, Paul. He's a little person in his own right." Heine sounded horrified.

"Yes, he is!" Rachel stormed into the room. "I can't believe you said that, Paul."

Paul looked devastated. "I'm so sorry, sis, I didn't mean for you overhear that. I would never knowingly upset you, not after everything you've done for us. And it doesn't mean I love him any less. It's just that sometimes I can see that bastard in his face. I know it's not his fault, and I know he certainly won't grow up like his father because you won't let him."

"Then don't ever say that in my hearing again." Rachel was still furious, mainly because the same thought popped into her head several time a day. She had loved Richie, short for Richard, ever since she'd held him that first time in her arms. The resemblance to his father had not been quite so obvious then, or she might not have bonded with him so easily. But as he'd grown up Richie had changed facially and, at the moment, he resembled his father more than her. At first she had railed at God for making her son look so much like that bastard – surely she had done the right thing in fighting for Richie's life, so why was she being punished? But eventually she had decided it was a good thing, because it would ensure she brought her son up to respect women and to fight for their right to equality. It would also remind her never to give up the search for enough evidence to bring him to justice.

"I'm sorry, sis, really I am," Paul said again.

Rachel was about to say more when she remembered Charles's threats about having Paul arrested if she reported him. She had no idea if that was what had happened, but she felt guilty anyway. She sat down opposite him and spoke firmly. "It's alright, Paul. I knew this would never be easy, and I do understand your feelings. But Richie is a child, he's not even five years old yet. The resemblance to his father will remind us to ensure he never grows up to be like him."

Paul smiled in relief. "You're right, sis. I'll never mention it again. I promise."

Heine patted Paul's knee and then turned to Rachel. "I attended a press conference today with someone you might be interested in meeting."

Rachel forgot about Richie for a moment and turned towards Heine. "Who is he?"

"He's a car dealer, a Vietnam veteran who seems just as passionate about their cause as you are. He's just introduced a special 50% discount on all his cars for others who served there too."

"That sounds interesting. What's his name?" Rachel frowned. "This isn't some attempt to match-make, is it?"

Heine laughed. "I wouldn't dream of it, Rachel." His face grew serious as he thought about the scars on Spanner's face and his pronounced limp. Not that he wasn't still quite a handsome man, he definitely had a commanding presence. He pushed his thoughts away and refocused on Rachel. "No, I just thought you and he might be able to work together to come up with some ideas to help the cause."

Rachel inclined her head. "Ok, give me his address and I'll call in and see him."

Heine smiled. "No need, I've suggested we all meet next Wednesday at our favourite restaurant. That will give you time to get a sitter."

Rachel shrugged. "Fine, I'll do that, then." She stood up. "Who wants some wine?"

CHAPTER TWENTY-SIX

Saigon, Vietnam

Lien hugged the children closer to her and prayed continually to Buddha to protect them. Their home was not far from the American embassy, and earlier they had heard numerous helicopters overhead and people screaming in the streets, but now all was eerily quiet. Lien didn't know what was worse, and she stared at Minh in terror.

Minh eventually stood up, walked to the window and peered through the curtains into the street. She could see North Vietnamese flags flying everywhere, but the streets were deserted other than... She frowned and peered through the glass.

"What is it, Minh?" Lien could feel her heart pounding with terror.

"There's a child sitting on the pavement, crying."

Lien stood up and joined Minh at the window. "Do you think he's lost?"

Minh sighed. "I don't know, but we can't leave the poor mite out there, Lien. I'll go and speak to him."

"Be careful!" Lien's terror increased.

Minh smiled. "I've had my life, Lien, death doesn't worry me. Wait here." Before Lien could say anything else, Minh had gone.

Omaha, Nebraska

Spanner sat in the restaurant waiting for his guests to arrive, his thoughts on what was happening in Vietnam. He'd watched the dreadful pictures of the last of the Americans fleeing the US embassy in Saigon on the television. Although he still didn't remember anything about Vietnam, he couldn't help feeling sorry for the population, which was now under the control of a brutal communist government.

"Hello, sorry we're late, we've been watching the news." Heine approached the table. Behind him were another man and an attractive young woman with long blonde hair and green eyes. Spanner stood up to greet them, his eyes on Rachel.

"Not a problem, I was only sitting here thinking about the awful pictures on the television, all those desperate people left behind…" he caught himself. "Sorry, I'm Steve Tanner, but everyone calls me Spanner." He smiled at her.

Rachel returned his smile. "Hi, I'm Rachel." Her smile faded. "Given why we're here, the events of today seem particularly poignant."

He pulled out a chair for her, and once she was seated he sat back down. "Yes, I keep thinking of all those men around the country watching their TVs and thinking about the waste of our lives, a waste that is still going on." He shook his head. "Sorry, I didn't mean to start this conversation quite so soon, I was going to be a good host first and offer you some drinks while you look at the menus!"

Rachel's smile broadened. "I think it's perfectly acceptable given today's events, but I would love a glass of wine please."

Rachel pretended to scan the menu while Spanner ordered the wine, but she was really watching their host. Despite his scars he was still an attractive man, and his passion for the cause was obvious. In some ways he reminded her of Martin and... Rachel frowned. For some reason she felt sure she'd seen him somewhere before, but she couldn't think where. She let the thought go and concentrated on the menu. She didn't need another damaged boyfriend. Martin had been enough for one lifetime. If Heine was matchmaking, he was wasting his time.

Spanner was finding it hard to concentrate on making small talk with Paul; his eyes kept drifting to Rachel. She seemed vaguely familiar, although he couldn't think why; perhaps he'd seen her at some demonstration. There was a natural pause in the conversation, and he turned to her. "So how did you get involved in the cause, Rachel?"

Rachel didn't answer for a moment. "It's a long story. I used to go on the anti-war demos in the early '70s. I was at Kent State University when the shootings happened." She ignored his gasp. "Then I met a guy on a demo, and we became close." She fell silent, wondering why she had mentioned Martin. She could have just left it at the anti-war protests. There was something about Spanner that made her want to confide in him. Rachel looked down at the table and tried to get a grip on her emotions. This was how it had started with Martin, she'd told him the truth about her pregnancy and look where that had got her. She looked up at him and changed the subject. "When were you in Vietnam, then?"

"1970, but I don't remember anything about it. I was blown up, hence the scars and gammy leg." He pointed at his stick, which she hadn't noticed. "And I lost my memory."

Rachel forgot her own misery. "That's awful. So you don't remember anything about your time out there? What about before you went?"

"Fortunately, the earlier memories gradually returned, but they stop at the Union Pacific rail station, where I went when I was drafted. I remember arriving at the station and getting on a bus, but that's it."

"That must be really difficult." Rachel wondered what it would be like to lose a part of your life. There were times she'd often thought she would like to forget, but now she wasn't so sure. She thought about what he'd said and suddenly remembered the day the school had taken them to the Union Pacific station and the large number of young men who had been drafted. There had been a man, good-looking, blonde hair and blue eyes who had smiled at her.

Rachel wondered where he was now and whether he'd survived. The thought made her sad, and she pushed the memory away and refocused on Steve. She couldn't bring herself to think of him as Spanner.

"I can't change it, so there's no point worrying about it. My memory will either come back or it won't." He shrugged. "My buddy Kurt saved me after the explosion, he works for me in the showroom now." He smiled, a twinkle in his blue eyes. "Apparently, we had a saying in 'Nam and that pretty much sums it up. Shit happens!"

Rachel laughed. "Yes, it does, and you're right. There's no point worrying about things we can't change."

"Or trying to change the past," Spanner added, looking straight into her eyes.

Rachel met his eyes and felt a shiver go down her spine. It was as if Spanner had dived into the depths of her soul and seen her darkest secrets. She felt herself blushing, but he was pouring some more wine now and seemed completely unaware of the effect he was having on her. She glanced across at Heine and was furious to see him smiling.

Spanner had looked away because he was suddenly aware that he was deeply attracted to Rachel, and it wasn't just her body. He wanted to get to know her better, to get inside her mind and reach out to her soul. He had the weirdest feeling he'd felt like that before about someone, but he couldn't keep hold of the thought and it vanished as soon as it had appeared.

Saigon, Vietnam

Chinh and Phuc entered the city several hours behind the army. They couldn't believe the last battle had been over so quickly and that they were finally in control of their own country. North Vietnamese flags had appeared everywhere and loudspeakers were already broadcasting the 10-point plan for the country, which included peaceful reunification, freedom of thought and worship and sexual equality. Prostitution and acting like Americans was banned.

Chinh smiled at Phuc. "Now we can look for Lien. Once our government has restored order, they will begin registering people. Lien will have to come forward or she won't be able to eat."

Phuc nodded. "That will be good, Commander." He had been furious when he'd discovered that Lien had left her room. At first he'd assumed she had just run out of money and he had looked for her among the homeless, but she seemed to have completely vanished. He had asked Chinh for help, but even he had been unable to find her, and eventually Phuc had reluctantly given up. After Da Nang had fallen to the advancing North Vietnamese army in March, Phuc and Chinh had renewed their search, looking everywhere, but there was still no sign of her or the child she must have had. It had crossed Phuc's mind that Lien might be dead, but Chinh had refused to believe it, berating Phuc whenever he'd mentioned it. Phuc had eventually decided it was not a good policy to argue with his commander, even though he found Chinh's obsession with Lien rather sinister.

Chinh could barely contain his excitement. His spies had told him years ago that Lien had gone to Saigon with an elderly lady called Minh. The spy had also told him that Lien had two children, both Amerasian. Chinh hadn't bothered to tell Phuc because he had a feeling the boy would run straight to Saigon to find his sister, and that wouldn't do. Chinh didn't want Lien frightened away, because he had plans for her. Now he was finally in Saigon, he was sure it wouldn't be long before he found Lien, and then they could be married. He had no doubt she would agree, because otherwise he would make life very difficult for her and this Minh woman.

The Bronx, New York

Jim finished his bourbon and waved at the barman for another.

"I think you've probably had enough, Jim." Lewis sighed. He'd known Jim was on a bender when he'd started drinking bourbon instead of his normal beer.

Jim peered at Lewis through his alcoholic haze, but he had drunk so much he didn't recognise him. All he saw was a young man who had probably never had to do anything difficult in his life. Jim felt his anger rising. This bastard had never had his life taken away, seen what Jim had, experienced hell on earth. As he glared at him, the face changed and Jim could see one of the men who'd burnt the orphanage. There had been two who had gotten away and Jim would never forget their faces. He could hear the screams of the children, the bullets throwing up dust from the dry ground, the shouts of his friends, and he reached for his weapon. It wasn't there. That bastard must have taken it. Jim moved towards the man, wondering why his face kept changing. The sounds in his head had changed now, he could hear people chatting. Why were they talking and laughing and not doing anything to help the children? The bar came slowly back into focus as Jim somehow fought off the flashback. He fumbled in his pockets. "Who are you to decide if I've had enough or not?" Jim finally brought out some dollar bills. "Just pour it until I've run out of money, ok?"

"Look Jim, I can't serve..." Lewis didn't get any further. Jim reached across the bar and grabbed him by the throat.

"I said pour me a bourbon or I'll fucking kill you. Understand?" He let go, suddenly feeling weak. He couldn't remember when he'd last eaten, not that it mattered any more. He just wanted to sink into oblivion, and the only way he could do that was to have another drink.

Lewis poured him another bourbon and stepped back, not knowing what to do. When Jim was sober, he was lovely, a real good guy. But his drinking was getting out of control again. Lewis didn't want to call the police on him, but if Jim kept on like this he would either kill someone or be killed himself. He was still thinking about it when Jim sank to the floor unconscious. Lewis came round the public side of the bar. “Give us a hand, Chris?”

“What are you going to do with him?” Chris was another regular, an old friend of Jim’s before his drinking had got out of control. He had watched the earlier encounter with growing concern.

“Put him in the back to sleep it off. Maybe I can find him some help.”

“Good luck with that, pal.” Chris straightened up and went back to the bar. Lewis peered down at Jim and then began going through his pockets, looking for something that might help.

CHAPTER TWENTY-SEVEN

Omaha, Nebraska

Spanner glanced across his office at Rachel, who was concentrating on some proposals he'd drawn up to persuade other businesses to give discounts to Vietnam veterans. He had been working with her for two months now, but still felt he knew nothing about her. Although his attraction to her had continued to grow, he hadn't yet plucked up the courage to ask her out, and he didn't know why. He didn't normally have a problem asking women out, but there was something about Rachel… He realised he had been staring at her for so long that his cigar had gone out. Spanner sipped his water and let out a deep sigh.

Rachel glanced across at him in concern. "Is anything wrong?"

"No, sorry, I…" Spanner took a deep breath. It was now or never. "Would you come out with me? On a date, I mean?"

Rachel stared at him in astonishment. After their first meeting she had been sure Spanner would ask her out, but he hadn't. Although Rachel wasn't sure she would have accepted, she would have at least have liked him to ask her. As the weeks had passed and they had continued to work together she was sure she wasn't imagining the attraction between them, but nothing had happened, so she had finally given up.

Spanner took her silence for a refusal and wished he hadn't said anything. He flushed and looked away. "I'm sorry, I shouldn't have asked..."

"Yes," Rachel interrupted.

Spanner's jaw dropped open. He looked up at her and then grinned. "Really?"

Rachel laughed. "I thought you'd never ask!" She blushed.

"I thought you might say no, and I didn't want to ruin our friendship."

"I'm sure we'll always be friends..."

Spanner stood up and walked around the desk towards her. Rachel looked up at him before allowing him to help her to her feet. He stroked her face tenderly. "I hope so."

Rachel gazed into his eyes. His touch was electrifying, sending shivers down her spine. He leaned forward and brushed his lips over hers. The movement was so gentle she was almost unaware of it. She felt her pulse quicken, and then his lips were on hers again and she forgot everything except the feel of his lips and the warmth of his body.

Spanner pulled back reluctantly, reached up and brushed a tendril of hair off her face. "I think we might be doing things in the wrong order…"

Rachel was about to argue when she suddenly remembered her violent reaction whenever Martin had wanted to go further than a lingering kiss. Her heart began pounding, she gave an uncertain smile and stepped back. "Yes, you're probably right." Rachel sat down abruptly and tried to control her breathing. Spanner looked down at her, wondering what had happened. One minute she had been responding to his kiss, the next she seemed to have switched off completely. He frowned. "I'm sorry, I didn't mean to overstep the mark…"

Rachel had her memories back under control now, and she managed to smile up at him. "You didn't, I just happen to agree with you that this isn't the place." She indicated the office windows which overlooked the forecourt.

Spanner relaxed. Obviously she just didn't want people watching them, and nor did he. "Would dinner tonight be alright? Is that too short notice to get a sitter?"

Rachel took a deep breath and repeated her mantra: *I won't let that bastard ruin my life*. It hadn't worked with Martin, however much she'd tried, but time had moved on and perhaps it would with Spanner. She had to try or that bastard would win. She forced another smile. "I'll ask Paul and Heine. Tonight would be lovely, thank you."

Ho Chi Minh City, Vietnam

Lien watched the children playing in the street and smiled for the first time in ages. Dung and An looked so much alike she still found it difficult to believe they were not related. She thought back over the last two months and marvelled at how quickly everything had changed. Minh had gone out to speak to the boy and a few moments later had returned with him, announcing he would be living with them because he had no family. Lien had been unable to hide her disbelief. "Don't we have enough problems?"

"He's a child. We can't leave him on the streets, Lien."

Lien looked at him more closely and was struck by the similarity to An. They could be brothers. "He said his name is Dung, but he doesn't know where his mother is," Minh continued.

Lien sighed. "How old are you, Dung?"

The boy shook his head. Lien looked back at Minh. "Did he have a birth certificate on him?"

Minh shook her head. "No, there's nothing. We'll have to try and register him."

Lien rubbed her forehead, her good mood fading as quickly as it had appeared. In the two months since the country had united under the communists, life had deteriorated rapidly. Two months of fear and increasing poverty, and they hadn't been able to register Dung at all. Because he was Amerasian no one was interested, and their last attempt had drawn the attention of the police. They had to report to the police station that morning and she was terrified.

"Are you ready?" Minh came out of the house with Vy. Lien nodded and called the boys.

"I don't understand." Minh stared at the policeman in confusion. "It's my house. You can't just take it away from me."

"We can do whatever we like. Your house is confiscated because you are guilty of associating with Americans. You and your family will be sent to one of our New Economic Zones so you can work for the state. It is a good opportunity for you to help rebuild our country."

"But we don't know anything about farming..."

"Or you can go to a re-education camp, if you prefer?" The man pushed some papers across the desk towards her and stood up. The interview was over. "You have two days to pack and leave or you will be arrested."

Minh was about to argue, but Lien grabbed her arm and pulled her away before she could say anything.

Lien waited until they were outside the police station before turning to Minh and putting her arms around the woman who'd become like a mother to her. "We'll manage, Minh, we have each other, and it's better than a re-education camp." When the policeman had threatened them with that, Lien had frozen with fear. She had spoken to a neighbour whose son had been sent to one. He'd managed to escape, but couldn't come home because they were looking for him. He now lived a perilous existence on the streets, never knowing when he would be arrested.

"But how will we manage?" Minh was still in shock. Everything she'd worked for over the years had been taken away from her by one stroke of a tyrant's pen.

Chinh watched from a distance and smiled. Having finally found Lien, his first thought had been to show up at the house, but then he'd thought about it more carefully. Lien was probably still angry about the bomb. It would be much better to wait until she was in a position where she was so desperate that she would be delighted to see him. He looked at the children and frowned. Obviously, the boys were the sons of the American, but who was the girl? She looked Vietnamese. There was no record of her marrying anyone, he'd checked. Chinh shrugged. It didn't matter, anyway. All that was important was that Lien was free to marry him.

Omaha, Nebraska

"Kurt Jackson. Who's this?" He hadn't recognised the number, although he did know the area code.

"You don't know me, I'm a friend of Jim Bonner. I think you know him too?"

Kurt's face lit up. "Yes, I do. Do you know where he is? I've been looking for him for months."

"He's in the Bronx, my bar to be precise. He's out cold now, but he's drinking real heavy and I'm worried about him."

"Give me the address and I'll drive down. I'm in Nebraska, so it'll be late tomorrow. Can you keep him there?"

"I doubt it, not when he wakes up. Do you want me to tell him you're coming?"

Kurt thought for a moment. "No, best not or he might disappear again. Is he likely to carry on drinking when he comes round?"

"Maybe, I suppose I could suggest it, but that seems a bit counter-productive."

"He probably will anyway, so just give him whatever it takes to keep him there. I'll pay when I get there."

Lewis smiled. "It's not the money, Kurt. He doesn't recognise people when he's drunk, it's like he's somewhere else. I'm scared of him when he's like that, to be honest."

Kurt took a breath. He knew exactly where Jim was, but he couldn't explain, not without having to face his own demons. "Yeah, he's back in 'Nam. I'll be there as soon as I can, ok?"

Kurt replaced the receiver and telephoned Spanner to tell him he'd found Jim and was on his way to collect him.

Omaha, Nebraska

"I'm sorry, Rachel, that must have been awful for you." Spanner was holding her hand across the table. Rachel's story had been so harrowing that for the first time that day he'd forgotten about Jim and whether Kurt had arrived in time to find him.

"I'm only telling you because I find it hard to… to be intimate because of it, and I don't want you wasting your time on me." Rachel felt strangely better after telling him about the rape and her treatment by the police and her parents. She hadn't mentioned Charles by name, because she didn't want Spanner feeling he needed to do anything if they ever bumped into him. It was unlikely, but now Charles was back in Omaha and working in the hospital it was always possible. Rachel hadn't mentioned Jamie and their ongoing quest to find justice either, because she didn't see the need.

Spanner squeezed her hand. "We don't need to do anything you don't want to, Rachel. We'll just take this at a pace you can cope with. It's you I want to get to know. Yes, I want to make love to you, but that's just a small part of loving you, so please don't worry."

Rachel stared at him in surprise and Spanner smiled. "Surely you must have guessed that I am in love with you?"

"No – I mean, I know you like me, but…"

He sighed. "You don't feel the same. then? It's alright,

you don't have to answer. Hopefully in time you will come to love me too."

Rachel took his hand again and smiled into his eyes. "I don't need to wait, Spanner. I think I already love you too." It was true – at least, she presumed this was love. It was certainly a feeling she'd never had before, not even for Martin.

Dong Bang, Tay Ninh province, Vietnam

"Please don't cry, Minh, we will manage." Lien had no idea how exactly they'd manage, but since the order to leave Minh had cried continuously and was barely eating. Now they had arrived at Dong Bang, Lien was terrified she would give up and die. "I need you, Minh," she pleaded. "I can't do this on my own, not with three children."

"We'll help, Mẹ." An tried to move one of the bags into the hut, but he couldn't even lift it.

Lien smiled through her own tears. "Dung, help An carry the bags from the cart, we need to get everything inside before dark." Her spirits had sunk when they'd arrived at Dong Bang – there was nothing there except mountains, trees and a few huts. Although being back in the country had briefly reminded her of her own village, there was none of the comfortable familiarity she remembered from her childhood. There was no market either, and Lien was grateful they'd stocked up on as much food as they could carry, even though the government had promised to provide food for three months. She had no idea how they were going to get more from the local town once that ran out, as they had used all their savings to survive since the end of the war. It would be months before they could eat anything they had grown, and first they had to cut down trees and clear the area of stones.

She helped the children move the last of their possessions into the hut and sent the boys out to collect twigs and branches so they could light a fire to cook. The heat and humidity were oppressive, and Lien was grateful that it wouldn't be long before they were in July and the weather would be more pleasant, although the lack of rain would make it harder to grow food. The rice was soon cooking on the fire, and Lien gazed into the flames. Perhaps she should have taken them all back to her village outside Da Nang instead. It would be another hard journey, but they would never survive here. She would talk to Minh in the morning when they'd all had some sleep. Perhaps things would look better in the morning.

Omaha, Nebraska

"I can't believe you two know each other." Jamie was staring at Rachel in astonishment. "Spanner is my oldest friend."

Rachel paled and looked at him in consternation. "I told him about the rape, but I didn't tell him Charles's name or that you are helping me."

"Why not? Spanner's the straightest guy I know. He would agree with what we're doing."

"But then I have to tell him that bastard's name. And what happens if we meet him somewhere? Spanner is starting to move in higher circles now; he could come across Charles when he's trying to raise money and help for Vietnam veterans. Spanner isn't the sort of guy to say nothing, is he? What if he attacks Charles? It could ruin everything we're trying to do."

Jamie bit his lip. He didn't like the idea of lying to Spanner, but Rachel was right. If Spanner knew the name of the man who'd raped her and gone unpunished, there was a chance he would go after him. "Ok, I won't say anything. When we bump into each other, as we will at some point, I'll pretend we've just met. I'm not happy about it, though." Jamie sighed. He also wasn't happy that Rachel was out of reach again, not that he'd ever really stood a chance. He knew Rachel didn't feel anything for him other than friendship, but he couldn't help his own emotions.

CHAPTER TWENTY-EIGHT

Omaha, Nebraska

Jim had been sober for several weeks now, and Kurt was beginning to think they might be getting somewhere, but he was permanently on edge, knowing his friend could fall off the waggon at any time. His own demons were perilously near the surface, the strain of watching Jim all the time wearing on him. Spanner had helped as much as he could, but because neither man would talk about their flashbacks and he hadn't been with them at the worst part, he couldn't do very much except employ Jim alongside Kurt and try and keep an eye on both of them.

"Is everything ok, Steve? You've been very distant." Rachel looked up to find him staring out of the window.

Spanner gave a tired smile. "Yes, I'm fine, love. Sorry. I'm just concerned about Kurt and Jim."

Rachel hesitated before saying what was on her mind. "I guess it's to do with Vietnam? Something that happened to them?"

Spanner nodded. "Yes. It was after I was injured, so I

wasn't there. But neither of them will talk about it, so I can't help."

"Perhaps we need to set up some kind of organisation that can help heal the minds of veterans?"

Spanner frowned and shook his head. "If we do that, people will think all Vietnam veterans are mad. It won't help their cause at all."

"But it's not their fault. Their minds are no different from their bodies. If they are physically injured they get help; so why not if their minds are wounded?"

Spanner looked increasingly agitated. "No! Maybe in the future people will be more understanding, but at the present time they don't want to know."

"People aren't going to be more understanding unless we bring it to their attention. They have to realise there's a problem among veterans that is caused by their military service and that it's no different from a physical injury. By not doing anything, we're just hiding the situation." Rachel pressed on, unable to see why Steve didn't agree with her.

"Sorry, Rachel, you could be right, but we have a hard enough job now without trying to change the public's perception of mental illness."

Rachel took in the stubborn set of Steve's jaw and decided to give up. She would try again later, because she was sure she was right. She just had to find a way of bringing Steve round to her point of view.

Dong Bang, Tay Ninh province, Vietnam

"Chinh?" Lien gaped at the man in the doorway. He was the last person she was expecting to see. He looked the same, his People's Army Vietnam (PAVN) uniform just as smart as she remembered, although it now had a shoulder board and she could see he had a higher rank than before.

She was suddenly conscious of how she must look after two months in the so-called New Economic Zone. She was thin and worn out, her hair unkempt, her clothes tattered and torn. "Is Phuc with you?" She was still furious with her brother, and she doubted she would ever forgive him for ruining her happiness, but she couldn't help asking after him.

"No, he's back in Ho Chi Minh City. I've been looking everywhere for you."

Lien suddenly remembered he was probably the one who'd given the order to blow up the bar and her expression changed. "Why?"

"Because I wanted to make sure you were alright, of course. I did look for you in Da Nang when our glorious forces took the city, I wanted to tell everyone that you were one of our people so you didn't get into trouble for being friends with the Americans. But I couldn't find you."

Lien stared at him, wondering what he really wanted. "You deserted me when I was pregnant and couldn't find another job. I ended up on the streets. Where were you then?"

Chinh felt his anger rise up. How dare she speak to him like that? He would have liked nothing better than to put her in her place, but if he lost his temper and hit her, she wouldn't do what he wanted. Instead, he managed to look shamefaced. "I'm sorry, Lien. I behaved disgracefully. I was jealous that you were having a child with the American."

Lien looked confused. "Jealous?"

"Yes. You must know that I like you, Lien. I have always liked you."

Lie didn't answer. Her brother's words about how Chinh had lied to her just so he could sleep with her were clear in her mind. She glanced behind him and saw the soldiers and guessed he was still important. It wouldn't do to upset him, but if he cared that much he wouldn't have left her to fend for herself. "Then why didn't you help me? Why did you leave me?"

Chinh clenched his fists but kept his expression calm. "As I said I was jealous, and I behaved badly. I'm here to put that right now."

"How?"

"Do you like it here?" Chinh ignored her question.

Lien gave a harsh laugh. "It's awful. There is no rain at the moment, so it's hard to get the crops to grow. We are all slowly starving because the help the government promised has not materialised. Our children work in the fields all day and can't go to school because there is none, and even if there was, we couldn't afford to pay for it."

Chinh looked suitably shocked, even though that was exactly what he had hoped she would say. "Then come back to Ho Chi Minh City with me," he said.

Lien fought to master her rising panic and confusion. "I can't leave my children, or Minh. She looked after me when I had no one."

"They can come back with you, of course."

Lien fought to keep her frustration out of her voice. "How would we live? We have no money, and I would not be able to get work because of the children."

Chinh waved a hand. "You don't need to worry about any of that, Lien. You can marry me, and then your children will be protected, and they can go to school."

"Marry you?" Lien nearly fell over in shock. She couldn't think of anything she wanted to do less – other than starve or work herself into an early grave leaving her children to fend for themselves.

"Is the idea so bad?" Chinh had clenched his fists again at her reaction.

Lien shook her head, suddenly realising that this could be a way out of the mess they were in. It meant she would have to endure his caresses, but perhaps she could close her eyes and pretend it was Spanner… "No, it was just a shock." She gave a wry smile and indicated her appearance. "I am not the girl you knew."

Chinh relaxed slightly. "You soon will be if you marry me. Imagine being looked after, Lien. No more slaving in the fields."

"And the children?" Lien still hadn't explained that Dung wasn't hers.

"They can come with us, of course." Chinh's eyes narrowed slightly. "I can see the boys are the American's, but who is the girl's father?"

Lien was about to explain that he was wrong when she realised this was the perfect chance for Vy at least to have a normal life without the disadvantage of having an American father. "I met a man in Da Nang while I was working in Minh's shop. He was killed before we could marry, which was why we moved to Saigon… Ho Chi Minh City, I mean." She held her breath. It wouldn't help An if he believed her, but at least she wouldn't have to worry about Vy anymore.

"Ah, I see." Chinh relaxed slightly. At least the girl wasn't Amerasian. He would pretend to accept the boys until they were married; then he would drive them out. The girl could stay. She looked like she would be pretty like her mother. If he ever got bored with Lien, he could always amuse himself with the daughter instead.

Omaha, Nebraska

Rachel returned Spanner's kiss with increasing passion. His hands moved over her breasts, and for a brief moment she was back in the tennis club. She froze, and Spanner immediately stopped.

"Sorry… I just…" she stammered.

"It's ok, if you want to stop you just have to say."

Rachel took a breath. She was determined to sleep with him and not let Charles spoil this for her. "No, I don't want to stop." She was sure if she could do it once with Spanner the bad memories would fade, and then everything would be alright.

Spanner resumed kissing her gently. It was Rachel who moved his hand back to her breast, and this time she found herself enjoying his touch. He lay her back on the settee and began stroking her legs. He was so gentle that she barely noticed his hand working its way up her legs until she felt his fingers on her panties, and again she pulled back, her breath coming in short gasps. Spanner immediately stopped. "Rachel, we don't have to go any further. This is beautiful, you laying here, my hands touching your breasts. Let's just enjoy the moment, alright?"

Rachel nodded, relief flooding her body. Then she sighed. "I was so determined…"

"We can go a little further each time, but not until you are comfortable with everything we do. I told you, it's not about sex, it's about loving you, and I don't need to be inside you to do that." He smiled down and tried to ignore the intense desire that was flooding his body. He wanted so much to make love to her, but he was determined not to push her too fast.

Rachel kissed him back and wondered how long it would be before she could let him go all the way. She'd never reached that point with Martin, they'd not had enough time. After his death she'd regretted not sleeping with him, but now she didn't. Now she was glad that she had saved herself for Steve. As long as he didn't get fed up waiting.

Dong Bang, Tay Ninh province, Vietnam

"How do you know him?" Minh watched Lien's face carefully. Lien had not told her very much about her past, other than her relationship with the American and how it had been destroyed when her brother had blown up the bar she worked in.

Lien sighed. She didn't really want to relive everything that had led up to the explosion, but Minh deserved some kind of explanation, especially if Lien decided to go ahead and accept Chinh's offer. Minh would be living with them, after all. "He was a VC commander near Da Nang. It was he who got me the job in the bar and wanted me to be friendly with the Americans, and he ordered the bombing."

Minh frowned. "Why would he do that if you were collecting information for him?"

Lien shrugged. "I think he thought I was getting too close to Spanner." It felt strange saying his name out loud again, and it brought back memories that she thought she'd buried.

"So what are you going to do?"

"I don't want to marry him, but what option do I have? If we stay in this godforsaken place we will eventually die. There's no future for the children, they can't even get an education. If we go back to Ho Chi Minh City they can go to school, the boys will be protected because of Chinh's status and Vy can live a normal life." She had already told her that Chinh had mistaken Dung for An's brother. She smiled at Minh. "And you will have an easier life."

Minh didn't answer for a moment. "But what about you? You will have to share his bed, be his property, do as he commands." She thought for a moment. "I am an old woman, Lien, do not do this for me. I can see it would be a better life for the children, but if you don't love him it will be hard for you."

Lien looked away. "My heart is frozen now anyway, Minh. It died when Spanner didn't contact me. At least this way the children will have some kind of future."

"When is he coming back?"

"In the next couple of days. I have to decide by then." Lien fell silent as she thought about her options. The thought of sharing a bed with Chinh made her shudder, but what choice did she really have? If she refused him, she had a feeling their already precarious existence would grow worse.

Omaha, Nebraska

Rachel closed the front door and walked slowly back into the living room. Another failure. She was surprised and grateful that Spanner was so patient. If she'd been him, she would have given up on her by now. They were progressing slowly, but she still hadn't managed to *go all the way*. Rachel grimaced; such a horrible expression, and one that was starting to seem like an unconquerable mountain.

She poured herself another glass of wine and thought back to Martin. They had seen so little of each other that sex had not really reared its ugly head. Perhaps it would have been better if it had – then maybe she would have been over her fear and not struggling so much now.

She walked upstairs to her bedroom and opened the closet where she kept all the boxes of evidence Jamie had given her. She reached underneath and pulled out the small diary from the brief time she had spent with Martin and began reading.

January 1971
Martin spent the weekend here and we discussed our plans for the cause. It's the first time we've seen each other since the march, our only contact has been by letter. I'm enjoying his company, but I'm not sure about some of his ideas, he seems to be much angrier than when I first met him. He kissed me but didn't try to do anything else, which was good because I'm not sure I am ready for anything more, not yet anyway. He is very good with Richie. He would make a good father if he wasn't so obsessed with getting revenge on the government.

February 1971
I don't know what to do. Martin is talking about planting bombs in politicians' offices to make them take notice of us. I argued that we were supposed to be protesting peacefully and he said where has that got us? He's right, but I don't see how killing people is going to make our point any better. Perhaps I should stop seeing him. It's only once a month, but what if he does something stupid and gets arrested? I can't afford to be involved. What would happen to Richie if I went to prison? Jenny thinks he has a screw loose. I don't think he has, but I do think something happened to him while he was in Vietnam that has affected his judgement. I will keep trying to talk him out of anything violent, but I am really worried. I think I will talk to Jamie and see what he thinks.

I didn't tell Jamie Martin's name or anything about him, just that it was someone I knew. He thinks I should report him and stop seeing him. But I couldn't do that, because a part of me understands why Martin is so angry. We have been peacefully protesting for years and not getting anywhere. But if Martin gets his way, veterans will be treated even worse than they are now. People already spit at us in the street and shout at us when we are out together where he lives, and we have been refused entry to restaurants and some shops because he is a veteran. That kind of thing is making him more and more angry and I don't know what to do to help him. If only the army could offer him some help, but they don't seem to want to know. The only good thing is that he never wants sex so I don't have to worry about that. Although there are times when I wish he would, maybe he would be less angry if we slept together. Even smoking dope doesn't calm him down.

March 1971

Martin was very quiet this weekend, I am sure he is planning something bad but he won't talk about it. He disappeared out four times over the weekend without telling me where he was going and barely had time for Richie. I saw one of his friends and he looked just as angry as Martin, he glared at me and then they went out. I haven't seen him before, he's not one of those who I met on the march. When they came back Martin was much happier though, and he even wanted to kiss me.

Oh God. Someone sent a bomb to the local senator's office and two people were hurt when they opened it. I can't help thinking that Martin was involved and eventually I asked him. He just laughed and said he wished he had been. I don't believe him.

I wrote to Martin today and told him it was over. I didn't want to, but I have Richie to think of. I feel so sad, as if my heart is broken, but I know I have done the right thing.

April 1971

There was a massive explosion in West Virginia today and several people were killed and injured. It was in a factory that made uniforms for soldiers. My heart is pounding as I am terrified this is something to do with Martin. Then I tell myself not to be so stupid. I can only pray I am wrong.

I am in shock and absolutely furious. Jamie came round to see me. He had followed me to find out who the man was and reported him to the local police. I understand he was just doing his job but to follow me! But even worse my darling Martin is dead, shot dead by the FBI yesterday while attempting to plant another bomb in the local government offices. He only did those things because no one would listen. I don't know what to do, the only person I can talk to is Jenny and I can't tell her everything, she'll be horrified. I have told her that Martin is dead though. She says I was lucky I finished with him when I did, and I know she's right. But what if the police want to talk to me? I can't tell them all the things he told me, about how he wanted to kill politicians can I? But how can I lie to them?

Rachel closed the book and replaced it carefully back under the boxes. She knew she should probably get rid of it, but it wasn't likely to be important to anyone now. Martin was dead, and she had waited apprehensively for the FBI to visit her. But nothing had happened, so she'd eventually allowed herself to relax and grieve for Martin and the person she'd almost become. She had eventually forgiven Jamie, but not herself. If she hadn't mentioned him to Jamie, he might still be alive, although she now realised he would have killed more people if he hadn't been stopped, and God only knew where she would have ended up. If only she had done something to stop him, to divert him from that self-destructive path. Rachel sighed. Jamie had told her there was nothing she could have done, and maybe he was right. That didn't stop her feeling sad and guilty, though.

Dong Bang, Tay Ninh province, Vietnam

Chinh waited in the forest and watched Minh leave the house. He called one of his soldiers over to him and whispered some instructions. The soldier nodded and disappeared. Chinh sat back and waited for Lien to appear. He had thought hard about the old woman and decided she would just be a nuisance. Not only would he have to support her, but she would be someone Lien could turn to if she wasn't happy. That would never to do. Lien should be totally reliant on him and no one else, so Minh had to go. She was old anyway, no use to the state. Her death wouldn't matter.

Half an hour later the soldier returned, Minh's lifeless body over his shoulder. Chinh smiled and indicated Lien's hut. The two men walked over to it and Chinh knocked on the door.

Lien opened it almost immediately and stared in horror. "No... *Minh*!"

"My soldier found her on the edge of one of the fields. It would seem she's had a heart attack." The soldier laid Minh on the ground. Lien knelt down beside her and leant over the lifeless body, tears streaming down her face. Minh's face was pale, her eyes closed, the life gone. Lien sobbed softly. Without Minh she would have starved, her children would never have been born, Dung would never have been rescued. Lien had no idea what she was going to do without her; now was truly all alone.

"I'm sorry. I will help you bury her." Chinh sounded very respectful, and Lien momentarily forgot her animosity toward him. She nodded and wiped her eyes before getting slowly to her feet.

"Thank you. Will you wait with her while I tell the children?" She walked back inside, closing the door behind her. Chinh scowled. That wasn't how he had expected the conversation to go. He had thought Lien would give him the opportunity to comfort her, not dismiss him and shut the door. But now was not the time to get annoyed. When she was married to him, Lien would treat him with respect. He took a breath and glanced down at the body. "Take her to the cemetery and start digging a grave. We'll be there in a minute." Fortunately, he had a higher rank than the man running the economic zone, so no one would question his orders or insist on a post-mortem. It wouldn't do for Lien to find out the old woman had been strangled. Not yet, anyway.

CHAPTER TWENTY-NINE

Omaha, Nebraska

Spanner licked his lips nervously and glanced across the table at Rachel, who was eating her soup. He had been planning this night for ages and now it was here, he was nervous. What if she said no?

"Are you ok?" Rachel was feeling equally uneasy. She could sense the tension in the air, and she was worried Spanner had grown tired of her. She wouldn't blame him if he had; she still hadn't managed to sleep with him. Perhaps he was fed up of waiting and wanted to end their relationship, but didn't know how to tell her.

Spanner nodded, then shook his head. "No, no I'm not. You know how I feel about you, don't you?"

"Even though I'm the world's most useless girlfriend?" Rachel put her spoon down and looked at the table.

Spanner frowned. "What do you mean?" There was a pause as he processed her words. "Oh… that."

"If you want to end it, I'll understand." She could hardly get the words out.

Spanner looked at her in shock. "Do you want to finish with me?"

Rachel shook her head. "No, of course not, but I'm not much good to you, am I?"

"Oh, for goodness' sake, Rachel, I've told you that isn't important," Spanner snapped, then took a breath. This was hardly the way he had envisaged proposing to her, but if he didn't say something soon...

Rachel stood up and picked up her handbag, fighting back tears. There was no point prolonging the agony. "I'm sorry, Spanner, I love you so much, but..."

"Will you marry me?" Spanner interrupted loudly, so loudly that the people at the next table looked up in surprise.

Rachel stopped and stared at him. "Marry you...?"

Spanner was suddenly aware that people were watching, and he wished the ground would open up and swallow him, especially as it looked like she was going to say no. He opened his mouth to say something, anything to persuade her that he loved her, but Rachel spoke first.

"You really want me to marry you?"

"Yes, goddamnit!"

Rachel started laughing, at first in relief and then with sheer joy. "Of course I will."

The sudden round of applause from the other diners in the restaurant caught them both by surprise, and Rachel blushed. Spanner laughed, and standing up, he took a quick bow before taking her roughly in his arms and kissing her.

The applause grew louder, although neither Rachel nor Spanner noticed, and then the head waiter was standing by the table with some champagne. "On the house, sir."

Spanner smiled down at Rachel and then turned to the other diners. "Thank you. I wanted my proposal to be different, but I never imagined it would be like this." There was a roar of laughter. Spanner beckoned the waiter. "I'll certainly never forget this night. Please will you all join me in toasting our future happiness? Waiter – champagne all round, please!"

Re-education Centre Outside Ho Chi Minh City, Vietnam

Phuc smiled at his reflection in the mirror. His new uniform, reed-green in colour and made from loosely woven cotton, with its shoulder boards and the thin loop belt from which hung his pistol, was extremely smart to his eyes. He wished Lien could be there to see how far he had come. He could hardly contain his impatience as he waited for Chinh to come back from Tay Ninh province. He couldn't believe that Chinh had finally found his sister after so many years. His thoughts went back to the day of the bombing, the last time Lien had spoken to him. He could clearly remember her fury when she realised what he'd done, but he hadn't expected her rage to last so long. He'd been sure she would get over her anger, so it had been a terrible shock to realise that Lien seemed to actually hate him and might never forgive him. On the one occasion he had tried to contact her after that fateful day, she'd raged at him that she was pregnant and that he'd left her children fatherless. Phuc had been so taken aback that he couldn't even think of the words to defend himself. Lien had taken advantage of the silence to hammer home her disgust with him and then told him she never wanted to see him or Chinh ever again.

Phuc's smile faded. What if she still felt the same way? She might tell Chinh to go away, and then he would never see her again. If Chinh was rejected, there was little chance he would tell Phuc where his sister was. Even now he wouldn't tell him, insisting that Phuc wait until he brought her back to Ho Chi Minh City. Phuc took a deep breath and tried to control his concern. Hopefully he was wrong, but until Chinh came back he wouldn't know, so there was no point worrying.

The knock on the door interrupted his thoughts. "Come!"

"Sir, there are some more prisoners coming in."

Phuc nodded. He had been in charge of the re-education camp for just over six weeks now, promoted after a mass escape under the previous commander. He was very proud of his new role in the PAVN. Re-education camps were not prisons, but institutions for those whom the state considered deserving of rehabilitation through education and socially constructive labour. His role was to monitor the political attitudes, work production records and general behaviour of those sent there, so they would return to help rebuild the country that years of war had virtually destroyed. Chinh had explained to Phuc that the country was bankrupt, because not only had the Americans frozen all $150 billion of Vietnamese assets in the US, they had also stopped Americans from sending money to support their children in Vietnam. Even more damaging, they had refused to pay the billions of dollars of reparations Nixon and Kissinger had promised and which the new Vietnamese government had been relying on. Thus his job was very important, as the more people they could get back to work helping rebuild, the quicker the country could recover.

There were three types of camps: short-term, long-term and permanent. Short-term re-education camps were normally 30-day courses that allowed detainees to go home at night and consisted of lectures teaching people to unlearn the old ways and learn about socialism. Level two camps lasted six months, and the detainees had to stay on the camp and provide their own food, although security was minimal; people could wander off, although they risked re-arrest and a stricter sentence.

Long-term re-education camps were the most prevalent and were for more educated individuals who were needed by the state. Phuc's camp was level three, a socialist reform camp. Its purpose was incarceration, indoctrination and forced labour, with sentences generally lasting three to five years. Phuc smiled as he remembered Chinh explaining that many of the inmates were educators, judges, writers, whom the government wanted to keep isolated from the rest of society, in case they used their influence to stir up opposition. They were unlikely to be released when their sentences were up – unless they were broken down enough to comply in educating the public about the glory of the communist party – but that was for the future. Many would die anyway from lack of food and medicine. His job was to ensure there were no more escapes, that those who were a threat to society were kept away from others and that the forced labour benefitted the country. He looked quickly through the paperwork of the new detainees – a couple of judges and a teacher – and ordered them to be brought in. This was his favourite part. People who once looked down on him were now reliant on his every whim, and Phuc loved his new power. The only thing missing was Lien.

Omaha, Nebraska

"I can't believe you've lied to me all this time." Emily's face was the colour of chalk. She'd never expected Mark to go behind her back, so to find out he'd been supporting Rachel for five years was a complete shock. Even worse, she'd found out from someone she disliked intensely. The woman had taken great pleasure in saying she had seen Mark with Rachel and another man in a restaurant.

Mark was perfectly calm. "I'm sorry I lied to you,

Emily, but I'm not sorry I've been seeing my daughter and grandson. Don't you think it's time you put this feud behind you? Rachel has done really well despite everything that happened to her, and her fiancé is a successful businessman. Why don't you come with us and congratulate her?"

"Us?"

Mark took a breath. "Paul and his friend have also been in contact with Rachel. It was Paul who found Rachel her job with the Democrats." He waited for the explosion.

"Paul and his *friend*?" Emily was no longer pale; her face was blotched red with fury. "You mean to say he's still seeing men after all the trouble we went to to keep him out of prison?" Emily shook her head in disbelief. "Sodomy is still a crime in this state, or had you forgotten?"

"No, I hadn't, but if he's discreet there won't be a problem." Mark was beginning to regret mentioning Paul's friend. He should have just said that Paul was visiting Rachel. He leant towards her, his eyes cold. "I hope you aren't going to cause our son a problem?"

"Of course not." Emily had no intention of getting Paul into trouble, but his *friend* was a different matter. But first she would have to pretend she wanted to see Rachel, or she wouldn't know who that friend was. "I know Rachel had a boy, Richard."

Mark raised an eyebrow. "She calls him Richie. Unfortunately, he looks just like his father… the man who raped our daughter."

Emily gasped, but Mark didn't give her a chance to argue. "He's the image of Charles Peterson, there's no doubting his parentage, so don't bother to try and say different."

"I was trying to protect you," she said, after a tense pause.

Mark shrugged. "Maybe. But we should have supported Rachel. Not tried to bully her into having an abortion."

"I only did what I thought was right for her. I didn't want her saddled with a child, being labelled..."

Mark cut her off. "The world has changed, Emily, and fortunately for Rachel it still is changing. A lot of people don't think that much about having children out of wedlock nowadays, including Spanner. That's his name by the way, or did you already know?"

Emily shook her head. Her so-called friend had delighted in telling her how the Steve Tanner who'd been all over the papers with his crusade for Vietnam veterans a few months earlier had proposed to Rachel in the crowded restaurant. Emily didn't know how she felt about Steve Tanner's cause. Personally, she couldn't care less about Vietnam veterans, but it did seem that he was a successful businessman who was making good money. It wasn't the life she'd wanted for Rachel, but it was better than her daughter deserved after everything she'd done to sabotage her own future. Perhaps it wasn't too late to salvage some of her plans for Rachel after all.

"So! Are you coming to meet them both or not?"

Emily took a breath and made a decision. She couldn't

run Rachel's life if she wasn't a part of it. "Yes, you're right. It's time we put this behind us and worked for our future."

Mark frowned. That wasn't quite what he meant. He shrugged. At least she was going to see Rachel, which meant he wouldn't have to sneak around anymore.

Ho Chi Minh City, Vietnam

The city hadn't changed much, but it was a welcome relief to be back in a crowded metropolis and away from the tiny hut in hell. Lien was still missing Minh, and the children didn't understand and kept asking for her. Lien blinked back tears; if only the woman who had become like an adopted mother to her hadn't died. She had no one to talk to about Chinh. Her instincts told her not to marry him, but her need for stability, for a safer future for her children, was telling her something different. So far he had been invaluable, finding her a small flat she could afford with the small amount of money she had left, and bringing her some furniture. She finished pouring the tea, handed Chinh a cup and sat down opposite him.

"Have you made a decision yet?" Chinh sipped his tea, his eyes boring into hers.

Lien looked at him and swallowed nervously. She could feel the sweat forming on her palms as she considered saying no. "I am very honoured that you would want to marry me."

Chinh's eyes narrowed. "Is that a yes, then?"

Lien managed a smile. "I would like to ask my brother's permission first; now that I know he is alive." It was the only delaying tactic Lien could think of.

Chinh relaxed. For a moment he had been sure she was going to say no, and he had felt his anger rising. "Of course. That won't be difficult. He's not far away." Lien's face lit up. Whatever her brother had done in the past, she needed his support now. "I'll arrange it," Chinh continued. Perhaps he had been wrong. Lien had seemed genuinely pleased to know her brother was quite close. "Once you have Phuc's blessing, I will begin making the arrangements. I will have to start with the paperwork. I will need a family book, your parents' names, and other family members, as far back as you can remember, so the state can verify you are a good person for me to marry. Phuc can help you with that." He took another sip of his tea, deep in thought. "Do the children have birth certificates?"

Lien hesitated. She couldn't produce the two she did have because it would show An and Vy were the twins. She would have to lie and then destroy their birth certificates. "They all have my surname. I did have all their birth certificates, but I have looked everywhere, and they have gone; I have lost them, they are not with my other paperwork."

Chinh frowned, then waved it away. "I am sure it will not be a problem." He would have to get all the children birth certificates before the wedding. He finished the last of his tea and stood up. "I will arrange for you to visit your brother."

"Thank you." Lien watched him leave, closed her eyes and tried to ignore the heavy feeling in her heart. Despite her intense misgivings, and unless Phuc could save her, it looked like her destiny was to marry Chinh.

Omaha, Nebraska

Rachel gave her mother a tentative smile. Her father had insisted on this meeting, or she would have refused. "Mother."

"Rachel, you're looking very well. And this must be Richard?" Emily stared at Richie and almost gasped. Mark was right. He did look exactly like Charles Peterson.

"Richie," Rachel corrected. She took his hand and pushed him gently forward. "Richie, say hello to your grandmother."

"Hello, Grandma. I am very pleased to meet you." Richie held out his hand.

Emily got over her shock and found herself smiling. "Hi, Richie. You are such a big boy!"

"I'm five next week. Are you coming to my birthday party?"

"I think that probably depends on your mother, but I would love to."

"Mom, can grandma come to my party?"

Rachel hid her exasperation and nodded. "Yes, of

course she can."

"Thank you. I'll look forward to it," Emily smiled

Rachel glanced at her watch. "We'd better go if we're not going to be late. Steve said he would meet us at the restaurant."

Emily looked slightly puzzled. "I thought his name was Spanner."

Rachel grinned. "Everyone calls him that, but I prefer to call him Steve."

"Spanner is much better!" Richie piped up and Rachel ruffled his hair.

"Do you like Spanner, Richie?" Emily asked as they climbed into the car.

"He's ace," Richie smiled. "He lets me sit in the driving seat and he said he'll teach me all about engines when I grow up."

"Really? That sounds nice, dear." Emily didn't sound particularly convinced. "Probably more fun learning to drive, though, than getting all dirty." She winked at him and Richie smiled.

"I think Grandma is right, don't you, Mom? I don't really like the smell of the engine."

Rachel gave an inward sigh. Her mother was already sticking her nose in. "I think it's a very good idea for Richie to know how things work, Mother. Steve is a very talented mechanic, he worked on loads of military vehicles and helicopters when he was in Vietnam."

"Oh, he's a Vietnam veteran then?" Emily's tone said exactly what she thought of that.

Rachel felt her temper rising. "Yes, Mother, and before you say anything else, he didn't choose to go, he was sent by the politicians you voted for."

"Have you agreed on a date for the wedding yet, Rachel?" Mark interrupted. Their eyes met in the driving mirror and Rachel gave a weary smile.

"No, Pop, we're going to decide today, but we're probably looking at next April. That's six months away, so plenty of time to plan. That will be alright with you guys, won't it?"

Emily looked horrified. "I need much longer to arrange it than that, Rachel. There's the wedding dress to be made, bridesmaids to choose, the venue to hire, invitation lists to write, then the invitations have to go out, we need to make sure the date doesn't clash with anything else or..."

"Mother!" Rachel interrupted Emily's monologue. "We aren't having a big wedding, just something small and intimate, close family and friends."

"But you can't –"

"I can do what I want, Mother. It's my wedding day, and this is what Steve and I want."

"Mark? Are you ok with this? Don't you want your daughter to have a big day?"

"Of course I do, honey, but it's up to Rachel and Spanner to decide." Mark tried to think of a way of changing the subject again, but then realised they were almost at the restaurant. He breathed a sigh of relief. "Anyway, you can talk to Spanner yourself – we're here now."

CHAPTER THIRTY

Re-education Centre Outside Ho Chi Minh City, Vietnam

"You understand what you have to do?" Chinh's eyes bore into his.

Phuc nodded. He would agree to anything to see Lien, even telling her that marrying Chinh was the right thing to do. For a moment, Phuc felt uncomfortable – then he pushed his conscience to one side. Going against what Chinh wanted would not only be stupid, it would be very dangerous. While he had the ability to help them both, he also had the power to make their lives miserable. "Yes, of course, not that it will be necessary. I am sure she can't wait to marry you."

Chinh nodded. "It would be madness to want to be on her own with three young children." He turned around and headed out of the office.

Phuc paced up and down the office, grimacing nervously while he waited for Chinh to fetch Lien. What if she hadn't forgiven him for killing the American? What if she really didn't want to marry Chinh? Her decision would affect him.

He liked being in charge of the re-education centre and would never forgive Lien if she ruined his life as well as her own. At first he wondered why Chinh had decided to bring Lien to the camp to see him; it would have been much nicer to have met her somewhere more private. Now he realised it was a subtle threat. If she didn't accept his proposal of marriage, she could find herself and her children in somewhere like this. Now he thought about it, Phuc realised her children must be Amerasian, so Lien needed Chinh's protection.

The door opened so suddenly he jumped. Lien stepped slowly inside, followed closely by the three children. Phuc took in the two boys' appearance and knew immediately that they were Spanner's children. Behind them came a young girl and he breathed a sigh of relief. At least she looked Vietnamese. "Lien… it's wonderful to see you again. I have missed you so much." He reached out his arms, and after a brief hesitation she stepped toward him.

"Phuc…" She allowed him to hug her and then pulled back. "Chinh said you are in charge here?"

Phuc smiled and nodded, searching for the respect he longed to see in her eyes, but he couldn't see anything except fear. He frowned. "Aren't you proud of me? Of what I've achieved since you last saw me..." He stopped abruptly, wishing he could withdraw the last sentence. The last thing he needed to do was to remind her of why they hadn't spoken for so long, not that she was likely to have forgotten.

"Proud?" Lien looked confused. "It's a prison..."

"No it isn't, it's a re-education centre. People who are sent here can be redeemed from their wrongful ways and be useful to the state. I am very proud to be helping our glorious country get back on its feet after the capitalist war that nearly destroyed us."

Lien stared at him in despair. Obviously Phuc hadn't changed at all. He still believed everything they told him. She could just about remember a time when she was the same. But now, she no longer believed anything anyone told her.

Phuc took a breath and changed the subject. "I am so pleased Chinh found you. We've been looking for you for years."

Lien shrugged. "I left Da Nang and came here to work. Then we were sent to one of the new economic zones, where we starved and worked ourselves to death for nothing."

Phuc winced. That sounded like a criticism of the state. He glanced around nervously, hoping no one had overheard. "You shouldn't say things like that, Lien, people might misunderstand you."

Lien gave a harsh laugh. "Why not, Phuc? There's only us here. Are you going to report me?"

Phuc looked horrified. "Of course not. Look, Lien, I don't want to argue with you. I've waited too long to see you again." He glanced at the children and tried to hide his distaste. "Aren't you going to introduce me?"

Lien had wondered if she should tell her brother the truth about the children, but the conversation so far had proved she couldn't trust him. "These are the twins, An and Dung, and my daughter Vy."

Phuc nodded curtly at the boys and smiled at Vy. He assumed Vy must be big for her age or the boys were small for theirs because they all appeared to be around the same age. He thought back and did the calculations. The boys must be nearly five, and she must be about a year younger. Lien was holding her breath and hoping her brother wouldn't ask the children's ages.

"Chinh has told me he wants to marry you."

Lien breathed a sigh of relief that Phuc had changed the subject. "Yes. What do you think I should do?" There probably wasn't much point asking, as she already knew what his answer would be.

Phuc hesitated. He recalled the expression on Chinh's face, the unspoken threat, all the things he'd seen Chinh do when people crossed him; then he glanced at the children and thought about the people who ended up in his camp. "I don't think you have any choice, Lien."

Lien looked at him sharply, astonished. After everything she'd heard him say over the past few moments, Lien had expected him to be enthusiastic about the marriage. But instead Phuc sounded reluctant, as if he wanted to advise her to do the exact opposite. She took a breath. "It is too dangerous to refuse, isn't it?"

Phuc nodded and glanced around nervously again. He lowered his voice. "Chinh will protect you and the children."

Lien sighed and her heart plummeted. "I'll tell him I have your permission, then." Just as she'd expected, fate had already decreed her future.

Omaha, Nebraska

"Hello Steve, I'm very pleased to meet you." Emily smiled up at the tall man before her. Her eyes roved over his vivid facial scars, and she wondered briefly what on earth her daughter was doing with someone like that.

"Spanner, please. It's lovely to meet you too. Can I call you Emily?" Spanner smiled and Emily forgot her critical thoughts. She could now see exactly why Rachel was attracted to him.

"Yes, of course you can."

Spanner's smile broadened. "I just want you to know that I love your daughter very much and I will always look after her."

"I'm sure you will." Emily found it hard to take her eyes from his.

Rachel smiled to herself. Steve had already charmed her mother. She watched as Emily made an effort and turned to Paul. "Hello Paul." Emily stopped thinking about how attractive Spanner was for a moment and realised there was someone standing with her son.

"Hi Mom, this is Heine Cohen, my friend." Paul smiled slightly nervously at his mother. What if she said something to upset him...?

"I'm very pleased to meet you, Heine." Emily somehow managed to hide her shock behind a smile. She searched frantically for something innocuous to say. "Have you known each other long?"

"I'm pleased to meet you too." Heine started to smile back before he met her eyes and almost took a step back at the fury he saw there. He took a breath and hoped he had imagined it. "It will be 12 years next month."

"12 years?" Emily found it even harder to keep her temper. "My... that's a long time." If he was telling the truth, it meant he had been with Paul when her son had been arrested, although for some reason he seemed to have escaped prosecution. Why? Emily stored that piece of information away for later and tried to concentrate on not losing her temper.

They all sat down, Spanner ordered some drinks and Emily decided to concentrate her attention on him. She needed him to agree to a proper wedding and she wanted to see whether he really was a suitable husband for Rachel. Paul and his *Jewish friend* could wait until later.

Emily watched Paul and his Heine laughing together and clenched her fists. If Paul wasn't careful, he would end up back in prison. What on earth was the matter with him? Couldn't he see how stupid he was being? It was bad enough knowing he was with a man, but a *Jew*? And one who was much older than him too. Obviously, it was the Jew's fault her son had chosen this life – he must have somehow brainwashed Paul into thinking what they were doing was normal. Unfortunately, she had to pretend to like him or she would ruin the opportunity to take charge of her daughter's life again. Emily finished her wine and made a promise to herself. She would accept her son was unnatural, but she would never accept a Jew into their lives.

Omaha, Nebraska

"I can't believe you let her talk you into having a big society wedding, Steve." Rachel was fuming that he'd given in to her mother. "We'd already agreed to have something quiet – now we have to wait until next September." Her mother had done it again. Within a couple of hours of being back in Rachel's life, Emily had taken over.

Spanner looked embarrassed. "To be honest, I'm not actually sure how she did it. One moment I was telling her I wanted something small, the next I was agreeing to the bridal event of the year!" He reached out his arms and pulled her close to him. "I'm really sorry, Rachel. I know you warned me... and I let you down."

He looked so forlorn that Rachel forgot her anger and hugged him back. "I don't suppose it really matters, darling. I suppose it might be quite nice to have a big wedding but, in future, we don't tell my mother anything until it's too late for her to interfere!"

"I'll go along with that." Spanner lifted her chin and gazed into her eyes. "I do love you, Rachel, and I am flattered that you can't wait to marry me."

Rachel smiled up at him. "And I love you."

His lips met hers and Rachel forgot all about her mother's interference.

Rachel lay back on the sofa and smiled up at him. Spanner gazed down into her eyes and smiled back. "Perhaps your mother should interfere more often?"

Rachel laughed. Even thinking about her mother couldn't dampen her happiness. For the first time since that awful night she'd forgotten her fear, there had been no flashbacks and she'd finally consummated their relationship. Steve had been so gentle, so loving, every touch taking her to ecstasy, to a place she hadn't expected. She was finally whole again. "Thank you."

He stroked her face. "What for?"

"For not giving up on me."

"I'll never do that, Rachel." He stared into her eyes. She wasn't the only person who was relieved. Spanner had waited so long to make love to her that he had begun to worry that he wouldn't be able to perform at all. He suddenly smiled. "Good job it's 1975 and not 1875, or we'd have had to wait until next September!"

Rachel laughed. "That would be dreadful." She was still laughing when another thought occurred to her. "Let's hope I don't get pregnant then… ruin all those arrangements my mother is making!" Spanner looked horrified, then he joined in her laughter. Nothing would give him greater pleasure than to know Rachel was pregnant, but it might be better to wait until after the wedding. He didn't want to fall out with Rachel's mother this quickly. Rachel reached up and put her arm around his neck. The thought of getting pregnant was quite exciting, especially imagining the expression of disbelief on her mother's face as Rachel yet again ruined all her plans.

CHAPTER THIRTY-ONE

Hi Chi Minh City, Vietnam, September 1976

"I don't want to go to school." An folded his arms across his chest and glared at Lien.

"Nor do I." Dung stamped his feet.

"But you have to go to school, or you won't learn to read and write." Lien tried to keep her temper. She had given up her freedom and married Chinh so that her children could have a better life, and now An and Dung were both refusing to go to school. "Why don't you want to go?"

"They don't want us there," An said eventually

"They call us names and throw things at us," Dung added.

"It true, Mẹ," Vy joined in. "Not me, I am ok, but the boys… everyone picks on them because they look American."

Lien sighed. She had hoped that being married to Chinh would have stopped that happening. But she should have known it wouldn't be that easy. Lots of schools wouldn't even take Amerasians; this one only had because of Chinh's position in the government. She knelt down and took each of the boys' hands in hers. "You must keep going to school so you can learn things. If the other children make fun of you, you must ignore them and work harder so that you are better than them. If they attack you, then you must protect each other."

There was silence, then An nodded slowly. "Ok, Mẹ." Lien turned to Dung, who glanced at An before nodding too.

"Good. Now off you go, or you will miss the bus – and don't forget your food." Lien watched them leave, swinging their xôi in the small bags, then sat down on the floor and cried.

Omaha, Nebraska

"You haven't told her, then?" Spanner smiled into the phone.

Rachel laughed. "No, I was going to, but in the end it seemed a bit mean. And it's not as if I can't get into the dress. It would have been different if the wedding had been next month."

Spanner glanced at his watch. "I'd better let you finish getting ready then, darling. I'll see you at the church."

"I'm almost ready, thank goodness. Not long now and we'll finally be legal!" Rachel blew him a kiss into the phone and replaced the receiver. She looked at herself in the long mirror and smiled. The wedding dress was full-length ivory silk, with long sleeves embroidered with lace and a silk tulle veil. Rachel had refused to wear white or anything too much resembling a meringue. Instead she had insisted on something she considered tasteful and her mother had found this, which she had to admit was stunning. There was no sign of the early stages of pregnancy.

"You look beautiful, you're positively glowing." Emily stood by the door admiring her daughter.

For once Rachel ignored her mother not knocking first. "Thanks, Mom."

"It's a good job I talked Spanner into having a big wedding, isn't it? You are far too beautiful to hide yourself away."

Rachel bit her tongue, quashed her irritation and smiled. Her mother had put everything into the wedding – it would be ungracious and rude not to show her appreciation. And she didn't want to spoil her own good mood by arguing with her mother. "It's a lovely dress, a wonderful venue and I'm sure it will be a great day."

Emily looked surprised. She had half expected a sarcastic reply. She smiled back in relief. "Yes, it will be. We'll show those democrats how to give a proper wedding."

Rachel bit her tongue, counted to ten so she didn't say anything and then glanced at the clock. "Perhaps you should go to the church now, Mom, make sure everything is ready. I'll go and see if Pop is ready."

"Alright, darling. I'll see you soon." Emily turned to leave, then stopped and looked back. "I am very proud of you Rachel; you look beautiful and I'm sure Spanner is a very good catch. You've turned your life around completely."

Rachel gave a wry smile. Steve had worked his charm on Emily at their first meeting, and by the end of the evening she was completely under his spell. Steve also had more patience than she did, which was good because it hadn't taken very long for her mother to start getting on her nerves.

Rachel took a long look around her old bedroom. She'd given up her flat and moved back in with her parents the week before the wedding. There were lots of memories here; most of the earlier ones were good, but after she'd been raped everything had changed. It felt strange to know she would never be back. Rachel took a breath and went to look for her father.

Ho Chi Minh City

"Why isn't my breakfast ready?"

Lien leapt to her feet. "Sorry, I was..." She stopped, unable to think what to say. If she said the boys were refusing to go to school, he would beat them when they came home. "I was thinking about my parents."

Chinh stepped towards her and grabbed her chin, pulling her closer to him. "Why? You have me now, you don't need anyone else."

Lien winced in pain. "I don't know, they were in my mind."

He stared into her eyes and then let go. "I'll be late, hurry up and get me something to eat."

Lien fought back her tears and hurried to heat up the pho bo she had made earlier. If only she could turn the clock back, she would never have agreed to marry Chinh. Even a re-education camp had to be better than the life she was living now. The boys were as terrified of him as she was; the only one he treated half decently was Vy. Lien wiped away her tears and tried to think of a way out. But nothing came to mind. If she tried to run away, he would soon find her. She had to have papers to move to another area, and even if she could get them, Chinh had so much power he would be able to find her. The only person she had in the world was Phuc, and he wouldn't help, not if it meant upsetting Chinh. She was trapped.

Chinh ate his pho bo quickly, his thoughts on the girl he would be visiting later. Marriage had not been as satisfying as he had expected. He'd soon grown bored of Lien in bed and had slept with a succession of other women since. Although prostitution was officially banned, there were plenty of women who would do what he wanted if he promised not to have them arrested. He was also fed up of supporting the boys and paying for their books and uniforms for school. Unfortunately, he would lose face if they didn't attend school because they were under his protection. If only they were a bit older, he could throw them out... Chinh finished eating and stood up. He would have to find a solution. Maybe if the house wasn't filled with children, Lien would be more interested in him.

Omaha, Nebraska

Emily sat back and smiled. The wedding was a great success: it had made all the newspapers and even the local radio station. The guests had included lots of well-connected people as well as some democrats. She hadn't had much choice about that as Rachel had insisted, but there was still time to work on her daughter's political allegiances. Emily sneered as she thought about the Democrat presidential candidate, the peanut farmer Jimmy Carter. As if he could run the country. Admittedly Gerald Ford wasn't the most exciting candidate they'd ever had, but surely people wouldn't be stupid enough to be taken in by a farmer from Georgia and his running mate!

Her eyes travelled slowly over the guests and came to rest on Paul and the Jew. Despite her best efforts, Paul was still with him. She had tried everything she could think of to separate them, from telling Paul she had seen Heine with other men, to stopping the reporter getting freelance work. But nothing seemed to work. She knew they argued, but they always seemed to get over any disagreements. She would have to find another way.

Re-education Camp Outside Ho Chi Minh City, Vietnam

Phuc finished the last of the paperwork and sat back, a satisfied expression on his face. Of the 14 prisoners up for sentence review, only one was suitable for release. He had increased the sentences of the others after reports of them speaking English, meeting in small groups, fighting and discussing politics and religion. He shook his head. The rules were so clear, he couldn't understand why they kept breaking them. Didn't they want to get out?

He reached for the mail and frowned. That was Lien's writing. He hoped there was nothing wrong. It was ages since he'd seen her; he had thought of visiting her several times but always changed his mind. The last time he had just turned up, Chinh had been very cold and Lien had been on edge the whole time. He had felt very unwelcome. He opened the envelope and read the short note quickly.

Dear Phuc
I wish you would come and visit again. Perhaps during the day when Chinh is at work? The children are all well, but I am very unhappy. I need to speak to you.
Please come, Lien.

Phuc sighed. He had guessed Lien would not be happy with Chinh, but what option had there been? If only she hadn't fallen in love with the American, things might have been different. Phuc thought back even further to when Lien had told the VC about the American patrol and they'd been ambushed. That had been the start. But if the past had been different, he wouldn't be where he was now. Unfortunately, Lien had sown the seeds of her own misery and he couldn't let her drag him down with her. Phuc glanced once more at the letter, screwed it up and threw it in the bin. He was wise to keep his distance – Chinh was bound to know if he visited Lien. He shuddered. She would have to sort her own problems out without his help. Chinh was much too powerful to upset.

Omaha, Nebraska

Rachel relaxed into Spanner's arms as they danced around the large ballroom. Thank goodness that was over. Now she and Steve could get on with their lives, away from her mother. She had introduced Steve to some of her friends at the Democratic party and she knew they were interested in him.

"Have you thought any more about becoming a councillor?

Spanner grinned. "You don't give up, do you?"

"No, because you know it makes sense." Rachel smiled up at him. "You would have some control over housing and employment, so you could push for special treatment for Vietnam veterans."

Spanner pulled her closer and didn't answer. When Rachel had first suggested it, he'd laughed and said he didn't have the right qualifications to be a politician, but Rachel had kept on, insisting that all he needed was a desire to make things better. The words had struck a chord with him as he thought about how angry he felt when veterans were discriminated against for being forced to go to a war against their will, and how no one had seemed interested in doing anything for them when they'd returned, damaged and asking for help.

"You are already standing up for them. You could have more effect if you were an elected official."

Spanner gave a theatrical sigh and smiled down at her. "If I say yes, will you stop nagging?"

Rachel smiled back. "Yes, I promise – well, for the moment anyway! Does that mean you are going to run?"

He nodded. "Yes, you're right. It does make sense."

Rachel hugged him tight, unable to conceal her delight. This was their first step. She had never forgotten her desire to change the world, but the challenge of being a woman, and one who had a child out of wedlock at that, would have defeated her before she could even get started. People would have focused on her, and not what she was saying. Working for the Democrats had only reaffirmed that reality, so she had almost given up on being able to do anything until she met Steve. It hadn't taken her long to realise his potential – she had just needed to give him the confidence to do all the things she had planned for herself. Now Steve had agreed to the first part of her plan, she would begin working out the next stage, which would be getting Steve to run for Mayor. Once he'd achieved that, she intended to start their campaign for entry into state politics, and who knew where that could end? Rachel had a brief vision of Steve in the White House, herself the First Lady, and a broad smile crossed her face.

Spanner grinned at the ecstatic expression on her face. He loved seeing the passion in her eyes when she talked politics and, if he were honest, the idea of running for office was rather exciting. It would be wonderful to be in a position to help people. Now he had agreed, he couldn't wait.

CHAPTER THIRTY-TWO

Ho Chi Minh City, Vietnam

"We don't want you here, get out of our children's classroom." Angry parents were shouting at An and Dung. One was even banging on the desk. "You are American scum." "Your mother mai dâm" "She should go to brainwashing class."

Vy watched in horror, but there was nothing she could do to stop them, she was too young. She glanced around and saw the teacher cowering in the corner and suddenly felt angry. She hurried over to him. "They're frightening my brothers." The teacher ignored her, so she said the first thing that came into her head. "My father and uncle will be cross."

The teacher paled, stepped forward and spoke to the parents in a low voice. Vy had no idea what he said, but it seemed to do the trick. The parents backed away and left the classroom. The other children sat down and watched expectantly. The teacher stared at An and Dung. "Sit in the corner away from the other children." The boys exchanged glances and did as they were told. Vy went to sit with them.

"No, not you, Vy. You go with the other children." The teacher looked furious, and Vy was scared, so she did as she was told.

An watched his sister move to the other side of the classroom and wished he understood why she was no longer his twin sister. When they had moved to the city his mother had told him that Dung was his twin now, not Vy, and that it was very important he didn't tell anyone the truth. An liked Dung, it was good to have a brother, but it was strange not having a twin sister anymore.

"I'm going to run away if we have to go to school." Dung wiped away his tears. They had left school and were walking slowly home.

An wanted to argue, but he didn't want to go to school either. "Where will we go?"

"I don't know," Dung shrugged. "Anywhere."

"You can't run away! Mẹ will be so upset, and Cha will be very cross." Vy looked scared.

"He's not my cha, even though we have to call him that." An glared at his sister.

"He's not my cha, either." Dung could still just about remember his parents, before they had left him. He didn't know why they had abandoned him, but now he thought it must have been because of the way he looked. He hadn't missed them when Minh and Lien were on their own, he had felt like one of the family. But now they were here with that awful man in charge of their lives, he missed his parents, his father in particular. Lien was still like a mother to him, when she wasn't frightened of Chinh, but he was cruel and Dung was terrified of him.

"Please come home..." Vy started to speak when the first stone hit An. He cried out, and then Dung screamed and she could see blood pouring down his face. Vy turned around and saw a group of boys picking up some small stones. "Stop! Go away!" Her screams fell on deaf ears as they began throwing them at her too.

Vy turned around to see that An was already running away, Dung close behind him. Vy ran after them, wondering why everyone hated her brothers so much.

Omaha, Nebraska

Jamie finished the last of his drink and watched Rachel and Spanner finish the end of the dance. He was pleased for his friends and he thought they were well suited, but he couldn't help how he felt about Rachel. He kept hoping that one day he would wake up and no longer love her, but so far it hadn't happened. For a moment he thought about her relationship with Martin Bremner and his brow furrowed. He was reasonably sure he had put the FBI off when they had come to the station asking questions about her. He had debated whether or not to tell her that she was now on the FBI radar, but had decided there was no point worrying her. She had been shocked enough by Martin's death and there was no proof she had been involved with any of the bombings. At least he hoped not.

"Enjoying yourself?" Jamie jumped guiltily, for a moment thinking the FBI had appeared, then realised Spanner was smiling down at him.

"Yes, it's a lovely wedding. Can I kiss the bride?" Jamie didn't know why he'd asked that. It would only make him feel worse.

"Of course you can." Spanner laughed.

Jamie stood up and gave Rachel an awkward kiss on the cheek. "I'll get some more drinks," Spanner said, then headed towards the bar, leaving Rachel on her own with Jamie.

"Here, take a seat." Jamie waited for Rachel to sit down before doing the same. There was an awkward silence, finally broken by Jamie. "Have you still got the boxes?"

Rachel shifted in her seat and nodded. It wasn't something she wanted to discuss on her wedding day, but Jamie had been so good to her, he had a right to ask. "Yes, don't worry. I moved them into Steve's house yesterday with the rest of my stuff."

"Wasn't he suspicious?"

Rachel shook her head. "No, he didn't even notice. They are in a safe place, and there's plenty of room for more if you get anything else."

Jamie breathed a sigh of relief. Rachel smiled. "You didn't think I would throw it all away, did you?"

"No, not really." He looked embarrassed. "Sorry, of course you wouldn't."

Rachel leaned forward and lowered her voice. "It's ok, Jamie, just because I'm married doesn't mean that I've forgotten what that bastard did to me." She glanced around, but Spanner was still at the bar. "I have every intention of making him pay one day."

Ho Chi Minh City, Vietnam

"What on earth happened to your face, Dung?" Lien pulled him into her arms and began gently wiping the blood away. She had hoped Phuc would get her letter and visit her today, but she hadn't heard anything. She returned her attention to Dung.

"I fell over," Dung lied, not wanting to upset Lien any more. Although things weren't the same now they had moved to the city, he still loved her.

Lien stared at them all in turn and guessed Dung wasn't telling her the truth. "You haven't been fighting, have you?"

"No, Mẹ."

Lien turned her gaze towards the others. "No, we haven't been fighting, honestly," An said truthfully.

"They haven't been fighting," Vy added.

Lien hesitated, then turned her attention back to Dung. "Come through here. Let's have a closer look."

She was just about to stand up when the door opened and

Chinh marched in. He looked at Dung in Lien's arms and felt his temper rising. "What's going on?" No one answered, so he repeated himself. "I said, *what's going on*?" He grabbed Dung's face. "Have you been fighting, boy?"

"N… no, Ch…Cha," Dung stammered in fear.

"He fell over." Lien finally spoke.

Chinh glared at her and then slapped Dung across the face, knocking him over. "Don't lie to me, boy." He turned to Lien. "Stop covering up for the lying American pig." He slapped her hard, making her cry out in pain, before refocusing his attention on the boys. "Now both of you, get to your bedroom. No food tonight for liars."

An and Dung didn't need telling twice and hurried away. Vy followed them. "Not you, Vy," Chinh shouted. "You can help your mother with the food." Chinh glared at her before walking away to the living room.

Vy waited for him to close the door before looking at the red mark on her mother's face and speaking. "Are you alright, Mẹ?"

Lien looked around in fear, but the living room door was definitely closed. She nodded. "Yes Vy, I am fine. Don't make a fuss, or Cha will be even more angry." She walked quickly into the kitchen, her heart pounding. She had to get out of this marriage before he killed her or one of the boys… or all of them.

PART FOUR

CHAPTER THIRTY-THREE

Ho Chi Minh City, Vietnam, 1987

Dung exchanged glances with An and indicated the man browsing through the stall in the market. An followed his gaze, then quickly nodded before working his way forward. The boys took it in turns to steal while the other acted as a distraction, or to prevent the victim from following. Today was An's turn. He bit his upper lip nervously before sidling up and lifting the wallet carefully from the unsuspecting man, then disappeared into the crowd. Dung followed at a safe distance and the two boys met up further down the road. An was already going through the wallet when Dung reached him.

"How much?"

"Enough to eat for a couple of days." An grinned, threw the wallet on the floor and they hurried away.

"Should we go and see our mother?" An finished the last of his bahn xeo, the succulent pork, shrimp, beansprouts and mixed herbs warming his thin body. It had been two days since they had last eaten. After their previous attempt at stealing had gone wrong, and they had only just escaped arrest, Dung and An had lain low in the slums of the city before daring to venture out again. They had been living on the streets for four years now, ever since Chinh had thrown them out when he found out they were no longer going to school.

"We'll have to make sure that khốn (*bastard*) isn't there."

"Con đẻ hoang (*whoreson*)," An spat. Chinh had made their lives a misery ever since he could remember. Continuous beatings and days and nights without food had replaced all his earlier memories with his mother and Minh. "Maybe we can persuade her to leave him."

Dung gave a harsh laugh. "We have tried, brother. She won't leave him because she is too scared."

"If our uncle would help Mother, she might leave." An continued to hope that one day they would be all be reunited.

"He's just as bad. He is terrified of the con đẻ hoang, can you not remember the way he behaved around him?" Dung scratched the scars on his arm caused by burning himself with a cigarette. They always itched whenever he thought about Chinh. His body was covered in scars, not only from Chinh's beatings but also from his own cutting and burning in an attempt to ease his pain. He knew An's was the same, although the boys never discussed it.

"What about Vy?" An smiled briefly as he thought about his beautiful sister. Vy still looked Vietnamese, which meant she had avoided the discrimination they had experienced.

An had been very confused when they first moved to Ho Chi Minh City and his mother had told him that Vy was no longer his twin sister and that Dung was his twin brother instead. It was only as he grew up that An realised why their mother had pretended that Vy had a different father. Now, An was pleased with his mother's decision. He would do anything to protect his sister, and he knew Dung felt the same.

Dung's face softened. "Vy has been trying to persuade Mother to leave for years, but she is scared too." His expression changed as he remembered how Chinh had looked at Vy when they were living there. "I think Vy should definitely leave."

An sighed. They had discussed this before and disagreed. Dung was sure that Chinh had inappropriate feelings for Vy, whereas An was sure he just liked her because she was Vietnamese. "I am sure you are wrong, brother."

Dung shrugged. "Let's hope you are right." He stood up. "Come on, let's see if it's safe to visit."

Omaha, Nebraska

Rachel listened to Spanner's latest speech and smiled. In just over 10 years, thanks to hard work and some luck, Spanner had risen rapidly through the politicians' ranks to the lofty heights of State Governor. Rachel could hardly believe things had been so easy, and she wished her father was still alive to see the success she'd made of her life. When she'd finally persuaded Spanner to run for councillor back on their wedding day, she had envisaged a glowing future leading all the way to the White House. Although she had been determined they would achieve greatness, she had never thought it would happen so quickly. Spanner's forthright manner, his obvious honesty and his passion for veterans had shone through to an electorate fed up with years of lies and spin. Now for the next step. It was the presidential election the following year, but two years later there would be the elections for the US Senate. If they started making connections now, Spanner could be in the running for senator. Rachel smiled and reached for some paper to make notes on, then cursed as the telephone rang.

"Hello?"

"Hi, sis." Paul's voice sounded strange, and Rachel frowned.

"Is everything ok, Paul?"

"No, no it's not. Heine has HIV."

Rachel nearly dropped the phone in shock. "Oh my God Paul, that's awful. How…? I mean…" She stopped, not sure what to say.

"If you want to ask how he caught it, it wasn't from screwing around," Paul snapped. "Sorry, I'm just fed up with people asking me if he's been unfaithful. He had to have a blood transfusion during an operation a couple of years ago, they think he caught it from that."

"I'm so sorry, Paul. Is he very ill?"

"He's in hospital with pneumonia. He probably won't make it." Paul's voice broke, and Rachel could hear him sobbing. She thought rapidly. She really didn't want to fly all the way to San Francisco, not when Steve would be celebrating his inaugural speech that evening. And could she really afford to leave the children? Rita and Bill would be fine, but Richie was being particularly difficult at the moment, not helped by her mother interfering as usual. On the other hand, who else could go to support him? Certainly not her mother.

Rachel fought to keep the frustration out of her voice as she spoke. "I can fly over today, if you like. You shouldn't be on your own."

"Would you mind, sis?" Paul sounded so pathetically grateful that Rachel felt guilty she'd even thought about not going to support him.

"Of course I don't mind. I'll sort out the children and then catch the first flight out. I'll ring you back when I know when I will be arriving."

"Thanks so much, sis. Can you leave a message on the answerphone? I'll be at the hospital."

"Yes, of course. I will pray for him, Paul." Rachel wondered what on earth had made her say that. It was years since she had thought of God. But it did remind her of something else. "What about Heine's family? Are they coming out?"

"Yes." Paul's voice had gone flat again.

"Oh..." Rachel forgot her unwillingness to fly out there

and started to feel angry. "They still won't have anything to do with you? That's ridiculous. You've been together now for over 20 years."

"As far as they are concerned, I don't exist. A bit like Mom does with Heine."

Rachel winced. It wasn't just Heine's family that was behaving badly. Her own mother was just as bad. She sighed. "It's so stupid, isn't it? After all this time, and things have changed so much."

"The world might have changed – well, some parts of it, anyway – but not some people. Anyway, I have to go now. Thanks again, sis. I'll see you later."

"Yes, I'll be there as soon as I can." Rachel replaced the receiver and headed downstairs to arrange for the nanny to look after Rita and Bill until Steve came home. She would ring Steve before she left, he would be back in his office by then. As she had no idea where Richie was, she would have to leave him a note.

Ho Chi Minh City, Vietnam

The door opened suddenly, making Lien jump. "An, Dung where have you been?" Her face lit up and she hurried over to hug them both.

"We've been around." An took in the bruise on her cheek and her black eye, both of which looked recent, and his heart sank. "Why don't you just leave him? You would be better off living on the streets with us."

Lien looked terrified. "You know I can't do that."

"Why not?" Dung shook his head. "My brother is right. You should leave."

"She can't." Vy ran in and hugged both the boys in turn. "Chinh has threatened to have you both arrested if she leaves."

"Why didn't you tell us?" Dung looked furious. If only he could get his hands on that worthless piece of shit…

"Dung is right, mother. You shouldn't stay here just because of us. We will leave the city; it will be hard for him to find us if we are not here. At least then you will be safe."

Lien fought back tears. "He would never let me leave. Let's talk of something else."

"Like whether he will let us come to your funeral when he has killed you?" Dung clenched his fists.

Lien gasped. "Please don't say that, Dung. Chinh will never do that. He just gets angry sometimes."

"Ha, he's a bully and should have been put down at birth." An was also furious. He took a breath and tried to calm down. "We could find a boat, maybe get to Australia?"

Lien gave a sad smile. "We would never have time to get out of the country before Chinh came looking for us." She paused. "Perhaps you boys should go, though, and take Vy with you." Lien had tried to convince herself that Chinh's attraction towards Vy was just in her imagination. She couldn't care less who he slept with outside the house – in fact, she welcomed it, because it meant he left her alone. She kept hoping he would find another woman to live with and leave her, but he never did. She had not been able to work out why, as he was obviously unhappy with her – and then she had realised he was not staying to be with her, but to be with Vy. He had always been nice to Vy, never beating or mistreating her, but lately she had noticed that he looked at Vy the same way he used to leer at her, and she had no idea how to protect her daughter.

Vy paled. "I could not go. If I did, Chinh would kill Mother."

Lien stared at her in shock. "What do you mean, Vy?"

Vy gazed at her mother and wished she could tell her the truth. That for years, whenever Chinh contrived for Lien to be out of the flat, Chinh had done things to her that she couldn't even bear to think about, let alone articulate. It had started when she was 10, just after he had thrown the boys out, and had continued ever since. The first time she had tried to push him off, not really knowing what he was doing, but sensing it was wrong. But Chinh had threatened to kill her mother and have her brothers arrested if she complained or tried to stop him, so she had stopped struggling and let him...

"Vy, what do you mean?" Lien repeated.

Vy hesitated. Perhaps if the boys hadn't been there, she could have found her courage and spoken, but she couldn't say anything in front of them; she didn't know how they would react. She forced a smile. "Nothing, just that Chinh is dangerous. I can't leave you on your own with him."

Lien looked at her carefully. For some reason she was sure Vy was lying to her, and she didn't know why.

"Then we should all go," Dung reiterated. "That way he can't hurt any of us."

Lien looked at the boys, then at Vy. She knew they were right, but she couldn't see how they could all leave the country without Chinh stopping them. He was too powerful. If she could get Phuc's help that would be different, but her brother was too scared of Chinh to do anything to upset him.

Omaha, Nebraska

Richie finished his bourbon and threw the cards on the table in disgust. Yet another hand he'd lost. He would have to ask Grandma Emily for some money to pay his debts or he would be in trouble. His mother wouldn't help, in fact she would be furious, but with a bit of luck he wouldn't need to tell her.

"Hope you're good for that, Richie?" Frank Belotti put his hand on Richie's shoulder.

Richie swallowed nervously. "'Course I am, Frank. You know my family's got plenty of money, right?" It was a poorly-kept secret that Frank was a member of the Mafia, and that he didn't take kindly to people not paying what they owed.

"Good, kid, I'd hate to fall out with you." Frank squeezed Richie's shoulder until the boy winced. "Especially as you shouldn't even be in here." Richie was below the legal age for gambling with cards, but being underage for something had never worried him.

"Mom's going pay for her little boy, is she?" one of the other gamblers jeered.

Richie scowled at him. "Why don't you put your money where your mouth is?"

"You gonna make me?" the man laughed.

"No, he's not. He's going home so he can sort out the money he owes me." Frank's tone brooked no argument. Richie shoved his chair back, stood up and leaned across the table.

"I'll be back next week, and then we'll see who's laughing."

"Out!" Frank put his hand on Richie's shoulder again and Richie raised his hands in surrender. "I'm going, ok."

"Nice going." Frank patted him gently on the back. "I'll see you tomorrow with what you owe, ok?"

It wasn't a request, and Richie nodded, his stomach churning uncomfortably. If his grandmother didn't help him out, he would have to go and stay with his uncle in San Francisco for a while.

Frank watched him go and cursed under his breath. Richie Hanson should never have been allowed into his card games, but because he was tall for his age, he looked much older and had managed to fool Enzo. By the time Frank had realised the boy's real age, he was already losing money and, knowing his family were good for it, Frank had decided to let him carry on. He shook his head. He should have gone with his gut and thrown him out as soon as he found out his age. Frank thought for a few moments and decided it wasn't worth risking it anymore. Richie would pay what he owed and then he would be banned until he was legally allowed to gamble away his family money. And if he didn't pay…

CHAPTER THIRTY-FOUR

San Francisco

"Keep going, Heine, please don't leave me." Paul sat by Heine's bed in ICU and watched as his lover's breathing became harsher and more laboured. Heine's health had gone downhill so quickly it had taken them both by surprise. They had moved to San Francisco nine years ago, after they had both decided it would be good to live in a place they felt comfortable together. Part of their decision had been a result of his mother's continual interference in his life. He knew she hated the fact he was gay, but she hated Heine even more. Paul couldn't work out why, as Heine was always polite and never retaliated, even when Emily was really rude. If only his mother had treated Heine like Rachel had, he would have been able to stay in Omaha, but her childish clumsy attempts to break them up had finally got through to him. Paul smiled briefly as he closed his eyes and recalled the conversation.

"I've had enough, Heine. I think we should move away from my mother."

"Are you sure?" Heine had looked concerned.

"If we stay here, sooner or later she will break us up, not because I believe any of her stupid lies about you, but because you'll get fed up and leave me."

Heine smiled. "I would never do that, but if you're sure about moving I can't say I'm sorry."

"Then you agree?"

"Yes. Let's move somewhere we fit in, where we don't have to apologise for who we are all the time."

"San Francisco?" Paul had been thinking about it for a while.

Heine smiled and nodded. "Yes, that sounds like the perfect place."

Heine squeezed his hand, bringing him abruptly back to the present. "You were lost in thought?" His voice was weak, but Paul could hear the worry in it.

"I was just thinking about when we decided to leave Omaha."

"Best thing we ever did."

"Yes." Paul fell silent again. Heine was right. They had been so happy until AIDS had come along to ruin it.

"I'm sorry, Paul."

"What on earth for?"

"For giving it to you."

Paul almost smiled at Heine's ability to still guess what he was thinking, something he had always been able to do.

Then he shook his head. "I don't mind. I don't want to live without you anyway. What would I do on my own?"

Heine didn't answer, but Paul could see the tears in his eyes. He squeezed Heine's hand tightly and fought back his own while he thought about how he would tell Rachel that he too was infected, his life expectancy dramatically reduced, despite desperate attempts by scientists to find a cure for a deadly virus that had killed so many of his friends.

Ho Chi Minh City, Vietnam

"We could try begging again?" An suggested, without much hope. They had tried that when they first found themselves on the streets and had not been very successful. Now they were older, they would probably fare even worse.

"If we're going to get a boat out of this shitty country, we need money. Proper money, we won't get that by begging," Dung snapped.

An nodded. "Yes, of course, you're right. We'll have to move around, though, and be careful, because if we steal every day we'll get caught."

Dung frowned. "You're right." He thought for a moment and an idea came to him. "Perhaps we should work separately, but whenever one of us is working the other should be somewhere visible where there are lots of people."

An looked confused. "I don't understand..." he began,

then he grinned. "Ah, so we can say it wasn't us if we get seen?"

"Yes – it will only work if we don't get caught in the act, though. We'll have to be especially careful and work out our targets in advance."

An sighed. "We normally just pick an unsuspecting person to rob. How will we know in advance?"

Dung smiled. "We won't target people, we will go for businesses instead. Then we can set up our alibis."

An thought about it for a few moments, then nodded. If they wanted to get out of the country, they would have to take risks. "Ok, let's plan."

Omaha, Nebraska

"More money, darling?" Emily looked concerned. "I don't understand why you need it. Your mother is very generous with your allowance. Surely you haven't spent it all already?"

"It's very expensive living up to our name, Grandma. I also lent money to some friends and they can't pay me back yet..." Richie held his breath.

"If they can't afford to pay you back, you shouldn't lend them money Richie."

"I know, but I felt sorry for them... you know how it is..."

"Mm, well I'm not happy. If you're stupid enough to lend your friends money, perhaps you should learn from that. It's not that long until the end of the month, after all."

Richie began to panic. If Grandma didn't give him some money, he would be in lots of trouble he could never talk his way out of. "It won't happen again."

Emily shook her head. Rachel was always telling her that she was spoiling Richie; perhaps she was right. He didn't seem to have much grasp of money, probably because she always gave into him. She made up her mind. "No, I really think you should learn from this."

Richie turned pale. "But you can't do this to me!"

"For goodness' sake, Richie..." Emily frowned. "What is it you aren't telling me, Richie?"

"Nothing."

Emily shrugged. "Then that's the end of the matter." She put her cheque book away.

"If I don't have the money, they'll kill me," Richie blurted out.

Emily blanched. "Who'll kill you?"

Richie shook his head, eyes wide with terror.

"If you don't tell me who you owe the money to, I definitely will *not* help you out!" Emily yelled.

Richie took a breath. "Frank Belotti."

Emily stared at him in disbelief and growing fury. "How the hell do you owe the mafia money?"

"I was playing cards..." He didn't get any further.

"That's illegal, you're underage!"

"I lied about my age at first, then... then I owed them money, so they let me keep playing so I could win it back."

Emily could barely control her temper. "How could you be so fucking stupid?"

Richie was shocked. He'd never heard her swear before. "I… I don't know." He dropped his gaze to the floor, unable to meet her gaze any longer.

Emily took a deep breath and got her temper back under control. Being angry wouldn't help. She gazed at him thoughtfully. "This is the last time, Richie. I can't keep giving you money. I take it your mother doesn't know about this?"

Richie looked horrified. "No."

"I'll deal with this, Richie. You can go now, and don't ever gamble again. Do you understand?"

"Yes – I mean no, I definitely won't, Grandma, I promise." He took a breath. "What are you going to do?"

"That's for me to know. Just go and leave me to deal with it." She could see the fear on his face as he turned to go. Good, if he was scared perhaps he might do as he was told. "Richie!" He turned back to look at her. "Keep away from Frank Belotti!"

Emily stared at the door for several seconds before picking up the telephone and dialling her private detective.

San Francisco, California

Rachel arrived at the hospital and made her way to ICU. She spotted Paul immediately and was shocked by his appearance. He looked so thin.

"Hi, sis." Paul stood up, and before she could hug him he indicated a chair opposite him on the other side of the bed and sat down again. Confused, Rachel hesitated and then sat. Perhaps he was worried about catching an infection which he could give to Heine?

"How is he?"

Paul looked into her eyes. "He's dying. It's only a matter of time now." He looked back at his lover and squeezed his hand. "Rachel's come to see you, Heine."

Heine opened his eyes with difficulty and managed a small smile. "Hi, Rachel. Have you come to say goodbye?"

Rachel blinked back tears and took his other hand. It was warm but lifeless, as if part of him had already gone. "You'll soon be out of here..." She stopped as he patted her hand and shook his head.

"No honey, I won't. You've been a good friend to us both."

"It worked both ways, Heine. If it wasn't for you, I wouldn't have met Steve." Rachel wiped her tears away and wished she'd come to see him earlier. "I wish there was something I could do." She listened to him wheezing and tears streamed unchecked down her cheeks.

Heine patted her hand again. "You can, honey. You can take care of Paul for me. He's going to need looking after."

"You know I will." Rachel squeezed his hand. "He can come and stay with us until he feels able to come home."

Heine turned his head towards Paul. "You haven't told her?"

"Told me what?" Rachel suddenly felt sick. "Paul?"

"I was going to wait..." Paul sighed. He knew Heine wanted him to tell Rachel because he was worried there was a chance Paul wouldn't say anything at all when he was dead. Paul could barely hold back his emotion. Even when he was dying, Heine was trying to look after him, make sure he didn't sink into despair and die alone.

"I have HIV too. I did the test when Heine first got ill."

Rachel's head felt fuzzy and she had to fight not to faint. "You can't have..." She shook her head, hoping she'd misheard. She looked down at Heine and then back at her brother. "Perhaps it's a mistake?"

Paul shook his head, but didn't answer.

She took in the pallor in his cheeks, the weight loss, his gaunt appearance, and she knew he was telling the truth. "Why didn't you say anything?"

Paul gave her a tired smile. "What would be the point? You can't do anything for me. There's no treatment, not yet anyway. Why make you miserable too?"

"I'm your sister... You'll have to come and live with us after..." She stopped, mortified, but Heine squeezed her hand again. "I'm sorry."

"Don't be silly, Rachel. I'm dying. Paul will be on his own. He will need looking after."

Rachel nodded. "Of course..." She trailed off. Now she knew Paul was HIV positive, it was obvious why he hadn't touched her. Then Rachel thought about the children and her heart skipped a beat. Although the experts now said you couldn't catch HIV easily, could she really take the risk of having Paul in the house with the Steve and the children?

Omaha, Nebraska

Spanner finished his cigar, switched over the television channel to catch the late news and let out a heavy sigh. The Iran-Contra affair was yet another stain on American politics, ensuring that the population trusted politicians even less. The Senate and House of Representatives had finally released a report blaming President Ronald Reagan for the whole affair – not really surprising after he had publicly admitted, in March that year, that his 'overtures' to Iran had ended up leading to an arms for hostages deal. Spanner shook his head in disgust. To give in to a hostile state that was holding your citizens hostage was hardly statesman-like behaviour.

But Spanner wasn't only annoyed that the *arms for hostages* affair, as it had become known, was still rumbling on. There were so many problems that needed resolving in the US, not least the treatment of veterans, but yet again it was another political scandal that was consuming media attention. His own inaugural speech as Governor of Nebraska had not made the main news – not that he'd really expected it to, but it would have been nice to have had some of his points aired by the news channels. Hopefully, the speech would be in the following day's state newspapers.

Spanner stood up, turned the television off and wandered over to the radio. Perhaps some music would calm him down. As Bon Jovi's 'Livin on a Prayer' filled the room, Spanner thought how much he missed Rachel on the rare occasions she wasn't there. He poured himself some bourbon and lit another cigar, a wry smile on his face as he thought about how Rachel had started nagging him to stop smoking. It was alright for her; she'd stopped smoking marijuana when she was pregnant with Rita back in 1976 and hadn't ever restarted. He had never given up his cigars, they had become his trademark and his crutch. Although he had developed a cough recently, Spanner had no real intention of giving the cigars up. He had to have some form of relaxation, after all, and he had been smoking them so long that he was sure they weren't doing him any harm.

He glanced at the clock and wondered what time Rachel would ring. He didn't want to go to bed until he'd spoken to her. He would have liked to say his own goodbye to Heine, but Rachel had gone so quickly she'd not given him the choice of going with her. Spanner thought quickly. Perhaps he would still have time to get there. He would tell Rachel he'd catch an early flight. He was sure she would be glad of his support, and he owed it to Heine. After all, without him, he and Rachel might never have met.

Ho Chi Minh City, Vietnam

Despite his decision to target businesses, Dung couldn't resist an opportunity when it presented itself. The man with the gold watch chain was concentrating on the stall, his eyes drawn by some antiques. Dung reached out, grabbed the watch, turned and ran straight into an undercover policeman. An watched in shock, then pulled himself together and disappeared into the crowd. There was nothing he could do for Dung, and there was no point getting arrested as well.

"What do you mean he's been arrested?" Lien slumped in the nearest chair. "What will happen to him?"

"I don't know... he'll be put in Mac Dinh Chi prison, I think." An was still shaken by how close he had come to being caught as well.

"You have to find a job, An," Lien murmured. If only Chinh had been a different sort of man, this might not have happened. He had forced the boys out of the home and onto the streets, pushing them into crime. Lien felt the tears forming, and for the first time in ages she thought about her parents. They would have been so ashamed of her.

An watched his mother crying and felt helpless. His childhood had been spent in in the shadow of her tears, and her despair over not being able to protect them from the monster she'd married.

"I'm so sorry An, this is all my fault. I have let you all down. I should never have married him."

"No you haven't, Mẹ, you did what you thought was best." He shrugged. "Shit happens!"

Lien paled. "Where did you hear that?"

An looked confused. "I heard someone in the market say it. I thought it was funny. Why?"

Lien gave a sad smile. "Your father used to say it a lot." She closed her eyes, and for a moment allowed herself to think of Spanner. He had been so gentle and loving. If only...

"If we go to America, Mẹ, we might be able to find him."

Lien shook her head. "It's too late for me, An, but you should leave. When Dung gets out of prison, you should all go – Vy too."

An nodded. "I had better make tracks before Chinh comes home." He gave her a quick hug and hurried away. Lien stared at the floor and knew she should make some effort to prepare an evening meal, or there would be trouble.

Omaha, Nebraska

Jamie finished reading the article about how DNA had convicted the Florida rapist, Tommy Lee Andrews, and wondered if that would be the answer to Charles Peterson. Rachel had continued to accumulate the case files he took to her, but there was never anything they could use. Charles was always careful to pick girls who the police could easily dismiss. Jamie had risen slowly through the ranks of the police force, and was now a captain. Several times throughout the years, he had thought about transferring to become a detective and investigating Charles himself, but he had always held back. Perhaps he should consider it again if it would give him the chance to nail that bastard. Jamie looked out onto his foggy garden and thought about the article he had just read. It would be best to wait a while and make sure DNA evidence wasn't challenged before suggesting anything to Rachel. He didn't want to get her hopes up only to have them dashed by some smart-ass lawyer.

He stood up and switched on the TV. Economists were still discussing the likely effect of the stock market fallback in October on Black Monday, followed by the Dow Jones Index fall two weeks later. Jamie listened closely, though without enthusiasm; unemployment was at its lowest level since July 1979, and he hoped they were wrong about a possible recession, because that could only mean rising crime. He was about to switch it off when Spanner appeared on his screen. Jamie smiled and turned the volume up. At least his friend was a politician worth listening to.

CHAPTER THIRTY-FIVE

Omaha, Nebraska

Richie climbed behind the wheel of his new car and smiled at himself in the driving mirror. His mother and Spanner had gone to San Francisco for Heine's funeral the previous day, leaving him on his own; well, other than his grandmother. But he wasn't too worried about Emily. He had always been able to twist her around his little finger. Richie's smile broadened. He had not heard anything from Frank Belotti, so he could only assume that his grandmother had paid him off. At first, he had been fed up that he could no longer play cards, but then he'd thought about it and realised he had been lucky. If his grandmother hadn't bailed him out, he would have received a beating, something that would have continued until he had either paid or worked off his debt. Richie shivered at the thought of his mother finding out just how close he had come to disaster. If the newspapers had learnt about him owing money to a member of the mob, it could have destroyed Spanner's political career, and his mother would never forgive him if that happened.

Richie thought about Rachel and thanked his lucky stars she hadn't found out about his gambling habit. Then he frowned. His mother had always been much stricter with him than Spanner. She certainly wouldn't have let him have a new car. But she was also much harder on him than she was with his younger brother. Admittedly, Bill was only eight, but Rachel did give him more freedom than she had given Richie at the same age. Perhaps it was because Bill was Spanner's son and Richie wasn't.

Not for the first time, Richie wondered about his real father. Rachel never talked about him at all, and he had no idea who he was. When he was younger, Richie had assumed that Rachel must have loved his father, or how else would he have been conceived? He would often fanaticise about him, imagining that he was a war hero who had died in Vietnam, which was why his mother was so single-minded in her fight for veterans. As he'd grown older, his fantasies had changed: his father was a famous professional footballer who had fallen in love with Rachel, and one day he would come and claim his son. He was a famous rock star, or an astronaut, one of the illustrious few who had gone beyond the Earth's boundaries. In all his fantasies his father didn't know he existed, but one day he would find out and come to find him. It was harder to find reasons for his mother's secrecy, so he had quashed any questions his mind had come up with. But now he was older, he was more realistic. The man was probably a nobody, maybe married, or just hadn't wanted to know. His mother had been young when she had given birth to him, so perhaps the man had led her on, taken advantage of her? Whatever the reason for his real father's absence, Richie had learned not to ask. In any case, Spanner was a good stepfather, much less strict than Rachel, and more importantly, there was no difference in the way he treated Richie and Bill.

"Can you give me a lift?" Rita suddenly appeared by the passenger door.

Richie grinned. Rita was only ten, but she was already showing signs of the teenager she would become, mainly because Spanner had a soft spot for his daughter. If his mother thought he was a problem, she would never cope with Rita, who had a mind of her own and was already very stubborn.

"Where are you going, Rita? Does Greta know where you are?"

"I'm going to see Jade."

"And Greta knows that?" Richie repeated.

Rita looked surprised. "Of course she does. It was her idea. She saw you get the car out and said to ask you for a ride, save her driving me over there."

Richie wondered if he should check first, then decided that would be ridiculous. What possible trouble could two ten-year-olds get up to?

Mac Dinh Chi Prison, near Ho Chi Minh City, Vietnam

Dung lay on his mattress and gazed up at the ceiling. He had no money to bribe the guards for outside work, so he hadn't left the cell since his arrival. He had quickly learned that if he followed the dai bong's (head prisoner) orders to sweep the floors and massage the older prisoners, they would leave him alone. He was lucky that the cell only had seven others in; some were very overcrowded. The police had come several times to interrogate him, wanting to know who he worked with. Dung had made up some names, but when the police had been unable to find them, they had tied him down and beaten him with rubber hoses. He had been unable to eat for days afterwards and lost even more weight, but so far he hadn't give them An's name.

The door opened and Dung's spirits fell. He couldn't take another beating.

"Out."

Dung stared at the guard and didn't move.

"You are free to go."

Dung still didn't move. How could that be?

"Don't you want to go?"

Dung leapt to his feet, ignoring his still-sore ribs, and hurried toward the door. Ten minutes later he was on the other side of the prison walls, a free man. Dung looked around and wondered why they had suddenly decided to release him. It wasn't as if he knew anyone who could pay off the prison authorities. Perhaps they were going to follow him to see where he went. He would make sure he wasn't being followed first, which meant several trips around the city, in and out of markets and apartment blocks. Dung smirked. He'd had years of practice at this. If there was anyone behind him, he would soon lose them. Then, once he was certain, he would go to the place he normally slept and see if An was there.

Lien watched from the other side of the road near the old presidential palace. She wanted to run over and hug him, but she couldn't afford to be seen anywhere near the prison in case someone reported back to Chinh. She would be in enough trouble if he found out she had paid the authorities off using money Phuc had lent her. She had told her brother that she had lost some money and she was terrified of what Chinh would do if he found out. Fortunately, Phuc had not questioned her too closely and had given her what she needed. If she'd known it would be that easy, she would have asked for more, enough for her children to try and leave the country, but it was too late now. Lien had no idea how she would pay Phuc back, but at least this way Dung was no longer languishing in prison and being beaten by the police.

San Francisco, California

"Are you going to ask Paul to come here for a while?" Spanner lay on their bed in the hotel and watched Rachel packing their clothes. Heine's funeral had been quiet, his family barely acknowledging Paul. There was silence, and Spanner frowned. "Rachel?"

"Paul's HIV positive." Rachel blurted out.

Spanner paled. "That's awful. I'm so sorry, Rachel. To find out today, as well…"

Rachel didn't answer. She knew she should have told him when he'd come out to say goodbye to Heine, but somehow she hadn't found the right time, and she could hardly admit now that she'd known for over a month.

Spanner stood up, walked over to Rachel and put his arms around her. She rested her head on his chest. "He should definitely come and stay with us, then. He'll need us, won't he?"

Rachel froze. "But what about the children?"

Spanner leaned back and looked confused. "What do you mean?"

"Would it be safe? The risks of catching it…" Rachel flushed under his scrutiny and looked away.

"The medical experts have explained that it can only be transferred through bodily fluids. Sharing a house with him isn't going to put any of us in danger. You know that, darling."

Rachel hesitated, choosing her words carefully. "The logical part of me knows that, but as a mother I can't help worrying. I know it's stupid." Spanner didn't answer, so she carried on. "And you know what people are like. We can't afford to have problems..." She stopped, not wanting to sound as if his political career was more important than her brother. But they had worked so hard to get Steve where he was. Something like this could put his career back years, or even destroy it completely.

"Darling, that's ridiculous. I'm sure nobody would even begin to judge us for looking after Paul."

Rachel sighed. Sometimes Steve was incredibly naïve. "Really? Look at Gary Hart. Forced to pull out of the Democratic presidential nomination race because of allegations about his private life."

Spanner laughed. "That's completely different, darling. Paul is ill, he will need someone to look after him. He can hardly go home to your mother, can he?"

Rachel shook her head. "Of course not." She was about to say more, when she remembered her promise to Heine. "Well, if you're sure...?"

"Of course I am. I wouldn't be much of a human being if I didn't want to help my own brother-in-law in time of crisis, would I?"

Rachel gave in. "Alright, darling. I'll ask him before we leave." She went back to packing. Perhaps she could persuade her brother to stay in San Francisco with his friends.

Ho Chi Minh City, Vietnam

"Dung...! What on earth?" An nearly had a heart attack when Dung arrived in the middle of the night, having walked around the city for hours to make sure he wasn't being followed. He hadn't seen anyone, but as he still couldn't work out why he'd been released he had decided to wait until it was dark before approaching An.

"*Sh!* I don't want anyone to know I am here."

"Have you escaped?"

"No, they suddenly let me go."

An furrowed his brow. "That doesn't seem right. Maybe the man dropped the charges?"

Dung shook his head. "I wouldn't think so, he was part of the trap. I thought they might want to follow me, but I haven't seen anyone."

An glanced around nervously, but the alley was deserted. "Are we leaving now, then? What about Vy?"

"We can't take her with us, not like this – it's too dangerous. And we don't have any money. I've been thinking, and this is what I think we should do."

An sat back and listened as Dung outlined his plan.

Omaha, Nebraska

"How could you be so stupid as to let her go shopping on her own?" Rachel glared at Greta.

"She told me she was going to visit Jade." Greta was still shocked that Rita had lied to her, let alone gotten herself arrested.

"If it hadn't been for Jamie, they would have ended up with a juvenile record." Rachel was furious. They had arrived back from Heine's funeral to find the house in uproar after Rita and her friend Jade had been arrested for shoplifting. She turned to Rita. "Are you completely stupid? What on earth were you thinking?"

"I didn't mean to steal it, Mom, I just forgot it was in my bag." Rita crossed her fingers behind her back and hoped her mother couldn't tell she was lying. This was all Jason's fault. He had dared her to steal something from one of the shops, and because she liked him and wanted him to like her back, she had done it. "I'm sorry, really I am."

"What was it doing in your bag before you paid for it anyway?" Rachel stared at her daughter, convinced she was lying. When Rita didn't answer she carried on, "It's not as if you didn't have enough money on you to pay!"

Rita fixed her eyes on the elaborately-patterned carpet and wished she could disappear into one of the colourful swirls.

"Are you listening to me?" Rachel snapped.

"Yes Mom, I'm really sorry." Rita repeated and then, seeing her father heading toward the study, burst into noisy tears.

"That's enough, Rachel. I'm sure Rita knows what she's done is wrong." Spanner came into the room, having just let Jamie out. "No more tears, Rita, there's a good girl. You've been lucky this time, so let's forget it now, shall we."

Rachel stared at him in disbelief. "Forget it? Are you serious? Do you know what damage she could have done to your career, not to mention her own life?"

"She's just a child, Rachel, and there's no real harm done." Spanner reached out his arms and Rita ran into them, snuggling into his waist.

Rachel shook her head, and was about to say more when she remembered the nanny was still standing there. "Take Rita upstairs, Greta, I don't want to see her downstairs for the rest of the day. She can go to school as normal, but no going round to anyone else's house for a month."

"That's a bit harsh..." Spanner started to say, before catching Rachel's expression. "Well, I suppose that's only right." He disentangled Rita's arms from his waist, leaned down and spoke gently. "You do have to be punished, sweetheart. But no more tears, ok?" He kissed the top of her head. "Now off you go, upstairs with Greta."

Rachel waited until they had left the room before rounding on him. "You're spoiling that child rotten. I can't believe you weren't even going to punish her?"

"I think the shock of being arrested was probably punishment enough."

Rachel shook her head. "It's bad enough my mother spoiling Richie every chance she gets, now you want to do the same with Rita?"

"It's not really the same, honey. Rita is still only a child. Richie is nearly a man."

Rachel could hardly speak, she was so angry. She took a breath and tried to calm down. "You are Governor of the State, you can't afford to have your daughter arrested for shoplifting, even if she is only ten. What if it reaches the newspapers?"

"It won't. Jamie took care of it."

"If you mean by paying everyone off, then that's no better is it?"

Spanner began to get annoyed. "Do you really think I would do that, Rachel? You don't know me very well, do you? I just meant that Jamie spoke to the store manager and suggested that because of the girls' age and their previously good characters, it would be best to let them off with a warning this time, rather than put them through the juvenile justice system where they would be mixing with real criminals."

Rachel flushed. "I'm sorry, Steve. Of course I know you wouldn't stoop to bribing people. I was just angry and worried, not only about your career but about Rita. I always thought Jade was a nice friend for her and a good influence.

Obviously, I got that wrong."

Spanner frowned. "You're making it sound like they did it deliberately. Rita said she forgot the T-shirt was in her bag?"

"Surely you don't believe that?" Rachel snorted in derision. "When I asked her why the shirt was in her bag before she'd paid for it, she couldn't answer me."

"But why would she steal? She could afford to pay for it."

"My question exactly," Rachel replied. "Maybe it was just a prank gone wrong, or perhaps someone dared her to do it?"

"What will you do, then?"

"Nothing. What can I do? If I start asking questions at the school, it will draw attention to Rita and make it all public. We'll just have to forget about it."

Spanner thought for a moment, then nodded. "I think that's best." He smiled suddenly, stepped closer and put his arms around her. "Shit happens, right?"

Rachel gave a wry smile, stood on tiptoe and kissed him. "Not anymore, if I can help it!" In future, she would keep a much closer eye on Rita.

CHAPTER THIRTY-SIX

Ho Chi Minh City, Vietnam

"Have you seen the boys?" Lien had waited for Chinh to go out before asking Vy.

"No, not for ages." Vy looked worried. Lien had told her that she'd paid off the prison authorities and Vy had been hoping that the boys would visit them. "I went to the place they normally sleep, but no one has seen them. Maybe they have left the city?"

Lien frowned. "That would be very hard to do without the right papers. And why would they do that? And not even say goodbye?"

Vy thought hard. "Maybe Dung thought his release was a police trap? If he did, he wouldn't come here in case he brought trouble on us."

Lien sighed. She hadn't even thought of that. "But what about An? He wouldn't need to worry about that?"

Vy couldn't answer that. Another thought crossed her mind. "You don't think they have left the country?"

"Maybe. It would be the best thing." Lien fought back tears. She would miss them both, but at least they would have a future somewhere else.

"Yes." Vy turned away. If only the boys had taken her with them. She wanted to protect her mother, but she wasn't sure how much longer she could stay here.

Omaha, Nebraska

"You can stay as long as you like, Paul." Rachel watched as Paul's friend Max helped her brother onto the bed. Even with Max's help, Paul was breathing heavily after climbing the stairs to the bedroom.

"Thanks, sis."

Rachel could hardly believe how much Paul had deteriorated in the months since Heine's funeral. If only she had listened to Steve and insisted he come and stay with them right away, but instead she'd persuaded him to stay in San Francisco in case he infected them. She felt sick with guilt and didn't know how she would ever forgive herself. Somehow, she pulled herself together and turned to Max, who had driven Paul all the way because he wasn't well enough to fly. "Thanks so much, Max. You can have the room next door, if that's ok?"

"That's perfect. I'll drive back tomorrow as I can't take any more time off work, but you know where I am if you need me."

"I don't know what Paul would have done without you." Rachel gave him a quick hug. She turned back to Paul. "I'll help you into bed."

"No need. I can manage as long as I take its slowly." He closed his eyes for a moment. "Don't forget to make sure I have all my own crockery, cutlery and toiletries." He took another deep breath and Rachel was relieved to hear the wheezing easing off.

She forced a smile. "Don't worry, we'll all be fine." She took a breath. "I'm so sorry Paul, I wish I hadn't talked you out of coming earlier."

"You were only trying to protect your family, Rach. I understand that."

Rachel flushed and blinked back tears. She hadn't realised he knew. "I..."

Paul gave a tired smile. "It's fine, sis, honestly. You don't need to feel guilty. In your shoes, I would have done the same thing."

Rachel wiped her eyes and stepped toward him. Before he could say anything, she sat down on the bed next to him and, ignoring his protests, put her arms around him and held him tight. He was so thin she could feel his ribs, and tears ran unchecked down her cheeks. "Don't die, Paul. I couldn't bear a world without you."

"I'm so sorry, sis, I don't want to leave you..." Paul fell silent and allowed himself to enjoy the warmth of the first human body he'd touched since Heine's death.

Omaha, Nebraska

"Jim…Jim…please don't." Kurt spoke with a calm he didn't feel. "It's ok Jim, we're back in the US, that's all in the past."

Jim was curled up in the corner of his bedroom, tears streaming down his face, the loaded gun pressed to his forehead. "I can't live with this anymore… I can't deal with the constant memories, the screams, the smell… Jesus fucking Christ, Kurt, it's in my head all the time."

"We can help, Jim – just put the gun down and let me help, please."

"No one can help, buddy. I have been to so many people who said they could help, and look at me!"

"Come and see Spanner, maybe he can suggest something. But please don't do this, or I will have this memory stuck in my head with all the others… is that what you want for me?" Kurt was running out of things to say.

Jim looked at him, his eyes empty. "Then go. Leave me alone."

"No, I can't do that, Jim. Would you do that, if it was me sitting there?"

"I can't keep living like this, Kurt. There's no future, nothing for me anymore."

"Yes, there is." Kurt searched desperately for something, anything that could give Jim hope. "What if we tried to find the VC who did it?"

Jim gave a harsh laugh. "How the fuck are we going to do that?"

"The country is opening up a bit, they are letting people out. I don't know, maybe we can go back over there, talk to people. If you give up, they'll get away with it."

"They already have."

"No, they think they have. I can see that little shit's face when I close my eyes too, Jim. Do you think you're the only one that's suffering? If you kill yourself, he's won."

Jim stared at him for what felt like an age, his mind turning over what Kurt was saying, before carefully lowering the gun.

Kurt exhaled slowly. "Come on, Jim, let's go and speak to Spanner. Maybe he'll know what to do."

Jim shook his head, the panic reappearing in his eyes. "I can't say it out loud, Kurt."

"No, ok, we don't have to." Kurt raised his hands. "I'll find a way of asking without telling him why, ok?" How he was going to do that, Kurt didn't know, but at least Jim had lowered the gun and no longer looked like he was going to pull the trigger.

CHAPTER THIRTY-SEVEN

En route to the coast, Vietnam

The two young men climbed aboard the railroad car and settled down in the corner to watch. While waiting at the station they had heard other people speaking of how bands of thieves roamed through the cars, robbing people and beating them up. Neither had anything worth stealing, but it was obvious their fellow travellers did. They were heading towards one of the remote fishing villages, where they hoped to find a boat to take them out of the country. But it all depended on what happened in the next few hours.

The train soon picked up speed, and as they left the city behind, four men appeared and started to threaten a group of their fellow travellers, a young couple with a baby. An and Dung watched the altercation for a few seconds before An stood up and moved towards them. Dung followed. "Leave them alone."

The leader of the bandits turned to look them up and down and laughed. "What are you going to do about it?"

An smiled. "If you don't go away, I will shoot all of you

and we will throw your bodies off the train."

The leader looked less certain, but he still didn't move away. After a few seconds, he resumed his threats on the couple. An sighed, pulled out his gun and pointed it directly in the face of the lead robber, ignoring the gasps of his fellow travellers. "Last chance..."

The leader hesitated, then backed away, followed closely by his three men. An let them move past him before speaking again, his voice calm and unruffled. "Don't forget to spread the word that the passengers in this carriage are protected by us."

They waited until the men left before sitting back down. Some of their fellow travellers nodded their thanks, but others just looked uncomfortable. A few moments later, the young man they had saved moved closer to him. "Thank you. I am Trang Hải Long, my wife is Trang Mỹ Di, and this is our daughter, Lan. Please accept this." Long pressed some money into his hand.

"Thank you. I am Nguyen Thanh An and this is my brother Dung." An lowered his voice. "I am hoping to find a fishing boat..." He left the rest of the sentence unspoken.

Long smiled. "We are too. Perhaps we could travel together?"

"Of course, that would be very agreeable to us." An glanced at Di and the baby who was sleeping soundly in her arms. "How old is Lan?"

"Five months." An expression of pride crossed Long's

face momentarily, to be almost immediately replaced by one of sadness. "My parents are dead; Di's have been moved to a re-education camp. We cannot stay in this country anymore."

An and Dung exchanged glances and An nodded. "No, there is nothing here." He fell silent, thinking about those he had left behind. Maybe one day, if they were successful, Lien and Vy would be able to follow them to a new life.

Omaha, Nebraska

Spanner watched as the Homecoming Act was finally passed and thought about all the Vietnam veterans he'd spoken to who would be celebrating that their children could finally come to America. No doubt there would be some veterans who wouldn't want their past arriving on their doorsteps, but on the whole, this was a good thing. Of course, they all had to apply for immigration visas by March 1990 or they wouldn't be allowed in, but he hoped it would help. He could still remember the awful television reports when Saigon fell, and he wondered how many of those Vietnamese who had helped the Americans had survived the communist regime.

He still couldn't remember anything about his time there, and although there were times when he thought it would be good to recall that time in his life, he'd adjusted to the fact that his memory would probably never come back. When he looked at other veterans, he knew he should probably count himself lucky that he couldn't remember; at least he didn't suffer from flashbacks and nightmares.

Omaha, Nebraska

Rachel stood at Paul's grave and thought about the last time she'd spoken to him. His condition had deteriorated rapidly after he'd come to live with them, and it wasn't long before they were employing a full-time nurse to look after him. For almost the first time in her life, Rachel was grateful her family had money. If they hadn't, Paul would have died alone on a hospital ward. Sadly, he had still died alone. Rachel had called in to see him on her way to accompanying Steve to a state function, but by the time she returned he had gone. She was glad she had kissed him goodbye, but she felt guilty she hadn't been with him at the end. Paul had supported her through the difficult times, and she had turned her back on him when he needed help. It didn't matter that she had finally seen sense – she had wasted months that she could have spent with him. She glanced at her father's grave and leant forward, kissed her fingers and placed them gently on the stone. It was eight years since his death, and she still hadn't grown used to the fact he was no longer around to support her. Her father and her brother, both gone. Thank goodness she had Steve.

"He wouldn't want you to be sad, Rachel, you know that." Spanner put his arm around her.

Rachel rested her head on his shoulder. "It's hard not to be. Things have changed so much. When I think about the problems his relationship caused at the beginning..." She fell silent, remembering Charles's threat to expose her brother. She'd never found out whether that was why Paul had been arrested. Then there was her mother. Rachel sighed as he thought about Emily. Right up until the end, her mother had refused to accept Paul's homosexuality. At least there had been some kind of reconciliation before he died, but Rachel knew that her mother still blamed Heine for her son's premature death.

Spanner hugged her tight. "Don't stay here too long, it won't help." He changed the subject. "I have to go; I have a meeting." He kissed her forehead and hurried away. The message from Kurt had sounded urgent. He hoped there weren't problems with Jim again.

Rachel watched him for a few seconds, then turned back to the grave. She was due to meet Jamie later to discuss another subject that she would rather forget.

Mui Ne, north of Ho Chi Minh City, Vietnam

"An, Dung – quick, come here. I've found a fisherman willing to take us. We have to leave now on the evening tide." Long turned towards the other two men and their wives who were also waiting in the shadows on the beach and beckoned.

An and Dung crawled out of the hole they had dug in the sand dune, waited while the other couples joined them and followed Long back up the wide sandy beach until they reached Di, who was waiting with the baby. Together they made their way quickly along the darkened harbour wall until they saw numerous boats rocking gently on the incoming tide.

Long peered into the darkness, grateful for the light from the half moon. "It's over there." He moved towards one of the larger woven bamboo basket boats with a steering oar. An stared at it for a few seconds and wondered if he was mad. The boat was big enough to carry five or six men and their fishing gear, but they would not normally go too far out. He was about to trust his life to this craft in the ocean.

"Khẩn trương lên (*hurry up*)," an older man waved at them urgently, and An reluctantly put his fears aside. He had no option, not if he was going to escape. There was no going back; not now. He let the other couples climb aboard with Long and Di, Dung also stepped on and then An moved forward, but the fisherman put up his hand. "Sorry, no more room."

"Don't be ridiculous." Dung stopped abruptly and spoke before An could say anything. "We're brothers, we go together."

"Not in this boat, not if you don't want to sink it."

"What's the delay?" Long spoke from further in the boat

"There's no more room, if the other man gets on it will

sink." The old man glared at him. "I told you only seven people."

"Hurry up or we'll all be caught." The urgent whisper came from one of the other men.

Dung sighed, turned around and prepared to disembark. "Ok, we'll try and find another boat then."

"No, you can't do that," An interrupted. "Go, brother. I'll find another way."

Dung looked horrified. "I can't leave you..."

"Make your minds up, we're leaving." The old man began untying the rope.

An reached out from the jetty and patted Dung's shoulder, a sad smile on his face. "It's fine Dung, just go. No one is looking for me..." He placed the gun in Dung's pocket, ignoring his brother's protests. "You might need it."

"But I..."

"Either get off or sit down." The fisherman threw the rope on board, climbed over the side and sat down by the oar. The boat began to move and An stepped away. "Bye, Dung. Look after yourself..." Dung remained standing, his eyes fixed on An as the boat drifted slowly away. A gentle wave rocked the craft, knocking him off balance. He sat down abruptly, and when he looked up again, An was gone.

Omaha, Nebraska

"Where is he at the moment?" Spanner looked horrified.

"He's ok, I've left him with a friend. I just wanted to ask you something."

"Go ahead."

"Is it possible to get back into 'Nam?"

Spanner grimaced and shook his head. "I doubt it. Why on earth would you want to do that? I thought you hated the place?"

"I do... it was just an idea."

"Kurt?"

Kurt gave a nervous smile. "I can't explain why, ok? It doesn't matter. Honestly. I'd better go, I don't want to leave Jim too long." He turned and hurried away before Spanner could ask any more questions.

"Ok, I'll call in later." Spanner called after him, then shook his head in bemusement. He had no idea why Kurt would want to go back to 'Nam. Surely he wasn't planning on taking Jim back there?

Ho Chi Minh City, Vietnam

"I can't find either of them." Vy stood in the kitchen and faced Lien. She had spoken to everyone she could think of, and no one had seen either boy for weeks.

"You've looked everywhere?"

"Yes, they are definitely not in the city… unless they have been arrested?"

Lien gasped and grabbed the counter for support, then she shook her head. "No, if they'd been arrested, I'm sure Chinh would have told us. He wouldn't have been able to hide his delight, you know that."

Vy nodded. "Unless he wanted to let us worry?" She paused. "No, you're probably right. He would much rather see our reaction. So where on earth are they?"

"Perhaps they have left the country?" Lien's face lit up.

"Let's hope so."

"You should go, too." Lien reached out and took Vy's hand.

Vy squeezed her mother's hand. "We've been through this, Mẹ. I can't leave you, and if you won't go…"

"Chinh will never let me leave him. He would turn the country upside down to find me." Lien stared at Vy and decided it was time. "If anything happens to me, there's something I want you to have. If you go into the garden and look under the rose bush I planted, there is a small box. It contains a ring."

Vy looked interested. "That sounds very mysterious?"

"It belonged to your father. His name was Spanner. I want you to have it. He gave it to me when he promised he would always love me." Lien closed her eyes for a moment and remembered the love in Spanner's eyes when he'd given her the ring. If only Phuc hadn't interfered… She opened them again and forced herself back to the present. "I hid it when I came here because I knew Chinh would take it from me." She took Vy's hand. "Promise me you will get the ring and try and go to America if I am not here. The ring might help you to find your father. He came from a place called Nebraska. He had a farm there."

"I promise." Vy wished she could persuade Lien to leave, but she understood why she was too scared to risk it. Unfortunately, Vy feared that Chinh's reaction to her own disappearance would be the same as if Lien had dared to leave him, but she couldn't explain that to her mother without telling her about all the other things Chinh was guilty of. There was no way she could bring herself to do that. It would break her mother's heart to know she had been unable to protect her daughter.

Omaha, Nebraska

"I'm sorry, Jamie, I've given it lots of thought and I can't do it. It's too late." Rachel paced up and down Jamie's office before stopping and staring at him. "I've never told Richie anything about his father. How do you think he will react when he finds out he is the result of a rape?"

Jamie leaned forward and frowned. "I understand that, Rachel, but surely you don't intend for him to carry on getting away with raping other women?"

"Perhaps he will get careless one day, and then he can be arrested."

Jamie laughed harshly. "What makes you think that? It's eighteen years since he raped you, we've had lots of similar complaints over the years, and he still hasn't been caught. When you married, you told me you wouldn't let him get away with it, and now you are planning on doing exactly that!"

"What effect do you think it will have on Steve's career if I go public now? It will be all over the media, it will destroy any chance he has of running for Senate. He's your best friend. Can you justify doing that to him?"

Jamie stared at her. "I understand you're scared, Rachel, but we have been collecting evidence for years in the hope we could prove what he did. And now we have DNA, we can do that."

"Can we?" Rachel sighed. "It will still be my word against his. He will just say that I consented, you know he will."

"Yes, if it was just your case I would agree, but we have evidence from twenty-three other women. He can't say they all consented and then suddenly changed their mind and reported him to the police."

"And you think every woman whose evidence we kept will want to go through the indignity of court after all these years? Many of them will be married, have children of their own; they might not have told their husbands. I never told Steve who raped me, how do you think he will react when he finds out it's someone he could well have met? I'm not even sure I can cope with being cross-examined in court about it, opening all those memories I have locked away, treated like a liar." Rachel took a breath. "But the main thing is Richie. I can't do it to him, it will destroy him."

"Then Charles will get away with what he did and what he's probably still doing." Jamie slammed his hand on his desk, making her jump.

"You haven't had any new cases for months," Rachel returned.

"That doesn't mean he isn't still active – more likely, the women are too scared of coming forward now he's a well-known heart surgeon."

"You forgot to add 'well-respected'," Rachel added sarcastically.

Jamie stood up and walked round the desk and stared down at her. "Well, he is, you've seen the articles I showed you in the medical journals."

"Which makes it even harder to take action against him. He will be able to afford the best lawyers; however many women appear against him, he'll find some way of wriggling out of it." Rachel turned away.

Jamie took a breath. He could hear the fear in her voice, and he knew there was a chance she was right. She had survived the assault, had made a new life for herself and Richie, and although he didn't agree, he could understand why she didn't want to risk everything.

"I'm sorry, maybe there will be another opportunity for you to use the evidence we have, but I can't do it now."

Jamie nodded. "Ok, Rachel. I would never force you to do anything you didn't want to, you know that." He smiled faintly. "As you say, he may get careless one day."

"Thank you." Rachel breathed a sigh of relief, gave him a quick peck on the cheek and left.

Jamie sat back and let out a deep sigh. His feelings for Rachel were never far from the surface, despite the years that had passed and the fact she was married to his best friend. He had long accepted there would never be anything between them, but for some reason his heart wouldn't listen to his brain.

Vietnam

An walked slowly back towards Ho Chi Minh City. It would take him days, but he didn't want to risk the little money he had left on the train. In any case, he wasn't in a great hurry to go back to the capital, not on his own. It had been bad enough while Dung was in prison, but at least there was a chance he would eventually return. His brother wouldn't come back from America or wherever he finally ended up. He also wouldn't risk writing to them in case Chinh found the letter and punished Lien and Vy. The chances were that he wouldn't ever hear from Dung again.

An was still walking when it occurred to him that he would need to be careful if he returned to the city. If Chinh found out that his brother had escaped, he would take it out on Lien and Vy. Both boys had been missing for a while now, so it might be best to leave it like that in the hope that Chinh wouldn't bother looking for them.

However, he didn't want to leave his family completely at Chinh's mercy – not that he could do much to protect them anyway, but he couldn't live with himself if he just moved away. He would have to find a way of keeping an eye on his mother and sister from a distance. But if he had to keep his head down, he needed to find a job of some sort. If he carried on stealing, sooner or later he would be arrested. Perhaps his uncle would help?

South China Sea

The boat rocked gently on the waves as they sailed east towards the rising sun.

"It's beautiful, isn't it?" Di pointed to the orange glow lighting the tranquil water.

Dung tried to find some enthusiasm for the wonderful sunrise, but he couldn't bring himself to relax enough to enjoy the view. He was still regretting leaving without An.

"Are you sure this fisherman knows how to steer a boat to the Philippines?"

Di smiled. "Of course, do you think we would have risked this with Lan if he didn't?"

Dung forced an answering smile. "No, of course not." He leaned forward to speak to the fisherman. "So, we just keep going east?" He still wasn't convinced. "What happens when the sun is high in the sky?"

The fisherman laughed. "Don't worry, I have a compass." He saw Dung's confusion and explained. "It will help me to keep the boat going east. Just pray that the wind keeps blowing." The last thing they needed was for the wind to drop and leave them without power. Dung nodded, and decided he had no choice but to trust the man to get them safely to land.

He glanced at his fellow travellers; the other two couples had barely said anything since they had left. They were older than him, the women well-groomed, the men in expensive clothes. Everything about them screamed wealth and privilege, and that they had nothing in common with an Amerasian criminal like him. Dung looked away and wished An was with him. It was like leaving behind his right arm.

Omaha, Nebraska

"Are you sure you're ok now?" Spanner patted Jim on the shoulder.

"I'm fine, just had a bad day." Jim hoped Spanner wasn't going to ask too many questions.

Spanner sighed and decided to change the subject. Whatever trauma his friends had suffered, they had never spoken of it to him, and he knew better than to ask now. "How's business?" When he had decided to go into politics full time, Kurt had taken over running all the franchises. Spanner's original idea had been to divide the management between his two friends, but when he'd realised how unstable Jim was, he had changed his mind. Spanner had not wanted to risk his business and the other veterans who made up the workforce, so he had made Jim Kurt's deputy instead. That way, Kurt was in charge.

"Good. We've taken on some more veterans, and we've also used some of the profit to help with a down payment on rent for a couple of guys who were down on their luck. It's all in the monthly report." Kurt was relieved to be talking about something else. "We're seeing another couple of guys today." He shook his head. "I can't believe we're still having to do this, Spanner, but homelessness is growing, not shrinking."

Spanner nodded; he knew the score. "Do they have any other problems?"

"Yes, one of them is an alcoholic, the other was on heroin for years; he's coming off now, slowly. But I'll keep an eye on them both."

"Thanks Kurt. You're doing a great job. I'll come and meet them all over the next few days, and don't forget I'm at the end of the phone if you need me."

"I know, but I figure you are pretty busy, so unless I'm really stuck I wouldn't bother you. I also do what you suggested – as one guy gets better, he helps with the next. It works really well."

Spanner smiled. "I might not remember 'Nam, but I do remember basic training and how we work better as a unit, all supporting each other." He would have liked to spend more time with the men he was helping, but Kurt was managing fine and he didn't want to interfere or make it look like he didn't trust him to do the job properly. Also, although his position might allow him to do more to help, it also made it harder for him to have normal face-to-face conversations with people; all they saw was his office.

Kurt smiled ruefully, and for a moment he forgot their current problems and thought back to how they had all met. "We sure were innocent." He shook his head in disbelief.

"If only we'd known," Jim added. There was no humour in his face, only pain.

Spanner frowned; he hadn't meant to put them on a downer. "Sorry, guys. It's all in the past now – let's concentrate on the future."

"Yeah, all in the past…" Jim exchanged glances with Kurt. Spanner felt a momentary flash of irritation at being excluded, then quashed it. He was the lucky one, the one who couldn't remember. If they needed him to know, they would tell him. Until then, he would do his best to support them and any other veteran who needed him.

CHAPTER THIRTY-EIGHT

South China Sea

"Dung! Dung! Quick, wake up!" Di's shout finally woke him from a deep sleep.

"What is it?"

"I think it's a pirate boat!" Long shouted in terror.

Dung pulled out his gun and peered in the direction Long was pointing. The boat was larger than theirs and bearing down on them at speed. Dung could count six men, and they were bound to be armed. His heart sank. Even if he was an excellent shot, which he wasn't, it was unlikely he could kill them all before they returned fire. He looked back in the boat, the wealthy men and their wives huddling together in one corner, the fisherman frantically trying to steer their craft away from the rapidly-advancing boat, Long picking up an oar to protect himself, Di holding Lan tight to her body, her face pale with fear.

Dung glanced around the small craft again; there was nowhere to hide except under the seat. "Quick, Di, lay down under here with Lan and try and keep her quiet." Di had only just crawled into the small space when the boat came close, a couple of ropes were thrown around the oar rests, and before they could react two men had tied knots and were trying to climb aboard. Dung aimed carefully and fired. To his relief, both men fell into the sea. He could hear lots of shouting, but he couldn't understand the language, and then came the sound of answering shots. Dung ducked automatically – the bullet ricocheted off the mast, narrowly missing Long. He heard a scream and watched as one of the wealthy men collapsed. A pirate grabbed the man's wife and began dragging her onto their boat – Dung fired, and he fell into the sea, taking her with him. The other man tried to fight off another pirate, but he was no match for him and his lifeless body was soon floating in the waves. His wife was screaming and clawing at the face of another pirate as he dragged her aboard his boat.

Dung stepped unsteadily forward, drew the knife out of the chest of the first wealthy man and threw it at a pirate trying to climb aboard. Above the sound of the waves crashing against the sides of the boat, he could hear the woman screaming on the pirate ship, and without thinking, Dung scrambled aboard. The woman was already naked, the man thrusting violently against her. Dung stepped towards him, placed the gun at the back of his head and fired, blood spurting all over the woman, whose cries grew even louder. Dung ignored her, turning his attention back to his own boat just in time to see the fisherman being thrown overboard and the pirate turning his attention to Long, who was trying to fight him off with an oar. As Dung climbed back on board, the pirate wrestled the oar away from Long and, before Dung could reach him, he had fired at close range.

Long fell back, blood blooming across the fabric of his shirt, and Dung went cold with horror. "*No*!" he shouted, aiming at the last of the pirates and firing. The splash was followed by a sudden silence that was deafening. Dung stood frozen in shock for several seconds, taking in the carnage around him. One of the wealthy men was dead, his eyes open, staring sightlessly at the night sky. He could count four dead pirates, he had seen one go overboard and there was one on the other craft. The other rich man and one of the wives had gone into the sea, and the other wife was still on the raider's boat. He could hear her sobbing. Dung took a breath and made his way towards Long.

"Are you badly hurt?"

There was no answer. Dung placed his hand near Long's nose but couldn't feel any breath. "Shit…" he swore and leaned closer. "Long, please speak to me…"

"Long?" Di had crawled out from under the sail, Lan sleeping peacefully in her arms. An wondered how on earth the baby had not woken during all the noise. "Long…?"

"I'm sorry, Di… I think he's dead." Dung could hardly say the words.

Di stared at him and shook her head. "He can't be. You're lying." Her voice rose an octave as she leant over Long's body and felt for a pulse. Tears ran down her cheeks.

"Long, please don't leave me..." Her sobs eventually woke Lan, who also began to cry. Dung peered around nervously. If there was one pirate boat around, there were probably others. "We have to get out of here in case there are any more of them. Let's get on board the pirate boat, it's bigger."

Di peered at him in shock and terror, and then down at Lan, who was still crying. The baby's cries seem to bring her to her senses, and to Dung's relief she nodded. She picked up her bag, moved to the other end of the boat and Dung helped her climb aboard the pirate craft. "I'll get as much food and water as I can, we don't know how long we'll be out here." He disappeared from sight. Di glanced across at the other woman, who was huddled in a corner, shaking. Di moved slowly forwards, intending to comfort her, but the woman suddenly leapt up, stepped towards the bow and jumped over. Di screamed.

Dung leapt back onto the pirate boat, a knife in his hand. "Di? What is it?"

"She just jumped..." Di's face was pale with shock and fear.

Dung cursed, then he took a breath. "There's nothing we can do, Di. I'm going to untie the other boat."

Di watched as the fishing boat drifted slowly away, tears streaming down her cheeks as Long vanished into the gloom. She sat down and cuddled Lan and, as the darkness gradually receded, she tried to pull herself together. "Can you steer this boat?" She stared up at him.

Dung shrugged. He had been asking himself the same question for the last hour. But there was no point worrying her. "I can do my best. Just concentrate on Lan." He sat down by the wheel and glanced up at the sky. To his relief, the sun was starting to rise, so he could at least make a start in the right direction. He realised Di was still watching him, and he repeated his earlier assurances. "I will do my best. See to Lan." As she moved slowly away, Dung peered ahead and tried to keep calm. He knew nothing about boats, and now he was stuck on his own, in a boat with a woman and a baby, in a sea that held more dangers than the weather.

Omaha, Nebraska

Spanner climbed the last of the stairs to his office and leaned back against the door of the stairwell, breathing hard. He had started taking the stairs instead of the elevator over the last few months in an attempt to get fitter, after realising he was becoming noticeably out of breath after the smallest of activities. He thought back to his first couple of months in the army and how fit he had been then, and shook his head. He really needed to get back in shape. He couldn't expect to be as healthy as he had been when he was twenty, but he was sure he shouldn't be this tired all the time. It wasn't as if he was that old; it must just be too much easy living.

He walked the last few steps to his office and sat down gratefully behind his desk. His leg was aching badly, but he was used to that. He reached into the drawer and took out one of his favourite cigars. He was sure Rachel was right and that smoking wasn't helping his breathing, but he couldn't make himself give them up, because they were a legacy of his days in Vietnam. Unable to remember anything of his time there, the cigars had become a symbol of his service, a link with the past.

He glanced through his in-tray and sighed. There were some veteran's letters in a separate tray – he would start with them.

Outskirts of Ho Chi Minh City, Vietnam

"What the hell are you doing here?" Phuc stared up at An in disbelief. He had just settled down to watch some television when the door to his apartment had opened.

An stepped in and glanced around the tidy room, taking in the expensive ornaments and comfortable furniture. It looked like Phuc was doing very well for himself. He had hidden outside and watched the apartment block for several days until he was sure Phuc lived alone.

"I need your help." An sat down on one of the seats opposite his uncle.

"You think you can just walk in here and demand things from me?" Phuc stood up, fury on his face.

"Yes, you're my uncle," An said, with more confidence

than he felt. "I want a job. It doesn't have to pay well, just enough so I can stay in the city and keep an eye on my mother and sister – something you should be doing yourself."

"How dare you –"

"I dare because you have done nothing to help your sister, my mother. You know what Chinh is like, but you don't ever go and see her, do you? Aren't you ashamed of yourself?"

Phuc flushed. "It's not that easy..."

An relented. "No, it isn't, is it? Chinh makes it impossible, and I understand that, Uncle, but I can't desert them as well."

Phuc sat down again, and gazed at him in silence for what felt like several minutes. Then he nodded. "I can get you some papers in another name, and I have a friend who owns a restaurant. I can get you work washing dishes there. Do you have somewhere to stay?"

An shook his head. "No, I am living on the streets."

"There are rooms to rent near the restaurant." He saw An's surprise and shrugged. "I eat at the restaurant regularly; I see the rental signs every time I go there. Come back in two days, I'll have the papers then and I'll have sorted the job."

An nodded and stood up. "Thank you, Uncle." He had almost reached the door when Phuc spoke again.

"Where's your brother?"

An turned around and smiled. "On his way to America."

Phuc paled. "He's escaped?"

"Yes. That's why I want to be near my mother and sister… in case Chinh finds out."

South China Sea

The sun was sinking slowly into the sea behind them, so Dung knew he was sailing in the right direction. In the bow of the boat Di was crooning softly to Lan, tears pouring down her cheeks. Dung sighed. It was days since they had cut the fishing boat loose, but Di was still grieving.

At least it was cooler now the sun had gone down, but there was no relief in sight. The cloudless skies and endless sunshine every day was taking its toll. Trying to make their water last was the biggest problem; he took a couple of sips and glanced at their dwindling supply. They wouldn't survive too many more days at sea. The water was almost gone, and there was virtually no food left. He held out the bottle to Di. "Would you like a drink?"

She nodded and took the bottle. "There's some bread left, if you want some."

Dung shook his head. "You and Lan have it, I'm ok."

"But what about you?"

"I'm…" He stopped abruptly. "Can you hear that?"

Di listened hard, brow creased with effort. "It sounds like a radio?" She peered into the growing darkness. "I can't see anything, can you?"

Dung shook his head. "No." He stood up and looked around.

"Maybe they will rescue us." Di's face had lit up.

Dung didn't answer for a few seconds. "It might be another pirate boat."

Di paled, held Lan closer to her and began trembling.

Dung reached into his pocket and pulled out his gun. He didn't have much ammunition left, so he could only pray it was a cargo ship or someone that would rescue them.

Ten minutes later, a large ship came into view on the horizon. Dung stood up again and began waving frantically. "Here, over here!" He knew they couldn't hear him – it was doubtful they could even see him – but he had to try.

"Dung!" Di suddenly screamed, and he spun around. While he had been concentrating on the ship, a pirate boat had appeared behind them. He pulled out his gun and fired wildly in their direction. He hit one man, then the gun stopped firing. Dung looked around for something else to defend them with, but there was nothing, and then there were men climbing on the boat.

Di backed towards him, screaming. One of the pirates grabbed her, pulled Lan from her arms and threw the baby into the sea. Before Dung could react, the man had shoved Di down on the floor and began clawing at her clothes. Dung tried to pull him off, but he was no match for the much bigger man. He fought hard, but within moments he was in the sea. The waves closed over his head, his mouth and nose filled with seawater and he began to sink slowly downwards.

Omaha, Nebraska

"Thanks so much for your help, Governor." The veteran was thin, his eyes full of tears as Spanner shook his hand.

"You don't need to thank me, it's us who should be thanking you for your service – and please call me Spanner."

"They said you were there too?" The man's eyes took on a haunted look.

Spanner nodded. "I was. But the explosion that gave me these," he indicated his scars and walking stick, "robbed me of my memory – so I guess it did some good, right?"

The man didn't smile. "You're lucky, sir, not to be able to remember. I mean, not about the injuries..."

"It's alright, my friends here would agree with every word. My injuries can be seen, yours can't, but we are here for you. You only have to ask, ok?"

"Thank you, sir – Spanner."

Spanner smiled and shook the hand of the next man. "Settled in ok?"

"Yes... Spanner... thank you so much..."

"No, please don't thank me. Honestly, I just want to help, so if you know any other 'Nam vets who also need our help, let Kurt know, ok? We can't work miracles, but we can help to find you a job and somewhere to live, and if you need it, we can get you medical help too."

An hour later, Spanner made his way back to his office. He enjoyed meeting the men they were helping, but he wished it didn't take them so long to see past his office and treat him like a fellow vet.

South China Sea

Dung could hear voices coming from a long way away. They gradually came nearer, and he opened his eyes.

"He's awake, sir."

Dung frowned. The man was speaking English, and he forced himself to concentrate. He glanced around; he appeared to be in a small room, but the whole thing was undulating gently.

"Glad you're back with us, son." The doctor hesitated, wondering how to tell him that the woman who had been on the boat was dead. "I'm Doctor Raphael. You're on a British cargo ship. I'm sorry to tell you this, but the woman on your boat is dead. She jumped into the sea when we arrived. We shot the man who was attacking her, but she just jumped. We searched frantically, that's how we found you. I'm so sorry. Was she your wife?"

Dung shook his head and spoke in English. "No… no, I was friend of Di and husband. We were attacked by pirates some days ago… husband was killed. Did you find Lan?" He saw the doctor's confusion and searched for the right words.

"Lan is baby?"

The doctor looked shocked. "Baby, what baby?"

"Men threw Lan into sea then attacked Di."

"No, there was no sign." The doctor sighed. That would explain why the woman had jumped. "You're not injured, so just rest until you feel able to move around."

"What happen me?" Dung had to know if they were going to take him back to Vietnam.

"We're on our way to the Philippines, so we will take you there. Are you trying to get to America?"

Dung nodded. "Yes." He frowned. "How you know?"

The doctor gave a wry smile. "Why else would you be risking your life in a fishing boat in the South China Sea?" He patted him on the shoulder. "Well, with a bit of luck you'll get there once you've spent some time in the Philippines."

Dung smiled back as the weight of the last few months fell from his shoulders. He'd done it. He was sorry about Long and Di and the baby, but if he really did get to America, he might be able to arrange for the rest of his family to come too.

CHAPTER THIRTY-NINE

Omaha, Nebraska

"Do you really think we have a chance of winning this time?" They were watching the Vice-Presidential debate between Republican Senator Dan Quale of Indiana and Democratic Senator Lloyd Bentsen of Texas taking place in Omaha. As Dan Quale insisted that he had as much experience in government as John F. Kennedy had when he sought the presidency in 1960, Rachel snorted. "That's ridiculous. Imagine trying to compare himself to Kennedy!"

Spanner was about to answer when Senator Bentsen replied, "Senator, I knew Jack Kennedy. I served with Jack Kennedy. Jack Kennedy was a friend of mine. Senator, you're no Jack Kennedy." Spanner and Rachel both burst out laughing.

"I saw a popular poll saying Dukakis was seventeen percentage points ahead of Bush."

Spanner shrugged. "I wouldn't bank on it, Rachel; the polls aren't always right."

"If they win again, this will be the third consecutive

Republican victory," Rachel mused. "I'm beginning to wonder if we can ever get back into government."

"Sure we can, honey; maybe even this time. Keep positive."

"Why don't you run for Senate in the next elections?" Rachel sat forward and looked at him. "You are really popular. I'm sure you could win."

"It's not that easy, Rachel." Spanner didn't want to admit that he had already been thinking about it, but had given up because the cost would be astronomical. "I don't have the kind of money you would need."

"Then we look for backing, it shouldn't be that hard." Rachel was becoming more enthusiastic by the minute. "You have lots of friends high up in the party. I'm sure they would support you if you let them know you were interested."

"I don't know..."

"Just think how much more you could do for veterans if you were a Senator." Rachel wasn't about to give up that easily. Whatever Steve said, she had a feeling Bush would be elected. Rachel needed something to take her mind off Paul's death and her refusal to go along with Jamie's plans to prosecute Charles. Planning an election campaign for Steve would be the perfect thing to occupy her.

PRPC (Philippine Refugee Processing Centre) near Morong, Bataan, Philippines

Dung had disembarked from the ship a few weeks earlier and had soon settled into the camp. He was provided with food, basic housing and medical treatment if he needed it, and was expected to attend classes and do two hours of voluntary community service every day. Dung found the classes difficult. He hadn't attended school since he was a child, and at first just sitting in a classroom brought back all the bad memories he thought he'd forgotten. This wasn't helped by the behaviour and attitude of some of his fellow Vietnamese, who continued to treat him as an outcast. He also had to keep reminding himself to answer to An's name; An didn't have a criminal record, so he'd had to keep using his name.

"You have to learn to read, write and speak English properly, An, or you won't be able to go to America, and when you get there you won't be able to work." Sandie Clarke was an Australian teacher employed by the UNHCR (United Nation High Commissioner for Refugees).

"I think I am too old now to learn," Dung smiled at her. Sandie was very pretty, and she was nice too.

"You're never too old, Dung. If you like, I can give you extra lessons?" Sandie knew she wasn't supposed to do that, but she had heard the other Vietnamese bullying and harassing him, and it made her angry. Some of the worst offenders were those from the High Officer Group, former government and military officials who had worked with the Americans, political prisoners who had come out through a Humanitarian Operation.

"You would do that for me?" Dung was astonished.

Sandie blushed. "I'll meet you later this evening, outside, at about eight." That would leave plenty of time before the curfew at nine-thirty. It would also help to keep him away from the drinking dens. Fighting and drinking were common in the camp, and the jail was usually full. Those sentenced for serious offences would forfeit their right to go to America.

"Thank you. You are very kind."

Dung watched her go back to the classroom and smiled. He would have to try harder now. He knew Sandie was right. If he didn't learn the language properly, he would struggle when he got to America, and the last thing he wanted was to end up living the same kind of life there as he had in Vietnam.

Ho Chi Minh City, Vietnam

An followed Chinh from a safe distance. He was reasonably sure he knew where Chinh was going, but he wanted to make sure. A few moments later he stopped, leaned back against the wall of a closed shop and lit a cigarette. Chinh was nothing if not predictable. Twice a week he visited the brothel, and from what An could see he always went with the same girl. An had started following Chinh a few weeks earlier, looking for anything he could use against him, but so far had found nothing. His mother wouldn't care that Chinh was using a brothel, she would probably be delighted Chinh wasn't bothering her. If she could simply have left him, she would have already done so.

Much to his surprise, An was enjoying working in the restaurant. Phuc's friend Dao Cam Be, the owner, was easy to work for. She had even suggested that he learn to cook and had given him a couple of lessons after work. An had tried, but soon realised that he didn't have an aptitude for cooking. His real talent had emerged after Be's delivery van had broken down and her normal mechanic wasn't available. An had offered to take a look, and in desperation, because she was losing money, Be had agreed. Despite never having worked on cars before, An had resolved the problem within moments, quickly spotting that a wire had come lose. Be had been so impressed that she had not only paid him a bonus, but had arranged for him to have some lessons when he wasn't working. An had discovered he had a passion for engines, and was soon working more at the garage than at the restaurant. He had just done his last shift at the restaurant, and from the next day he'd be working full time at the garage.

An put out his cigarette and wandered slowly back to the

room he was renting. If he could only find something he could use against Chinh that would allow his mother and sister to leave, he would be completely happy – but so far, all Chinh seemed to do was to visit the brothel. He would just have to keep following him and hope something would come up.

Houston, Texas

"Good heavens, if it isn't Rachel Hanson." Charles Peterson sat back at his desk and stared at her in what she assumed had to be fake astonishment. He must have known it was her because she'd had to give her name when she made the appointment. Rachel sighed. Charles hadn't changed much; his hair was thinning slightly on top, but the arrogance was still there. Unfortunately, it was like looking at an older version of Richie. She pushed the thought away and concentrated on why she was here.

"Rachel *Tanner* now." Rachel fought back her revulsion as memories of the last time they were together flooded her mind. She glanced around his office, the expensive décor, the original oil paintings on the walls, and wondered how much of it Chares had actually earned and how much was paid for with the Peterson money. "You've done well for yourself."

"I could say the same about you, married to the Nebraska State Governor. Obviously didn't mind you having a bastard in tow, then?" He laughed.

Rachel walked towards his desk and sat down. "I'm so pleased you brought up our son, Charles. The child who is a result of the night you raped me. The child who you owe me seventeen years of child support for. I've come to collect."

Charles burst out laughing. "You've got some balls, Rachel. I'll give you that. What makes you think I'm going to pay you anything?"

Rachel smiled. "DNA, Charles. You're a medical man, I'm sure you understand how easy it would be to prove you are my son's father." She was pleased to see the smile fade from his face. She pressed on. "I could take you to court for the money, but I am sure you would prefer to come to an arrangement."

"Are you really trying to blackmail me? If you think you've got a case, take me to court." He stood up. "Now get out!"

Rachel didn't move. "I had a feeling you might try to wriggle out of your responsibility, so I thought I would remind you of the publicity that me going to court would generate. Once it reaches the media… I am sure there are a few other girls raising your bastards. Would you like me to name a few of them?" Rachel had used the files Jamie had given her to trace some of the women. At least half a dozen had children with ages that fitted in with the dates of the complaints against Charles.

Charles glared at her, then sat down again. "The publicity wouldn't do your husband any good either."

Rachel smiled. "I think most people would think he's a nice guy for taking in someone else's child. You on the other hand..."

Charles slammed his fist down on the desk, making her jump. "You *bitch*..."

Rachel raised her eyebrows. "Well?"

"How much?"

Rachel smiled, reached into her handbag, and pulled out a piece of paper with some numbers written on it. She slid the paper across the desk.

Charles read it and let out a harsh laugh. "That's ridiculous."

Rachel shrugged and stood up. "Ok. I'll see you in court, then."

Charles waited until she had almost reached the door before shouting after her. "Ok! I'll write you a cheque."

Rachel breathed a sigh of relief and turned back. She made no attempt to hide the triumph in her eyes as she took the cheque. "Goodbye, Charles." As she left the room she remembered her promise to Jamie on her wedding day that she would make Charles pay; she hadn't meant like this, but it was something. It also gave her another degree of leverage over him, as he wouldn't like his Republican friends to know that one of their biggest financial backers had also backed a Democrat.

Rachel hurried to the bank. She didn't think he would change his mind and try to cancel the cheque, but there was no point taking chances. Now she had the money for Steve's campaign, she would start looking for Democrats to support him.

Charles watched her hurrying away and tried to control his temper. No one blackmailed him and got away with it. He thought for a moment and then smiled. He knew exactly how he would get his revenge on Rachel.

Ho Chi Minh City, Vietnam

"How dare you not tell me that An had left Vietnam?" Chinh stormed into the apartment and slapped Lien hard across the face.

Lien staggered under his blow, put her hand up to her stinging face and stared at him in shock. "I don't know what you're talking about?"

Chinh hit her again, this time knocking her to the floor. "Don't lie, you stupid bitch. He's in the Philippines. My contact tells me their immigration department has been investigating him." He kicked her hard in the stomach. "Where's the other worthless scum?"

Lien shook her head. "I don't know, I swear."

"Lying bitch." Chinh kicked her again, then pulled her to her feet and slapped her hard across the face, breaking her nose.

Lien could feel blood pouring down her face, but all she could think of was that her son had escaped.

"What are you doing?" Vy rushed in and tried to pull him off. Chinh shoved her to one side, knocking her over.

"That worthless scum An has escaped, and I want to know where Dung is."

"Escaped?" Vy could hardly hide her elation.

Chinh took a menacing step towards her. Vy tried to back away. "I don't know. We haven't seen either of them for years." She got to her feet. "It's true – you have to believe us."

"You're both liars." Chinh turned his attention back to Lien and began shouting. "Answer me!"

Lien raised her head and smiled. "Even if I knew where he was, I would never tell you." She spat at him.

Vy gasped in horror. What on earth was the matter with her mother? She would only make Chinh even more angry. She was about to speak when she realised Chinh was undoing his belt.

"No – she didn't mean it –"

"Shut up, whore." Chinh punched her hard on the chin, sending her sprawling, then turned back to Lien and raised his belt.

Vy tried in vain to pull him away, and eventually succeeded. But instead of stopping his assault, Chinh grabbed Lien and yanked her to her feet. As Vy watched, he dragged Lien towards the door of the apartment, and before she could react, he had shoved Lien down the concrete stairs.

Outskirts of Ho Chi Minh City, Vietnam

"I'm so sorry, An." Phuc knew the words were totally inadequate, but he was struggling with his own guilt.

"And he got away with it?" An could barely speak, he was so angry.

"Yes, he told the authorities that Lien slipped and fell down the stairs... Vy backed him up, she didn't have any choice. But she told me what had happened."

"Is it safe for me to visit Vy?"

Phuc shook his head. "If you want to do it without him knowing, then I would say no. But does it matter if he sees you now?"

An stared at him for several seconds without speaking. "Yes, it does. I do not want him to know I am still in the city, because I am going to make him pay."

Phuc looked uneasy. "What are you going to do?"

An gave a harsh laugh and his eyes bore into Phuc's. "I don't know yet, but he will regret the day he ever married my mother."

Phuc swallowed and cleared his throat. "Do you want me to let Vy know you are here?"

An shook his head. "No. She would not betray me on purpose, but who knows what Chinh will do to her if he thinks she knows where I am? Better she thinks I too have left the country."

CHAPTER FORTY

Omaha, Nebraska, 1989

"So, Reagan's Department of Veterans Affairs Act has finally come into effect." Rachel sighed and switched off the news. Although she was pleased there was some recognition of veterans, a part of her wished it had been brought in by Democrats, rather than Republicans. Even better if Steve had been involved.

"Yes, let's hope it does what it's supposed to." Spanner had read through the legislation carefully and he had his doubts. Its remit wasn't much different to that of its predecessor, the Veterans Administration set up in 1930, and he had a feeling it had only been passed to avoid alienating large numbers of military voters.

"You don't sound very happy?" Rachel stared at him in surprise. She had been expecting him to be jumping for joy.

"Oh, I am. I'm just not sure it's going to make that much difference on the ground, the place where the help is really needed. The Republicans are determined not to let the state expand any further, and unless it does, it can't help people, not really. I think it's just window dressing, to be honest, but hopefully I'm wrong."

Omaha, Nebraska

"I'll get you the money, I swear." Richie cowered in the corner of the room, his face turning puce from the pressure of the man's hands around his throat.

"I told you not to gamble in my premises ever again!" Frank Belotti yelled at him, before ordering the man to let go.

Richie gasped air into his lungs gratefully, his face returning slowly to its normal colour. He breathed in deeply again, and then doubled up in pain as Frank punched him in his stomach. "What the fuck were you doing in my casino?"

"I'm sorry, I… I just wanted to play cards." He tried smiling. "You know how it is…"

Frank shook his head. "No. I don't. You're a fucking idiot, and I don't need you fucking up my business."

"I won't, I swear…"

"Your family can cause me problems, and I don't need that hassle."

"They won't – I'll get the money."

"How are you going to get the money, shitface, without getting it from your family? And if you do that, I'll have the police breathing down my neck again, like they were last time!" Frank hit him hard again.

"I'll tell them not to bother you." Richie gasped.

Frank grabbed him, lifted him up by his shirt and slammed him against the wall. "You'd better sort it and quick. You understand?"

"Yes… yes." Richie stared at his own reflection in the large mirror. He was so close he could see the fear in his eyes.

Frank abruptly released him and Richie crumpled to the floor, sweat pouring off his face. He would have to go to his grandmother. No doubt she would shout at him, but at least she wouldn't beat him up.

Frank waited until Richie had left and then opened the door. "Was that alright?"

Charles laughed. "Perfect. Nice touch slamming into the mirror so I could see the fear in his eyes. I thought he was going to shit himself." He handed Frank some money. "For your time."

Frank grinned, pocketed the money and watched Charles leave the room.

Charles made his way out of the club. It had taken a while, but he'd found a way to get Richie gambling again. Angela had been quite difficult, she had taken a lot of persuasion to dump Richie, but she'd done it eventually. Charles smiled. If Rachel thought he was going to pay for her Democrat husband to get elected, she could think again. By the time he'd finished, all the money he'd given her would have gone to Frank Belotti, a known member of the mob. Not a good look for a prospective senator.

Ho Chi Minh City, Vietnam

Vy cowered in the corner of the bedroom and prayed that Chinh would soon go to work. It was nearly six months since he had murdered her mother, and she hadn't been allowed to leave the apartment since.

"Make sure you have dinner on the table when I get home." He grabbed her chin and forced her to meet his eyes. "Don't forget I have people watching, so don't try to leave – or you know what will happen to you."

"I won't, I promise." Vy knew exactly what would happen, she had the scars on her back from his belt from when she had run away before to prove it. She hadn't tried again; she was too scared. If only she could get a message to her uncle. Phuc had always been nice to her, unlike her brothers who he seemed to hate. But without being able to leave the apartment she couldn't beg for his help.

The door slammed and she let out her breath shakily. At least she would be on her own for a few hours. Vy stood up and walked slowly into the kitchen. The bedroom was a constant reminder of her mother. Chinh had specifically forbidden Vy from throwing anything away, telling her that the traces of her mother would remind her what would happen if she lied to him.

Vy sat down on the floor and cried. There was still no word about Dung. Obviously Chinh had not been able to find him – the temptation to gloat about that would have been too much for him. Vy allowed herself a small smile. When Chinh had found out that someone had paid her brother's prison sentence, he had thrown things around the apartment, but he hadn't suspected that Lien had been responsible because he knew she'd had no money. Fortunately, Chinh had assumed that it was someone in the gang Dung worked for, otherwise he would probably have taken out his anger and frustration on Vy, even though she wasn't responsible. She shivered. If only she knew where Dung was it would give her some comfort, but he was unlikely to come to the apartment, it was much too dangerous. She would just have to pray he was safe.

Omaha, Nebraska

"You promised me you wouldn't gamble again, Richie. You'd stopped for ages, why on earth have you started again? Or have you been lying to me?" Emily sounded more disappointed than angry.

"No, I did stop. I… I…" Richie fell silent.

"I want an explanation, or I'm not bailing you out."

"I split up with Angela."

Emily stared at him in disbelief. "You split up with your girlfriend of, what is it… three months? And you were so upset you decided to go and blow $5,000?"

Richie nodded. Put like that, it did sound pretty pathetic, but last night he'd been devastated.

"You didn't think of just getting drunk and screwing some other girl like any normal man would do?"

"I'm sorry..."

Emily shook her head. "No, I'm sorry, Richie. I can't keep bailing you out, not without speaking to your mother first." She saw his expression and decided to explain. "I promised your mother I would tell her if you did this again."

Richie paled. "She knew about the other time?" He felt sick. "You said you wouldn't tell her."

"Yes; we agreed I would deal with it and that there was no need for her to get involved." Emily paused. "Get out. I need to speak to your mother so we can decide what to do next."

Emily waited until he'd left the room and then picked up the phone.

Ho Chi Minh City, Vietnam

Chinh had been standing outside the apartment block for an hour, waiting to see if Vy disobeyed him and went out. He had been doing the same thing every day since he had killed Lien. Chinh smiled as he thought about Lien's last day. She had got what she deserved, finally. He had suspected from the very first time that she was a traitor, but he had wanted to fuck her, so he'd turned a blind eye. He had hoped that once would be enough to get her out of his system, but she had continued to haunt his dreams when he was asleep and his thoughts when he was awake. Because of that, he had given her the benefit of the doubt when she'd cultivated the American.

Deep down he had known she had been playing him, but because of his feelings he had allowed her to get away with it until Phuc had confirmed his suspicions. Then he had finally acted, convinced that without the American she would fall into his arms, but instead she'd told him she was pregnant and, as much as he wanted her, he couldn't even bear to look at her swollen body, so he'd walked away. He had never forgotten her, though, and after the war he'd genuinely thought they could make a fresh start – and they might have done, if she hadn't chosen her sons over him. That was why he'd turned to Vy for comfort. It hadn't mattered that she was little more than a child; he had no such scruples. His only regret was that Lien had died without knowing what he had done to her precious daughter.

"Let me know if she goes out or anyone comes to visit her."

"Yes, of course. You know I will, sir." The elderly neighbour was only too happy to spy for Chinh in the hope of favours.

Chinh walked slowly towards his car. In some ways, it was disappointing that Vy didn't attempt to disobey him. He would just have to find another excuse to punish her.

Omaha, Nebraska

The television in the corner of the office was broadcasting the news about demonstrators marching in Washington, demanding legal abortions.

"Are you ok, honey?" The phone was ringing but Rachel was ignoring it, seemingly fixated on the news.

Rachel started. "Yes, sorry." She suddenly realised the telephone was ringing, but still made no attempt to answer it. "It was just reminding me of Richie."

Spanner nodded. "Your parents…"

Rachel gave a wry smile. "Just Emily, actually. I don't think Pop would have thought about it. Emily was always the driving force." In the last few years Rachel had begun referring to her mother as Emily, as if to distance herself from their relationship. "Ironic when you think how close they've become." The phone had gone quiet now.

"She's the only grandmother the kids have now." Spanner's parents had both died within a year of each other. His father first, from a heart attack, and his mother from a massive stroke. They hadn't been that much older than he was now. He brought his attention back to Rachel. "Richie was closer to my parents than the others because he's the oldest. He missed them when they died, so it was only natural he would transfer his affection to her."

"I get that. And I wouldn't mind if she stopped interfering. We spent ages encouraging him to go to college to study engineering and she talked him out of it."

"He does seem happy though, honey. Maybe your mother was right. Richie was never that interested in engineering, perhaps he is better suited to journalism."

"Maybe, but that wasn't her decision to make, was it?"

Spanner sighed and picked up his newspaper again. He understood why Rachel was so annoyed, but her mother wouldn't change now, and he was fed up being caught in the crossfire. He winced at a sudden sharp pain in his chest and made a mental note not to eat so much spicy food late at night. Perhaps he should see a doctor; he was sure indigestion shouldn't be this painful. It wouldn't hurt to check.

He was still thinking about it when the phone started again. This time Rachel automatically reached for it. There was a brief silence then she exploded. "For Christ's sake, Emily. You said you'd sorted it!" She slammed down the phone and shoved the papers on the desk onto the floor.

"Rachel, what on earth...?"

"Richie has been gambling again."

Spanner stared at her in horror and felt his temper rising. "I thought your mother had that under control – that's why we decided to stay out of it, pretend we didn't know. If he owes that mobster more money..." The sharp pain in his chest had come back with a vengeance, and he grimaced in pain.

"Don't worry, I'll speak to him this time." Rachel was

so angry she could hardly speak. She hadn't blackmailed Richie's father for money to give it all to some gangster to pay off his gambling debts. "He'll wish Belotti had got hold of him by the time I've finished with him." She stood up and reached for her handbag, then realised that Spanner looked very pale. "Are you ok?"

"Yes, just indigestion I think." He started to reach for the tablets he kept in his drawer, but the pain was now spreading down his arm and into his shoulder. He gasped, and Rachel forgot her anger with Richie. "Do you want me to call 911?"

Spanner forced a laugh, even though the pain was getting worse. "I'm sure it's just indigestion..." The pain grew stronger, sharp, as if someone was stabbing him, then everything went black.

"Steve!" Rachel screamed as he collapsed on the floor. She rushed over to him and checked his pulse before picking up the phone, dialling 911 and trying to stay calm. "Ambulance... Hurry, please. My husband, Steve Tanner..." she gave the address, "yes, he's the State Governor... he's collapsed with chest pain." She listened to the questions and answered as best she could. "His face is grey... his breathing is very shallow... his pulse is barely there." She fought back tears. "His father had a heart attack a few years ago, it looks like that." She replaced the receiver and hurried back to Steve, who was still unconscious. "The ambulance is on its way. Please don't die, darling." Tears streamed down her face. "I can't live without you... Steve..."

CHAPTER FORTY-ONE

Re-education Camp Outside Ho Chi Minh City, Vietnam

Phuc finished the last of his paperwork releasing several RVN soldiers and officers who had been in the camp since the end of the war, and sighed. They were now free to go to America, unlike him who was stuck in a country he hated. People like his brother-in-law had completely ruined the country and corrupted so many of their youth, promising them a utopia and instead removing all their freedoms and condemning them to lives of poverty and fear. If only they had been able to see into the future all those years ago, Lien might still be alive. He had spent the best years of his life serving a cruel repressive regime, and he couldn't see any way out. No doubt to those incarcerated in the camp, Phuc seemed to have a pretty good life, but he was just as much a prisoner as they were. He couldn't express an opinion that didn't agree with the regime, he couldn't travel without permission, nor could he leave the country to start a new life.

Phuc gazed at the papers of those men who were finally being allowed to leave his camp and envied them. He stood up and walked over to the window, and thought about Lien. She had seen the light long before him and he had ruined that for her – he had allowed his jealousy to get the better of him and let Chinh manipulate him into killing the man she loved. He had then wasted years hating her sons, and not supporting her, and now Lien was dead and An was hiding under false papers, vowing revenge. Although he couldn't see how his nephew could possibly avenge Lien's murder without being killed. Dung had at least escaped, but the chances of ever seeing him again were remote. Even worse, because of his fear he had left his niece at the mercy of the monster who had killed his sister.

Phuc took a breath and wondered if he should risk going to see Vy. But what if she refused to see him? He could hardly blame her; he had abandoned her and her mother. Or worse, what if Chinh saw him there? He had been quite clear in his warning for Phuc to stay away. He rested his head in his hands. He was grateful his family weren't still alive to see the way he had behaved to his sister. They would be so ashamed of him. He was worthless.

Omaha, Nebraska

"I'm so sorry, Mom." Richie was almost as pale as Spanner had been when he had collapsed. "I wouldn't have done anything to upset Spanner, you know that."

"But you did. It was the shock of hearing about your gambling that gave him the heart attack!" Rachel snapped.

"That's not entirely fair, Rachel," Emily interrupted. "Obviously, Spanner already had a problem, or he wouldn't have had a heart attack."

"Oh well, that's alright then." Rachel rounded on her. "My son owes the mob more money, despite you saying you sorted it out, but it's not his fucking fault. Jesus fucking Christ," she ignored her mother's shocked expression, "stop making things worse. Richie doesn't need any encouragement to behave like an asshole. You can pay this latest lot off, I don't see why I should, seeing as you had assured me you had it sorted." She turned back to Richie, stepped towards him, her eyes boring into his. "And as for you. If you ever gamble again, I will personally hand you over to Belotti and tell him he has my permission to do whatever is necessary to teach you a lesson. Have you got that?"

Richie paled even more. "Yes, Mom. I'm sorry, really I am."

"Don't keep saying that!" Rachel screamed at him. "He could have died. Do you understand that?"

Richie nodded his head vigorously. "Yes, yes, I do, I

promise. Please, Mom…"

Rachel stared at him for several seconds, then threw her arms around him and hugged him close. "I'm sorry, Richie. I know you didn't mean this to happen, but all actions have consequences. At your age, Steve was in Vietnam fighting for his country. You have no idea how lucky you are. Please don't waste your chances."

"I won't, Mom, I promise." Richie hugged her back, relieved that she seemed to have forgiven him.

Emily watched silently. Rachel really needed to get her temper under control. Blaming Richie was very unfair, even if he had broken his promise to her as well. It wasn't as if Spanner had died, after all. He was would be home in a few weeks.

Omaha, Nebraska

"I'm sorry, I don't understand. Are you saying that Steve could have another heart attack at any time?"

"Your husband's heart is quite damaged. Lifestyle, smoking and the explosion that injured him twenty years ago have all taken their toll. Ideally, he needs a heart transplant but there is a long waiting list. We've put him on it, but it will be some time before he is able to have one. In the meantime, he needs to stop smoking and take things a bit easier. Less stress!" David Mulcahy, the cardiologist, smiled, trying to be reassuring.

Rachel stared at him. "But he's going to run for Senator."

David frowned. "I wouldn't advise it, not as things are."

"But I'm not about to die immediately, am I?" Spanner spoke up.

"No, of course not."

"Then I'll carry on with my life. Yes, I will stop smoking... but I'm afraid sitting around doing nothing would be more stressful than fighting for senate."

"But Steve..."

"But nothing, Rachel. It's my life, and although I appreciate you're worried, I can't stop now. I need to keep fighting for veterans. If I don't, who else will?" He reached over and patted her hand. "I'll be fine. I have plenty of things left to do yet, I promise."

Rachel looked at David, who eventually shrugged. "Alright, Spanner. But please stop smoking, as that will make a difference, and for goodness' sake try not to get too stressed."

Spanner stood up and shook his hand over the desk. "Thanks for everything, David, you've been great."

Rachel followed suit, her mind churning with concerns for the future. She wanted Steve to carry on running for Senator, but not at the expense of his health. She turned back. "How long will he have to wait for another heart?"

"It works on need and the availability of the right heart, so I would say at least another year maybe two, unless he gets worse."

"That long?" Rachel looked shocked.

David sighed. "We can only use donated hearts, and the number that becomes available each year is much less than the number needed."

"Are you really sure you still want to run for Senator?" Rachel asked as they walked slowly back to the car.

"Yes, of course, honey. I admit I wasn't certain when you first suggested it, but I've had plenty of time to think about it since then, especially while I was in hospital. There are so many things I want to do. I can't give up now."

Ho Chi Minh City, Vietnam

Phuc stood across the road from the apartment block and tried to find the courage to see if Vy was in. He was entitled to visit her – Chinh couldn't stop him seeing his niece. Phuc clenched his fists. Who was he kidding? Chinh could do whatever he wanted. Phuc had seen exactly what Chinh was capable of, and he still had the nightmares.

His thoughts returned to the funeral, the last time he had seen her. Vy had not had much chance to speak to him after Lien's death, but between sobs she had told him that Chinh had beaten Lien and then thrown her down the stairs. Vy's distress had been made worse because she'd had to back up Chinh's story that Lien had slipped and fallen. The authorities had of course believed him. Phuc had been so upset at his sister's death that for once he had forgotten his fear and confronted Chinh. His courage hadn't lasted long, not after Chinh had threatened him. Phuc swallowed nervously as he remembered Chinh's hands around his throat, but it was the whispered words he'd spat venomously in Phuc's ear that had made sure the younger man would never say anything.

Phuc turned away. It wasn't worth the risk.

Omaha, Nebraska

"It's incredible, isn't it?" Rachel and Spanner were watching television coverage of the Berlin Wall coming down. People had been streaming across the wall for days now, the world transfixed at the collapse of something that had been a symbol of the Cold War for so long – scenes no one could possibly have predicted, even a week earlier.

"I can't remember a time it wasn't there."

"Nor me. I can remember Kennedy standing there and making his speech back in the '60s."

"Apparently this was all a bit of an accident," Spanner smiled, gesturing at the screen. "The man who made the statement was supposed to have said that East Germans needed to apply for visas the next day to travel, but he didn't have time to read his notes properly. The reporters were there asking questions, and he said that private travel outside the country could now happen without prerequisites starting from now. Because it went out live on TV, people from all over East Germany flocked to the wall."

"Bet he was in trouble!" Rachel laughed.

"Yeah, apparently when thousands of people appeared clambering to cross, he couldn't get any orders either to open the gate or open fire, so he eventually decided to open the gate."

"It was that close, then?" Rachel looked troubled. "It could have been a massacre."

"No, I don't think he had enough men to realistically prevent the gate opening. Fortunately, he did the right thing."

"So, what happens next?"

Spanner thought for a few moments. "I suppose Germany will be reunified, and maybe the Soviet Union will collapse; not immediately, but I think it will happen." He was silent for several moments, thinking about all the men who had died in Vietnam fighting against the soviet-backed north.

"Do you think the world will finally be at peace?" Rachel was thoughtful.

Spanner gave a wry smile. "I'd love to think so, but I'm sure there's some maniac somewhere getting ready to cause a problem. The man who started all this change is coming to address the US Congress next week."

"Lech Walesa?"

"Yes."

"History in the making," Rachel murmured thoughtfully. She glanced across at Steve. He looked much better now, and his last couple of check-ups had not shown any further problems, but she still worried.

As if reading her thoughts, Spanner smiled at her. "So, when are we going to start my campaign then?"

"You still want to?"

"Damn right I do. With peace in Europe, we can start looking at withdrawing our troops and spending more money on our own country and our veterans, starting with expanding the Department of Veterans Affairs!"

CHAPTER FORTY-TWO

Ho Chi Minh City, Vietnam, 1990

Vy checked again that there was no one behind her and hurried into the Vietnamese Ministry of the Interior, the first stage for an interview with the American Orderly Departure Program and, hopefully, acceptance by the United States. After her mother's death Chinh had terrorised her into staying with him, and with no one she could ask for help, Vy had become resigned to her fate. Chinh had kept her a prisoner for virtually a year before finally loosening his hold over her, and it wasn't until she went to the market that she had heard about the Homecoming Act and the fact she could apply to go to America. Vy was grateful that Lien had never told Chinh that she was Amerasian or he would never have let her out, not in time to apply anyway.

Vy had wasted no time in going to apply for an American Immigration visa. Her name would appear on a valid household registration, so she wouldn't have a problem there. Her problem would be Chinh, but she had a feeling that when he found out who her father was, he wouldn't want anything to do with her. She just had to make sure he didn't kill her before she could leave. Once she filled in the forms, Chinh would soon get to hear, and then she would be in danger unless she left. Vy had worked out a plan. She would fill in the Orderly Departure Forms which would then go to the local neighbourhood leader, and from there they would go up the chain to the Ministry of the Interior. Unfortunately, Vy knew this would cost money, because many of those who worked in the Ministry wanted a little encouragement to ensure the forms continued on their way. Vy didn't have any cash or anything she could sell, so she had decided to go to her uncle and ask for his help, not just for money but for somewhere to hide until the papers came through. Since her mother's death Phuc had distanced himself from Vy even more, but she had no intention of letting him wriggle out of his responsibility to her.

Houston, Texas

Charles read the report from his private detective and cursed. It seemed Richie had not been near any of the clubs since Belotti had beaten him up. That damn husband of Rachel's having a heart attack had obviously frightened him off. He would have to find a way of encouraging him back if he was going to ensure his money wasn't used to back a fucking Democrat. Charles thought back over everything he knew about his son and wondered which buttons he could press to produce the best results. There was no girlfriend on the scene, he appeared good at his job… Charles smiled as an idea came into his head.

Houston, Texas

"Run!" his fellow gang member yelled at Dung, who didn't need telling twice. He was already running as fast as he could away from the federal officers who had suddenly appeared from nowhere.

"There must be an informer," Tiger panted as they turned the corner and disappeared into a large block of apartments, where he hoped they would be able to get lost. "How else did they know where and when the crack was being delivered?" He raced up the concrete steps, followed closely by Dung.

"I don't know." Dung was gasping for breath by the time they reached the third floor. "But who?" The gang were all Vietnamese. They'd known each other since the camp in the Philippines, and met up in the US as agreed. "I can't see anyone of them grassing us up."

"Well, someone fucking did, An." Tiger pulled him into a corridor, flattened himself against the wall, put his fingers to his lips and pulled out a knife. "You got your gun?"

Dung nodded, looked around nervously and prayed the officers would not come looking for them on this floor. At least he was used to answering to An's name now. He couldn't remember the last time anyone had called him by his real name.

He let out a shaky sigh. His plans to settle in America and lead a useful life had come to nothing. The authorities had sent him to a small town in Texas where there were no other Vietnamese. At first Dung had tried to find work, but no one would employ him. Eventually running out of money, he had lost his accommodation and ended up on the streets. It was then he had remembered Tiger and some other men and how they had agreed to meet up in Houston. He had nothing left to lose, so he had stolen a wallet and boarded a train to Houston.

Omaha, Nebraska

"Put the gun down or we'll shoot." The police had surrounded an apartment block in one of the less affluent areas of the city after reports of a man shooting a rifle from the roof. He hadn't actually hit anyone yet, probably because he appeared to be drunk.

"The bastards are getting closer! We need to open fire!" The man yelled, swaying precariously near the edge.

"Put the rifle down and move away from the edge." The policeman continued to speak calmly, his finger resting loosely on the trigger. He had no idea who the man was talking to – there was no one else in sight.

"If we don't shoot soon, they'll overrun us, sarge." The

man raised the rifle and took aim.

"Sir, put the rifle down." There was a noise behind him, and the policeman spun around, finger tightening on the trigger.

"It's alright, officer, I've been sent by the State Governor to try and talk him down." Kurt held out a piece of paper with the Governor's stamp on it. The officer read it carefully and nodded.

"Good luck. But if he starts firing, I'll have no option but to shoot."

Kurt nodded and turned his attention to Jim, who was becoming increasingly agitated. "Jim, it's ok, they're retreating." He raised his voice. "You can stand down."

"No, they're coming closer. If they find us, they'll kill us. We have to survive, to tell the world what we've seen..." Jim began to cry.

Kurt wondered if he dare breathe a sigh of relief. If Jim was crying, perhaps the flashback was coming to an end. "We're going to retreat now Jim, they've gone. It's safe to put the rifle down, trust me."

Jim hesitated, then his eyes slowly refocused. He glanced around in confusion. "What happened? Where am I?"

"You're ok, just lower the rifle and we can go home, ok?"

"I don't think..." the officer began.

"Shut up," Kurt snapped, then turned back to Jim. "It's ok, buddy, just put the rifle down and we can go."

Jim looked at him, then at the police officer. "He could

make it all go away, Kurt."

"No, he can't, Jim," Kurt spoke quickly in desperation. "You know how you feel after 'Nam. Do you want this guy to feel the same because he has to shoot you?"

Jim lowered his head. It would be so easy. All he had to do was to raise the gun and the officer would shoot. He would be at peace.

"For fuck's sake Jim. How are we going to find those bastards if you're dead? We're the only witnesses; if you're gone, it's just my word against theirs."

Jim gave a harsh laugh. "We're never gonna find them. We can't get back into that shit country, so how the hell can we make sure they pay?"

"We fucking won't if you're dead. If you're alive, who knows what will happen in the future."

Jim stared at him and tried to work out which was more important, revenge or peace.

Houston, Texas

Dung didn't mind not getting any money from the botched drug collection, he was just relieved that he hadn't had to use the gun. The DEA had searched the corridors below them, knocking on several doors while he and Tiger had edged their way cautiously up the stairs. They would probably have been caught, but someone else had fired at the officers and their attention had been diverted from Dung and Tiger, allowing them to slip away.

"We need to find out who told them we would be there." Tiger was pacing up and down.

"It could have been someone from the cartel," another man suggested.

"Not according to them. They are furious and threatening not to do business with us again." Tiger stopped pacing and glared at the six men seated on the floor. "One of you is a traitor, and when I find out who it is, you will be begging me to kill you."

"One of the other drug gangs could have done it," Dung suggested nervously.

"But they had to get their information from someone here." Tiger looked at each man in turn, trying to discern from their expressions who had betrayed them. They all met his gaze, and eventually he looked away. He was sure one of them was guilty, and he was determined to find out who it was. Unfortunately, he had to plan the next pick up soon or they risked losing their regular customers, and it had to go well, or they would have no credibility left with their suppliers.

"An, stay here with me. The rest of you go home, I will send for you when I need you." He waited until the men had gone and then turned to Dung. "We have to be really careful next time, or we will be out of business. I will contact our suppliers and find out when the next shipment is coming in, and then we can plan a pick-up."

Dung nodded. "Do you really think one of our men betrayed us?"

Tiger shrugged. "How else did the DEA know where to find us?"

"But why now? We have been running this for nearly a year with no problems. This shipment wasn't any bigger than normal. I still think the leak is from the supplier."

Tiger thought for a moment. "You could be right. But we can't prove it."

Re-education Camp Outside Ho Chi Minh City, Vietnam

Phuc stared at Vy in astonishment. He hadn't seen her since Lien's funeral, an occasion he had hurried away from as soon as he could, citing pressure of work as an excuse to get away from Chinh. After Chinh's threats towards him, he had decided it was safer not to see Vy. There was nothing he could do to help her, so why risk everything he had? Although Phuc had worked his way up the system, Chinh far outranked him and he knew he was no match for the older man.

"I need your help to leave Vietnam and go to America."

"How are you going to do that?" Phuc looked confused.

"I'm Amerasian. My father was Spanner, my twin brother is An. Dung was just a boy we rescued. He happened to look like An, so mother pretended he was An's brother. She wanted me to have a normal life."

Phuc paled in shock. How could he have got it so wrong... and then his eyes lit up. "You're Amerasian?" He studied Vy carefully. He couldn't really see anything of Spanner in her, but it didn't matter. Vy could be the answer to his future. "Can you prove it?"

Vy shook her head. "No, but you can. You can get me a new birth certificate."

Phuc nodded. He couldn't quite believe his luck. "Yes, I can, and I can grease the wheels so your application goes through quickly." Vy looked surprised that she hadn't had to argue her case more. Phuc smiled. "But only if you take me with you. Relatives can go too, as I am sure you know." He debated whether to mention that An was only a few blocks away, but decided not to, not until he'd spoken to him.

Vy stared at him in shock. She hadn't known about relatives. "We don't have to stay together once we get there; it's just to get us into the US."

Vy thought for a moment, then nodded. If Phuc came with her, there was a chance they might actually get away – he had all the connections and the money. She would be stupid to say no. "Ok, but I have to stay with you while it's being processed. If I go home, Chinh will kill me, like he did your sister."

Phuc nodded again. She was right about Chinh, and he wasn't about to let that bastard take away his only chance of freedom. "Agreed. You're right not to trust him." He tilted his head, mind racing. "Do you need to collect anything?"

Vy shook her head and looked him straight in the eyes. "No. I am sure you will buy me some more clothes?" Fortunately, her father's ring was outside the apartment in the garden. It would mean going back to collect it, but she would wait until she saw Chinh go to work before retrieving it. There was no reason to tell Phuc about it.

Phuc thought hard for a few moments. "I'll hide you somewhere in one of the working parties outside the camp until Chinh stops looking for you. By then, the paperwork should be done and we can leave."

CHAPTER FORTY-THREE

Omaha, Nebraska

"The doctor said…"

"The doctor said I should try and carry on as normal, Rachel. I can't just sit around and wait to die. I'm on the list for a heart transplant, and in the meantime, I will take the medication they have given me and do my best to carry on, ok?"

"Ok, I'll shut up." She stood up on her toes and kissed him. "I'll get the newspapers, see how they reported last night. Poor Jim. He was in such a state when Kurt got him home."

"But he survived." Spanner sighed. "I wish they would tell me what's going on."

"It must be pretty bad if Kurt won't tell you." Rachel picked up the newspapers and began skimming through the headlines. The first couple were sympathetic; she breathed a sigh of relief, and then came to the third one, and her heart skipped a beat. Rachel reread the headline, then checked the by-line. What the hell was Richie thinking? She was vaguely aware the phone was ringing, but she couldn't deal with that now.

"What is it?" Spanner was halfway across the room to answer the telephone.

"You'd better read this. But you have to promise not to get angry."

Spanner laughed. "I can't promise that until I've seen it, but the newspapers don't normally wind me up. Most of it is garbage anyway, and the intelligent voters normally treat it as such, you know that."

"Not when it's written by your stepson." Rachel was still trying to digest the content, to check whether the poison was only in the headline.

"*No charge for Governor's gunman friend.*" Spanner stared in disbelief, not at the headline but at the by-line next to it. *Richie Hanson.* He would have expected such a headline from the Republican newspapers, but not from one that was normally supportive, and certainly not on an article apparently written by his stepson. He was about to answer the phone when he changed his mind. It could be the newspapers, radio or TV, and until he spoke to Richie, he was not prepared to speak to any other media outlet.

Outskirts of Ho Chi Minh City, Vietnam

"Vy has left Chinh, I am hiding her until she can leave the country." Phuc smiled at An, who wiped a dirty hand across his oil-stained face and frowned.

"How can she leave the country?"

"The American Homecoming Act." Phuc saw his confusion and quickly explained.

An's frown deepened. "But if her name and address have to go on the forms, won't Chinh be able to trace her from there?"

Phuc shook his head. "I have paid for her papers to be hidden."

An looked astonished. "That must have cost a fortune?"

Phuc looked embarrassed. "I think I owe to it your mother to help. And anyway, relatives can go as well, so I am going with her. You could come too."

An's pulse quickened at the faint flicker of hope. The thought of leaving Vietnam was so tempting. Then he remembered his vow to take revenge on Chinh for his mother's death, and he reluctantly shook his head. "I can't, not until I have found a way of avenging my mother."

Phuc stared at him in exasperation. "But surely escaping Vietnam and going to America will be revenge in itself, won't it?"

An thought for a moment, then shook his head again.

"No. I can't leave until he has paid for what he's done." He smiled. "But I would like to see Vy now she is not with him."

Phuc nodded. "I'll bring her to your room tonight." He hesitated. "It's not too late to change your mind, An. I can get you put on the application form."

An shook his head. "I know you have said the papers are safe from his eyes, but I can't risk letting that bastard know I am in the city and I don't want to go into hiding, not yet, not until he has paid the price for killing my mother and abusing my sister. Taking the papers out and adding me might endanger you both... the papers could be accidentally seen by someone... you know what it's like."

Phuc thought for a moment. It was obvious An wasn't going to listen to him, but perhaps Vy could persuade him to drop the idea of revenge and leave with them. Yes, An had a point; it would be a risk adding him to the forms, but Phuc knew how Chinh operated, and even if An did find a way of getting revenge, he would never get away with it. Chinh had too much power. An would have to kill Chinh to have any chance of surviving and obviously that wasn't his plan, or he would have already done it.

An watched his uncle leave and wondered if he was making a mistake. Perhaps he should just forget all about revenge and just take the opportunity to leave. Then he remembered his childhood, the misery Chinh had put him through, how he had treated them all, the beatings he had received for no reason and how his mother had been forced to watch, and his resolve hardened.

Ho Chi Minh City, Vietnam

Chinh had turned the city upside down, but there was no sign of Vy. He had even checked the Homecoming Act applications, but her name wasn't among them. None of his informants had seen her, except the elderly neighbour who said she'd seen Vy digging in the garden. Chinh had gone to check and found signs of disturbance around the rose bush – not much, though, so whatever she had been looking for must have been quite small.

Chinh sat back and wondered briefly if Phuc had anything to do with Vy's disappearance. Then he shook his head. No, Phuc was too much of a coward to go against him. There had to be another explanation. Perhaps the other brother, Dung, was involved. Chinh stood up and stepped towards the filing cupboard where he kept the most important files. Dung had somehow left prison, and Chinh had never found out who paid for that. He would start by looking into the boy's contacts.

Omaha, Nebraska

"I swear it isn't what I wrote." Richie was almost crying. "My article was completely different, explaining and supporting what Kurt did. You don't really think I would write something like this?"

"Then how come it's got your by-line on?" Rachel was furious and not prepared to listen to any more excuses. "Spanner has done everything for you, and this is how you repay him? At least have the guts to admit it!"

"But I didn't write that. I went straight to the editor when I saw it, but he just said that all articles on the front page have to be edited first, so I resigned. I don't know why it was changed or who did it, but I didn't do it, you have to believe me."

"So now you're out of a job, too. What the hell have I done to deserve a son like you!" Rachel spat, and immediately regretted her words. She took a breath. "I'm sorry, that was uncalled for." She thought for a moment. "You are telling me the truth? You didn't have anything to do with that article?"

"No, Mom. I wouldn't do that to Spanner, even if he didn't have a bad heart."

Rachel thought hard. If Richie was telling the truth, it meant someone had used her son to get to Spanner, to cause mischief. But who? Any one of their Republican rivals could be involved and it would be impossible to prove. The only thing they could do was to put out something else, something telling the real story. Steve would have to do some TV interviews, call a press conference, engage in damage control. She glanced at Richie who was still looking distraught. “Alright, I believe you. I think someone is probably using you to get at Steve. I’m sorry you’ve lost your job. I know you loved it.”

Richie shook his head. “I’m not, I can’t work somewhere that treats their staff like this. I’ll find another place, in a paper that supports Spanner.”

Rachel gave a small smile. “I would offer to help, but you don’t need it. You’re a good journalist.”

Richie sighed. “I *was*… God knows how this will affect me. The man who shit on his family. Hardly makes me seem very trustworthy.”

Rachel’s smile broadened slightly. “I am sure you will find something, Richie, don’t give up. As Steve would say, *shit happens*!”

Richie gave the ghost of a smile. “I’ll start looking now.”

Rachel watched him leave, a melancholy expression on her face. Unfortunately, he was right. It would reflect badly on him, but there was nothing she or Steve could do to help without making things worse and giving the Republican media even more ammunition.

Outskirts of Ho Chi Minh City, Vietnam

Vy stepped into the room and stared in astonishment at the man standing by the window, smiling at her. Phuc hadn't said where they were going or why, just that he had a surprise. For a moment she thought it was An, then she remembered her brother was no longer in the country. "Dung?"

An's smile broadened. "Don't you recognise your own brother, Vy? I was beginning to think I would never see you again." He stepped towards her and hugged her.

Vy snuggled against his chest, unable to believe her brother was safe. Eventually she drew back. "I don't understand. I thought you were in the Philippines… that's what set Chinh off… " She fell silent, unsure if he knew about their mother.

"It's a long story. Dung and I were going to escape together, but there wasn't enough room in the boat, so he went on his own. He was the one with the criminal record, it seemed the sensible thing to do. I assume that once he reached the Philippines, he decided to use my name to help him get into America because I don't have a criminal record."

Vy was still confused. "Have you been here all this time, then? Do you know about the Homecoming Act?" Vy stopped and took a breath. "Sorry, it's just been so long. I can't believe you are here." Tears appeared in her eyes. "You know Chinh killed Mẹ?"

"Yes. Yes, to all of your questions. Phuc told me about Mẹ." An put his arms around her and held her tight, before pulling back and staring into her eyes. "You need to leave for America with Phuc as soon as possible."

Vy wiped her eyes. "What about you? Why don't you come with us?"

"I have something I need to do here first."

Vy frowned. "I don't understand. What could be so important... oh, is it a girl? Are you married?"

An laughed. "No, it's not that." He glanced at Phuc and then back to her. "I can't tell you, but it is very important, and once it's done, I will leave – I promise."

"But there is a time limit on applications." Vy held his hand tight. "Come with us, please."

"I can't, Vy, but I will find a way of leaving, I promise." He kissed her forehead and then held her tight again. "It's so good to see you, sister."

Phuc backed towards the door. "I'll leave you both to catch up. I'll be back in a couple of hours, ok?"

Vy watched him leave and turned back to An. "He's been very helpful. Much more than I expected. I'm so pleased he's been good to you as well."

"Perhaps he's mellowed with age," An laughed. Then his smile faded. "It's a shame our mother isn't here to see the change."

Vy nodded. "She felt very let down by him. I don't know all the details, but I think it's a bit more than him just encouraging her to marry Chinh. Did she ever say anything to you?"

An shook his head. "No, nothing." He sighed. "We'll probably never know now. Perhaps it's for the best." Planning revenge against Chinh was hard enough.

"Oh! I nearly forgot. There's something you should see." Vy fished inside her jacket and pulled out the chain around her neck. An could see a ring on it. "It's our father's ring. Mẹ told me it was hidden under the rose bush in case I ever found a way to leave Vietnam. I dug it up from the garden. It might help me find our father when I get to America. His family had a farm in Nebraska, and the ring came from his mother's family." She undid the chain and passed it to An.

An read the inscription inside before handing it back to her. Lien had impressed on all the children that they should never mention Spanner for fear of Chinh overhearing. An wondered briefly where his father was now, then pushed the thought away. He obviously hadn't cared about them, or he wouldn't have deserted their mother.

Outside Houston, Texas

The last two pick-ups had gone to plan, and Dung was feeling more confident. Tiger seemed to have forgotten his suspicions, and everyone was more relaxed as they waited in the darkness off the highway for the delivery to arrive. Dung peered into the darkness and spoke softly. "Tiger, there's a truck approaching."

"I see it." Tiger raised his voice slightly. "Everyone get ready. We need to get the stuff off and loaded as quickly as possible. Keep your eyes open. Anything suspicious, yell, ok?"

There were murmurs of assent and then the truck approached. Dung watched as the vehicle pulled off the highway and stopped near them. Two of the men took up positions behind and in front to keep guard while Dung moved forward with Tiger, his hand clutching his gun just in case. The driver climbed out and hurried around to the back, spoke a few words to Tiger to confirm he was in the right place and then opened the back.

"Hands up! Federal Officers. Don't move..."

Dung stared in horror as men came streaming out of the back, rifles raised, and he glanced at Tiger. To his horror, his friend was smiling as he raised his hands, and Dung swore. "You fucking bastard, it was you all along."

Tiger shrugged. "They pay better..." He didn't get any further as Dung opened fire, killing Tiger and two officers, and then ran. His shots had taken them by surprise, but within seconds they were firing back, and he felt a sharp pain in his leg, knocking him to the floor, the gun flying out of his hand. Dung tried to get up, but he was too late – the gun was kicked away from him, his hands roughly handcuffed behind his back and a man was shouting something in his ear about being under arrest.

Ho Chi Minh City, Vietnam

An smiled to himself as he finally came up with the perfect way to get his revenge on Chinh. Having followed him intermittently for the past few months, he'd accepted that Chinh wasn't up to anything that he could use to destroy the man's career. In any case, his grievance against Chinh was personal, so his revenge would have to be something that reflected that. The idea had come to him weeks earlier, but he had pushed it to one side, not sure if he could actually do something so violent himself. But now he had spoken at length to Vy and she had told him some more things about their mother's life with Chinh, he no longer had any reservations. In fact, he would enjoy it, especially as he knew Vy was hiding the way Chinh had treated her. He and Dung had always had their suspicions, but now he was sure they had been right.

The next step was to enlist the help of the prostitute Chinh saw regularly. It might take time to get her on side, but he was not in a rush. Vy and Phuc had left the country, they were safe. Thanks to Phuc's new identity papers, Chinh had no idea An was in the country, let alone the city. In any case, it was over a year since his mother's death, so he was unlikely to be top of the list of suspects. An put out his cigarette and walked back into the garage, a smile on his face. He was planning to enjoy every moment of his revenge.

CHAPTER FORTY-FOUR

Ho Chi Minh City, Vietnam, 1991

Chinh zipped up his trousers and looked down at the naked girl lying face down on the bed, her hands and feet tied to the posts. He grinned and slapped her bottom hard, leaving another red mark. "I think a little bonus is due tonight, Loan. I'll see you next time." He threw some notes on the pillow before leaving the room and closing the door quietly behind him. A couple of minutes later, the door opened and the brothel owner hurried in and untied her.

Loan sat up and picked up the extra notes Chinh had left on the pillow before rubbing her wrists and ankles where the rope had dug in.

"Are you ready for the next one?" Since Chinh had started using Loan exclusively, the brothel owner had treated her with more respect than before. Chinh was an important client who paid well, and whose presence protected her business from having to bribe the local police to leave her alone.

"No, I think I'll take the rest of the night off." Loan

was sore, and it would be nice to spend the night with her daughter for a change.

Thi scowled and was about to argue. Then she thought about all the benefits of having Chinh as a client, and forced a smile. "Alright. I'll see you tomorrow. Don't be long getting dressed, one of the other girls can use this room."

Loan watched her go in relief and stood up. There weren't many advantages to servicing Chinh; he was often violent, although he was careful never to leave any permanent marks on her body. But he paid well, and that meant she could have the rest of the evening off. She wanted nothing more than to escape her life, take her daughter and disappear, work in a shop or restaurant, anything not to have to sleep with any more pigs. But earning enough money to disappear was not easy. She had thought about working for herself, so she wouldn't have to share her money with Thi, but she knew it wasn't feasible. Working in the brothel meant more safety, not only from the clients but also the police.

Loan finished dressing and headed for the door. No point day-dreaming about a better life – women like her didn't get lucky.

Federal Detention Centre, Houston, Texas

Dung stared at the walls of his cell and wondered how on earth his life had come to this. When he'd left Vietnam, he had been determined to make a new life for himself and then try and bring the rest of his family to America as well. He'd had so many hopes and dreams, and now they had all crumbled to dust. He had let everyone down, but soon it would be all over and he would be at peace.

Dung shivered and tried to ignore the terror rising inside him. The court had found him guilty of killing two federal officers as well as Tiger, and had sentenced him to death. He was now awaiting his execution.

He glanced at the writing materials he had been given and smiled bitterly. If only he had someone to write to. He was hardly going to write to his family – better they never knew what had happened to him. His only company was a radio, which he left on even though he wasn't really listening to it.

Dung stood up and began pacing up and down, his thoughts on his life in Vietnam. Perhaps he should have stayed there. He sat down again and tried to listen to the radio, hoping it would take his mind off his predicament. He was only half listening when something caught his attention. Dung frowned. Spanner? Wasn't that the name of the man Lien had claimed was Vy and An's father? Dung listened more closely, but the speech was too fast for him to understand. He would have to ask his attorney.

PRPC (Philippine Refugee Processing Centre) near Morong, Bataan, Philippines

"How did you get on?" Phuc asked as soon as Vy arrived back after her interview. She was soaking wet from the incessant rain, but she was smiling.

"My English is good enough for me to be an assistant to Bernard Cotterill, the camp writer."

Phuc had no idea what a camp writer did. "What's that mean?"

"He is writing a book about the refugees in the camp. He needs an interpreter to help him." Her eyes shone with excitement. "What about you?"

"I can help with administration," Phuc answered.

"That's great." Her smile faded. "How long do you think we will be here?"

Phuc sighed. "I have been asking around and it would seem we could be here for months, so I think the best thing is to forget about moving on too quickly, be grateful we are no longer in Vietnam and learn as much as we can so we are ready for our new lives."

Vy nodded. "I wish An was here too, Uncle."

"I know, Vy, but we both tried to persuade him to come with us."

"I just wish I knew what was so important that he wouldn't take the opportunity to escape."

Phuc hesitated. She probably had a right to know what her brother was planning, but there was no point telling her because she would only worry. "He didn't tell me either," he lied. "I guess we will just have to trust him and hope that he makes it out soon."

"But if we've left here, how will he find us?"

"I am sure the camp will pass on any correspondence, especially if we ask them to," Phuc said reassuringly, and Vy smiled again.

"Yes, of course, I hadn't thought of that." She suddenly stepped forward and hugged him. "Thank you for all your help, Uncle. I couldn't have done this without you, and although he isn't here, at least I know that An has a better life now, thanks to your help."

Phuc didn't answer. He thought about Lien and how he'd failed her and her children. "I have not always behaved honourably or looked after my family, Vy. I will never forgive myself for the way I treated your mother. But now I have been given another chance, and I want to use that for good." He felt tears forming and blinked them away. "I am sorry I didn't help you or Lien. I can't turn back the clock or undo things I have done. If I could change the past, I would never have let her marry Chinh." He wasn't sure if that was true, but he liked to think he would have found the courage to stand up to Chinh. Then he thought about the devastation on Lien's face when the bomb went off and she thought Spanner was dead and he felt sick. He could never tell Vy about that. He pushed his guilt away, gave a wry smile and tried to lighten the mood. "You see, your uncle does know he made mistakes."

Vy smiled. "It's all in the past now, Uncle. Let's look forward, not back." Phuc wasn't the only one who had reasons to forget the past.

Omaha, Nebraska

"You again? You're not allowed in." The doorman tried to block his entry, but moved aside as Frank Belotti appeared.

"Hello Richie, you'd better come in."

Richie looked surprised. He had half expected to be barred if he was recognised, but he didn't know any other clubs, and for some obscure reason this place felt like home when his real home rejected him. His mother had finally believed him, and Spanner had said the same, but he still felt guilty, even though he hadn't done anything wrong.

Frank shrugged. "If you want to have some fun, who am I to stop you? If I did that with everyone, I'd be out of business, right?" He stood back, Richie stepped inside the door and his brain fog cleared almost instantly. He would play some poker, and when he won, he would play roulette for a while.

"Want some company?" The girl was long-limbed, with dark hair and brown eyes.

Richie smiled at her, his worries briefly forgotten. "I'd love some, how are you at cards?"

Frank watched them head towards the card games, his brow slightly creased. Charles Peterson had insisted he let the boy back in, said he would make it worth his while, so who was he to complain? He had also suggested finding the boy some company, so Frank had obliged. He wondered why Charles was so insistent in letting the boy gamble away his parents' money, but then decided it was none of his business, as long as the State Governor didn't make trouble for him, and Charles had been adamant he wouldn't. As Richie sat down, Frank caught a glimpse of him in profile and inhaled sharply. The boy strongly resembled Peterson; maybe they were related somehow, although he had never heard any rumours to that effect. And if that was the case, why was Charles so intent on ruining him?

Ho Chi Minh City, Vietnam

"All you have to do is tie him to the bed." An smiled at Loan. He had watched her for several weeks, trying to work out the best way to approach her. She had a small child, a girl of about three years old who was looked after by an older woman he discovered was Loan's mother. He could threaten them, but he didn't want to lower himself to Chinh's standards. Eventually, An had decided to hire her for the evening and persuade her to help him.

Loan stared at him. He could see the fear in her eyes, but also something else he couldn't identify. "He will kill me or have me shipped to one of the army brothels if he even finds out I was talking to you about him."

An reached out and took her hand. "He won't find out. Why should he? This is the first time I've hired you, there's nothing for him to find out." *And he would be dead anyway*, but he obviously couldn't tell her that.

Loan thought fast. This could be the answer to her prayers. But she had to protect herself and her daughter. Her useless mother wouldn't look after the girl if anything happened to her. She would dump the child on the nearest street corner or sell her to some pig so she could get drunk. "What if he refuses?"

An raised an eyebrow. "Is that likely?"

Loan shook her head. "No, we have done that before, but he normally tells me what he wants."

"I am sure you can persuade him."

Loan took a breath. "What's in it for me?"

"42,000 Dong?"

Loan smiled. "Make it 100,000 and I will do it." She saw his face and shrugged. "I don't know what you have planned, but I imagine it will be hard for me to work here again?"

An hesitated, but only for a few moments. It would be virtually all the money he had saved up, but it would be worth it. "Ok, a quarter now and the rest after I spend some time with him."

Loan thought carefully. "And you knock me out and tie me up."

An looked horrified. "I can't..."

"Then they will not think I am involved."

An nodded slowly. He wasn't sure if he could hit a woman, especially one who hadn't done him any harm, but he understood her logic. "Ok, that makes sense." He peeled off some notes.

Loan took them and their eyes met. "You've paid for the evening... do you want to do anything?"

An shook his head. He had achieved what he'd come for. "No, it's ok, thank you. Enjoy the rest."

Laon smiled, lay back on the bed and opened her legs. "You're sure?"

An grinned. She was right – he had paid for her time...

Federal Detention Centre, Houston, Texas

"You are sure he is a State Governor?" Dung asked again.

His attorney, J.P. Woodford, sighed. "Yes, that's why it's news."

"Can I write him?"

The attorney frowned. "Why would you want to write to him?"

"I think he knew my mother in Vietnam." Dung replied, taking the attorney by surprise.

Jonathan shrugged. "I guess you can, not sure what he can do to help you though."

"But if I write him, you will mail, please?"

The attorney nodded. He couldn't see why it would a problem; after all, he was being paid by the state to represent Dung, and that meant doing what he could to have the man's sentence commuted to life. Dung was a model prisoner, never causing any trouble and always polite. If he thought this man could help him, why not? "Ok. You write to him and I'll see it gets mailed."

Dung waited until his attorney had gone before sitting down on his bed and picking up the pen and paper he had been given. He thought carefully about what to say. His English was not good enough to write at length; he would have to keep it short and to the point and hope that would be enough.

Hi Spanner
I sorry to bother you, but think you will want to know this. You not know me, but you know my mother Lien in Vietnam. She tell me you in love with her but after bomb when you hurt she no hear from you again. She tell me you are my father. I am in big trouble, they going to kill me soon. Can you help your son please.
Nguyen Thanh An

Dung finished writing and then read through what he'd written. It was very short, but he didn't trust his English to write any more. If this man really was An's father, surely he would at least want to see his son, even if he couldn't help him. If he visited, then Dung could tell him about the rest of his family and maybe he could help them get to America. Then at least he wouldn't have failed completely. It wouldn't matter if he subsequently found out that Dung had lied about being his son, not if he could reunite him with his real children.

CHAPTER FORTY-FIVE

Omaha, Nebraska

The coughing spasm finally finished. Spanner closed his eyes and tried to steady his breathing. His cough was definitely getting worse, as was the breathlessness.

"I thought you'd stopped smoking." Rachel had arrived in his office just as he finally managed to catch his breath. She shook her head.

Spanner looked apologetic. "I'm sorry. I thought one wouldn't hurt." He started coughing again.

Rachel raised her eyebrows. "Really? I think you should at least go to the cardiologist and get something for that cough, get him to check you over as well."

Spanner nodded. "I will. Can you make me an appointment this morning?"

Rachel blinked in surprise. She'd been expecting a long argument about why he couldn't do it immediately. "Is there something you're not telling me?"

Spanner hesitated, then nodded. "It's probably nothing, but I think the breathlessness is getting worse. I'm struggling to walk upstairs now." He saw her expression and tried to reassure her. "It could just be an infection, it's the time of year for that."

"Yes, I'm sure you're right." Rachel somehow spoke the words calmly despite the rapid beating of her own heart. She had noticed him breathing heavily several times lately but had pushed her worries to the back of her mind, dismissing them as nothing important, refusing to accept his symptoms were getting worse.

"Good, let me know what time and I'll be there." He glanced at the clock. "I have to go, Rachel. Operation Desert Storm has begun. Airstrikes have started against Iraq."

Rachel stared at him in shock. "I knew Congress had agreed to use force to liberate Kuwait, I just didn't expect it to happen so quick."

"Well, having got pretty much the whole world's agreement, I guess they didn't see any point in waiting," Spanner replied. Like Rachel, he had mixed feelings about the US getting involved in another foreign war.

"Do you think there will be protests?" For a moment Rachel was back in the 1970s, reliving the heady days of the anti-Vietnam War demonstrations.

Spanner gave a wry smile. "Even if there are, I don't think we could go and join them!"

Rachel forgot her worries about his heart for a moment and laughed. "I can just see the headlines, *Nebraska State Governor attends anti-war demo!* I'll ring the Dr Mulcahy and make you an appointment." She was quiet for a moment, then she added, "And then I think I'll go home and check on the children."

Spanner raised an eyebrow. Rachel smiled. "I just want to make sure they aren't planning on demonstrating."

Spanner laughed. "I can't see Bill on any protest march, can you? At twelve years old, his only interest is cars." His expression changed. "Rita, on the other hand… How old were you when you skipped school to go to the Moratorium to End the War demo in the city?"

Rachel sighed. "Sixteen, but kids grow up a lot quicker these days." They exchanged glances. Rita was nearly fourteen now and had always been headstrong, and she was stubborn like her mother.

"You're right. Go and check she's not planning anything." The world had changed since he'd attended demonstrations. Protests were rarely peaceful these days, even if they set out to be. They were often taken over by groups with other agendas and, as much as he would be proud to have a daughter who felt strongly enough about something to demonstrate, his overriding concern was to keep Rita safe.

PRPC (Philippine Refugee Processing Centre) near Morong, Bataan, Philippines

Vy sat quietly on a seat in the camp, thinking about the people she had met that day. The rain had stopped, and the noises from the nearby jungle reminded her vaguely of her childhood in Vietnam and the life they had shared before Chinh came along and ruined everything. She couldn't remember very much, but she did remember her mother laughing a lot, and she could recall playing in the fields with An and Dung. Vy sighed heavily, pushed her own memories away and thought about the stories she had listened to since working with Bernard. Her own life after Chinh had been bad enough, but hearing the awful stories other refugees had told Bernard, she was now able to put it in some kind of perspective. Tales of abandonment, cruelty, lives spent on the street or in prison because of their appearance...

"Are you alright? You look very sad."

Vy smiled up at Diem, a young black Amerasian who had begun speaking to Bernard just before they finished for the day. He was due to come back and finish his story the following day. "I was just thinking about the stories I have heard over the last few weeks."

Diem inclined his head. "If they are like mine, it must be very difficult for you to listen to them all."

Vy nodded. "I thought my life was hard, but hearing the dreadful stories has made me realise that I have had it relatively easy, although my brothers didn't."

"Did they look like you?"

"No, they were tall and looked like Americans, so they were picked on." She fell silent, thinking about An and wondering where he was.

Diem sat down next to her. Vy turned to him. "It was worse for you being black, wasn't it?"

Diem nodded. "I think so. We stood out more, I guess, because of our skin. They called me bastard and... other words. I slashed myself all over with a razor to try and numb the pain, so then people saw the scars and thought I was a troublemaker. I tried to kill myself several times. Then when I was seventeen, they told me I had to help arrest illegal street vendors, but I refused. They weren't doing anything wrong, so why should I harass them? So they arrested me and sent me to Duyen Hai district." He gave a wry smile. "The state farm for Agricultural and Industrial Education and Labour. It was nothing more than a forced labour camp."

"What did you do there?"

"I dug ditches to let the water in to irrigate the crops. It was salt water, so then we collected the salt. I escaped after a few weeks and went back home, but because I had been arrested my name had been removed from the family register, so I couldn't stay there." He stopped and smiled at her. "You will hear all this tomorrow, so why don't we talk of something else?"

Vy smiled back. "Like the future?"

"Yes, what are your plans?"

"I would like to be a teacher."

Diem looked surprised and then nodded. "I am sure that's a good idea."

Vy felt irritated at his surprise, although why she should care about the opinion of someone she had only just met, she didn't know. "You don't think I would make a good teacher?"

Diem gave an apologetic smile. "I'm sorry – yes, I do." He hesitated and then said what was on his mind. "I was just thinking that you are a very good listener, and that maybe you would work with people who have problems, that was all."

It was Vy's turn to look astonished. "I hadn't thought of that."

"I didn't mean to..."

"No, I think you're right." Vy's face had lit up. "I could help people from Vietnam settle into the United States – well, I can once I have got used to it myself." Her brain was rushing ahead. She could make a big difference to people like Diem and all the others whose stories she had heard if she trained to do something like that.

Diem watched her with a combination of amusement and tenderness. He could see the passion in her face, and it was inspiring and contagious. For the first time ever, Diem felt he could do something with his life. If she could have this much effect on him after only a few moments in her company, what couldn't she achieve? Diem realised he was staring at her, and he flushed and looked away. Vy glanced across at him and smiled. "Thank you, Diem. It's a brilliant idea. I can't wait to find out how I can do this." Her eyes met his and she felt a strange warmth spreading through her body. The heat lodged in the pit of her stomach, and she wished he would kiss her. Vy pulled herself up suddenly and turned away. What on earth was she thinking?

Diem leaned forward, her lips were so inviting… then suddenly she was looking away, and he stopped abruptly. What the hell was he doing?

Omaha, Nebraska

"He's getting worse again, and I don't know what to do to keep him sober," Kurt sighed. "I'm sorry to lay this on you again, Spanner, especially after the last time, your health and the newspapers and everything, but I'm out of ideas."

Spanner shook his head. "Don't be silly, Kurt. Jim's my friend too. And don't worry about the media, they can piss off. I will always help my friends, and the media can't stop me trying to help a Vietnam vet." It was a good thing Kurt didn't know he had just returned from the doctor, or about his prognosis, or he definitely wouldn't have come to him for help.

Kurt relaxed slightly. "He's definitely sliding backwards again. He seems ok and I start to think we're over the worst and then... then he suddenly goes off the rails again."

Spanner thought for a moment. "Look, I know that something happened while I was in hospital, and that neither of you want to talk about it." Kurt opened his mouth to say something, so Spanner raised a hand. "Wait, hear me out. If you really don't want to tell me then that's your call, but if that event is causing Jim's problem, I can't help unless you tell me something, even if it's not all of it."

Kurt stared at him and took a breath. "It's not that we don't want to talk about it, more we can't, because... because it's so fucking awful, just thinking about saying it out loud..." Kurt felt the sweat breaking out on his forehead and he stopped.

Spanner looked concerned. "Ok Kurt, I don't want to make things worse..."

"They burned an orphanage... the VC... with the kids inside... we saw the faces of two of them... the ones who did it... " Kurt spat out the words.

Spanner's face paled, but before he could speak Kurt continued. "I see their faces in my sleep, when I'm awake, I smell the burning flesh, hear the screams..." He slumped to the floor, tears streaming down his face. "We couldn't stop them, Spanner... we couldn't stop them... oh, Christ... we hid because there were too many of them and they would have killed us, but we shouldn't have, we should have tried." He looked up. The anguish on his face broke Spanner's heart. "Why didn't we do something?"

Omaha, Nebraska

"We could go to San Francisco or Washington on January 26th? They're holding big rallies on that day. It's a Saturday, I checked, so we wouldn't need to skip school." Rita put down the leaflet she'd picked up from a demonstrator outside the school.

"How on earth are we going to get there?" Jade looked sceptical.

"I've got money, and we could stay with Max."

Jade frowned. "Max? Oh... your uncle Paul's friend?"

"Yes. I'm sure he wouldn't mind." Rita was already planning how she would ask him. She had only met Max twice, once when he had brought Paul to live with them and again at the funeral, but she was sure he would be happy to help.

"What about your parents?" Jade still wasn't convinced.

"What about them? Mom skipped school to go to demos against the Vietnam War with her hippy friends in the 1970s, even Pop went on them. They can hardly object if I am following their example."

"No, I guess not. Ok, I'm in," Jade grinned. "What do we tell our parents, then?"

"You can say you're at my house, I'll say I'm at yours. We'll leave Friday afternoon. Come on, we'll go downtown and book our flights."

"Aren't you going to ring Max first?"

"No, I'll do it when it's all fixed." Rita had no intention of ringing Max until they reached San Francisco airport. She didn't want to risk him talking her out of it, or even worse, telling her mom.

Omaha, Nebraska

Spanner had finally calmed Kurt down and the two men were sitting quietly in his office. "I'm sorry, I shouldn't have asked," he said eventually. "I understand now why you didn't want to talk about it."

"You were right, though. Until you knew what we were facing, you couldn't help."

Spanner sighed. He still wasn't sure how he could help. It wasn't as if he could turn the clock back, and they couldn't even go to Vietnam and look for the perpetrators. He understood now why Kurt had asked. Then something clicked. "Ok, I have an idea. The Homecoming Act and other things have enabled lots of Vietnamese to come to the States over the past couple of years. Perhaps I can get you access to immigration records and you and Jim could go through them. It's a long shot, but you just might see these men. If not, at least you're doing something."

Kurt stared at him and his face lit up. "That's a brilliant idea. I could leave Jim to do that while I take care of the business. He got a better look at them than I did. It will also keep him busier longer if he's on his own."

Spanner nodded. "There will be thousands of files. Obviously you only want the men, so that will cut it down a bit."

"Anyone over eighteen," Kurt added. "Vietnamese men don't show their age. If they have come here, they'll probably lie about their age."

"I'll see what I can do. Are you sure you're ok now?"

Kurt nodded and stood up. "Yes, I'm fine. The thought that we may actually find these bastards has helped me, so hopefully it will have the same effect on Jim."

"It might not turn up anyone, Kurt. It's more likely they are still in Vietnam, so don't get your hopes up too much."

"I know, but just knowing we're doing something, even if it is several years too late..."

"You did what you had to do to survive, Kurt. You shouldn't feel guilty about that. If you and Jim had died, they would have got away with it because there would be no witnesses. Maybe you survived for a reason."

Kurt thought for a moment, then smiled. "I wish I'd told you years ago. Can I tell Jim?"

Spanner was reaching for the phone. "No. Wait until I've got permission first. We don't want to get his hopes up and then find I can't make it happen."

CHAPTER FORTY-SIX

San Francisco, California

"So what made you think of coming here, girls?" Max looked decidedly uncomfortable, having suddenly received a phone call from Rita late at night to say she and a friend were at the airport and could he pick them up.

"We've come to join in the protests against the war tomorrow."

"Ah... of course. Do your parents know you're here?"

"Of course," Rita lied. "Mom was going to ring you, but I said I would do it when I got here."

Max took his eyes off the road and looked closely at her for a few seconds before concentrating on the traffic again. "Yeah right, Rita. Is that true, Jade?"

"Er… I guess…" Jade blushed and then fell silent.

"Well, I'm sure she would agree – she and Pop were always going on demos in the seventies. We just didn't want to bother her… not with Pop being ill and that..." Rita trailed off.

"You can stay the weekend, girls, and yes, you can go on

the demo tomorrow, and I'll come with you to make sure you're both ok. But I am going to ring your mom to let her know where you are."

"But..."

"But nothing. It's either that or I turn the car around and put you both on the next plane back!"

Rita looked at Jade and sighed. "Ok." There would be hell to pay when they got back, but at least they could go on the demo.

PRPC (Philippine Refugee Processing Centre) near Morong, Bataan, Philippines

"I think that's an excellent idea, Vy." Phuc smiled at her. "What made you think of it?"

"I was talking to Diem, he's one of the people who told his story to Bernard. He suggested it."

Phuc frowned. "Diem is black, isn't he?"

Vy looked at him sharply, her anger rising. "What's that got to do with anything?"

"Nothing, I was just asking." Phuc glared at her and tried to keep his temper. Vy's face had lit up when she had mentioned Diem. Obviously, she liked him. "He has lots of scars..."

"Yes, he's black and yes, he's slashed himself with a razor

because the Vietnamese made him feel so bad about the colour of his skin. You of all people should understand what that's like."

Phuc realised he'd made a mistake. "I do – I was just a bit concerned that he might cause trouble, that's all."

"Why should he? He wants a new life in America just like the rest of us."

Phuc didn't answer immediately, although he felt concerned. He had never seen Vy look quite so animated about any of the other people whose stories she had listened to. But he also recognised the stubborn expression on her face. It reminded him of Lien. He would have to tread carefully, or he would risk making things worse.

Omaha, Nebraska

"What does that mean?" Rachel stared at Steve in horror.

"Just what it says, honey. My heart's aging much faster than I am and I need the transplant sooner rather than later. He's going to put me up the list."

Rachel sat down and tried to fight back tears. "How long?"

"I guess it depends on how soon a heart becomes available." Spanner sat down beside her and hugged her. "It'll be ok, honey, they'll find one."

Rachel didn't answer. She would go and speak to Chris and see if he could pull a few strings. She wouldn't tell

Steve though, because he would never agree to jumping the queue. She was trying to think of something positive to say when the telephone rang. "Oh, for goodness' sake." She stood up, walked over to the desk and picked up the phone. "Oh, hi Max... yes, it has been ages..." She listened carefully, then her face darkened. "What?"

Spanner stood up. "What is it, Rachel?"

Rachel covered the receiver. "Our daughter and her best friend Jade are in San Francisco so they can go on the war protest march tomorrow."

Much to her chagrin, Spanner burst out laughing. "Really? I wonder where they got that demonstrating spirit from."

Rachel glared at him, then began laughing as well.

On the other end, Max raised an eyebrow. He was sure he could hear laughing. He was about to speak when Rachel started talking again. "Hi Max, sorry about that. I was just telling Steve... er, don't tell Rita we were laughing, will you?"

Max smiled. "No, of course not. I'm just pleased you're not fuming!"

"Well, I am, but as Steve reminded me, I did the same thing back in the seventies so I can't really say too much." She changed the subject. "Are you sure you don't mind them staying?"

"No, and I'll go with them tomorrow, to keep an eye on them."

"Thanks Max, that's really kind of you, and I am sorry they bothered you."

"No sweat. At least they decided to contact me and didn't just crash anywhere."

Rachel smiled. "Let me know if you're out of pocket, and thanks again." She put the receiver back and glanced at Steve. Within moments they were both in stitches, their laughter ringing around the room.

PRPC (Philippine Refugee Processing Centre) near Morong, Bataan, Philippines

Phuc sat in the office where he was helping out and tried to work out what to do about Vy's interest in Diem. Vy was like her mother. If he told her not to do something, there was a chance she would do it just to spite him. He didn't object to Vy having a boyfriend, but their lives would be hard enough when they got to American anyway. He could remember when the Americans were in Vietnam. They seemed to hate their black people even more than they hated the Vietnamese, at least that was how it had seemed to him. He had been reading American newspapers since they had arrived in the camp, to help him get used to the country where they were going to live, and unfortunately things didn't appear to have changed that much. If Vy decided to marry a black man, they would never be able to have the new lives they wanted.

Phuc sighed and wished he could come up with a solution that didn't involve someone getting hurt. Unfortunately, Vy was his priority, and if that meant hurting Diem, that was what he would have to do. If he didn't, Vy could risk ruining everything.

Omaha, Nebraska

Spanner replaced the receiver after talking to Kurt and smiled. At least he'd managed to do something constructive. Kurt was on his way to speak to Jim now, and hopefully that would give his friend something to do to occupy his thoughts and keep him off the self-destructive pathway he was on. Spanner glanced at the clock and stood up. He had better get ready for the campaign rally or he would be late, and that wouldn't look good. He hurried to the door, ignoring the ache in his chest.

He reached the lift, pressed the button and waited, his thoughts on Kurt and Jim and how awful it must be to be living with what they'd experienced – and they were just the tip of the iceberg. How many more veterans were suffering with little help? If he could get elected, he would make a concerted effort to try and help more. Spanner glanced up at the floor indicator and wondered why the lift was taking so long. He would be late if it didn't hurry. It would appear to be stuck on the ground floor. His pulse rate quickened. He should have left earlier. Perhaps he should use the stairs? He was still trying to decide what to do when he realised that his arm was aching and the pain in his chest was getting worse. *Oh shit,* he murmured. Not now… not when he was on his own, when most of the staff had gone home… He turned away and tried to walk back to his office, he needed to get to a phone… but the pain was too much, and he collapsed on the floor.

CHAPTER FORTY-SEVEN

Omaha, Nebraska

Jim stared at the massive archive of files and wondered where on earth to start. His first reaction to Kurt's news had been to shake his head and say no. He couldn't spend his whole day thinking about those bastards. But gradually Kurt had talked him round, and now he was feeling quite enthusiastic. Maybe Kurt was right. If they'd acted at the time, they wouldn't have made any difference, just gotten themselves killed, and then there would have been no witnesses, but now… now he could dedicate the rest of his life to finding the murderers. His thoughts turned to Spanner and he shook his head. Thank goodness the cleaner had found him in time. Maybe there was a God after all. She had been loading her cleaning materials when the door had closed, and the lift had shot up to Spanner's floor. Exasperated, she had hurried up the stairs and found him collapsed on the floor. They had rushed him to hospital, and he was now recovering, although the prognosis wasn't good. Spanner needed a heart transplant, or he wouldn't last much longer.

Jim took a breath. One of the last things Spanner had done was to get him access to these files. It was time he got on with it.

Omaha, Nebraska

"It's all my fault…" Rita sobbed uncontrollably. "If I hadn't gone to San Francisco…"

"No it isn't, darling. Don't be silly." Rachel hugged her daughter tight. "Pop was ill, you know that. It had nothing to do with you, his heart just gave up." She let go, and leaning down, she wiped Rita's tears away. "No more tears, darling. He will get the heart transplant he needs and then he will be as good as new."

"You promise?"

"I can't promise anything, Rita, you know that. But you need to be strong for him, we all do. Come here Bill, give me a hug. Then we'll go and see your Pop."

"He will be ok, Mom, won't he?" Bill hadn't moved from his chair; his normally tanned face was pale.

Rachel wanted to reassure them both, but she didn't want to lie either. "It's in God's hands now…" She sighed. If only it was up to her, a heart would become available immediately and Steve would have the operation and be fit and healthy again… if only…

Ho Chi Minh City, Vietnam

An glanced anxiously at his watch again and wondered where Chinh was. He had always arrived on time before. What if he knew An was waiting for him? Maybe Loan had told him... He breathed a sigh of relief as Chinh came hurrying into view and disappeared into the brothel.

An waited a few moments, then made his way around the back and crept toward the room Chinh would be using. Loan had left the blind slightly up as he'd requested, and he could see her binding Chinh to the bed. An took a deep breath and tried to steady his nerves. He could feel the knife against his skin and the sweat forming on his face. He forced himself to concentrate on his mother and Vy. That was why he was there. To take revenge.

He peered back through the window. Loan was naked and sitting astride Chinh, who she had also blindfolded. An grinned. That was a nice touch. He would give her a bonus for that. He took another breath and let himself in.

"What...." Loan called out in pretend surprise. An drew back his fist and punched her hard. She fell on the floor, eyes closed. An had no time to check she was alright, Chinh was already struggling against his bonds. An grabbed a handful of tissues from the box by the bed and stuffed them into Chinh's mouth before he could cry out. Once he was satisfied Chinh couldn't make any noise, he grabbed Loan's stockings and used them to tie her up. He was relieved she was still unconscious. He pulled out the meat knife, taken from the restaurant kitchen earlier that day, so he knew it was sharp, and leaned over Chinh.

"You think you are untouchable, Chinh, but you aren't..." He raised the knife and held the blade against Chin's testicles. "I do hope you enjoyed your last fuck."

Chinh's struggles became more violent, his moans louder, but not loud enough to worry anyone outside.

An sliced one testicle off. He fascinated to see how easy it was. He looked at Chinh's face, but it had appeared he had passed out. An shrugged. It was a shame, but he didn't have time to wait for him to come round. He sliced the other testicle off, pulled the tissues out of Chinh's mouth and shoved both testicles in.

CHAPTER FORTY-EIGHT

Omaha, Nebraska

Rachel let herself into Spanner's office and sighed. There was so much unopened mail despite the secretary's best efforts to keep up. She sat down and began going through it slowly. Most of it wasn't important, things that could be dealt with by other departments. Some of the personal letters, though, would need to be dealt with. She began writing replies to letters, explaining that Spanner was in hospital and that their problem would be passed onto others to deal with, when she reached the one from the Federal Prison in Houston, Texas. Rachel frowned. Why on earth would someone in Texas be writing to the State Governor in Nebraska? She opened the envelope and began reading.

Ho Chi Minh City, Vietnam

An watched Chinh gasping for air for a few seconds, then became aware that Loan was regaining consciousness. Sadly, he would have to go before Chinh woke up. An hurried towards the window and let himself out. He had already worked out his escape route, and he hastened through the deserted back streets towards the river and threw the knife in. He glanced nervously around, but there was no one about, so he walked quickly towards some waste ground he had identified a few days earlier. The city sounds were more muted here, and he crossed quickly to an old deserted garage where there was a large metal drum. An was relieved to see both the bin and the small bottle of petrol he had left behind it, were undisturbed. He quickly took off his blood-soaked outer clothes and threw them in, followed by the petrol, before setting fire to them with his lighter and hurrying away.

It wasn't until An was halfway back to his room and the adrenaline finally wore off that the enormity of what he had done hit him, and he bent over and retched, again and again.

Omaha, Nebraska

Five minutes later, Rachel was still reeling from the shock – not only from the fact that Steve had a child, but that this child was on death row in Texas. What the hell was she going to do? She knew Steve still had no memory of his time in Vietnam, which would explain why he hadn't contacted this Lien person while he was in hospital. But he was much too weak for her to tell him this now. It could cause another heart attack, and he wouldn't survive that. If only he could have a heart transplant. Not that there was anything he could probably do to help the boy. If he was on death row, he had probably done something to deserve it. Rachel shuddered, imagining the headlines if Steve tried to intervene in another state's justice system. He'd faced enough of a backlash from the media for trying to help Jim. He had survived that because he was popular, but even if his health was good, his political standing would suffer too much for him to do anything. She glanced down at the letter again. Perhaps this An was lying… her heart suddenly quickened as an audacious idea popped into her head.

Rachel took a breath and tried to talk herself out of it. No, it wouldn't be possible. Even if it was possible, to do what she was thinking would be despicable. Steve would never forgive her if he found out. She put the letter safely in her handbag and tried to get on with the rest of the correspondence, but the idea wouldn't leave her, and eventually Rachel decided to stop and try and work out a way it could be done. Then she realised she knew exactly how, if she was brave enough.

Outskirts of Ho Chi Minh City, Vietnam

An grabbed the newspaper from the young boy, handed over some money and hurried back to the garage to read it. He was expecting to see his attack on Chinh on the front page, but there was nothing there. He scanned through the paper quickly and eventually found a small piece stating that a government official, Hoang Kim Chinh, had been injured in an accident and was recovering in hospital. An felt sick. How on earth could Chinh have survived? And even more worrying, why were they reporting the assault as an accident? He threw the paper in the bin, stepped outside the garage and lit a cigarette.

"Everything alright, An? You look very pale." My, the garage owner, had arrived back from collecting some spare parts and was watching him carefully.

An jumped. "No, no I'm fine. Just having a break."

My looked An up and down, his scepticism evident. "Mm, well, I have the parts here now, so you can put that out and give me a hand."

"Yes, of course." An stubbed the cigarette out and followed My back into the garage. His hands were sweating and his legs trembling. What if Chinh came after him? He was supposed to have died. If the newspaper report said it was an accident, it must be on Chinh's orders. An shivered. If only he had listened to Phuc and Vy. He could be enjoying freedom. Instead he was stuck in the same city as a brutal maniac who would now be looking to get revenge on him. And for what, exactly? He could admit to himself that he had enjoyed having Chinh at his mercy for a brief time, but once the euphoria had worn off he'd felt disgusted. Castrating the bastard hadn't changed anything – it hadn't brought his mother back and it hadn't undone Chinh sexually abusing Vy.

An glanced back towards the door, half expecting armed police to come rushing in to arrest him, but everything was quiet. He turned his attention back to the engine he was working on and tried to concentrate on something else.

Federal Detention Centre, Houston, Texas

Dung stared at the four walls of his cell and wondered how long it would take to get an answer to his letter. He knew there was a chance that Spanner wouldn't reply to him. After all, he had not bothered to get in touch with Lien after the explosion, so perhaps he had just used her, pretended that he loved her and taken the opportunity to go home and forget all about her. If that was the case, then he would just throw Dung's letter in the bin.

Dung lay down and prayed for the first time in years. Surely An's father wouldn't let his own son die?

Houston, Texas

"I thought our business was concluded." Charles glared at Rachel, who was waiting outside his consulting room.

"I have a one-off proposition for you." Rachel indicated his room. "I wanted to discuss it in private."

Charles debated whether to tell her where to go, but curiosity got the better of him. He opened the door. "Come in and get it over with."

Rachel followed him inside. "Can you lock the door? Make sure we're not disturbed." Rachel wasn't sure how he was going to take her proposal, but she didn't want anyone interrupting.

Charles shrugged, locked the door and walked over to his desk. "Well? I'm waiting."

"I'll give you all the evidence I have against you if you do one thing for me."

Charles sat down at his desk, and watched her closely for a moment before speaking. "How do I know I can trust you?"

"When I tell you what I want you to do, you'll know you can trust me, because it won't be in my interests to do anything against you."

"Go on, then."

Rachel took a deep breath and fixed her eyes on the floor. "Steve needs a heart transplant. You're a very good heart transplant surgeon. He can't wait too much longer, another heart attack will kill him, but there's no donor hearts available at the moment." She stopped and looked up at him. "I know where you can get a heart."

Charles stared at her in disbelief. "Are you mad? You can't pick a heart up from the market."

"Not quite from the market," Rachel replied, "but almost."

There was a long silence. Charles was curious, despite himself. "Go on then, where's this heart?" he asked in a dismissive manner.

Rachel quickly explained how she had found a Vietnamese refugee on death row through Spanner's work with veterans and Vietnamese refugees. Before Charles could comment, she continued, "Organs, including hearts, are often taken from prisoners on death row for research, so that will give you a reason to be there. He has no family, so the only people likely to be watching the execution are the Governor, his attorney, the guard to carry out the execution and the doctor. If you can convince the doctor to help, you can be waiting for the heart in the ante room behind the death chamber. Only the heart would still be beating."

Charles stared at her in disbelief. "Are you mad? I could get struck off for what you're suggesting, or worse."

"And you could get struck off if I take all my evidence to the police. I also have a record of you paying me money for my silence. And your Republican friends won't be too pleased to know that your money is being used to back a Democrat!"

Charles shook his head. "You won't go through with it. Spanner would never get elected if any of this came out."

Rachel shrugged. "He won't get elected if he's dead, either, so I don't have anything to lose."

Charles shook his head. "It would never work..." he muttered, but his brain was already thinking of ways in which he could do it. The challenge appealed to him, and knowing that Rachel had nothing else on him would be a great relief. "What about the hospital?"

Rachel shrugged. "You are their senior heart surgeon; they aren't going to argue with you if you say someone has died. It might take some cash to keep people quiet, but you're not short of money."

"When is the execution due?"

Rachel frowned. "I don't know, but as a doctor you could ask if they have any executions coming up, as you would like to harvest the heart for research."

"How do I contact you?"

"You're a heart transplant specialist, you can contact me at the hospital where Steve is."

Charles stood up, walked to the window and stared down at the city while he weighed up the risk. Although his face was impassive, inwardly he was fuming. No one ever got anything over him… at least no one had before Rachel. Despite her assurances, how could he be sure that she would hand over all the incriminating evidence? He couldn't let her think she'd won again or she would be back whenever she felt like it, and who knew what other outrageous things she might demand.

He caught sight of her reflection in the window and his focus shifted. The years had been kind to her, she was still very attractive. He wondered idly what she was like to fuck now – obviously a little more experienced than before. She probably knew all sorts of tricks… his upper lip curled and his expression darkened. His trousers suddenly felt tight as he thought of the perfect way to put himself back in the driving seat and stop her even thinking about blackmailing him in future. His smile broadened. The hospital security team had insisted on fitting cameras in his office for insurance purposes, despite his objections that his consultations were confidential. Eventually a compromise had been agreed that gave him control of the cameras via a button under his desk, and control of any material that was filmed via a computer in the cupboard located in the corner of the room. The cameras remained off unless he switched them on.

He turned towards her. "I'll go along with your plan, providing you do something for me."

Rachel's eyes narrowed. "Like what?"

Charles leaned towards his desk, secretly pressed the

button switching on the camera and walked towards her. As he drew closer, he began undoing his zip. "You give me a blow job for old time's sake, and we have a deal."

Rachel stared at him in disbelief and then burst out laughing. "Are you serious? Do you really think I would touch you with a bargepole?"

Charles shrugged, took out his erect penis and began stroking it. "You don't have to touch it... just open your mouth."

Rachel shook her head. "You're mad."

"And you're desperate. Isn't your husband's life worth a few sucks, a little teasing with that viperous tongue of yours?" He stepped towards her, careful to keep her in view of the camera. He could edit out the coercion afterwards. "Come on Rachel, a quick blow job and you'll get everything you want, and we never have to see each other again."

Rachel stared at him in desperation, but she couldn't think of a way out. Yes, she could carry out her threat to expose him, but he could retaliate by telling everyone that she had tried to blackmail him into stealing the heart of a refugee on death row to save her husband. Even if she denied it and Steve survived, he would be ruined. The mud would stick. "You swear you'll do the operation?" she spoke eventually.

Charles didn't answer straight away. He was enjoying himself so much he was having trouble controlling himself, and he didn't want it to be over too quickly. He wanted to savour every moment. He took a breath and tried to think of something else for a moment. When his erection had shrunk, and the immediate sense of release had passed, he allowed himself to look at her again. The fear, disgust and loathing in her face was enough. He leaned towards her and ran his fingers over her lips. "Yes." He rested his hand heavily on her shoulder, pushing her down. "Kneel." His voice was hoarse with lust, his eyes glazed. Rachel closed her eyes and tried to pretend she didn't care. After everything else she was prepared to do, this was nothing. A few moments' discomfort and he would save Steve.

She knelt down, raised her head and reluctantly opened her mouth.

"Open your eyes."

As she obeyed, Charles forced himself inside, his fingers grabbing her hair, knotting it round his hands, drawing the strands tighter and tighter, making her gasp in pain. Charles thrust back and forth, harder and harder, his fury at her impudence for daring to blackmail him mixing with his lust, faster and faster until he finally exploded. Sensing she was about to spit him out, he let go of her hair and held her mouth closed until he saw her swallow. Then he let go.

Rachel collapsed on the floor and tried to hide her tears. She wouldn't give him the satisfaction of crying. Charles got his breath back and smiled down at her. "Well, that was fun, wasn't it?" He zipped up his trousers, walked back to his desk and surreptitiously switched off the camera.

"I'll be in touch when I know when the execution is, and when I've worked out how to get the doctor to do what we want."

Rachel staggered to her feet and nodded. She felt numb, but somehow she would have to forget this, or he would win. "I'll wait to hear from you." She walked to the door and let herself out.

Charles walked towards the cupboard where the computer was, a smile on his face, and began reviewing the camera footage. A few minutes later he was hard again, his trousers cutting into his groin, and his smile was even broader. Rachel might think this was the end, but it wasn't. He was back in charge now, and he had something he could use against her if she reneged on their deal.

PRPC (Philippine Refugee Processing Centre) near Morong, Bataan, Philippines

"A drink with you?" Diem looked surprised but pleased, and for a moment Phuc felt guilty at what he was planning to do.

"Yes, I thought we should get to know each other better. I wasn't very friendly towards you at first, and I'm sorry. I was just looking out for my niece."

"I didn't take offence. In your position, I would do the same. Vy is so precious. She has been a such a help to me."

Phuc looked confused. "I don't understand?"

"People look at me and all they see is my skin colour, the razor slashes and scars, and they think I am just a troublemaker – so they either avoid me or attack me." He shrugged. "Vy helped me see that I am worth more than that. I don't mind admitting that I was scared of going to America, but now I am looking forward to it."

"What are you going to do there?" Despite himself, Phuc was interested.

Diem looked slightly embarrassed. "I have discovered that I have a talent for cutting hair, so I am going to get some work with a salon and then eventually start my own."

Phuc blinked at him in astonishment. Diem laughed. "Yes, I know I don't look like everyone's idea of a hairdresser, but I am hoping people will not judge me for how I look."

Phuc found himself smiling. "I am sure you'll be successful."

Diem nodded. "I hope so. It will be so exciting, won't it? They told me today that my application has been accepted, and I am leaving in a couple of days. I am going to San Francisco. I was just on my way to tell Vy."

Phuc hesitated. "You are going to America in a couple of days?"

"Yes. Shall we have a drink first or..."

"No, let's go and find Vy. You can come and share our meal." Phuc suddenly realised that he couldn't sabotage Diem's chances of a new life. In any case, he wouldn't be a threat anymore because he would be in America. The chances of them being sent to the same place were miniscule, and once he had gone, Vy would forget all about him.

En route to Omaha, Nebraska

Rachel was grateful she had to concentrate on the road, or she had no idea what she would have done. She was still in shock that yet again Charles had sexually abused her – only this time she had let it happen, she had even gone along with it. Despite the copious amounts of water she'd used to swill out her mouth, and the numerous peppermints she'd eaten since, she could still taste him, and she wondered if that would ever go. It had taken her years to get over the rape, but this time she didn't have the luxury of waiting for the pain to fade. She had to carry on as normal, pretend everything was the same as it had been when she'd left Omaha that morning. She wanted to pull over, find a bridge and jump off – but she couldn't, she had to get back. Steve would be waiting for her.

For a moment, she forgot Charles and thought how much she loved Steve, and how much she needed him. She must make sure he never found out the lengths she had gone to. A wry smile crossed her face as she wondered which of her sins he would consider worse. Blackmailing a rapist into stealing a heart from the son he knew nothing about, or consenting to give the rapist a blow job. Tears pricked her eyes and she fought them back angrily. If she crashed the car now, Charles would have won. He would have forced her into being unfaithful to the man she loved and not had to do anything in return.

Her expression hardened and she wiped away the tears. Let Charles think he had won, let him have his few moments of triumph. Once he had done what she wanted, she would see that he paid for everything. And she would do it in such a way he would never suspect her… not until it was too late for him to retaliate, anyway.

Omaha, Nebraska

"Can't keep you away, can I?" Frank watched as Richie sauntered through the club with one of the hostesses on his arm.

"I'm on a lucky streak, can't waste it!" Richie was high on his success; he was already up $10,000. At this rate he wouldn't need to worry about getting another job.

"Enjoy, it won't last long!" Frank muttered under his breath. Charles had paid him well to ensure Richie crashed and burned and ended up owing him thousands of dollars. Angel had done her job well; it appeared Richie was already half drunk, and drunken men didn't make very good card players. Charles had also had him buy up a debt from some guy in Texas. Frank wondered briefly what game Charles was playing, then shrugged. It wasn't any of his business, and as long as he wasn't out of pocket...

PRPC (Philippine Refugee Processing Centre) near Morong, Bataan, Philippines

"Uncle? You're back sooner than...?" Vy stopped abruptly when he saw Diem and smiled.

"I bumped into Diem and he tells me he is off to San Francisco in a couple of days, so I invited him to have a meal with us to celebrate."

Vy gasped, stepped forward and hugged Diem. "You have your papers? That's so exciting."

"Yes, isn't it? I can't wait, and I am so grateful to you, Vy." Diem hugged her back and smiled at her.

"You have been waiting ages, I am so happy for you."

Phuc was watching carefully. Vy really did look pleased for Diem. Perhaps he had read too much into their relationship.

"I will miss you, but once I am settled, I will write to you with an address." Diem was still smiling at Vy.

"That would be wonderful, then we can keep in touch and you can tell me when you are the proud owner of lots of hair salons!" They both laughed. "Come on, you can help me get dinner."

Phuc watched as they went into the kitchen. America was

an enormous country, with millions of people – what harm could it do if Diem did write to Vy? If she found out he was trying to run her life, she would be furious, and Phuc didn't want to fall out with her; he was enjoying having her in his life. Perhaps he would just keep out of it.

Omaha, Nebraska

Richie stared at the cards in total disbelief. One minute he was winning and then... He didn't even dare contemplate how much he owed. "Any chance of some credit? I'm good for it." If only he had another hand, he was sure he could win back what he'd lost.

The dealer shook his head. "You'd have to take that up with the boss."

Richie nodded and swallowed nervously. There was no way Frank would give him credit. He stood up.

"Going somewhere, Richie?" Frank was standing behind him, his eyes cold, face unsmiling.

"I'll find the money Frank... you know I'm good for it..." Richie looked over Frank's shoulder searching frantically for a way out, but he was trapped. Two of Frank's enforcers were already in place.

Frank leaned forward and lowered his voice. "Let's not create a scene, Richie... it's not good for business." He took Richie's arm. "We can talk in my office." Before Richie could say anything, he found himself being led towards the back of the casino, Frank's hand gripping his arm like a vice, the two enforcers following behind, their faces expressionless.

"I can get you the money..." Richie began as one of the men closed the door behind them.

"No you can't, Richie." Frank grabbed him by the neck and shoved him up against the wall. "Your grandmother made it quite clear that if you got into debt again, she would not be bailing you out."

"Then why did you let me back in?" Richie spat at him, then regretted his hasty words as Frank's fingers tightened around his neck and he began to suffocate.

Frank suddenly let go. Richie gasped in air gratefully, doubling over spluttering and coughing. Frank watched him for a few moments, then grabbed him by the hair and pulled him upright. "You owe me $7,000 Richie. You can't pay me, so you're going to do a little job for me instead. Capiche?"

Richie nodded. "Yes... yes."

Frank stared into his eyes. "Good." He turned away and picked up a piece of paper. "You are going to pay this man a visit for me."

Richie glanced down at the paper and registered the address. "It's in Texas...?"

"You scared of crossing the state line?" Frank raised an eyebrow and Richie shook his head.

"No." Richie was already planning what he could tell his mother about why he was going to Texas.

"And you won't tell anyone where you're going, will you?" Frank's eyes bore into his.

"No... no." Richie took a breath. "What do I say to him?"

Frank gave a cold smile. "You're going to threaten him."

Richie paled. "Threaten him?"

Frank leaned forward and spoke quickly for several minutes before stepping back. "Capiche?"

As Richie hesitated, Frank slapped him hard across the face, knocking him back against the wall.

"Yes, ok, I'll do it." Richie used his hand to wipe the blood from his mouth.

Frank smiled and patted him on the shoulder. "Good."

Richie took a breath. "And if I do what you want, is my debt cleared?"

Frank was about to nod when he remembered Charles's last condition. "You are to stay away for at least a year."

Richie frowned. "Stay away? I don't understand..."

"You will not come back to Nebraska for at least a year. It's not difficult to understand, Richie."

"But what excuse can I give?" Richie was horrified. How could he leave his mother when Spanner was in hospital? "My stepdad's dying... I can't leave my mom..."

Frank shrugged. "Not my problem. I'm sure you'll think of something, because if I see you back in Omaha before that, I will find another way of collecting your debt."

CHAPTER FORTY-NINE

Omaha, Nebraska

Spanner finished reading the newspapers in his hospital bed and smiled. At least this had been a quick war and America was on the winning side again. But it wasn't all good news. Although Kuwait had been liberated from seven months of Iraqi occupation, the oil fields had been set on fire by their retreating troops.

"Morning Spanner, how are you today?"

Spanner put the paper down and smiled at his stepson. "Hi Richie, you're early." His face lit up. "Have you found a job?"

Richie shook his head. "No, not yet."

"Still can't find anything, eh?" Spanner gave a sympathetic smile. "You will do soon, Richie. Don't let it get you down."

Richie shook his head. After Frank's ultimatum he'd thought hard, and the only excuse he could come up for leaving was for a job. "I've got an interview in California. I don't know if I'll get the job, but I figured it was worth going. Maybe leaving the state is the answer." He hated lying to Spanner, but he had no option.

Spanner smiled. "Good for you. I think that's a really sensible idea. You can't stay at home forever. What did your mom say?"

"She wasn't very happy, but she understands." Rachel had been furious at first, claiming that it wasn't fair to leave Steve when he was so ill, but eventually she'd agreed and even been supportive. Richie had been so relieved he hadn't wondered at his mother's sudden change of heart.

"Good luck, Richie. Let us know how you're getting on. It's very boring in here!"

Richie sighed. "I'm sorry to leave you when you're like this."

"Nonsense, you have your life to lead, and it's not the first occasion I've spent time in hospital." He watched Richie go and closed his eyes.

He had dozed off when Rachel rushed in. "Darling, I have great news," she blurted out.

Spanner was instantly alert. "What, what is it?"

"They have found a heart for you. Isn't that wonderful? I'm so thrilled. Unfortunately, it's in Houston, Texas. You will need to be transferred to Houston, and they will do the operation there." Rachel spoke rapidly, her face flushed with excitement.

Spanner felt relieved and apprehensive all at once. "How will I get to Houston?" he asked.

"They will fly up here tomorrow and they will take you there, honey. You'll have the transplant the next day."

"You will come with me, love, won't you?" he asked anxiously.

"Of course," she said, "but I will have to travel separately. The ambulance aircraft is small, so I can't travel with you." Catching the mournful expression on his face, she kissed him on the cheek. "I will be there for the operation, darling, don't worry."

"Where is the heart coming from?"

"Not sure my, love," Rachel said. "They wouldn't tell me much, but I believe it was some sort of accident." She looked downwards, terrified that Steve would see the lie on her face. "Darling, you will be healthy again!"

There was no going back now.

Ho Chi Minh City, Vietnam

An had been living on his nerves ever since the night in the brothel, but nothing had happened, and he was gradually starting to relax.

"Can you deliver this car to Da Nang for me?" My finished wiping his hands on a towel and indicated the new Suzuki Vitara sitting on the forecourt.

An's face lit up. He rarely had the opportunity to drive even though he had passed his test over a year ago, one of the first things he had done when My took him on full time. "Yes, please."

My laughed and threw him the keys. "The address and

all the necessary paperwork are on the front seat. Drive carefully."

An slipped into the driver's seat and started up the engine. It would be good to get out of the city; perhaps he could finally relax for a while.

Houston, Texas

"I can't pay," Doctor Jefferson Carson pleaded. "Just a few more days, please."

Richie leaned forward and put the tip of the knife against Jefferson's throat. "Sorry, the people I work for don't have any more time to give you."

"But I don't have any money, and I don't get paid until the end of the month..." Jefferson searched his mind frantically for some way of getting rid of the mob's debt collector.

Richie shook his head and drew the knife back, and then suddenly stopped. "Maybe there is a way you could get out of this."

"How? I'll do anything... well, almost anything..." Jefferson tried a small smile.

Richie did not return the smile. "I'll set up a meeting for you. Wait here."

"Here?"

Richie grabbed Jefferson by the hair and replaced the knife on his throat. "You aren't planning on going anywhere, are you?"

"No! No, I'll wait."

Richie let go, put the knife back in his pocket and walked slowly away. He hoped he had done enough to pay his own debts. He would have liked to watch what happened next, but he daren't risk it.

Charles smiled to himself and put the camera away. He now had more material to prevent Rachel double-crossing him, and he would deprive her of her precious bastard if necessary. Charles waited until Richie had driven away before crawling out of the bushes, smartening himself up and walking confidently towards the prison doctor.

PRPC (Philippine Refugee Processing Centre) near Morong, Bataan, Philippines

"I will miss Diem, but at least he's finally out of here." Vy finished clearing the breakfast dishes away.

"You'll probably get a letter from him soon," Phuc smiled.

"Let's hope so." Vy was about to say more when she heard the mail arrive and Phuc went to get it. A few seconds later he ran in, his eyes alight. "They've come!"

Vy stared at him and then the penny dropped. "Our papers?"

"Yes, look." He handed her a sheaf of papers and Vy quickly flipped through them, hoping they would be going to San Francisco or at least California. Her face fell. "We're going to New Orleans."

"Isn't that exciting?" Phuc watched her closely. Obviously his first instincts had been right. "If you're worried about hearing from Diem, Vy, they will forward any mail on to our new address."

"Yes, of course they will." Vy smiled. "I will need to go and do some reading about New Orleans and see what opportunities are there."

Phuc smiled and turned his attention back to his own papers. In two days, they would be on their way. He couldn't wait. And if any letters arrived from Diem for Vy, he would just have to get rid of them. The boy would soon lose interest if Vy didn't reply.

Houston, Texas

"I can't do that!" Jefferson stared at Charles in terror.

"Of course you can. I will approach the governor and ask permission to use the prisoner's heart for research. All you have to do is to switch the final injection for some more anaesthetic or water or anything else that's innocuous, it doesn't matter as long as it's not potassium chloride so he doesn't have a real cardiac arrest. Then you flip the ECG switch off, so it looks like he's dead."

Jefferson thought frantically but he couldn't think of any way out. "And if I do this my debt is paid?"

Charles nodded. "Yes. That will be it. Obviously, if you tell anyone what you've done, your wife and daughter will get a visit."

Jefferson paled even more but nodded. "Ok."

Charles breathed a sigh of relief. "Phone this number as soon as you have a date, and I'm sure I don't have to remind you not to speak of this to anyone."

Jefferson swallowed nervously and nodded again. Charles smiled and walked slowly away.

Omaha, Nebraska

Jim sat back and rubbed his eyes. He had been looking at endless pictures of Vietnamese men for days and not seen anyone that even vaguely resembled the men he was looking for. The phone rang and he reached for the receiver.

"Hi Jim, it's Kurt. Just to let you know, Spanner has been moved to a hospital in Texas so that he's ready for a heart transplant if one becomes available."

"Is that good or bad?"

"Don't know. I guess it's good; at least they aren't giving up on him."

"True."

"Any luck?"

"No, nothing yet, but I'll keep looking. I've barely scratched the surface."

"Are you doing the most recent first?"

"No, I thought I would start with the early ones and work forward. It's going to take months, I think. Fortunately, the numbers coming in have dropped, so there aren't as many recent ones." Jim yawned. "Sorry, obviously need more coffee."

"Ok, I'll speak to you later. I'll be at the office until seven if you want me."

"Ok, bye." Jim put the phone down, glanced at the clock and picked up the next file. He'd make some coffee once he'd finished this pile.

New Orleans, Louisiana

Phuc looked around their new home and breathed a sigh of relief. They were finally free of Chinh and of anything to do with Vietnam. It would be hard starting over, but they would have help and at least they could always change cities if they weren't happy. They wouldn't have to fill in pages of paperwork before doing anything. It was a strange feeling.

"It's odd, isn't it? Knowing we can come and go as we please?" Vy echoed his thoughts. She hugged herself. "I can't believe we're really here at last."

Phuc laughed. "Well, we are, and unless we go and get some food, we'll spend our first night hungry!"

"Trust you to think only of your stomach!" Vy punched his arm playfully.

CHAPTER FIFTY

Federal Detention Centre, Houston, Texas

Dung had finally accepted that Spanner was not going to come to his rescue, was not even going to bother to answer him. There were only a few days left before his execution now, and he was becoming resigned to the fact that nothing was going to save him. Despite his attorney's attempts to keep up Dung's spirits, he could tell by the look in J.P's eyes that he had also given up hope that Dung would be granted clemency. He wondered what his sister was doing now, and whether his family had heard that he was in America or whether they thought he was still in Vietnam. He hoped they still thought about him. Jonathan had said he could write to them, but Dung had decided not to. Better they thought he was living his life somewhere happily, than know the truth.

Houston Heart Hospital, Texas

Rachel sat by Spanner's bed and held his hand. The hospital had informed them that the heart would be available later that day and the transplant would take place that evening, and now they were waiting. Rachel was relieved that Charles hadn't put in an appearance.

"If I don't make it..."

"Don't say things like that, Steve. You will be fine. I know you will." After all her scheming, she couldn't even think about anything going wrong.

Spanner smiled. "Rachel, I'm sure you're right, but I just wanted to tell you that I love you, and the years we've spent together have been the happiest of my life." He closed his eyes and wondered if his damaged body would really survive such a massive ordeal.

Rachel stared down at him and prayed he would be alright. If he died, then it would all have been for nothing. Her thoughts went briefly to the young man who was going to die, but she couldn't find any sympathy for him. He had killed people, he had been sentenced to death. At least this way he could atone for his crimes by doing something good. Spanner could do so much for other people if he was given the time to do it. Her decision was definitely the right one, although it would have to remain a secret forever, because she knew Steve would never see it the same way as she did.

Federal Detention Centre, Houston, Texas

Jefferson was shaking with fear. Even though he knew there was little chance of him getting caught if he was careful, he was still terrified, and he was also wracked with guilt about what he was about to do.

Jefferson had thought hard about what he could put in the final injection, and finally realised that if he used anything different from the three drugs normally used for the execution, it would show up in the autopsy. The only thing he could do was to cut down the amount of anaesthetic in the first injection and use the remainder as a substitute for the potassium chloride. That way, the drugs found in the body after death would be correct. Unfortunately, it meant the prisoner would not be completely unconscious, so he would feel the full effects of the paralysing drug. It would be excruciatingly painful for several moments while everything shut down, but there was nothing else he could do. Although he had tried to convince himself that the prisoner was a murderer and therefore not an innocent, he couldn't stop the guilt. He glanced at the clock. It was time to go.

Jefferson walked slowly towards the execution suite where Charles was waiting. Jefferson let him into the small ante room, gave him a gown and mask and then walked through to the execution chamber to wait for the prisoner.

New Orleans, Louisiana

Vy checked the mail and sighed in disappointment. She had been hoping that she would have had a letter from Diem by now. It was weeks since they'd arrived, and even longer since he'd gone to San Francisco.

"Are you still expecting him to write?" Phuc managed to look concerned.

Vy shrugged. "I was sure he would. Perhaps it's got lost, or they haven't forwarded it on from the Philippines."

"Or he has started his new life and it doesn't include you, Vy," Phuc said, as gently as he could manage. "I'm sorry if that sounds abrupt, but maybe it's time you forgot all about him and got on with your life, like he obviously has."

"You're probably right," Vy smiled. "It's not as if I don't have plenty of friends." She had found work in the local community centre helping fellow countrymen and women settle into their new home. Diem had been right, it was the perfect job for her, and she would have loved to tell him so, if only he would write. "I'll see you later. Bye, Uncle."

She hurried out the door and Phuc watched her go with a sigh of relief. It was a good job she had been at work when the envelope had arrived. Phuc had immediately hidden the letter and waited until he knew he had the apartment to himself before opening it.

My dear Vy,
I hope this letter finds you and your family well and that you too are now in America. This is my address at the top so you can write back. I love San Francisco and can't wait to show it to you. I have a good job in a big salon and although my wages are not large, I get very good tips. Please write soon and let me know where you are and we can make arrangements to meet up.
With very best wishes to my good friend
Diem

Phuc had debated what to do with it. He could just throw it away, but there might be an occasion when he needed it. He couldn't imagine why he would want it, but he had grown cautious over the years and reluctant to do anything that he might regret. Perhaps it was best to keep it, just in case. He had hidden it among his own papers and hoped that Diem would soon get the message when he didn't get a reply.

Federal Detention Centre, Houston, Texas

Gabriel Adams and the other guard escorted Dung slowly towards the execution chamber. It was only Gabriel's second time as executioner, and he could already feel the sick sense of dread forming in the pit of his stomach. He knew it was part of his job, but it was the part he liked least. Gabriel took a deep breath and tried not to imagine what the prisoner was thinking. If it was bad for him, it must be a million times worse for the prisoner. He glanced at Dung, but the prisoner's face was expressionless. Gabriel looked across at Shaun Nicols, his fellow guard, but he just appeared bored. Gabriel wondered briefly if he could swap the execution with Shaun but then realised that wasn't likely. Shaun was lazy and would never do anything he didn't have to. Gabriel took another breath. Obviously he couldn't get out of his duty, so he might as well just accept it.

Dung's heart was beating rapidly with fear, but his mind was surprisingly calm. He knew there would be no last-minute reprieve now. Obviously, An's father either didn't believe him or didn't care. There was a chance Spanner hadn't received his letter, of course, but it no longer mattered. Dung's long struggle to survive in a world that hated him because of how he looked was finally over. He reached the chamber and looked out at the governor and J.P. watching through the glass. The governor had told him they would witness his final moments. Dung wondered how it would affect his attorney to see a man die, and then put them out of his mind. Gabriel gestured for him to lie down on the gurney, a padded stretcher normally used for transporting patients, and then he was strapped down. Dung had refused a chaplain. God had done nothing to help him in life, so why would He help him after death? Dung no longer really believed in an afterlife; he doubted whether he would see his blood relatives, and he wouldn't recognise them anyway. His last thoughts would be for his living family, and his hopes that they would have a better life than he had.

Dung lay on the stretcher, stared up at the ceiling, and wondered how long it would take and whether he would feel anything. The tears ran down his face and he thought of Lien, Vy and An. Jonathan had told him it would be very quick. The anaesthetic would knock him out and then it would all be over. He glanced up at the doctor who was there to certify his death and watched as he nodded to the prison guard. Dung was briefly surprised, then he remembered the governor explaining that the doctor never administered the injections because killing people was against his Hippocratic Oath. He felt the guard take his arm, and then the prick of the needle as the sodium thiopental was injected into his arm. Dung automatically began to count, expecting to lose consciousness in the twenty seconds the attorney had told him, but although he felt drowsy he was still aware of his surroundings. Maybe he had counted too quickly? Dung was about to say something when he felt the second injection, pancuronium bromide, enter his system and then suddenly he was in excruciating pain. He tried to let them know he could still feel everything, that he was still conscious, but he couldn't move anything, he was paralysed. The pain grew worse. Dung wanted to scream, but he couldn't. He felt like he was drowning... he couldn't breathe... the pain went on and on... sharp agonising pain that grew worse... then mercifully, everything finally faded away.

The guard injected the third injection. The doctor checked the ECG that was attached to Dung, glanced at Gabriel who was looking out at the viewing area and then carefully flipped the ECG lead off so the machine showed that Dung was dead. Jefferson nodded to the governor and spoke clearly. "He's dead." He turned to the Gabriel. "Give me a hand to get him out of here."

Gabriel looked slightly confused. This might only be his second time, but he was sure it had taken longer last time. But he wasn't a doctor and the prisoner looked dead, so he nodded and helped Jefferson wheel the body out into the antechamber where Charles was waiting.

"I'll wait until he's finished, then call you." Jefferson spoke with authority and Gabriel hastily left the room. The last thing he wanted was to see the other doctor remove the prisoner's heart. He couldn't shake the horrible feeling that the first injection he'd given the prisoner hadn't worked properly – he was sure he'd seen panic in the man's eyes before he'd finally died.

Charles had already prepared the ice water and potassium. Within two minutes he had opened the chest cavity, carefully removed the heart, and placed it in the cold box to preserve it. He glanced across at Jefferson, who was staring at the blood that was pouring from the open wound, seeping unchecked onto the pristine floor.

Charles shoved him in the back. "For fuck's sake, help me clean up or they'll smell a rat."

Jefferson somehow pulled himself together, reached for the cleaning fluids and cloths and began wiping up the blood.

Local Community Centre, New Orleans, Louisiana

Vy finished writing the letter to the refugee camp and put it out with the rest of the mail. She had kept it short, explained that she was expecting a letter from Diem and could they pass her address on to him, just in case his letter to her had gone astray or not been forwarded on to her. She had sent the letter from the community centre, because she knew her uncle would have tried to stop her. Despite his attempt to hide his antipathy, Vy had guessed that Phuc didn't like Diem, and so would be delighted if he didn't keep in touch with her. She could have told him to mind his own business, but she couldn't see any point in falling out with him, especially as there was a faint chance he could be right and Diem had indeed forgotten about her. If that was the case, it would also be less embarrassing if he didn't know she was chasing after Diem.

She turned her attention to the first of the day's cases and forgot all about Diem as she read through the file. From the little she read in the file, it seemed like it would be an impossible case after so much time and with so little information.

"Hello Hanh, please sit down and we'll have a chat." Vy waited for Hanh to sit down before adding, "I've had a quick look in the file… it might be difficult after so much time. I don't want to get your hopes up."

"I know, but if I don't try, I will never forgive myself." Hanh gave a timorous smile.

Vy took a breath. "Ok, let's start from the beginning. How old is Mai, and when did you last see her?"

Hanh looked embarrassed. "She was born in 1970 and I put her in an orphanage because she was Amerasian. You know what it was like over there, it was the same before the end of the war. I had no money, and my parents refused to support me, so it was either that or leave her on the streets or in the countryside somewhere to die. I couldn't do that. I thought she would be safe in the orphanage."

Vy frowned. "There's nothing about an orphanage in the file, Hanh. It just says that Mai was given to another woman to look after."

Hanh twisted her fingers together. "I said that to the man who interviewed me because I felt ashamed. I thought he would judge me."

Vy cursed under her breath. She could guess who Hanh had seen, and it wasn't the first time someone had lied to him because he wasn't very sympathetic.

"What's the name of the orphanage?"

"It was the Nhà của ánh nắng, House of Sunshine. I liked the name." Hanh looked even more embarrassed. "I was only fifteen." She looked down and peered at Vy through her eyelashes.

Vy reached out and patted her hand. "You don't need to be ashamed, Hanh. It wasn't your fault."

To her horror, Hanh began to cry. "My father sold me to a man who provided girls to American soldiers. But when I got pregnant, he threw me out because I couldn't earn any money, and my family disowned me because I had dishonoured them." Her sobbing grew louder. Thu suddenly put his head around the door. "Is everything alright?

Vy glared at him. "Yes, we are just talking." She waited for him to go and eventually he took the hint. Hanh glanced warily behind her before standing up. "I should go."

"No, you shouldn't. Don't take any notice of him, Hanh. I take it Thu was the man you saw before?"

Hanh nodded, but she still looked uncomfortable and Vy felt sick suddenly. She had seen that expression on her own face after Chinh had... Vy pushed the memories away and was just about to ask Hanh if Thu was behaving unprofessionally when she changed her mind. She would need to get Hanh's confidence and trust first if she wanted to get the older woman to confide in her.

"You said you thought the orphanage would be safe? What happened?"

Hanh hesitated and then sat back down. "It caught fire,

early 1971. Some of the children escaped, but others were killed." She fought back tears. "If she is dead, I will accept that, but I just need to know."

Vy reached out and took her hand. "I understand that, Hanh, and I will do my best to try and help you. But I can't make any promises, as long as you understand that."

Hanh smiled through her tears and squeezed Vy's hand. "Thank you, thank you so much."

Vy watched her go and wondered where on earth to begin. Then she smiled. The author who was collecting stories from those in the refugee camp would be a good place to start; he might have spoken to someone who had been in the orphanage.

CHAPTER FIFTY-ONE

Omaha, Nebraska,
Six months later

"Your tie is crooked." Rachel smiled up at Steve, unable to believe how quickly he had recovered from the heart transplant.

"It's fine, honey. You're just nervous."

"And you're not?"

Spanner grinned. "Of course I am. I always get nervous before a big speech, and it's worse this time because I haven't done one in a while – not to mention, this is the big one."

Rachel nodded. He was right, this was the rally that would either get him the backing he needed, or spell the end of their dream. She took a breath. If it didn't work, then everything would have been in vain.

"It will be ok, honey, and if it isn't, then I'm still State Governor."

"And you're still alive." Rachel felt sick. How could she possibly have thought everything she'd done was in vain if he didn't become a senator? The most important thing was that Steve had recovered and should have a long and healthy life ahead of him. She suddenly hugged him tight, taking him by surprise.

"Are you alright, darling?"

"Yes, sorry, just a bit nervous. I know how long you've been working for this."

"*We've* been working for this. We're a partnership Rachel, we always have been." He glanced at the clock. "And now we'd better go, or we'll be late, and that won't be a good look," He shook his head and smiled.

"What is it?"

"I just remembered that was what I was thinking when I collapsed, that I would be late and where the hell was the lift!" He took one last look in the mirror. "We do make a very handsome couple, Mrs Tanner." He gave her a quick kiss on the forehead. "Come on, let's go."

Da Nang, Vietnam

An sat back and glanced around the new garage. He couldn't believe My had trusted him enough to put him in charge of his new garage. My had branched out into selling cars as well as repairing them and had suggested An run his new premises in Da Nang. He was even more delighted to be away from Ho Chi Minh City and his fears that one day Chinh would find him. If only he could share his news with Vy. But he couldn't write to her, because he didn't know where she was. An frowned. Or could he? It probably wouldn't be too difficult to find out where the refugee camp in the Philippines was. He could write a letter to her there and ask them to pass it on if she was in America.

An thought hard. Would Chinh be able to monitor letters going out of the country, especially to the Philippines? The bastard must have worked out where Vy had gone by now. Perhaps he should wait until he could find a way of mailing a letter outside the country. An let out a heavy sigh. He was probably overthinking things, but he couldn't help himself. He had a good life now; no point ruining it by not being careful.

New Orleans, Louisiana

Vy wasn't yet home from the community centre. Phuc was sitting quietly on his own reading the newspaper, the television providing background noise. He had finally found a job working as a clerk in an import and export company. It wasn't particularly interesting, but it paid quite well. Phuc finished his dinner, put down the newspaper and glanced up at the television.

The local news had finished, and the main news was now on, the newsreader droning on about politics which Phuc didn't really understand. He stood up and was about to switch the television off when his heart skipped a beat. He stopped abruptly and stared at the screen in disbelief. It was Spanner, he was sure of it. He turned up the sound and waited impatiently for the reporter to state the man's name and why he was on the television. The camera showed more footage of a large rally and he realised that Spanner, if it was him, was running for Senator in a place called Nebraska. Phuc slumped back down on his chair in shock and listened to the rest of the report. It didn't tell him any more except to confirm that it was Spanner.

Phuc sat back and thought hard. Spanner had obviously done well for himself. Why hadn't he written to Lien after the explosion? He was sure he had loved Lien. Then he remembered how he had tried to break Spanner's trust in Lien, to make him think she was lying to him. Perhaps that had worked and that was why he hadn't contacted her again. Phuc looked up at the screen again, but the news had moved on. Should he try contacting Spanner – he might be able to help Vy – or should he leave well enough alone? What if Spanner knew who was responsible for the bomb? He could be opening a can of worms… He walked into the kitchen and reached for a bottle of beer. He would think carefully before rushing into anything. Fortunately, Vy hadn't been home and, as far as he knew, she didn't know anything about Spanner. He was pretty certain Lien had not spoken about Spanner once she married Chinh, in case one of the children mentioned him and set Chinh off into one of his murderous rages.

Omaha, Nebraska

"Well, that was a great success." Rachel replaced the receiver again and smiled across at Spanner. The phone hadn't stopped ringing all the evening with offers of support. "You have more than enough backing now. We're on our way!"

Spanner took her in his arms and spun her around. "And it's all thanks to you, honey. I could never have done it without you."

Rachel snuggled into his arms and began to relax. Everything was going to plan. Then she remembered Charles and her smile broadened. She had given him everything, as she'd promised – at least, he thought she had. In fact, she hadn't actually given him anything of use at all. Despite having made the promise to give up all her evidence, Rachel had known she couldn't do that to Jamie or to all those women who had suffered at his hands, so she had painstakingly set about fabricating some evidence files complete with clothes and underwear, and that was what she'd given him. Then she had taken the real evidence and placed it in a bank vault, as she was no longer comfortable having it all in the house, just in case he decided to have someone break in and steal it. She smiled up at Spanner. "Let's go to bed. I think we should celebrate, don't you?"

New Orleans, Louisiana

Vy finished her paperwork and glanced at the clock. She had some time until her next appointment, she would have a quick look at the newspapers. Five minutes later she had dropped the paper on the floor and was staring at the ring on the chain around her neck in shock. Her father was state governor of Nebraska and he was campaigning to be a senator. She was sure it was him, even though she only knew his nickname and the state he had lived in. There couldn't be two men called Spanner in Nebraska surely? And she had his ring as proof. She had to go and speak to him. Find out why he had deserted her mother and left her with his children, why he hadn't made any attempt to contact them. Vy took a breath, stood up and left her office.

Thu was sitting at the reception desk and he looked up in surprise.

"I have to go."

Thu frowned at her. "You've got another appointment."

"It's urgent, I... I can't explain but I will be away for a few days, not sure how long yet." She was already moving toward the door.

"What about your clients? You can't just leave them!" Thu yelled in exasperation.

"I'm not going for good, just for a few days." She suddenly remembered Hanh would be coming in the next day. Of all her clients, Hanh was the one she didn't want to trust to anyone else. She thought quickly. "Tell Hanh I will be back as soon as I can. I haven't abandoned her, but I have to go. Tell her to wait for me to get back, she doesn't need to see anyone else." Vy reached the door, and before he could say anything else, she had gone.

Omaha, Nebraska

Jim rubbed his eyes and drank some more coffee. He had been looking through the files for months now and not found anything. He was beginning to think it was a waste of time. The bastards were probably still in Vietnam, if they were alive. They probably wouldn't have needed to flee the country. He looked at the remaining files and shrugged. He might as well finish, at least the flow of refugees had slowed considerably. Another couple of months would probably do it.

He reached for the next file, yawned, took a sip of his coffee and opened it. The coffee went down the wrong way and he began choking. Jim stood up and moved away from the desk and coughed violently. Eventually he recovered and stared down at the file. His heart felt like it was beating at twice its normal pace, he was struggling to breathe, and his hands and legs were trembling. He would never forget the face staring up at him. It was with him every waking moment and in his dreams.

He picked up the telephone and dialled out. "Kurt?"

Kurt sighed. He had a mountain of paperwork to get through, he hoped Jim wasn't on a downward spiral again. "Hi buddy, how's it going?"

"I've found one of them."

There was a brief silence, then Kurt cleared his throat. "Did you say you've found one of them?" His voice sounded hoarse and he swallowed.

"Yeah, the younger one. He's staring up at me now, the fucking bastard... He's here in the US."

"How old is the file, Jim?" Kurt asked urgently.

"Why, what fucking difference does that make?"

"If it's really old, he might have moved from the address that's in it."

Jim checked quickly. "No, it's this year. I'm going to pay him a visit."

"Wait Jim, where is he? I'll come with you."

Jim hesitated. "Why? Don't you trust me?"

"Of course I do, but he might be armed, or be in a gang or something. We need to take it slowly, go and do a recce first..."

Jim thought for a moment. "Yeah, ok. When can you be ready to leave?"

"In a couple of hours. I need to get someone to cover the business. Where are we going?"

"Louisiana. I'll meet you at the airport."

New Orleans, Louisiana

"You can't just arrive and claim you're his daughter." Phuc stared at Vy in shock.

"Yes, I can. And I have proof." Vy was busy packing.

"What proof?"

Vy stopped and pulled out the ring that she wore on a chain around her neck. "Mẹ gave it to me before that bastard killed her. It's Spanner's ring, he gave it to her to show how much he loved her." She showed him the underside. "Look, it has his family name on."

Phuc looked closely and could just make out the words *Karla Herz* and a date: *1879*. He was shocked and couldn't think of anything to say for a moment. If she did get to speak to Spanner, he might tell her that Phuc had planted the bomb – he couldn't allow that. He would have to go with her; that way, he could make sure Spanner didn't say anything against him. "I'd better come with you."

Vy looked at him in surprise. "Are you sure? What about work?"

"I'll tell them I'm sick. I'll go and sort out some clothes." Phuc hurried into his own room and breathed a sigh of relief. At least if he was there with her, he could control the conversation.

CHAPTER FIFTY-TWO

Omaha, Nebraska

Spanner looked around at the huge crowd and raised his hands. The cheers grew louder and he turned towards Rachel, who was standing off stage. He beckoned her and she came forward. Spanner took her hand and raised it. The clapping increased, cheers reverberated around the large auditorium and he leaned towards her and gave her a quick kiss. "I can't believe how well it's going, can you?"

Rachel shook her head. "No, you are obviously saying what they want to hear. It's amazing. isn't it?"

They stood drinking in the applause for several moments, then left the stage and headed towards the back room where there was a reception for everyone who wanted to stay. Spanner and Rachel walked up to the far end and sat down gratefully, enjoying the few moments of peace before the doors opened and the crowds flooded in.

"Is it alright to let them in now?" one of the security guards called up from the door.

Spanner looked at Rachel and she nodded. "Yes, go ahead."

The door opened and a man and a woman walked in. Spanner's welcoming smile froze on his face. His head started buzzing, his chest felt tight and he was suddenly somewhere else. He could hear screams, a strange whirling noise reverberating around which he belatedly recognised as a blast wave, then into the chaos in his head he could see a girl walking in slow motion towards him. He frowned. "Leni? Is that really you?"

Rachel stared at him, turned towards the Vietnamese man and woman who were still walking towards them, and then back to Spanner. "Steve? Are you alright?"

Spanner ignored her. He was still staring down the room. "Leni..." He spoke softly, a puzzled expression replacing the shock. And then everything suddenly came crashing back into his brain... Vietnam, the helicopter missions, picking up and dropping patrols, the rockets chasing them across the sky, the VC, blood, napalm, picturesque villages, the smell of burning sewage and rubber, jungles filled with murderous traps, China Beach... and Leni. Spanner stood up. "Oh God... Leni? I had forgotten you... I'm so sorry..." He fell silent and shook his head as the memories continued to flood into his brain and he fought to put them in some sort of order.

"Steve, what the hell is going on?" Rachel was becoming alarmed. She yelled at the security guards. "Don't let anyone else in. Get them out. No, not them…" She yelled as the guard moved toward the Vietnamese couple. "Quick, find a doctor." The guards began making everyone else leave, while one used his radio to find a doctor. She turned back to Spanner. "Steve, talk to me. Is your memory coming back?"

Spanner was still staring into space and didn't answer, so she turned to the Vietnamese pair. "Who are you?"

"I'm Vy. From Vietnam. This is my uncle Phuc. Spanner is my father."

Rachel's hand went to her throat. "Oh God… not another child," she whispered.

Vy looked confused, but decided she must have misheard. "After the explosion, he just forgot about us. He didn't contact my mother at all."

"He lost his memory... after the bomb… couldn't remember anything about Vietnam at all…" Rachel felt the need to explain. Phuc breathed a sigh of relief. If Spanner couldn't remember anything… His relief was short lived as Rachel pulled herself together and carried on talking, anything to cover up her earlier mistake. "You must resemble your mother, Vy. It looks like it has triggered his memory. Was she called Leni?"

"Lien." Vy was looking confused now. "What do you mean he couldn't remember?"

Rachel sighed. "The bomb. He was badly injured, and it gave him amnesia." She turned back to Spanner again and paled. He looked awful. She reached out a hand and took his arm. "Steve... Steve! Do you know where you are?"

Spanner took his eyes off Vy and stared at Rachel. He tried to speak, but the dizziness was getting worse. He felt sick and then everything went black.

ABOUT THE AUTHOR

Gavin L James was born in Ireland and now lives in North West England. He is interested in the history of the 20th century, music, golf and travel.

Printed in Great Britain
by Amazon

56956378R00373